JADED VISIONS

T. L. JONES

JADED VISIONS

An Imagine House/Starving Writers Book – Subsidiary of
Truesource Publishing

Published by arrangement with the author

Truesource Publishing: Dallas, Texas

Imagine House Publishing: Dallas, Texas

www.truesourcepublishing.com

www.facebook.com/truesourcepublishing

ISBN : 978-1-932996-37-1

Printed in the United States of America.

Published in Dallas, Texas.

For more information on T. L. Jones go to...

www.tljonesauthor.com

ABOUT THE AUTHOR

 T. L. Jones lives in southeast
Texas with her husband Dave,
her dog Zeus, and an African
Grey Parrot named Herman. She
is a former police officer, and
through her career in law
enforcement has acquired
valuable insight into criminal
behavior. Her experience in law
enforcement and her fascination
with the paranormal has
supercharged her creative juices
into writing. Jaded Visions is her
first novel.

This book is dedicated first and foremost to my late friend and author, Butch Grant. Butch told me time and time again, I could do this. Though gone he is not forgotten. Also to my wonderful husband, Dave for all the encouragement and patience through this wonderful roller coaster ride.

ACKNOWLEDGMENTS

I would like to acknowledge the following people for their help and or support with this book: Officer Dave Jones, Darlene Castillo, Mary Durr, Joelle Cruz, Robbie Jones, Lisa Jordan, Kay White, Betty Jones, Bobby Adams, and if I forgot anyone, please forgive me.

A special thank you goes to my son Joseph Durr. Joe, all your hard work has been greatly appreciated, and you will never know what it means to me. I love you son.

I would also like to thank my editor Allee Wesolowski.

Better keep yourself clean and bright; you are the window through which you must see the world.

~ George Bernard Shaw

1

IT was a day like any other day for Jade Hamilton. The twenty-four-year-old recent college graduate was ready to begin life. Small, petite Jade, with golden hair and sweet, almond-shaped brown eyes, sat in her living room, dreading the next few hours and what would happen to her and the small child waiting across the street.

The sky was a brilliant blue and the weather chilly but livable. Children played in the park across the street, and she heard their laughter and their screams of delight.

She sat in her house watching, listening and knowing what had to be done.

Jade was going to have to face yet another dilemma.

Getting up slowly, never taking her eyes off the park or the children, and with dread strong in her heart, she walked out of the room and opened the front door.

As she crossed the street, Jade saw the little girl.

Why did this have to happen now? Jade was beginning a new career, a new life. She was the newest member of the Croft, Sealy and Mooney Private Security Firm.

Jade wasn't like most people; she knew things she shouldn't and could see things happen before they actually occurred.

Jade called it a curse in the beginning, but her father took time and patience with her, explaining what a gift she had been blessed with. The more she listened to her dad, the more it made sense and the more she could see it as just that: a gift.

The private security firm was going to pay big for Jade's

gift. However, they were completely unaware of it; they wanted her because she finished in the top in her class. Her recent degree in criminal justice was the first step in getting her unusual ability out there. To be used as it should be. The degree didn't mean a thing to her, but helping people did.

Jade was only ten when the visions began. She had been sitting at the desk in her bedroom putting a puzzle together when she had her first vision. She wasn't sure what had happened. One minute, she was putting a puzzle together, and the next, she was seeing her mother getting into the car and connecting her seatbelt as she backed out of the driveway. A large truck slammed into the side of the car, instantly killing her mother. The young age afforded no comfort to Jade and the life she was destined to lead.

Jade tried repeatedly to keep her mom home that day, even lying, saying she was sick and needed her mom there. Jade of course didn't know the accident would truly occur.

But it did.

Jade told her dad of the "dream" the day of her mother's funeral. At first, Walter Hamilton, Jade's father, told her she didn't really see anything and that she was just in shock. Walt was always and still was the unyielding and protective father. He was a handsome, strong, and virile man with silvering hair and the same brown eyes that Jade possessed. He was always there, always guiding his precious Jade.

Of course, Jade had more visions and shared them with her dad before they happened to prove to him that she was cursed.

After a fishing accident with one of the family friends, Walt began to give credence to Jade's visions. He even helped Jade try to prevent the incidents from happening.

In one such vision, Jade saw a young girl from the local diner, Beth Ann, walking on the sidewalk when a motorcycle jumped the curb, striking Beth Ann and killing both her and the driver.

Jade and Walt sat in the diner, in Beth Ann's section, until they watched the motorcycle pass by. Jade had to plead with Beth Ann to stay until she and Walt finished their dinner. She liked Beth Ann and wanted to make sure she stayed safe. Of course, they took their time, and Beth Ann became anxious to leave, knowing she was off shift already, but Beth Ann took pity on Jade, knowing she had lost her mother six months earlier.

That was the cost of living in a small rural town; everyone knew everything about each other. Or so they thought...

That night, on the news, Jade and Walt heard about the motorcycle driver and the accident they could not entirely prevent. He held Jade and explained how they had saved Beth Ann and that it was a blessing the gift provided. Jade understood but was still hurt over the dying driver. She thought she should have been

~ 8 ~

able to do more.

Jade knew it took both her and her dad there to keep Beth Ann in the diner. No one else could help her, as no one else knew her secret. No one else *could* know her secret.

Walt told Jade that she wouldn't be seen or thought of as normal if she told anyone. He stressed time and time again that she should tell no one. All through high school, college, friendships, relationships, Jade never told anyone. Ever!

Shaking herself from her memories, Jade brought herself back to the present, focusing again on the task at hand.

*There...*Jade saw the girl standing all alone, so tiny and so vulnerable. She was wearing a blue sweat suit and staring at a backpack that was on the ground.

The corner park was a popular place for the neighborhood children. It was huge, with a playground area, walking trails, a boardwalk for skating, and a large open area for flying kites or playing fetch.

Today there were a lot of kids, a few parents, an ice cream truck, a police woman talking to a couple of teenagers on skate boards, and people with their dogs.

As she approached the little girl, Jade could feel the heaviness growing in the pit of her stomach.

She was a beautiful little girl. Jade knew that her name was Emmie, knew she was six years old and that she had long shiny brown hair, beautiful green eyes—almost the color of emeralds—and that she was so small in size she could have been four instead of six. Jade's visions would supply information above and beyond need, on occasion.

Emmie turned and watched Jade walk up to her, and Jade extended her hand. Jade smiled and the little girl picked up her backpack and reached for the outstretched hand.

Jade slowly walked away, holding Emmie's hand, guiding the child away from danger. No one tried to stop her. With her heart pounding and her palms sweating, Jade simply couldn't believe it was going to be this easy.

They walked to her car, which was parked in front of Jade's house. The keys were already placed in the car for a quick getaway. Opening the rear driver's side door, she helped Emmie in and seat-belted her tightly. The little girl never said a word. She was so trusting, just as Jade knew she would be. Jade got in and started the car. The small sedan sprang to life quietly. A graduation gift from her dad, Jade silently thanked him again for the car, the down payment on her house, and actually just her life in general, which has been made too easy by a loving and overprotective father.

Watching Emmie through the rearview mirror, Jade smiled and began to hum a tune that was meant to keep the child from being frightened. The tune was familiar to Emmie and she began to hum along with Jade. 'The Itsy Bitsy Spider' filled the car while Jade drove away.

Jade had planned the trip in detail when the vision first came to her. She would take Emmie to the small coastal town of Ivory Bluff, in Texas. A rented cabin would provide enough time to give her the answers she needed. This time, she not only needed to save the child, but she also needed to keep herself from being arrested for kidnapping.

The drive to Ivory Bluff would take a few hours, but the scenery would more than make up for the drive. Beautiful, old oak trees lined both sides of the Texas highway. The serene landscape gave Jade plenty of time to calm her pounding heart. She constantly watched for any vehicle that could be following them. An unknown killer was out there—waiting.

The miles went by quickly. Both occupants, deep in thought, failed to notice the surrounding landscape change from rural countryside to coastal beauty. The drive ended faster than Jade realized. Had it really been only hours since putting this child in the car and thus changing her life forever?

Jade pulled into the driveway of the rented cabin while looking around to make sure they had not been followed. Everything appeared to be all right. Jade looked at Emmie.

"Well, this is it," she said softly, calmly. Emmie sat quietly, looking at her. Smiling, Jade got out and helped Emmie get out, and together they walked to the cabin, hand in hand.

Emmie still had not said a word and Jade was beginning to wonder what the child was thinking. After all, Emmie was six years old, able to talk, even to reason to a certain extent, yet she hasn't asked Jade who she was, where they were going, where her mom and dad were...nothing!

Jade knew she had to be careful of what she said and how she acted. She didn't want to scare Emmie.

They entered the cabin and looked around. It was small and quaint. It was a log cabin and very open, having a well furnished living area, two bedrooms, a cute loft, and a small kitchen—all in all, quite homey.

Emmie then turned to Jade. "Are you the lady the angel told me about?" Her innocent little face was finally looking for answers.

Jade just stared at the little girl.

"It's all right," Emmie said. "I know you're going to keep me safe."

Jade knelt down and looked Emmie in the eyes. "What angel?" She asked in confusion. Emmie smiled and explained that she'd had a dream last night in which a beautiful woman was going to take her away so that she wouldn't be harmed. She further explained that in her dream, an angel told her this. She told Jade that she wasn't scared.

"Did you tell your mom and dad about the angel?"

"No. The angel told me not to."

Jade digested this information with trepidation. Did Emmie have a gift too? Could Jade be that lucky? Jade shook herself from her thoughts and chose not to comment on the angel. "What's in the backpack, Emmie?"

"Aw, well, just a jacket and my baby doll." Then with gleaming eyes she said, "I know you're gonna take very good care of me because you're the beautiful woman the angel was talking about. What's your name?"

"I'm Jade," she said and shook hands with Emmie. Delighted, Emmie giggled.

They took their time looking around the cabin, inside and out. The beach wasn't far away and they could hear the crashing of the surf. The air had the tangy smell of salt that tells you you're near the ocean. After a quick look around, Jade took Emmie into one of the bedrooms and helped her to settle in.

The room was perfect for a little girl. The window dressings were white with an abundance of pastel colored butterflies. The bedding matched with cute, butterfly-shaped decorative pillows. The furniture was white with etched butterflies here and there. On the headboard, butterflies danced around, and the canopy was topped with even more butterflies, beautifully embroidered. This was the most perfect bed for a little girl's room.

On the walls were water color paintings of pretty meadows, spring flowers, and, of course, butterflies. "Emmie, this is your bedroom while we're here. Do you like it?"

"Yep, it's pretty, but where's all the toys?" she asked as she walked in a circle, checking every nook and cranny.

"Hmmmm, I don't think we'll be here long enough for you to miss your toys."

Yawning loudly, Emmie crawled up and sat down on the bed. "I like this room. Butterflies are soft," she said, yawning yet again.

Laughing, Jade said, "I'll be in the next room if you need anything." Walking out and closing the door, she wondered how long Emmie would remain so easy to deal with. Not having much time in the company of children, Jade had no idea what to expect from Emmie. Resigned to draw from common sense, Jade acted out of desperation with little thought of the potential behavior of a six-year-old. It was going to be easy with this kid. She was not a whiney kid, from the look of things, and Jade was beginning to relax a little.

She went into the other bedroom. This room was just as

nice, but it suited an adult. The furniture was pine with a massive four-poster bed, a chest of drawers, and a chair by the only window. The walls were the same pine inside as out, and a frilly valance and blinds covered the window.

Satisfied with her bedroom, Jade went to the car and got the suitcases and the food. Dragging everything inside, she decided to use this opportunity to settle in. Putting the refrigerated items away, she moved restlessly to the bedroom, not bothering with the pantry food.

Jade unpacked her suitcase. She had not brought a lot of clothing, but enough for two or three days, along with cosmetics, a toothbrush, her hairbrush: the usual things one packs for a short trip. She did the same for Emmie. Slipping back into the child's room, Jade looked with wonder at the now sleeping child. Everything would work out. She'd make sure. This little girl would be fine and so would she. Worrying about Emmie's parents and wanting to contact them to reassure them she was fine was strong in Jade's mind. But she knew that would have to wait. She wondered if they were searching already—of course they would be. She knew that she and Emmie were too far away, and safe for now, so she pushed the thoughts from her mind and quickly began putting away the few items of clothing she had purchased for Emmie.

Jade made her way to the small bathroom in the hallway between the bedrooms. She put all the toiletries and necessary items away and then went to the kitchen for a quick finish up.

Jade was not the best cook, but she could get by. She just hoped Emmie was not a picky eater. Digging out a snack consisting of a Snickers candy bar and can of Pepsi, Jade thought about what she had done. She had to call her dad and explain where she was and why. He would be upset that she did this without his help but she couldn't take a chance of him being charged with kidnapping too. She'd probably need him to help her get out of jail later.

Jade settled in and called her dad. Explained the vision she had received just two days ago. She told him of the little girl being strangled, that she didn't know who was strangling the child because she couldn't see the killer's face. She told him of the information given in her vision about finding the little girl in the park and about her name being Emmie, and that she was six, and would be wearing a blue sweat suit. Walt was full of questions, and she did her best to answer them. After explaining each detail given and each detail the vision lacked, she continued, "Dad I need you to watch the TV for anyone pleading for Emmie's return and to let me know who they are. I have every intention of returning her and telling them why I had to do this. I feel so bad at how they must be suffering over this." Jade was filled with guilt at the pain she must be causing these parents.

"Jade, please just take her to the cops and tell them what you know—just don't tell them how you know it. They'll protect her and you won't have to worry about breaking the law."

"Dad, don't you think I've already thought of that? The authorities would turn Emmie over to her parents, and I don't know if the killer is one of them."

At length, the conversation ended with Walt not knowing where Jade had taken the little girl. That was how Jade wanted it and how she knew it had to be. The less he knew, the better off he would be.

~

Tied in knots from the stress and strain of the day, Jade knew she had to relax or suffer one of her infamous migraines. Knowing details were needed to bring this ordeal to an end, Jade closed her eyes and began breathing deeply, slowly—letting the vision come back:

He didn't appear to be a big fella. She still could not see the would-be killer's face, but his hands were around Emmie's throat, choking harder and harder. Emmie didn't struggle, didn't utter a sound, she just lay there looking into a face that was shadowed.

Choking with fear for the child, Jade looked for clues in this vision. Where are they... in a house, a car, a building, a school? Why can't I see more? This vision is so dark. Dig deeper... look around. Find a windowpane, a mirror, something to reflect the image of the face. Why can't I see more? I cannot allow Emmie to go home until I know the identity of the killer!

Struggling for answers she knew would not come to her just yet, Jade let the vision slip away.

Frustrated and not the least bit relaxed, she went through the vision in her mind. Being twenty-four and having had visions for the better part of fourteen years, she could control them to some degree. She knew how to bring the vision back and hold it for a while. She also knew the limitations on these visions. No matter how hard she tried, she could not get details that were simply not there—like the face of this would-be killer. No matter what she tried, she couldn't see it.

She gave up and went to get a couple of aspirin for her headache.

Meanwhile, Walt felt so helpless, and that was a feeling no father ever wanted to feel. No one would understand Jade's need to give so much of herself for others. He knew she didn't date or have much of a social life, but he knew that the special person meant for her would come along at the right time and that she wouldn't be alone forever. In the meantime, Jade had him, and he had Jade. He was so proud of his daughter for using her gift to help others.

He remembered Jade telling him that she knew how to stop a vision before seeing the whole thing; she learned this early on and how she could control it. He had softly encouraged her to use her gift for other people. He explained that it was given to her for a reason and that she should invite the visions and do what she could to help those in need.

He worried about her being lonely and in solitude too much. After all, what would happen to her when he died? It would happen—it happened to everyone eventually. *The right one for her will come along soon.* Walt knew this deep in his heart. He knew Jade would be alright. He held onto that thought in order to keep his sanity.

~

Jade and Emmie sat down to a dinner of hotdogs and potato chips. While they ate, Jade tried to explain to Emmie why they were there at the cabin. She began by saying, "Emmie, I don't want you to worry about anything." Smiling, she continued. "I'm a friend of your mom and dad's. It's okay for you to be here with me."

"Do you know the angel too? And why do you look kinda like her?"

Jade didn't really understand this angel business but said, "The angel was there to take care of you, just like I am doing now. But no, I don't know the angel. What did she tell you?"

"She just told me that there would be a beautiful woman coming to get me and that I should go with her and that she would take good care of me." Turning her face sideways and looking up she continued, "She said if I didn't go, then I could be hurt."

Emmie looked over at Jade, smiling and appearing so at ease with this virtual stranger. Jade had to protect this child no matter what the cost to her. She wasn't sure about this angel stuff, and she didn't want to get into that just yet, but Emmie wasn't giving her a choice. "Did she say why you would be hurt? Or how?"

"No. I think she just wanted me to go with you."

"Why?"

"I'm not sure. But you came to get me, and that's all I know. So what!" She sat up on her knees and placed her little meaty hands on her hips, looking directly at Jade.

Laughing at this Shirley Temple act Jade replied, "You're right, honey. Hurry and eat your hotdog before it gets cold". Jade picked up her hotdog and took a bite. She needed time to think.

~

After dinner, they went for a walk. Along the beach, Emmie would run into the surf every now and then. Jade had folded up their pant legs, and they each carried their shoes and socks. This was a quiet, empty stretch of beach, allowing Jade to let her guard down and relax. The beach, with its lulling sound of waves, was always a favorite place for Jade. A lot of thinking and figuring things out could be done just sitting on the beach, listening to the sounds of the sea and to the seagulls while watching the water crash over the sand. Thoughts could run away from Jade if she let them, and she would sit for hours, unaware.

Jade loved the palm trees and the scratching sounds the fronds made when rubbing against each other. She reveled in the salty, tangy smell of the air. Everything seemed clean and fresh. No sad or worrying thoughts were allowed to enter her mind while she was in her favorite place.

Emmie looked thoughtfully at Jade and, in a rush, said, "You know, I'm kinda glad you came and got me."

"Why?"

"My mommy and daddy fight all the time. Last night I heard Daddy telling Mommy they were in trouble. I was going to take my piggy bank out to Daddy but I heard the door slam, and Daddy was gone."

This child was endearing herself to Jade. Innocence was a good thing to have sometimes. "I know your daddy would have appreciated your help. That was so sweet of you." Jade wondered how much this child would know; Jade so desperately needed an answer but didn't want to cause more worry for Emmie. "When your mommy and daddy fight, is it about money?"

"Money, and Daddy's job."

"What kind of work does your daddy do?"

"I don't know, but Mommy always tells him to get a new job."

"Well, don't you worry, little one, everything is going to be just fine." Jade's heart grew heavy at the thought of this child and all that her six-year-old brain was trying to cope with. Jade jumped up and took Emmie's hand. "Run," she yelled as she pulled the girl behind her. They ran a good distance before they both fell to the ground, gasping for air. Laughing and lying there side by side, the freedom to be so careless was intoxicating at first, but the danger that was lurking reared its ugly head.

"We need to get back to the cabin. It's getting dark," Jade said sitting up.

The sun was setting into a spectacular sunset of crimson, orange, yellow, and blue, with all the colors mingling to make this the best and most beautiful time of the day.

A strong breeze was beginning to blow in, and the air brought a chill with it. Emmie's pants were wet from the surf and Jade didn't want Emmie to catch a cold. Grabbing her hand, Jade pulled Emmie to her feet. "Come on, kiddo, let's get back."

They skipped back to the cabin hand in hand, singing children's songs.

Jade gave Emmie a bath and tucked her in for the night. Sitting on the edge of the bed, she told Emmie a children's story. They quietly laughed and giggled together as Emmie snuggled closer to Jade, listening intently to every word, until sleep overtook the tired child. When the deep breathing continued and Jade knew she was asleep, she leaned over, kissing Emmie's forehead as she pulled the covers up and quietly left the room.

Taking a seat in a big overstuffed chair in the quiet living room, Jade once again telephoned her dad. Walt told her there had not been anything on the news about a missing child. Jade couldn't believe this.

"Where did you take her from, and where were her parents?"

"I took her from the park across the street from my house." Jade thought for a minute, realizing that there weren't any adults around Emmie. Where had her parents been? She couldn't ask her, as Emmie was already asleep. "I assure you, Dad, I'll find out in the morning when she's awake. Thanks for everything, and I'll call you tomorrow."

After brief goodbyes and the realization that she was tired but not quite ready for sleep, Jade went to the small bathroom and removed her makeup. While she brushed her teeth and hair, she thought once again about Emmie's parents. The guilt for their suffering right now could become overwhelming for her if she allowed it. Her decision that there was something strange about them not being on the news, begging for the safe return of their child by now, had her wondering yet again where they could've been while she stole their daughter.

Walking into her bedroom, she picked up a book she had placed on the nightstand earlier. She read every night before going to sleep; it was her relaxation technique for a sound night's sleep. Looking at the book now and knowing she couldn't concentrate enough to read, she sat down in the chair by the window. The question of Emmie's parents had continually crept into her mind, and concentration on the book would be out of the question. She finally laid the book aside and went over the park scene in her mind yet again.

Knowing all too well she was too tired to make sense of anything tonight, she crawled onto the bed, covered herself with the comforter and willed herself to sleep.

~

Jade was an early riser. Breakfast already made, she went to get Emmie. Opening the door to the bedroom, she could see Emmie was not asleep but was sitting on the floor, rocking her baby doll and singing a song. Jade stood there for a long moment and watched the child lovingly holding the baby doll like a mother would hold her child. Jade watched as she got up and placed the doll on the bed, covering the doll and kissing her forehead. Smiling, Jade opened the door further, barely stepping in, and said, "Emmie, come and eat some breakfast."

"Okay, but I have to potty first," Emmie said, turning to look at Jade.

"I'll see you in the kitchen then." Nodding her assent, she turned to leave.

Jade was making plates and setting them on the table when Emmie walked into the kitchen. "Good morning, Emmie," she said, her beautiful face smiling at the child.

"Mornin', Jade," Emmie said as she crawled up and onto the chair. "Hrrrrmph!"

"You could've asked for help to get in your seat kiddo," Jade said, laughing at the red-faced girl.

"Why would I?" Hands on her hips again, "I'm six!" She said it with her defiant little look, daring Jade to say anything about her being so small.

Jade took the hint and changed the subject as she cut up her eggs. This morning's breakfast consisted of eggs, bacon, and toast with jam. Jade took this opportunity to ask Emmie what her mom and dad's names were.

Emmie looked at Jade strangely saying. "You don't know your own friends' names?" Then she started giggling.

Jade was embarrassed. This child caught onto something so simple before Jade had caught on herself. Looking at Emmie, she said, "Of course I know their names. I just want to see if you do."

"My mommy is Amy, and my daddy is James. What do you call them?" she asked with a smart mouth edge to her voice.

"Well, silly, I call them Amy and Jimmy."

Emmie looked stunned. "You call my daddy Jimmy?" she asked in awe.

"Yes, why?" Jade said hesitantly.

"No one calls my daddy Jimmy. Daddy said only little boys are called Jimmy."

Jade laughed, caught again. "I've known your daddy since he was a little boy, so I've always called him Jimmy."

No last name –I need a last name!

"Emmie, what is your whole name?"

"Emmie Louise Linderhoff. What's yours?"

Linderhoff –thank goodness! "Jade Jolene Hamilton. And we need to eat—our eggs are getting cold. Yuck! Cold eggs are terrible," Jade laughed.

~

After breakfast, Emmie went to her room to play with her dolly. Jade cleaned breakfast dishes and went to sit in the living room, deciding to call her dad. Maybe he would be able to find a telephone number or something for Emmie's parents. Picking up the phone, she called Walt.

"Dad, will you see what you can find out about James and Amy Linderhoff? They are Emmie's parents." Jade was proud of her newfound discovery.

"I can call Ryan. Did you ask her where her parents were yesterday?"

"No, I was busy trying to get names. I'll work on that. So you'll call Ryan about this?"

"I'll call him and see what he can find out, and I'll call you back."

"Thanks, Dad. I'll wait to hear from you. Hey, don't tell Ryan too much, but just give him enough to keep his curiosity down, okay?" Jade hung up, remembering Ryan. He was only a couple of years older than her and had been a good friend to her dad. She met him in passing a few times but had never really taken the time to get to know him. He was a nice looking guy, she remembered. He was a police detective with the St. Joseph Police Department. St. Joseph was a small, rural Texas town. During her college years, she didn't take much time for anything but studying. She made the dean's list every time, and now, as she thought about it, knew what it had cost her: a social life, boyfriends, and simply friends in general. She vowed to make time for a social life if she didn't end up in prison.

Jade turned on the TV and was searching for a newscast when photos of a man and woman were shown. Jade stopped surfing the channels to see what the photos were for.

Her blood ran cold when she heard the report. "*Two bodies have been found but not yet identified. An unknown male and female were found dead on the east side of Charleston Avenue early yesterday evening. If anyone has information concerning the identity of either one please contact the local police department.*"

She didn't need names to know these would be Emmie's parents. Jade turned the TV off and called Walt back. "Dad, I just saw a report about an unknown male and female found dead last evening." Jade was upset and excited, causing her voice to be too loud.

"I know, honey, I just saw it too. See if you can get a description of Emmie's parents from her without letting anything slip." Emmie walked into the living room while Walt was talking. Holding the doll, she looked at Jade.

"Are you okay? I heard you yelling."

"Dad, hold on a minute. Yes, sweetie, I'm okay. Wanna play a game?"

"Uh, okay." She sat down on the floor at Jade's feet. "What kinda game?"

"We're going to play a memory game. Can you tell me what your mommy looks like?"

Talking about her parents put her at ease. "Yeah, my mommy has brown hair to here," she said, holding her hands to her shoulders, "and she has brown eyes. She is very pretty, and daddy always calls her Skinny Bones."

Jade knew from this description and the photos on TV that the female body would be that of Amy Linderhoff. "That is a very good description of your mommy, now try your daddy."

Emmie laughed and said, "Well, daddy has brown hair too, but his is really short. He has green eyes like mine, and he has big muscles. Daddy told me they called me Emmie because our eyes are the same color as emerald stones, and daddy calls me his little Emerald Emmie."

"Thank you, sweetie, you play this game too well. You can go play again." Jade reached down and pulled Emmie to her feet. Emmie smiled before she turned and walked down the hallway.

Stopping just short of her bedroom, she turned to Jade, saying, "Hey, you didn't have to answer anything. What kinda game is that?"

"The grown up kind, sweetie." Smiling still, Jade continued, "Sorry, but you play so well that I didn't have anything better to say than you did." She held her breath. *What a stupid answer*, she thought. But it worked. After Emmie was out of sight, Jade turned back to the telephone. "Dad, the descriptions Emmie just gave'll match the male and female found."

Now Walt was concerned for more than the possibility of Jade being charged with kidnapping. "Jade, stay inside until you hear from me. I think we have a major problem here," he said as he hung up.

Jade paced the floor. Why hadn't she been given more information in this vision? What was going to happen to Emmie? The little girl was safe now, but if she had been with her parents only yesterday...

2

WALT realized after disconnecting with Jade that he didn't have a telephone number for her. She'd forgotten to give it to him. He would just have to wait for her to call him again.

He telephoned Ryan Douglas. Ryan and Walt met when Walt had a fender bender that Ryan had witnessed and stopped to take care of until a uniformed officer arrived. They hit it off right away even though Ryan was only in his twenties. They had kept in touch ever since and even had an occasional lunch together.

Jade and Walt usually handled visions together without help from anyone. This time would be different. Walt dialed St. Joe's PD and waited for Ryan to come on the line. Hearing the young detective answer, Walt said, "Ryan, I have a problem, but I can't discuss it by phone. Can you come over?"

"I'm working a case right now. It'll be a while. But I'll get there as soon as I can. I'm sorry, but this is a very important case, and I can't just drop and go."

"Ryan, this may be a matter of life and death! I'm sorry, but I don't know what else to do."

"Walt, this is a big mess I'm dealing with here. Can't you tell me over the phone?" Ryan was worried, as he knew his friend wasn't the drama type.

"I would, but I have a lot to tell you, and I don't want to get into it over the phone. I know you're busy, but, Ryan, I think Jade is in trouble and I really need your help."

"Walt, I promise I'll be there as soon as I can. Give me a bit and I will try to sneak out."

Walt didn't want to leave home in case Jade called back. He waited for Ryan because he knew that Ryan would eventually be able to drop whatever it was that he was doing and come over. Walt walked around his big, old house. The old Victorian had four bedrooms. It was really too big for him, but it was Jade's childhood home, and he just couldn't bring himself to sell it. Feeling on edge, Walt turned on the TV and surfed the channels to see if anything else came on about the dead couple. He was watching a report on the couple when Ryan rang the door bell. Walt let him in. Sometimes Walt found it hard to believe that Ryan was as young as his daughter. Ryan was a good-looking young man with black hair and blue eyes, and he was easily 6' plus. His body was thick-set, and his face held a strong, chiseled jaw line. "Do you want something to drink?"

"No, I need to get back as soon as I can. What's up?" Ryan searched Walt's face for the answers.

"Let's sit while I try to explain everything." Walt led Ryan into the living room where the reporter on TV was still showing photos and asking for the public's help.

Ryan looked over at Walt. "That's my pain in the ass right now. That's the case I'm working on. So, now you understand how I couldn't just walk out?"

Walt was not entirely sure that Ryan was indeed the right person to talk to about this.

"Ryan, what do they know about that couple? Any information about them that you can share with me?"

"All we know right now is that the couple was murdered near the park, and it's believed to be a drug deal gone bad."

"Drugs?" Walt asked, looking and feeling scared. What had Jade gotten herself into? Walt was reeling now, and was not sure what to say.

Ryan looked at him, concern in his voice, "Are you all right? You're white as a ghost."

"Ryan, you're gonna want to sit down while I explain the fix I'm in."

Hesitantly, Ryan sat down while looking to Walt for answers. He knew that this wasn't going to be good.

Walt began with Jade. "I know you don't know my daughter well, but she is very special and all I have."

"Is she okay? Walt, you're not making much sense here. What the hell is going on?" Ryan knew his old buddy was in trouble.

Sitting and thinking quickly while trying to put thoughts into words, Walt blurted out, "Jade has visions. You know, of impending events. I have always encouraged her to keep this

~ 22 ~

knowledge to herself, but…"

Ryan had a look of disbelief on his face, just as Walt knew he would. But, to his credit, Ryan did sit there and listen while Walt went into detail about some of the visions and how he knew they existed. Ryan was fascinated with the story Walt told.

"Why are you telling me all of this, Walt?" Ryan, concerned his friend was suffering from delusions, continued to listen to the story that Walt unfolded.

"The couple on TV, Ryan, they have a daughter named Emmie, and Jade had a vision concerning Emmie, which she acted on."

"What? You know who they are?" Ryan was stunned. "Who are they?"

"Their names, I believe, are James and Amy Linderhoff. Emmie is with Jade. She told Jade their names and described them to her. Jade made it seem like they were playing a game, so the kid doesn't know her parents are dead. Jade told Emmie she was friends with Amy and James so she wouldn't be frightened at being with a stranger."

Ryan collected himself and opened his cell phone. Looking Walt in the eye he called the precinct and asked for his partner, George Dunleavy. George and Ryan had been partners for the last two years. George was nearing sixty and was teaching Ryan everything he knew.

"Hey George, it's Ryan. I need you to check and see if anything has come back on the prints we ran through AFIS on that couple." AFIS was the Automatic Fingerprint Identification System that law enforcement officials used to identify prints taken in cases like these.

"Well, we won't have any information back until this afternoon. Why?"

"I'll explain later." Ryan hung up and looked at Walt, still in disbelief of the story of visions, but trying hard not to show his friend his thoughts. "Walt, where is Jade?"

"I don't know where she is. I don't even have a telephone number to call her. I'll have to wait until she calls me again."

"What do you mean you don't know?" The disbelief was evident in his voice.

"Well, shit, Ryan, when she took Emmie, she went somewhere, and she is refusing to tell me where. She thinks she's keeping me out of trouble by doing this on her own."

"Look, I have to get back, but I'll call you soon. I need more information, and Jade may have the answers. Try to get a specific location for them."

"I will. Thanks, Ryan, I knew you would help, and I know we can trust you." Walt stood to shake hands with Ryan.

"Walt, you've given me a lot to take in here, and I'll do

what I can. But visions? It's not that I don't believe you, but come on."

"Ryan, trust me, I know how it sounds, but it is true. All of it."

"Walt, you can trust me with this. I won't tell anyone, but Jade needs to get that kid to me now, and I have a million questions for her! I cannot believe she just took this kid and didn't have a clue what she was going to do afterwards. Is she mentally unstable, Walt? I mean, does she take meds or anything I need to know about?"

"Why, hell no, she isn't mentally ill. Why would you...?" He stopped and took a deep breath. He knew how this sounded, and to a cop it must sound even worse.

"Look, Ryan, I will do what I can to get her back here. As soon as she calls, I'll let you know." The two men shook hands, and Ryan left.

~

Going straight to the precinct, Ryan's intention was to get information on the Linderhoffs. If they were into the drug scene, there would be something on them in the system.

Ryan found that James Linderhoff had been arrested the previous year for a controlled substance charge. The photo of James Linderhoff in the computer system was indeed that of the male subject found yesterday.

Ryan had been a detective with the St. Joseph Police Department for two years and a patrol officer for six. He and George had been partners as long as Ryan had been a detective. George had been with the same department for the last thirty years and a detective for the last twenty-five years. They worked well together, considering the age difference. George kind of took Ryan under his wing. He really liked the "kid."

George was rounding the corner just as Ryan got to it and was almost knocked off of his feet as they collided. A big, powerful man even at sixty, George was a sight to see. At 6'6", he was a hulking man with white hair. His face not as lined as most at sixty, and he was still a good looking man.

"Hey, what's your hurry, Ryan?" George practically yelled as the pain hit him, making him instantly angry. He grabbed Ryan, holding him up while they both got better footing.

"I have to talk with you right away. We have a break in this case." Ryan said excitedly.

"What are you talking about? Where the hell have you been?" George was irate that Ryan had nearly taken him out only a second ago. A fall at his age could be detrimental to his health.

He hated growing old.

"I'll explain everything in a sec. Come on, let's head to the office." Ryan turned and left George standing there.

George pulled himself together and followed Ryan to the office that they shared: a moderate sized area with two desks and a wall of file cabinets. Family photos for both Ryan and George lined three shelves on the wall behind the door. The two desks were overflowing with files, and each held a computer. Chairs sat in front of each desk, and a small round table with four chairs occupied one corner.

Ryan leaned against his desk with his arms folded across his chest and looked George straight in the eyes.

"George, what I am going to tell you has to be kept between us until I get more information." Ryan filled George in on the information Walt had given him but left the visions out. "Jade is friends with Amy and James Linderhoff, and she has their daughter with her."

"What? We need to talk with this Jade. Where is she? Shit, and the kid! How old is the kid?" George was stunned.

"Walt is trying to locate her. He saw photos on TV and called me because he knew Jade was friends with the couple. He knows Jade has the kid with her."

"How much have you told Walt?"

"I just told him that the couple had been murdered near the park and we believe it may have been a drug deal gone bad."

"That's it? You didn't give him any other information?"

"No. I know what I can and can't say." Ryan stood straight up, looking and feeling offended.

"Good. I want to speak with Jade. I also want to speak with the child." George turned his back to Ryan and rifled through some papers on his desk.

"I know. I told Walt we needed to find Jade as soon as possible. I'm going back to his house to wait. I'll call you as soon as we know anything on her whereabouts. Oh, here's some information on James I found on a previous drug charge. George, call my cell when the information from AFIS comes in." Ryan gathered his files and headed for the office door.

"I will. You call me as soon as you know where they are!" George said, preparing to go check on the AFIS lead.

~

Walt was still waiting for Jade to call when Ryan arrived. The two were sitting in the living room exchanging ideas about the situation when the phone rang.

"Dad, I thought you were going to call me. What's going on?" Jade was angry.

Walt smiled, letting Ryan know that it was Jade on the phone. "I was going to, but you didn't give me the number." They both laughed at that. Then he began explaining to her what he and Ryan had discussed. "Jade, it's very important that you tell us where you are so we can be on our way there. You're not safe."

"No, Dad—I can't tell you where we are. You'll be putting yourself in danger of being arrested as an accomplice."

"Ryan needs to talk with you and Emmie. Jade, he knows everything. I told him about the visions and why you have Emmie with you. I had to tell him everything."

Stunned and not quite sure what to say, she held the phone tight in both hands and took a moment to collect her thoughts and keep her anger in check.

"Jade?" He was worried. Maybe he should have told her he shared her secret in a way that would not incriminate her or make her seem as though she were not lucid. He blurted it out like it was no big deal. He knew it was a big deal. Damn, he needed to stop and think before he did anything else to frighten her. "Baby?"

"Dad, I can't believe you told this guy about my...my...you know. He's probably just going along with everything because he wants to get his hands on me and arrest me."

"Jade, come on—I told you that I know Ryan. You need to listen to me. Where are you?"

Ryan grabbed the telephone and started talking to Jade. "I know you don't know me very well and have no reason to trust me, but you have to bring that child back here and do it now. I have a lot of questions that you need to answer, and I need you here in person for this interview." He stopped and listened. Total silence. "Jade?" Jade hung up. She had not said a word to Ryan, and now he feared he had blown the best lead he had. "Damn it." He tossed the phone on the table and hung his head. "She hung up," he said, not even bothering to look up.

"Don't worry, Ryan, she'll call back, but don't grab the phone like that. Jade's uneasy with the fact that her secret is out. I shouldn't have told you before talking with her first."

~

Jade was more afraid now than ever before. Walt, her rock and her life, had told her secret without even discussing with her the implications of someone knowing that she was different.

Emmie chose that minute to walk into the living room. She looked at Jade with big tears in her eyes. "I want to go home!" she hiccupped on a sob.

Jade walked over and picked her up, hugging her tightly. "Why do you want to go home?"

"I miss my mommy and my daddy. I need to see them and hug them." she cried.

Jade held the child to her. "Soon, little one, soon." *What was she going to do now?*

Jade took Emmie to the kitchen, and they made cookies together. Emmie was soon laughing and had forgotten about home, at least for the moment. Jade was brainstorming the entire time they were baking, trying hard to keep herself cheerful for the child's sake. She could not tell Emmie she would never see her parents again. She could not tell her anything for certain—not even that she was safe, because right now Jade didn't know if either of them were indeed safe. She didn't know anything, except that she had taken a child without permission, that the child's parents were now dead, and that someone else besides her father now knew her secret.

~

Ryan waited at Walt's house for what seemed like hours for the phone to ring. When it finally did, Walt grabbed it and was relieved to hear Jade's voice.

"Dad, what have I done?"

Walt began speaking soothingly to his daughter, explaining the importance of her bringing Emmie back and talking to Ryan. Finally, after hashing it out from both points of view—both hers and Walt's—she decided she would bring Emmie to her dad's house tomorrow. They hung up and Walt told Ryan that she would be there tomorrow. The two men agreed that Ryan should come a little after two, thereby giving Walt time to put Jade at ease and to not overwhelm Emmie.

"Oh, and Ryan? Make sure your badge and gun are hidden, too," Walt said as the thought occurred to him.

"No worries, Walt, I know what I'm doing. I'm a pro at this. Trust me," he laughed.

Ryan left and headed back to the precinct. George called his cell phone just before he pulled into the station's parking lot.

"Hey, we got their names! You were right—it is Amy and James Linderhoff. I cannot believe we have this break so soon. We're trying to contact a next of kin right now."

"George, I'll be in the office in a few minutes, okay?" Ryan had to make sure Jade was protected until he knew how she was involved in all this.

3

AFTER dinner, Jade bathed Emmie and once again told her a night time story.

"When are we going to see my mommy and my daddy?"

"Maybe tomorrow, okay?"

"Can I call my mommy?"

"No, sweetie, they're not home right now. Try to get some sleep, okay?"

Emmie hugged Jade and lay down to sleep while sighing and turning over on her side. Jade ran her hand down Emmie's long hair.

"I'll take you home soon," she whispered.

Jade then returned to the kitchen to clean the cookie mess and put the food away. She had to make sure Emmie was asleep before she tried to make her vision come back. She was hoping for more detail, more information, more anything.

At the same time that Jade was thinking of recalling her vision, her father was beating himself up for betraying Jade's secret to Ryan. He hoped that he really knew Ryan as well as he thought he did. Ryan now had the power to hurt Jade–Walt had given him that power.

He would never forgive himself if Ryan used this against Jade. Walt had poured his heart out to Ryan on Jade's behalf. He was the one to always say, "No one must ever know your secret, sweetie." Walt prayed with all his heart that Ryan was the kind of man he thought he was: trustworthy.

~

Jade went into the bedroom and put on her PJs. While performing her nightly ritual of taking off her makeup and brushing her teeth and hair, she went through the day's events.

Walt had actually shared her secret with this guy – who was a police detective, of all people. Police officers were the hardest people to try and reason supernatural occurrences with. What kind of man was Ryan? Her father talked about him with such respect, but was he trustworthy? He seemed nice enough the couple of times she had run into him when she was with her dad, but she didn't have any idea what he was really like. She had to have faith that her dad knew what he was doing. He was always there for her and always gave her good advice. Why question him now?

She lay down on the bed and decided to give the vision another try. Closing her eyes and breathing deeply and slowly, she let the vision overtake her mind: *A small girl lying on her back on…carpet? The little girl is Emmie and she's wearing a blue sweat suit, the same one she had on in the park…Emmie is staring at the person that is choking her…Why is she just staring, why isn't she struggling, why isn't she making sound…Is she dead?*

Of course. Her eyes are lifeless; her struggles have stopped. The person is so angry that they won't stop choking her. What could this child have done to anger someone so much?

The area is well lit…is that sunshine? Wait, yes, it's not carpet, it's grass; they're outside. Look at the hands strangling Emmie—man's hands definitely, not a big man though; the hands are small. A tattoo on his right hand on the wedge between the thumb and forefinger…what is it of? Focus, look harder. What is the tattoo? Screaming…where is the screaming coming from?

Jade sat up and listened.

The screaming was not in the vision. It was Emmie. Jade's blood chilled at sound of the screaming. Jumping up, she ran to her.

Emmie was screaming and flailing around on the bed. Jade grabbed Emmie and held her. "Shush, you're okay, you're okay now, baby."

Emmie woke up and looked at Jade. Tears were streaming down her cheeks.

"Emmie, what were you dreaming of?"

"The angel was back and told me that Mommy and Daddy were never coming back."

"Why would the angel tell you that?"

"I don't know, but the angel said you would take care of me. She said I should stop asking to go home and that you are my

~ 30 ~

home now. What does the Angel mean?" Emmie looked up into Jade's face with her own face full of wet tears.

Jade looked at Emmie and realized that she did not have the first idea about how to tell a six-year-old child that her parents were dead. "I don't know where Jimmy and Amy are right now, but, Emmie, you can stay with me as long as you want to."

"Are my mommy and daddy okay, Jade?" she asked with hope in her eyes.

"I don't know, honey. I don't know." This was not the time to break this child's heart. Sometimes lying was allowed, right?

Nothing else was said. Jade lay down with Emmie and held the child while she slept. Going over and over the vision in her mind while she lay there, nothing of it made sense to her yet, except that Emmie did not struggle in the vision because she was already dead. The tattoo – why couldn't she see what the tattoo was? Jade lay there for a long time, not moving, as she was afraid to wake Emmie. What would tomorrow hold for them? Finally sleep came: no dreams, no visions, just fitful sleep. Jade awoke to daylight and a sleeping left arm. The pins and needles feeling would stop as soon as she could shake her arm.

Moving off the bed slowly and as quietly as possible while trying hard not to wake the sleeping child, Jade was not ready to face more questions that she couldn't answer. She went to the bathroom and washed her face, brushed her teeth and then her hair, and searched for clothes. Jade heard Emmie moving around in her bedroom before she came into the hallway.

"Jade, where are my clothes?" she yelled down the hall.

"Hang on, I'll be there in a minute." Finishing up her morning routine, she went in to help Emmie find an outfit for the day. While Emmie dressed, Jade brushed the girl's long hair into a braid. Leaving Emmie to brush her teeth, Jade went to make breakfast.

She decided oatmeal and orange juice would have to do this morning. There was a lot to get done before they left for her dad's house. Jade sat with Emmie while she ate, but did not eat much herself. Her stomach was tied in knots. "Honey, where were your mom and dad while you were playing in the park?"

"Mommy took me to the park. Then, I saw her and Daddy with the ugly man. I was sliding down the slide, and Mommy said she would be right back. Then Mommy, Daddy, and the ugly man walked to the parking lot. I didn't watch them because I was playing. Then you came, and I knew that you were the lady the angel had told me about."

"I didn't see either Amy or Jimmy when I came to the park. Who is the ugly man, Emmie?"

"I don't know his name. Every time he comes to my house, Mommy and Daddy fight. He must be a bad man."

"Let's play the memory game again and tell me what the man looks like."

Emmie sat there for a few minutes then said. "He's ugly, he's mean looking, ummm, he has black hair, and I don't know what color his eyes are. Oh, oh, but he has a drawing on his hand," she said excitedly.

"Drawing? What drawing?"

"I don't know, it's funny looking." She grabbed her hand and put her finger between her thumb and forefinger. "It's here," she said.

Jade held her breath. Afraid to say the wrong thing, she just said, "Okay, go get ready. We're going to my dad's house today."

Jade cleaned the kitchen and then telephoned her dad. "We're on our way," she said when he answered.

He was relieved to hear Jade's voice. He'd had nightmares last night. "Be careful, honey." He thought she sounded a little better today. He would have to tread lightly. No more blurting things out. He would take his time and think everything through first.

"I will, Dad. We'll see you in a few hours."

"A few hours? Jade, where the hell are you?"

"Dad, don't ask. I'm not going to tell you. We may need to stay here longer, and I am not going to pull you any deeper into this than I already have."

"Jade, I am your father, and I want to help you. We need to be honest with each other about everything. That's why I told you I shared your secret with Ryan."

"Dad, I'm not saying we are hours away. I'm just saying we will see you in a few hours."

"Okay. Be careful." He hung the phone up and looked out the living room window. Where was she? Why did she feel that she couldn't tell him? He stood there a while, just watching the quiet neighborhood. Nothing was moving, no cars, no people, no animals—absolutely nothing.

~

Jade settled Emmie in the rear car seat, and they left the security of the little cabin hideaway. She was trying to figure out the right way to explain their meeting with her dad and Ryan. Emmie was steadily watching Jade through the mirror. Her eyes were so full of questions, but Jade still didn't have any answers. Figuring that she'd better start a conversation with Emmie and hopefully stave off the questions that were sure to start, she asked, "Emmie do you have family besides your mom and dad?"

"Yeah, my Aunt Annie. Annie's going to school."

"Do you know the name of Annie's school?" she asked hopefully.

"Yeah, the school is named 'college,' silly."

"Oh. Does Annie have kids?"

"No...Jade?"

"Huh?"

"Can I go home so I can see Harry? I think he's hungry and scared."

"Who is Harry?" Her heart began to pound rapidly. Was there another child?

"Harry's my dog."

"I didn't know you had a dog, Emmie. Why don't you tell me about Harry?" Whew, that was too close for comfort. Strange...why would another kid pop into my mind?

"He's a big dog. He is so smart, and he can sit and shake paws. He even rolls over if you tell him to. I miss Harry."

Now Jade had another problem: Harry! She didn't even know Emmie's address. Would a six-year-old know her own address? "I'll take you home later and we will take care of Harry together." Jade drove on with her mind still going in circles. She would have to tell Emmie the information soon. First things first—Jade was going to meet with Ryan. And Ryan knew her secret. What was he thinking about her? Did he think she was crazy? Would he want proof that she had visions? He would of course want proof, as he was a cop! How was she supposed to appear normal and hold a normal conversation with him when he knew her secret? Hell, too much thinking could hurt one's self-confidence. She just needed to let it go. Emmie was still watching her through the mirror, so she decided to try and explain this trip to her dad's house. "Emmie, we're going to see my dad. His name is Walt, and he is very excited to meet you. He will probably ask you all kinds of questions, but you don't have to answer anything you don't want to." Emmie looked frightened, and Jade felt her heart crumble. This poor child...what was going to happen to her?

"Is your daddy mean?" she asked quietly.

"No, sweetie, he is very nice, and I think you'll like him. Do you have grandparents?"

"Yeah, my grammy is in New York, and my nanny is in California."

"No grandfathers, or grandpas?"

No, Gramps died, but Grammy says he's alive in our hearts. Do you have a grammy or a gramps?"

"No, mine died a long time ago. My mom died too, but your grammy is right because my mom lives on in my heart." Jade knew they were almost to her dad's house. She felt panic rise and decided to stall a while. "Hey, do you like ice cream, kiddo?"

"Oh yeah!" she yelled excitedly.

Jade felt that Emmie needed more time. She knew that she did. They drove around the block from where Walt lived to a popular ice cream parlor. Parking the car and going inside, she hoped to keep her panic under control. "What's your favorite flavor of ice cream?"

"Strawberry."

"Do you want a cone or a sundae?"

"A cone, please," she answered as her face lit up with a huge smile and dancing eyes.

"Okay, one strawberry ice cream cone and one chocolate ice cream cone it is." Jade sat Emmie down on a chair. "Wait right here, okay?" Turning to the young girl at the counter she ordered the two cones. While she waited, she kept her eyes on Emmie. She looked so little and alone sitting there with her short legs dangling, moving back and forth with anticipation. Once again, the thought went through her mind: what would happen to this child? Jade paid for the ice cream and grabbed napkins on her way back to the table. Emmie smiled big when she saw the cones.

"Yum...my cone," she said as she reached for the pink one and began licking it with enthusiasm. "Everyone likes chocolate, but Mommy says only special people like strawberry."

"Your mommy sounds like she knows a lot about ice cream. I like strawberry, too, but only sometimes. I have to be in a special mood for strawberry ice cream."

"Mmm," was the only sound Emmie made while she happily ate her ice cream.

Jade enjoyed hers, too. Watching Emmie eat her cone was an absolute delight. They sat just looking out the window, eating their ice cream cones. Then Jade turned and asked, "Are you afraid of policemen, Emmie?"

"No. Mommy always says that if you need help, you should always find a policeman to help you. Why? Are you afraid of policemen?"

"No, your mom is right. Policemen are there to help us. Let's get going, honey. Come here and let me wipe your face and hands." After she got Emmie cleaned up they went to the car.

They drove in silence the short distance to Walt's house. Jade kept watching for anything unusual, making sure they weren't followed. She decided as soon as they got to her dad's house that she would tell him Emmie has enough to deal with for now, and maybe they could put Ryan off for a while.

Emmie looked at Jade through the mirror. "Everything is okay," she said it as if to reassure Jade. How cute was that!

"I know sweetheart, but why do you say that?"

Emmie looked at Jade with almost grown up eyes. "I know you'll take care of me, so everything's okay."

"You're right, I am going to take care of you," Jade agreed. "Can you tell me where you live?"

I live in a house near my school. My mommy made me learn my address for school. It's 1255 Maggie Lane. Where do you live, Jade?"

"I live across the street from the park where you were playing. Do you remember where the car was parked when you got in?"

"Yeah."

"Well, I live there."

"Oooh, you have a pretty house. Mommy said one day we would have a pretty house, too."

They arrived at Walt's house, and Jade turned to reassure Emmie, "Now remember, Walt is my dad and he's very nice; you'll love him. He'll be like a grandpa to you." Smiling at the little girl, she said, "Also, Emmie, there'll be a policeman coming to see us. He's going to help us find out about your mommy and daddy, okay? Ready?" Jade kept her smile in place.

Walt opened the front door and stood on the porch waiting for them to get out of the car. Jade helped Emmie out and the two walked up to greet him. Walt hugged Jade, holding her tighter than usual.

"I'm okay, Dad," Jade assured him.

Walt released Jade and looked down. "You must be Emmie."

"Yes, sir," Emmie replied. She then held her hand out and said, "It is very nice to meet you, Mr. Walt."

Walt laughed and, kneeling down, he hugged her. He looked at Jade and said, "She is absolutely adorable."

"Yes, she is," Jade said, squeezing Emmie's hand.

Walt picked Emmie up, and they all walked into the house. Looking at Jade, he could see all the strain and stress that his daughter had been experiencing. Jade smiled at her dad and shook her head. "It's all right, Dad. When is Ryan going to be here?"

"In a while. He and I decided to give you and Emmie time to settle in."

Emmie and Jade went into the living room and sat down side by side. Walt went to the kitchen to get drinks. Emmie wanted milk, and Jade, a Pepsi. Walt would have something stronger but only because he needed to settle his nerves before Ryan got there. He knew that Ryan was going to be hard on Jade, and he hoped his little girl was up for it. She looked so rough and tired right now.

Jade looked around the room and remembered when she was a child. This room used to be so huge to her, but now it was a normal size living room. Everything always seemed bigger when she was a child. This house was her home: the books lining the shelves beside the fireplace, the overstuffed chairs and comfortable sofa, the family pictures everywhere she looked, the picture of the lovely face of her mother smiling at her that felt so reassuring, the beautiful trellis outside that was filled with climbing roses of every color, and the ivy strung throughout that went all the way to the third floor roof—this was her home.

Walt was also remembering when Jade was Emmie's age. He slowly walked back to the living room. Setting the drinks on the table and plastering a smile on his face, he asked, "Emmie, what grade are you in?" He handed out the drinks.

"First grade, sir."

"How old are you?"

"I'm six. How old are you, sir?"

Both Jade and Walt laughed. "Too old!" he replied with a smile that could dazzle women of every age. Walt sat down across from the girls. He would give them a few minutes to rest and then show Emmie the surprise he had for her. He loved children and wanted Jade to marry and give him many grandchildren. He knew that in time she would, and he would just have to be patient. He leaned forward and drained his drink. "Emmie, come on, I want to show you something." Walt took Emmie by the hand and walked her to the back door, showing her the tire swing he had made for her in the backyard. "Do you want to go play?" he asked.

Her little face lit up once again with that huge smile that she was capable of, and she flew out the door, running to the swing.

"Do you need someone to push you?" Jade asked.

"No, I'm six!" she yelled without looking back.

He turned to Jade, "Good, this will give us time to talk before Ryan gets here."

Jade didn't want Emmie out of her sight. "Let's sit here on the porch, Dad. I don't want to leave her out here alone."

The day was another beautiful one: blue skies, no clouds, birds chirping, and everything in the world seemed right. It would be, if only Jade could be strong enough for what was to come.

"So what have you found out?" Walt asked. "Ryan is going to have a lot of questions. Do you feel up to it?"

"Sure. I've been trying to get answers from Emmie, but she's so young and smart. I'm trying to get information from her without giving anything away but she picks up on things so quickly that I'm afraid to ask too much. I hope Ryan is good with kids. I did get her address, and I know her mom and dad were with a man at the park. Emmie is quite observant for being only six. She's already asked me if her mommy and daddy are okay." Jade was so nervous; talking rapidly as though she didn't want to be interrupted before she said everything that she was thinking.

"Jeez, what did you say?"

"Nothing. I just held her and let her cry herself to sleep. Dad, she says an angel talks to her. She knew I was coming to get her, and she told me she knew that I would take good care of her. She says the angel told her that her mommy and daddy were not coming back. Why would an angel do that? What do you make of all this?"

Walt looked reflectively at the little girl swinging. "I think she knows more than she is saying and trying, in her six-year-old way, to let you know that she knows. I think the angel is her way of telling you: she knows."

"Oh, I get it. There isn't an angel and it's just her way of coping? Wow...I thought that she might have a gift too," Jade said.

"Exactly. Well, that would be my guess, anyway."

"I had the vision over and over, trying to see more, and I think Emmie laid there being strangled without fighting because she was already dead. I know the killer has a tattoo on his right hand. You know, like in the wedge between his thumb and forefinger, but I can't tell what the tattoo is. Emmie called it a drawing when she was trying to describe the 'ugly man,' but she didn't know what the tattoo was either. I still can't see his face. Dad, this is the worst vision I've ever had. I can't see important things—the things I need to see."

"Hey, Jade, look at me!" Emmie was swinging and laughing. She was so delighted with that simple tire swing.

"Yay, look at you go! Thanks, Dad, she's having a ball. That swing was a good idea."

"I was hoping it would give us time to talk before Ryan got here. I know you're worried because of the information I shared with him, and I know I should have talked with you first, but we need Ryan and in order to get him on our side. I had to be completely honest with him. He didn't even make jokes about the visions; he listened and then asked that you bring Emmie to talk with him. Of course he wants to talk with you too, but I think he is more interested in talking with Emmie. Have you told her about Ryan?" He was trying to put her at ease and lessen the strain that he could see in her eyes.

"I told her that a policeman was coming over to see us. I hope Ryan will go easy on her. I never confirmed to her that her mommy and daddy were dead."

"Jade, I can make some lunch. Are you hungry, honey?" A change of subject might be just what she needed.

"No thanks, Dad, but let me ask Emmie." Standing up, she yelled out, "Emmie, are you hungry?"

"Nooooo, I don't want to get off the swing. Please let me stay out here!"

"Okay, we're going to stay right here until you're ready to

come in. Just be careful, okay?"

"I will."

Sitting there quietly and watching Emmie swing, they were both in deep thought. Each trying to put the other at ease, but neither was succeeding. It was strange for both of them—they had always been so at ease with one another, so this tension seemed unbearable to both.

"There's the doorbell. You stay here with Emmie, and I'll get the door." Walt took the opportunity to escape.

"Dad, please ask Ryan to take his time with Emmie. I'm afraid she's fragile right now." Jade felt her heart stop when the door bell sounded again. She hoped she was ready for this. She was more worried about Emmie, but she couldn't stop her heart from hammering in her own chest.

"I will. I'll be right back." Walt hurried to the door and taking a deep breath, he opened the door with a smile. "Hey, Ryan, you're right on time. We're all out back. I made Emmie a tire swing, and Jade didn't want to leave her out there alone. Is it okay with you if we sit on the back porch?"

"Walt, before we go out there, has Jade said anything to you? Was she able to get anything from Emmie?"

"Come on, Ryan, Jade will tell you everything she can. She's worried about Emmie, though. She asked that I tell you to go easy. Have you dealt with many kids?"

"Don't worry. I'm a professional, and I'll be gentle, I promise."

"Do you want a drink before we head out back?"

"No thanks, Walt, let's just get this over with so you and your family can get back to normal."

4

JADE was pushing Emmie on the swing when Ryan came out. At first, she was unaware that anyone had come out of the house. She was completely focused on Emmie, leaning over and speaking into her ear something that made Emmie laugh as she swung away.

Ryan stood there, staring. He didn't remember Jade looking so vulnerable, so tiny. Realizing, not for the first time, what a beauty Jade was. How had he known Walt as long as he had and never taken the time to get to know Jade as well?

She was petite, not more than 5'3", Ryan guessed, and no more than 110 pounds soaking wet. Looking at her, he could not believe she actually thought that she had visions. After all, only loony tunes thought that, didn't they? Ryan just knew that when he talked to her she would probably be a real lulu. Even though she looked normal, he had dealt with enough to know that looks could be deceiving. *Wait... wait...* Ryan thought. What was he doing? Didn't he just tell Walt he was a professional? He needed to get his head in the game and handle this investigation as it needed to be handled.

"Uh—Jade? Come on up here," Walt said, knowing it would be better for everyone to get this over with.

Jade turned and saw her dad and Ryan. She felt sick to her stomach; this was really happening. She reminded herself to stay calm. "Emmie, you keep swinging for a while." Walking to the porch, she felt really even more sick. This was not going to be easy.

"Is that guy your brother?" Emmie asked, leaning

backwards in the swing.

"No, sweetheart, that's the policeman I told you was coming to see us." Jade stopped walking and looked at Emmie.

"He doesn't look like a policeman. Where's his gun?"

"I don't know honey. I'll be right there on the back porch, okay? If you need anything, just yell." Turning, she began what felt like the walk to the gallows.

Walt watched Jade, knowing how uncertain she must have felt. "Jade, you remember Ryan Douglas, don't you?"

"Of course—hello again, Detective Douglas." At least her voice didn't give away her emotions.

"Ryan, please...and may I call you Jade?" Ryan was even more taken with this beautiful creature up close. He watched her slight nod of assent and found that he had a hard time catching his breath. She had really grown up over the last two years. Ryan took in her hair, which was the color of spun gold, and her chocolate brown eyes, and her cute little pointed chin with a dimple in it. Her eyes were shaped like almonds and held the longest lashes he had ever seen. It was a face of beauty, yet it was one filled with innocence. Trying hard not to show his thoughts, he got down to business. "Let's get this going," he said, watching her. "Let's sit down and relax. We'll take this slowly and get to know each other somewhat before we move on to Emmie and her parents. I want you to know that I will do whatever needs to be done to gain your faith in me. I want you to be comfortable. You can trust me, okay?" His steady eye contact took in every bit of her body language. He knew she was nervous, but he wondered why.

Jade was going to get through this the best way that she could. She was not going to give in to her fear and run like a scared child. She tipped her face up and meeting him eye to eye, she said, "Ryan, I can only tell you what I can tell you. You will believe what you believe. It's that easy."

"Wow, Walt—she's incredible!" Ryan said, with a smirk on his handsome face.

"Yes, she is. Thank you." Walt saw his little girl put on the brave front and held hope that she would deal with this just fine.

"I know that Dad told you I have visions. Let me explain my visions before we get going on this, okay?" Best to jump right in with both feet, she thought to herself.

"I think that's a great place to start," Ryan replied, while privately thinking: here we go with the visions again. Good God...

"Alright, well, here goes—I see things before they happen. I sometimes can stop them from happening, and sometimes I help them to happen. It just depends what the vision is."

"Okay, wait. Your visions—are they dreams?"

"No, I'm awake when I see them. Usually."

"How long have you had them?"

"Since I was ten—I saw my mom's accident just hours before it happened."

"I know. Walt explained some of the visions you've had. He shared some of your successes with me. I hope you don't mind."

Jade blushed and looked over at Emmie.

Walt looked at Ryan to see his reaction. Ryan was looking at Jade with such interest Walt felt the need to leave them alone. Getting to his feet he went for the door. "I'm going to get a drink. Anyone else want one?"

"No, thank you," Ryan and Jade said at the same time. Walt went into the house, closing the door and smiling to himself. Maybe Ryan is the right one for more than this investigation, he thought to himself, smiling. Walt was full of wicked thoughts about Jade's future. He had been worried about her earlier, wondering about her social life, or rather the lack thereof. He liked Ryan. Ryan was a good young man. The two of them had a lot to offer each other. He just hoped they could see farther than the tips of their own noses, as they could be a match made in heaven. This was the wrong circumstance in which to start a relationship, but whatever it took...

"Jade, tell me about the vision you had with Emmie and her family."

"I didn't have a vision of her and her family—just of Emmie."

"You never saw her parents in this vision?"

"No. Five days ago I was sitting in the park across from my house. I go there just to sit and watch people sometimes. It's a nice park with wonderful views. I remember I was sitting there, watching a couple of kids skateboarding, when the vision began. I saw a beautiful little girl in a blue sweat suit being strangled. The little girl was just lying there, not fighting, not crying out, but instead just staring at the face of the person that was choking her. I knew her name was Emmie, but I don't know how. Sometimes I get facts with my visions. It's knowledge that I just *know*. I don't fully understand how it all works, but I can control it to a certain degree. Anyway, Emmie's name and age are two of those facts. I knew the little girl would be at the same park in two days. I also knew that I would have to keep her safe. I didn't know how I was supposed to do this; I just knew that I simply had to. I went to the park the next day and listened to all the kids, trying to hear the name 'Emmie,' but I heard nothing. Then, I rented a safe place to take the child, filled two suit cases—one for her and one for me. The next day, when I knew Emmie would be there, I sat in my living room watching the children play in the park. Then I saw her. I left my house, went to the park, walked up to Emmie, and she took my hand. We walked to my car, and I drove away."

Stunned, he asked. "You never saw her parents?"

"No," she replied. Ryan...he was easily 6'4, with a nice body, thick, but not fat by any means, black hair, and, upon closer inspection, the bluest eyes she had ever seen. He had a strong, chiseled jaw line and sexy, pink-colored lips. He was not more than 29 or 30. No wedding band, but that didn't mean anything...

Stop this, Jade told herself, *you have enough problems right now!*

"She wasn't there with any adult? She was just in this big old park playing all by herself?"

"I never saw anyone with her, but I asked Emmie about that. She told me her mommy took her to the park, and her daddy and a man showed up. Emmie said they went to the parking lot, leaving her on the slide. Then I showed up and she left with me, not seeing her parents again."

"Has she asked to go home, or where her mommy and daddy are – anything at all?"

"Yes, but I keep putting her off. I know she has an aunt. Her Aunt Annie goes to college somewhere around here, but I don't know where. I also know that Emmie has a grandmother in New York and one in California. She has a dog named Harry, and she lives at 1255 Maggie Lane. She said that she doesn't know the name of the man that her parents went to the parking lot with, but that he is an ugly man and that he causes her mommy and daddy to fight a lot. She is a very smart little girl. She's scared and trying not to show it. I need you to help me with this, but not at any cost to her – no cost that we can help, that is. I know that she already has more to bear then she knows or is even capable of understanding. She thinks her parents and I are friends. I didn't know what else to tell her."

"You don't know her parents, do you?"

"No."

"After seeing the photos on TV, did you remember seeing them at the park?"

"No."

"Then how did you know it was them?"

"Because I saw the pictures, and then I asked Emmie to describe them to me."

"Do you think you can pick the man out of a mug shot book?"

"No. I never saw his face. I just know he has a tattoo on his right hand in the web between his thumb and finger."

"A tattoo of what?"

"I don't know. I couldn't see it clearly. Emmie calls it a drawing, but she doesn't know what it is either."

"What did you intend to do after taking the child from the park?"

"I don't know, I was going to keep her safe and call her parents to try to explain. I don't know..."

"Okay. Why didn't you call us?"

"I don't know who the killer is. I wasn't even sure it wasn't one of her parents. You would have given her back to her parents and thought I was nuts..."

"Yeah, you're probably right. Okay, we need to figure this out so I can help you stay out of trouble."

"Can't we just say I was friends of the Linderhoffs, and I took Emmie with me, and that her mom and dad knew she was left with me? I can say that I left them at the park and had not seen them since."

"Yeah, but what about Annie? She won't know you, and she'll say she's never seen you before. Besides, we don't want you near the Linderhoffs that day." He paused, thinking for a minute. "Does Emmie know what drugs are?" he asked, looking back at Jade.

"I don't know. I didn't ask her anything about that. Why?"

"We believe this was a drug deal gone bad."

"What are you going to do with Emmie? I want her here with me until I know she is safe. If we stick to this story, I can keep her a while...can't I?"

"I have to find Annie first. She's the closest next of kin." Ryan sat there looking at Emmie trying to figure this out. Everything Jade said made sense to him, even the visions—though he couldn't believe he was giving any credence to visions.

"I need to talk with Emmie alone." Jade looked at Ryan with such vulnerability that he had to put her mind at ease. "I promise I'll be gentle with her. Does she know her parents are dead?"

"No. I haven't told her anything except that I was friends with them, and they knew she was with me."

"Why don't you go in with your dad and let me talk to her."

"At least let me stay and tell her who you are, okay?"

"Sure, okay."

"Emmie?" Jade stood and walked to the edge of the porch.

Leaning backwards in the swing again, holding on for everything she was worth and laughing loudly, Emmie said, "Yeah, Jade?"

"Come here, sweetie, I want you to meet someone."

"Dang it, okay, hang on." She reluctantly climbed off the swing like a champ. She was having so much fun. She came running up the porch steps with a big smile on her face. "Hi, who are you?" she asked, looking up at Ryan.

"Emmie, this is Ryan. Remember the policeman I told you about?"

"Yeah."

"He needs to talk to you, okay? Don't be afraid." Jade gave her fingers a light squeeze.

"I'm not afraid of him," she said, still smiling at Ryan.

"I'll be in the house with Dad if you need me, okay?"

"Okey-dokey!"

"Hello, Emmie," Ryan said, leaning down to pat the top of her head.

"Hi."

"Emmie, come sit over here and talk to me." Ryan patted the chair next to him.

"Okay, but I need to go swing again soon. You can swing, too, if you want to."

"Cool, I just might do that," he said, watching her climb into the chair. "Emmie, how do you know Jade?"

"I just met her. My angel told me about her."

"Your angel?"

"Uh-huh."

"Tell me about Jade and your angel, Emmie."

"Okay, so see, I had a dream of an angel, and the angel told me about a beautiful woman. Jade is the beautiful woman. You think Jade is a beautiful woman?"

Caught off guard at this little girl's maturity level, he laughed and answered, "Yes, I do, honey."

"Well, she is going to help me not get hurt," she said it so matter-of-factly that Ryan had to laugh. "Why would you get hurt?" he asked calmly.

"The angel told me if I didn't go with the beautiful woman, I might get hurt. Oh, and she said my mommy and daddy aren't coming back. Why won't they? Are they mad at me?"

"No honey, they're not mad at you. When did you see your mommy and daddy last?"

"At the park. My mommy takes me to the park all the time."

"Did your daddy take you, too?"

"No, Daddy and the ugly man came to the park and talked to Mommy."

"The ugly man?"

"Yeah, he has a drawing on his hand, and he's bad."

"Why do you call him the ugly man?" Ryan asked, laughing at her candidness.

"Mommy and Daddy always fight when he's around."

"What do they fight about?"

"I don't know. Stuff."

"Emmie, have you ever seen the man give anything to your mommy or daddy?"

"Sometimes he would give Daddy presents."

"Presents?"

"Yep."

"What kind of presents?"

"I dunno. They always were wrapped up."

"In pretty paper, like for your birthday?"

"No, dumb brown paper, like a bag, kinda."

"Did your daddy ever open them so you could see them?"

"No. Mommy said it was stuff for big people, not kids, so they said I didn't need to see them. I know Daddy liked them though."

"How do you know he liked them?"

"'Cause when the man would give them to Daddy, he would laugh, and they would shake hands or hug sometimes. Mommy was scared of the ugly man. When he came over, Mommy would take me outside or to the park sometimes. Then, when the ugly man left, Mommy would cry or tell Daddy he needed to get a better job."

"Emmie, did you ever see your daddy smoke?"

"Smoke what?"

"You know – cigarettes or things that smelled funny?"

"No. Mommy said cigarettes are bad for you."

"Were your mommy or daddy sick a lot?"

"Daddy was. How do you know that...are you my daddy's friend too?"

"No, I don't know your mommy or your daddy. I am trying to help you find them."

"Oh, are they lost?" Her eyes turned fearful.

"I'm not sure yet. Do you know the ugly man's name?"

"No. My daddy always called him a bad name."

"What was the bad name?"

"I'm not allowed to say it."

"It's okay Emmie, I need to know. We won't tell anyone you said it."

"Daddy always called him Asshole. But not when he was there, just when he was talking to Mommy."

"What did your daddy call him when he was there?"

"Umm, I don't know."

"Think, honey. Think really hard."

"Umm, I have to think 'cause it was funny."

"Take your time."

"Where's your gun?"

"It's right here inside my jacket. See?" Ryan opened his jacket so Emmie could see the gun in his shoulder holster.

"Oh yeah, wow, is it real?"

"Sure is. Now think: what did your daddy call the ugly man?"

"I think he called him Mickey, you know like Mickey

Mouse, but I don't know his other name."

"Mickey?"

"Yep."

"Do you think you could pick Mickey out of some pictures I could show you?"

"Oh yeah, I could draw you a picture of him too."

Laughing, he said, "Okay, maybe later. Jade tells me you have an Aunt Annie?"

"Yep."

"Do you know Annie's last name?"

"Uh, you mean like mine is Linderhoff?"

"Yes, sweetie, is it Annie Linderhoff?"

"No. It's Annie Armstrong."

"Armstrong, you're sure?"

"Yeah, I'm sure."

"You have been a champ, kiddo. Thanks for your help, but I might have to ask more questions later. Is that okay?"

"Sure. You're cute, Ryan. I like it when you smile."

"Gee, thanks! I think you're cute too. You want to go swing some more?"

"Yep, you wanna swing too?"

"Maybe later, okay? I need to talk with Jade again."

"Okay." She eagerly jumped off the porch and ran for the swing.

He watched her run to the swing and pull herself up. Pushing hard with her legs in the air, she finally had it going. Opening the back door he said "Walt, Jade—come on out."

Ryan could tell that Jade had been crying. He tried hard to quell his empathy for her. Why did she have this effect on him? Usually he could care less what people thought; he just did his job and left them to deal with whatever they had to deal with. This one was different. It hurt him to think he was causing her pain.

Jade tried to hide her fear. "Well, she sure doesn't look any worse for the wear."

"Oh, she's delightful. Not afraid of strangers, that's for sure."

"Did you tell her about her mom and dad?" she asked, not really wanting to know.

"No. I want to find out more information and have answers for her. I know she's only six, but she's smart as a whip. She has such a cute personality for someone so young." Ryan began making notes. He needed to do something. Watching the fear cross Jade's face, he felt he needed busy work, and so he made notes.

Jade excused herself and went to talk with Emmie. Walt watched Ryan writing furiously and smiled. This was turning out to be interesting—very interesting indeed.

Ryan needed to find out about Annie. Was she James'

~ 46 ~

sister or Amy's sister? Where was she going to school? Would she want to take Emmie until everything was taken care of? Who was this man? Were they dealing drugs? Where did Jade fit in? Did she know more than she was telling? Could the visions be real? His heart said yes, but common sense said no way. He was good at reading people. She seemed sincere, but right now, her ass was in a crack, and self-preservation would naturally take over. She said in her vision the child was being strangled. The parents were strangled, and that information had not been released. Was she in with the killer and knew what was going on and instead saved the kid? He would have to check and see if she had a record. Then he would get her and Emmie down to the station to look at mug shots. Ryan watched Jade with Emmie. She was definitely protective of the child. They were laughing, and Jade was pushing her in the swing. They were singing and having a good time. Ryan hated to interrupt the two. He stood up. "I believe I have what I need right now. Keep them here. I'm going to the station to check out this information, and I'll be back soon." He turned and touched the door handle. "Oh, by the way, how old is Jade?"

"She's twenty-four. Why?" Walt was curious. What was Ryan thinking?

"Just needed it for my report. I'll see you soon." He looked back to the swing one more time and then opened the door.

"They'll be here for a while. You be careful." Walt wondered if Jade would stay but didn't let on to Ryan that he was afraid she might leave again. Ryan left, and Walt sat there watching the girls play. Would Jade be safe if this were a drug deal gone wrong? Did she have any idea what she had gotten them into?

Walt went inside, and Jade finally felt herself relax. What had they talked about? She'd tried to hear but couldn't. Ryan didn't even say goodbye to her. Did he think she was guilty of something? Jade finally released a breath that she didn't even know she'd been holding. Wow, Ryan was a good looking man. Why hadn't she noticed that before today? He seemed sweet and caring, but would he really help them? Could he really help keep her out of jail?

5

RYAN called George on his way to the station. "Look up Jade Hamilton, white female, twenty-four years of age. I don't know her birth date. Just run her in the blind and see what you get. And do you have any leads on a sister of either James or Amy Linderhoff, name of Annie?"

"No. Are you sure she's a blood relative?"

"Yes. Her name is Annie Armstrong. She's going to college somewhere near here. Run her name in the blind too. I don't know how old she is, but judging from the Linderhoffs, she should be in her twenties."

"Why are you interested in Jade?" George was getting a bad feeling about this.

"I just want to make sure she doesn't have a criminal history, that's all."

"I thought you knew her. Are you on your way back?"

Shit. Not thinking again. Get your head out of your ass! Ryan was berating himself for not keeping his head in the game. "I do know her, but she's been away at college, and you never know about college kids, right? Anyway, just run her in the blind and see what you get, okay?"

"Okay, no problem. I'll go take care of that now. How long before you get here?"

"On my way. I shouldn't be too long. Thanks, George." Ryan hung up. He needed to get with the game plan and stay there. What the hell was wrong with him?

George picked up the piece of paper he had been writing on and went to dispatch. He spotted Denise through the glass window. He liked Denise. She was a good dispatcher. "Hey Denise," he said with a big smile on his face.

"Oh lordy, what do you want?" she asked, looking at him with questioning eyes. He needed something, she knew. Detectives didn't come just to chit-chat—they always wanted something.

"Are you too busy to run a couple in the blind for me?"

"Am I busy? I'm a dispatcher...what do you think?"

George laughed and slapped Denise on the shoulder. "Okay, you got me there."

"Yeah, I do. What's up? Who do you need checked out?"

"I need a couple of females run in the blind. I don't have a date of birth on either, but I do have names and approximate ages."

"Okay, who are they?"

"Hamilton, Jade; white female, twenty-four years of age, and Armstrong, Annie or maybe Anna; white female in her twenties."

"Can you give me a minute?" she asked, finishing up what she had been working on.

"Sure. I need a complete criminal history and all."

"Are you going to wait in here, or do you want me to call your office?"

"How long do you think it will take?"

"About ten minutes. Is that okay?"

"Yeah, I'll wait right here."

George didn't know how dispatchers dealt with their jobs. They almost had to have eight arms and two brains to accomplish all they needed to do. The radio was going off with officers running traffic, the telephones rang incessantly, and the 911 system rang off the hook, not to mention the public walking up to the window, wanting to ask questions or make appointments with someone. These dispatchers were underpaid and understaffed, giving up their days off more often than not, and yet they still appeared to have a sense of humor. It totally amazed George.

He would stand there and wait until Denise could get his information, and he wouldn't try to rush her. He had great respect for a good dispatcher.

Denise handled two more telephone calls and three radio dispatches but finally handed the information to George.

"Thanks, I know you're busy and all, but I really needed this." He used his charming smile—the one that made women feel like they were special. He knew how to get what he wanted.

"Yeah, whatever...get out of here; I have work to do." She blushed and smiled back at him.

"I know, thanks again." George headed back to the office

to wait for Ryan.

While waiting he made some inquiries on Annie's possible college. He knew they needed to find her and let her know about the Linderhoffs before their names were released to the media. That would be a hell of a way to find out your brother or sister had been murdered and that your niece was missing. Well, not missing, exactly, but she wouldn't know that.

George called two of the three colleges in the area before Ryan walked in. No luck so far. He waved his hand at Ryan, giving him the sign to wait a minute, as he dialed the third.

Ryan sat down at his desk and looked over his notes while he waited for George to get off the phone.

George gave his name and credentials to the person on the phone and then asked if Annie Armstrong attended school there. Ryan watched as George began to write something down and his heart started to pound. Thanks to Jade, they were going to make some headway in this investigation. Ryan heard George ask for Annie's schedule, and then he thanked who he had been talking to and hung up. "Ryan, Annie attends St. Joseph's Community College. She will be there in the morning. Her classes begin at 9:40."

"Great job, George. What did you find out about their histories?"

"Jade doesn't have a criminal history. Here's the return for her drivers license. Annie also doesn't have a criminal history. This investigation is going full speed now. What are we going to do about the kid?"

"I don't know. Jade wants to keep her and is with her for now."

"You know that we can't let her do that if this aunt wants her and is the closest blood relative..."

"Yeah, I know. We need to check California and New York for the grandmothers. I don't know which is which, as far as the states go. I'm sure Annie can help us with that."

"Yeah, we just need to make sure the media doesn't release any names yet." George was shuffling papers around on his desk.

"I'll call my buddy Lenny over at the news station and explain what I can. He'll help." Ryan was looking through his phone numbers.

"Okay, so what did you find out?" George was anxious.

"Emmie doesn't know the name of the suspect. She said that her dad calls him Mickey. She and Jade will be coming in to look at mug shots today or tomorrow. Did you find a driver's license for Annie?"

"There are four Annie Armstrongs in their twenties. We'll have to wait to get more information. Or we could skip the school thing and go to these four addresses," George suggested.

"No. Right now I want to work on some mug shots for Jade and Emmie to look at. This guy is supposed to have a tattoo on his right hand. So, I guess we start there."

"Ryan, you know a lot of the detention officers don't bother with tats. They just get the photos. This won't be easy," George said.

"I know, but this guy had to have been in and out of here a dozen times. What one detention officer doesn't get, the next one might."

"You've got a point. Okay, let me look for all the suspects with tattoos on their right hands while you call Lenny." George turned to his computer.

"Great, let's get started." Ryan was hopeful that they would have their suspect soon.

George pulled up a computer program that would eliminate anyone without a tattoo on their right hand. The computer began to scroll through the names. The number at the bottom of the page was climbing rapidly.

Ryan telephoned Lenny and explained as much as he could, asking Lenny to stop showing the photographs of the couple and to call if any information had been received but not to release any information on the victims. Lenny agreed and didn't bother to ask any questions. He knew that Ryan had told him all that he could at this point. They had always worked well together; a little mutual respect went a long way. Lenny got a lot of leads for his news stories from Ryan, and he wasn't about to put a kink in that chain, no matter what. Ryan hung up the telephone and looked over at George. "How's it going?"

"I'm compiling the list, and it's going to be quite long."

"I think I'll call Walt and see if he can get Jade and Emmie in here today. Do you think you'll have that list done soon?"

"I think it'll take about two hours to finish the list then get all the photos together."

"Ok, it's five now, so what do you think—eight tonight, or just wait until tomorrow?"

"We need to go find Annie in the morning...after that we don't know if she'll take Emmie."

"You're right. Let's go with tonight." Ryan went to get them a cup of coffee and then telephoned Walt. "Hey, Walt, it's Ryan. Is Jade still there?"

"Yes, Ryan, they're both still here. Do you need to talk to her?"

"No, I just wanted to see if you could get the two of them down here around eight tonight."

"Hang on just a minute and let me ask, okay?"

"Sure."

Walt turned toward Jade. "Ryan's on the phone; he wants to know if you and Emmie can go to the station tonight around eight?"

Emmie got excited when she heard this. "The police station, cool! Come on, Jade, let's go!"

Jade smiled at the little girl and nodded her head "Alright, tell Ryan eight will be fine."

Walt grasped the phone and confirmed, "That's fine, Ryan. They'll be there. Can I come along?"

"Sure, great. We'll see y'all then." Ryan looked at George and confirmed that they would all be there tonight.

"Hey, I'm going to print the list with what's done so far, and if you would, start getting the photos, okay?" George was worried about time. This is gonna be a long list. He sighed.

"Damn, are there that many perps with tats on their right hands?" Ryan said. "Shit, I'll get the photos together." He took a swig from his coffee. "Do you think we actually have the suspect here in our system?" Sitting his coffee cup back down, he looked at George.

"If this is indeed a drug deal of some type, then yes, I believe he'll be here."

"What information are you using to get that list?" Ryan had never learned to compile a list like this. It was useful information and he wanted to learn.

"Oh, your usual: male, white, tattooed hand, previous drug charge. That type. Why?"

"I've never put a list like this together, so I just wondered. I've made a photo lineup, so I'm assuming you just take the printed information and enter the names in the program, and it will match a photo to the name, right?"

"Yeah... Boy, I guess I need to let you start doing more of your own work!" George said, laughing.

"Hey, easy now! I do a lot of work—I just leave the technical things for you."

"This coffee is great. What happened, did we hire someone new?" George asked, taking a big swallow.

"I made it." Ryan leaned down and smelled the fresh brew.

"You're kidding! I think you should make it more often. Usually it's not even drinkable. Here—I have one hundred fifty names so far. This list is still going like crazy." George handed the papers to him.

"Wow, you weren't kidding when you said a couple hours. I had no idea there would be so many." Ryan took the list from George and looked through the names.

George leaned back in his chair, clasping his hands behind his head. He said "So, Ryan, what's Jade like? Didn't you say she knew the Linderhoffs?"

"Yeah, she was a friend of theirs. She hasn't known them long. She's really nice, a lot like her dad, but beautiful. Man, George, she's a tiny, petite thing. She really cares about the kid and apparently will do whatever it takes to protect Emmie. Jade has the prettiest smile...not that she smiles all that much. I think I would have to say she is the most delightful creature I've seen in a long time," he said, looking up at the ceiling and picturing Jade in his mind's eye.

"Whew. Well, okay then...sorry I asked," George laughed. He had never seen Ryan so taken by anyone.

Ryan realized what he had just said and how he said it. Shit, he would never hear the end of it. "Hey, don't take any of this out of context. I didn't mean anything more than what I said. I don't want you to make too much out of this." Ryan felt the heat rise up his neck.

"I don't think I am. Are you feeling guilty or something?" George had that knowing look on his face, which was quite smug, actually.

"No. I just want to make sure you understand. I only think of Jade as a witness; a useful tool in this case, nothing more."

"Sure. Okay." George was still laughing.

"Oh, whatever, George. You're the one that's married. Not me." Ryan was getting huffy and didn't know why he was letting George get to him like this.

"Exactly, but..."

"Oh no, you don't. I should have known better than to say anything."

"Hey, don't get your panties in a wad. I'm just giving you a hard time. Take it easy, man. I think it's funny you're acting, like, all poetic and shit." George knew he was gonna pay for this in the long run but, he still had to razz Ryan. That's what partners did.

"Yeah, yeah, whatever." Ryan went back to his computer and got to work, deciding that was safer than talking right now.

~

Walt was grilling hamburgers for dinner. Jade was in the kitchen, slicing tomatoes, lettuce, and onions, and Emmie was playing on the swing. Everything was as it should be right now. He was thrilled the girls were there. Watching Emmie swing, he thought he would do whatever it took to keep them safe.

"Dad, what do you think I should tell Emmie about going to the police station?" Jade asked, coming outside with her veggie tray. Setting it down on the table, she turned to look at Emmie.

"I don't think you need to worry over much. She was pretty excited about the prospect of going to the PD. I would just tell her she's going to look at photos to try and find the man who was with her parents," he said, trying to keep it simple for her.

Jade would keep it simple. The less said, the better, she thought. Hmm.... "Yeah, I think you're right about that. Emmie, come on, honey, it's time to eat." Jade watched as Emmie climbed off the swing.

They all sat on the porch and ate dinner together. No one was talking or worried about anything at the moment. It was peaceful...leisurely. It felt good to Walt. He loved having Jade home, and Emmie was an added pleasure.

Dinner was soon finished, and everyone was stuffed. The stress level had dropped considerably for Jade. She watched as Emmie took her last bite. "Emmie, go get washed up. We have to go soon," Jade said.

"Okay." Jumping off the chair, she ran to the door. "I liked the hamburger. Thanks, Walt."

"Well, you're welcome, kiddo. It was pretty good, wasn't it?" he asked, smiling.

"Yep!" Then she was gone.

"She is too cute, isn't she?" he asked Jade.

"She is a cutie. We need to go by her house, though. Did I tell you about Harry?"

"Who?" His forehead creased with frown lines.

"Harry. Emmie has a dog; I didn't know about him until earlier today."

"We can't just leave the dog there...he'll starve. Are you going to stay?" He wasn't sure he wanted the answer.

"I thought we would go back to the cabin for a while," she said hesitantly.

"Why?" Walt pushed his plate back.

"I'm not sure who the killer is. I don't want him to see Emmie. He could still hurt her, and I can't let that happen." Jade was getting defensive.

"I really don't think you need to worry about that. Stay here. That way, I can help you keep an eye on her."

"No, Dad. We can't do that to you."

"What's that supposed to mean? I'm your father, and I would love for you to stay here, both of you."

"Oh, Dad." Jade was worried about causing her dad stress. He was getting older, and she worried about his health. Not that he ever had a sick day, but...

"Just think about it, Jade. If you go back to this, this cabin, you may be too far away if you need me," he reasoned.

"I'll give it some thought. I promise," she said, reaching across the table and patting his hand. She stood and began clearing the dishes.

Taking an arm load of dishes and leftover food to the kitchen, she enjoyed the feeling of normalcy.

The phone began to ring. "I'll answer it!" Walt said, beginning to get up.

"I've already got it," Jade yelled from the kitchen. "Don't worry about it. Hello?"

"Jade, it's Ryan," he said cautiously.

"Oh, hey, Ryan. What's up?" she asked, surprised.

"I just forgot to ask if you wanted photos of tattoos to look at. I mean, since you don't know what this guy looks like, I can get tattoo pics for you."

"The tattoo is the only thing I can pick out, so yeah, that would be great."

"Alright, I'll have only tat photos for you. Did you explain to Emmie what I need?"

"No, but I will before we get there. While you're on the phone, I have a question," she said hesitantly.

"Okay."

"Um, Emmie has a dog named Harry. We need to feed him and she misses him. Can I legally go to her house?"

"She will be with you, right?"

"Yeah."

"Then go ahead. Just don't touch anything you don't need to. Get the dog and the dog food and leave. You are taking the dog, right? I mean you don't want to go every day to feed him and let him out."

"Oh no, I mean, yeah, I'm taking him with us. I don't want to go there every day. What about letting her get some of her things?"

"No. Don't take anything but the dog and dog food. We haven't been there yet. There may be clues that we need. As a matter of fact, can you wait until tomorrow?"

"Why?"

"George and I will go there tonight after you leave here. Then you can let Emmie take whatever she wants to tomorrow. We can feed the dog while we're there."

"Are you going to put that yellow crime scene tape all over the place?"

"No, why?"

"I think it would scare Emmie."

"Oh, no, we won't need to do that. It's not the crime scene. I don't think we will even need to fingerprint anything, so there won't be black powder everywhere either."

"Thanks, Ryan."

"I didn't do anything. See you guys soon, then."

"Yeah, goodbye." Jade hung up. Thankfully, he was easy to deal with. Police officers could be arrogant and just plain hard to deal with. Ryan was making this as easy as possible for her, and she knew that. She figured she may as well have her talk with

Emmie to explain why they were going to the police station tonight and to see if she wanted to stay here or go back to the cabin.

Taking the newspaper out to her dad, she finished clearing the table. "I guess I'll go have that talk with Emmie about tonight. That was Ryan wanting to make sure Emmie knew what to expect. You enjoy your paper, Dad." She smiled and patted his shoulder. Walking into the kitchen just as Emmie came out of the bathroom, she set the dishes in the sink and turned to Emmie. "Hey, kiddo, just thought you might want to chit-chat about the trip to the police station tonight."

"Are we gonna see Ryan again?"

"Yes, we are. He's going to show us some pictures. He wants us to see if we can find that bad man for him." She watched Emmie's face for signs of fear and found none.

"Why...does Ryan have a picture of the ugly man?"

"Well, honey, we're not sure that he does. He is trying to find out what the ugly man's name is and maybe even where he lives. We're going to try and help him do that, okay?"

"I don't wanna see him, but I'll try. Do you know him too?" She asked, looking up at Jade.

"No, I don't know him. I'm just going to look at the pictures with you. Okay? You know it will just be a picture, and no one will actually be there, right?"

"Yeah, I know. Can I go swing now?"

"In a minute. I need to know if you want to stay here tonight or go back to the cabin."

"Stay here. Stay here!" Emmie said jumping up and down.

Walt laid the paper aside and went into the kitchen. "You sure sound excited. What's up?" he asked Emmie, rubbing the top of her head.

"I'm staying here, Mr. Walt. Yay! Yay! Yay!" she said, doing a little dance. Walt and Jade both laughed at her.

"Emmie, I'm sorry, but it will be too late to go to your house tonight to get Harry. We'll have to go in the morning," Jade said when the jig was over.

"Why? I miss Harry. I want him." Pouting her lower lip and placing her hands on her hips, she looked pitiful and angry.

"I'm sorry, sweetie, but we'll be at the police station too long, and it will be too late."

"Oh. Alright. I hope he's okay." She sat down on the floor and began drawing circles with her little, chubby finger.

"Harry's fine. You'll see." Jade reached down and lifted Emmie to her feet. "Dad, is it okay if we bring Harry back here tomorrow?" Jade thought the dog could be a problem.

"Sure. It'll be fun. Is Harry an outside dog or an inside dog?" he asked Emmie.

"An inside dog. He has a house and everything. He has a

door to go in and out of the kitchen. He has to potty outside. Yuck. I wouldn't wanna potty outside." Scrunching her face, she made sounds of disgust.

Jade and Walt just laughed at the remark and the face that Emmie made.

'We have a little time yet; do you want to go upstairs and pick out a bedroom for the night?" Jade asked, still laughing.

"Okay." Forgetting the swing, she ran to the stairs.

The house was a two story, and all the bedrooms were on the second floor. That was always fun for Jade as a child. She used to slide down the stairs on her belly, and her mom would inevitably catch her and scold her. The second floor had four bedrooms, an office, three bathrooms and a game room. Jade always wanted brothers and sisters when she was little, but it just wasn't meant to be. The downstairs had two formal living rooms, a formal dining room, a kitchen, a den, a powder room, and a sun room. The house was very large, and Walt used to say it was way too much room for just him and Jade, but it was home, and Jade was born there. Walt would never sell the place—too many good memories.

"Dad, we have about a half hour before we have to leave. Is it okay if I leave Emmie here? I think I need to take a walk to try to clear my head."

"Sure, honey, she'll be fine."

"Thanks, I won't be long." Jade walked to the front door. Turning back to her dad she said, "Dad, I know this is quite a mess I've got us in, and I just want to say thank you for everything. You've always been there for me, and I'm sorry about all of this."

"Everything is going to turn out okay. Don't fret so much." He walked over, opened the door, and gave her a slight shove. Laughing, he closed the door.

6

OUTSIDE, the fresh, cool air hitting her face was exactly what Jade needed. She walked down the street, and before she knew it, she was sitting on a curb. *The hand with the tattoo again, and this time a pretty, young, dark-haired woman is sitting in a living room, and he's in the hallway. He has a knife in his hand. He's slowly walking toward her. Who is he? Why can't I see his face? Who is she, and what did she do to him? The cat--he's going to trip over the cat. He's focused on the girl and doesn't see the cat. Running in the path of this man, the cat seemed oblivious to his presence. Ha! He trips and falls and the woman jumps up, and, upon seeing him, she begins screaming. Oh, the screaming is so loud! He's on the floor still. Is he hurt? She's running for the door.* "Go!" Jade urges, silently. *He's up and running after her. He grabs the back of her head and, grabbing her by the hair, is pulling her back.* "What do you want? Why are you doing this? Who are you?" *The girl, sobbing, keeps asking all these questions, but he doesn't say a word.*

When the street came back in focus, Jade was confused; sometimes her visions happened at the most inopportune times. Realizing what had just happened, she tried to put this new information into perspective and remember it all. She had to tell Ryan. Who was this new victim? Where did she fit into the drug deal? Getting up, Jade looked around to see if she was being watched. Everything appeared to be normal. Walking back to her dad's house, Jade had the eerie feeling she was being watched. Turning repeatedly, she looked around. Knowing the killer was out there somewhere but not knowing who or where he was chilled her to the bone.

"Dad!" she yelled, coming through the front door.

"Right here." He came out of the living room, looking at her with worry. "What is it?"

"We have to go now! Where's Emmie?"

"She's still upstairs. Honey, what's wrong?"

"I had another vision with the ugly man. Emmie? Come on, we have to go," Jade yelled up the stairs.

"What happened? Was it Emmie again?"

"No, it was a young woman. I don't know who she is." Jade was flushed and her heart was beating like it would jump from her chest. "Emmie, come on!" she yelled again.

"Jade, calm down and tell me what you've seen," Walt said.

"Not now, Dad, we gotta go," Jade said as Emmie reached the bottom of the stairs. Taking Emmie's hand, she led the way to the car.

Walt drove, and Jade sat looking out the passenger window, deep in thought. Emmie sat in the back seat, quiet as usual. Walt couldn't keep himself from looking over at Jade. She was pale. He wanted to know what it was about the new vision that caused her to panic. He knew that he would have to wait. Right now, he knew, she needed time to sort through her thoughts, and he would give her that time. Pretty soon all hell was going to break loose. He could feel it.

~

At the station, Ryan and George had just completed the list with the photos. After a fresh cup of coffee, they were ready. It was almost eight, and Ryan hoped they were on their way.

"George, I'm going to the front desk to let the officer know we're expecting Jade so they'll let her in," he said, standing up.

"Well, okay, I'll just sit here and wait for you to get back." He was being a smartass, as usual. "I need a minute to relax anyway. I have to call Doris, too." Actually, he did need to let his wife know it would be another late night. After all these years, he still called to let her know he would be late.

"The old ball and chain? Sure, call your wife, and I'll be right back," Ryan said, laughing. He knew George was being a smartass, and, in an attempt at being one himself, he realized just how stupid he sounded. Shaking his head, he made his way to the front desk and left word with the desk officer that Jade Hamilton was expected. The desk officer would call his office when she arrived.

Walking back to his office, Ryan thought of more

questions he'd need to ask Emmie about Annie. He didn't know if she was James' or Amy's sister. He didn't know if she lived in a college dorm. He didn't know a lot of things. He hadn't been using his brain earlier because he was practically tongue-tied from seeing Jade. He really needed to get his head into this investigation. He was sure George had noticed the change in him. Look how he went on and on about her when George asked what she was like. What was he thinking? He wasn't—that was the problem. He would, though. Beginning now, he vowed silently, he would not let her affect him like this. He was a grown man, for goodness' sake. Ryan walked in just as George was getting off the telephone.

"Doris says hi," he said, leaning back in his chair with his long legs on his desk.

"She's such a sweetheart. I don't know why she puts up with you."

"Puts up with me? It's the other way around. Wait till you get married. You'll see." George said, shaking his head in disbelief.

"What? Get married! I'm the eternal bachelor, remember?"

"So you say. I see you've changed, and quite quickly too," George laughed.

"I've changed?" Ryan looked at George like he'd grown a second head.

"Hey, take it easy. I didn't mean anything by it. I think it's great. Every good man needs a good woman," George said, laughing so hard that his stomach hurt and he had to lower his legs to the floor.

"Oh my God, leave it alone, George." Ryan knew he was in trouble now. He would never hear the end of it. He knew George heard him earlier. He should have kept his mouth shut. Dumbass, he thought of himself again.

"I'll let you know if you're in trouble after I see you and Jade together." George was having too much fun now. The phone rang.

"Whatever, George, answer the damn phone. I'm going to the front desk to get Jade. I know that's the call. See ya." Ryan made his escape quickly. Why did he let George get under his skin? Hadn't he already made up his mind not to let Jade get him all twisted again?

Approaching the front desk, he saw them standing there. "Hey, Walt, Jade, Emmie. Come on back. Officer Carter, can you find me some visitor badges?"

"Sure thing, Detective Douglas, give me just a sec." Searching through a drawer, Officer Carter pulled out three badges and handed them to Ryan.

"Thanks," he nodded to Carter. Turning he asked, "How was the ride over?" He handed each of them a visitor's pass.

"It was quiet," Walt said, looking at Ryan. He turned his eyes toward Jade and hoped that Ryan would see and get the hint that something was wrong.

"Jade, are you okay? You seem a little lost in thought." Ryan did notice and wanted to know what was going on.

"I'm fine, just a little side-tracked. We need to talk, in private," Jade said.

"Sure, just let me help Emmie with this badge real quick." He leaned down to pin the badge on her. "Okay, guys, you need to leave these on while you're here. Come on, I'll take you to our office. Do you want coffee or anything?" he asked. Jade and Walt both declined. Emmie asked for a soda.

"No Emmie, you don't need a soda. Would you like some water?" Jade interrupted.

"No, never mind," Emmie sighed.

Ryan and Walt laughed as they walked ahead of Jade and Emmie.

"Never hurts to try," Walt said to Ryan. They continued to laugh.

As they walked into the office, George stood up. Ryan introduced his partner and greetings were exchanged.

"George, Jade needs to talk with me privately, so could you begin explaining things to Emmie and Walt?" Ryan asked.

"Absolutely. Come on over here, guys, to this table." He pointed to the small table in the corner.

Emmie stood there staring and not moving. "Emmie, are you okay?" Jade was worried. She had never seen Emmie react like this. Emmie still just stared at George. Not moving, not answering, but just staring at George.

Ryan walked over to Emmie. Leaning down he whispered in her ear. "He's kinda big and scary isn't he? But he won't bite, I promise."

George was a big hulking man with white hair and glasses that almost made his eyes appear to be popping out of his head. George got this reaction from kids a lot. He should have stayed sitting down; he knew better. He walked over to the table and sat in one of the chairs, trying to make himself appear smaller. Ryan took Emmie by the hand and walked with her to a chair and helped her into it. She still just stared at George. George looked at her, trying to soften his face by smiling, then held his hand out for her to shake. "Hi, Emmie, I'm Ryan's partner, George."

"How did you get so big?" Emmie asked with awe in her voice and still staring.

"I ate all my vegetables when I was a kid," George said, laughing.

"I don't like vegetables," Emmie said. "How tall are you?"

"I believe I'm 6'6". At least, the last time they measured

me, I was."

"Wow. You could touch the ceiling without a ladder," she said in awe.

"Yeah, I could, but the Captain wouldn't like that. I would get it dirty, and then they would have to paint it." George was trying to get her comfortable. He wasn't used to dealing with kids. They were always in awe of his size. He preferred to deal with adults—he always had the intimidation thing going for him. George looked over at Walt and just shook his head. "I try so hard," he said, smiling, and getting a laugh from everyone but Emmie.

George began explaining the process to Walt and Emmie, and Ryan took Jade into the next office over. They usually used this room for interrogations, so it wasn't well furnished or comfortable. He offered her one of the plain grey steel chairs, and, leaning against the wall, he crossed his arms over his chest and said, "Tell me what's going on." He was looking down at her compassionately.

"I had another vision. This one's different than Emmie's, but it's the same man."

"When? What was it?" he asked, disbelieving.

"I went for a walk to clear my head after dinner, and I found myself sitting on the street curb after my vision. I saw the man with the tattoo standing in a hallway, and he had a knife in his hand. I could see a young woman in another room; I believe it was a living room. The woman didn't know he was there. He began walking toward her with the knife, and a cat came out from somewhere. The man fell over the cat, hitting the floor hard. The woman saw him and ran screaming for the door. He got up and grabbed her by her hair, pulling her back. She was crying and asking him who he was, why was he doing this, those kinds of questions. Then suddenly I was focused on the street in front of me. That's pretty much it."

"Do you have any idea who she is?"

"No, I've never seen her before."

"Did you recognize the house?"

"No, I've never been there. Is this man a serial killer?" Fear ran down her spine.

"No, I don't think so. You say he had a knife?"

"Yes."

"What did the knife look like?"

"It was...um...oh, the blade was about four inches long, with a black handle. It had weird notches cut out where the serrated edge would be."

"You mean there were spaces in between each notch?"

"Yes. It was a wicked looking knife. The blade was gleaming, and he was determined. We have to find out who she is

~ 63 ~

before this happens." She shivered.

"Okay, hang on, how do you know it hasn't already happened?"

"Because I get the visions *before* they happen. Usually well in advance."

"Do you remember what the woman looked like?"

"Yes, she was in her early twenties, had long dark brown hair and a really pretty face."

"So if you saw her again, you would know her?"

"Without a doubt." She nodded her head.

"Let's look at these photos we have and get that going. We have to take this one step at a time."

"You have to find this girl tomorrow. I think after that it will be too late."

"Okay, let's do what we can. Right now, that means trying to find out who the killer is." He tried to calm her down. "I'll do my best, but you stay out of this as much as you can. Let us handle this guy." He steered her toward the door.

"I can't sit back and wait for this girl to die. I won't."

"I'm not asking you to. We will find her." Ryan and Jade walked back into the office. Everyone was talking and getting on famously. Emmie was busy looking at mug shots. Walt and George were talking and every now and then stopped to answer a question that Emmie had.

Ryan walked over to his desk and grabbed a pile of tattoo photos. He walked over to Jade, pulling a chair out for her, then sat down beside her. "These are photos of just tattoos. Some are on different body parts beside the hand, but I want you to look at the tats and see if any of them look like the suspect's."

"Alright." Jade took the photos.

"Jade, do you want some water?" He touched her shoulder lightly.

"No, I'm fine, thank you."

Walt and George stopped talking and were watching Ryan and Jade. Emmie was oblivious to everyone, busily looking at photos.

Ryan looked over at the guys and shrugged his shoulders. Walt understood more than George did. George still didn't know about the visions, and Walt was sure Ryan wouldn't tell him.

Jade looked through photos until she thought her eyes were going to start spinning. Nothing looked remotely like the tattoo she'd seen. Emmie, quite the little trooper, kept looking picture after picture, occasionally making a funny comment about a mustache or a nose or some flaw on the person.

After what seemed an eternity, and with all the photos reviewed, Ryan rubbed his neck and then stretched. While thanking them for their cooperation and effort, he saw the worry in

Jade's eyes as she waited for him to tell them they were free to go. It was almost ten now, and Ryan and George still had to go to the Linderhoff's residence before calling it a night. "Just a few questions before you guys leave," Ryan said.

"Sure," Jade said.

"Actually, the questions are for Emmie. Are you up to a couple more questions, kiddo?"

"Uh-huh." She stood there waiting though she looked tired.

"Your Aunt Annie...does she live in a school room or does she have a house?"

"She has an apartment on the second floor."

"Is she your daddy's sister?"

"Nope, my mommy's."

"Can you describe her to me? I mean, tell me what she looks like?"

"Oh, she's pretty. Almost as pretty as Jade."

Jade blushed, and Ryan looked at her, smiling. George and Walt watched them and then looked at each other with knowing smiles.

"Aunt Annie has dark brown hair, longer than mine. She's skinny like Mommy. I don't know how old she is, but she's mommy's baby sister."

"That's great, honey, thanks." Standing up and turning, he offered to walk them all to the front desk. "I know it seems like we didn't make progress tonight, but believe me, we did." He looked Jade square in the eye as he talked.

When they arrived at the front desk, he took their visitor badges, handing them to Carter. Then, going to the front door of the station house, Ryan told Jade not to worry and that he would call her first thing in the morning about Harry if she would give him her number.

"The girls will be staying with me for a while, Ryan, if you need to talk to them."

"That's really good news. I was hoping they would. Besides, I'll know how to get a hold of Jade if I need to." Ryan looked relieved.

"That's true. I didn't think about that," Walt said.

"Get home safely. I'll be in touch." He opened the front door for them as they left.

Walt walked the girls to the waiting car. He knew Jade had told Ryan about the new vision and wanted to know about it himself. Jade was quiet, but they couldn't very well talk with Emmie in the back seat. He would wait until Emmie was in bed for the night. Then he would get answers.

~

Ryan and George left the station and headed for the Linderhoff house. It was a good thing they were going at night. Maybe the neighbors wouldn't see them, and nosy neighbor gossip wouldn't start. Everything needed to stay hush-hush for a while still.

Annie had yet to be contacted, and people were always trying to add their two cents. They arrived at 1255 Maggie Lane around eleven thirty. It was a cute little cottage with gingerbread trim. Not what you would expect a drug dealer to live in, but that still remained to be proven.

The house was pitch black, no lights left on. Ryan and George walked around back to enter. They would probably have to break a window to get in. They sure didn't need anyone seeing that. They opened the gate to the backyard and heard Harry start barking. George stopped and looked at Ryan.

"It's okay, it's only Harry." Ryan forgot to ask what kind of dog Harry was.

"He sounds big. What kind is he?" George wasn't fond of dogs. He didn't like this at all.

"Yeah, he does, but Emmie said he's a cute house dog."

"You didn't ask what kind he was, did you?" George knew this could be bad.

Harry came around the corner of the house, lips rolled back, and barked deeper than the guys heard at first: a huge poodle. He must have been three feet tall and around seventy-five pounds. Ryan and George stopped in their tracks. They couldn't shoot this dog. Harry was all the poor kid had left. George jumped behind Ryan. "You deal with this. I can't believe you didn't know how fucking big he is," George gritted through his teeth.

Ryan reached his hand out cautiously toward Harry, palm down. Calmly and quietly, he said, "Good boy, we're not going to hurt you." By keeping his voice soft and speaking to Harry nicely, he hoped the dog would come around. "That's it. Good boy." Harry inched his way toward Ryan's hand. Lips no longer rolled back, Harry didn't look threatening or mean any longer. "Come on, it's okay. That's it. Come on." Ryan kept coaxing Harry.

George looked at Ryan in amazement. "You're crazy. I wouldn't put my hand out there like an hors d'oeuvre."

"Shush, he's coming around. Don't scare him. Come on, Harry, come here. That's it, boy." When Harry sniffed the hand, Ryan slowly raised his hand and began petting him. "Okay, stay put, George." Ryan said, still in the sweet, quiet voice. "He's just a big old baby. That's right, Harry, you're just a big old baby." After petting and rubbing Harry for a few minutes, Ryan felt they were safe. "George, go on around Harry and see if you can get in. I'll hold him here until you do."

"Thanks, man. I have a thing about dogs, especially the ones that roll their lip," he said as he moved around the dog that was now licking Ryan's hand. He checked the back door. It was locked, of course. He looked around. The back of the house had several windows and one door. The door was solid wood on the lower half with a doggie door cut out and several small panes of glass separated by strips of wood on the top half. Realizing they would have to break out a small window pane in the door, he took his suit jacket off and wrapped his hand so he wouldn't cut himself and punched the lower left pane. He reached inside, turning the dead-bolt and releasing the door lock.

After George went inside, Ryan quit petting Harry and followed. Safely inside, Ryan turned on the kitchen light.

"Amy was a clean housekeeper. You gotta give her that," George said.

"Yeah, watch yourself. Here comes Harry through the doggie door. Jeez, George, you could have come in that way and not broke anything. That door is huge."

"Well, hell, it has to be. Look at the size of that mutt." George was feeling a little frazzled.

"Harry's not a mutt. He's a Standard Poodle, which are very smart dogs."

"Yeah, yeah, come on, let's look around. And if that dog bites me, it's your ass."

They decided to stay together so if anything was supposedly missing, they were alibis for each other. When they entered the living room, it was a disaster. Everything was turned inside out. The sofa cushions had been ripped open, books thrown around, tables turned upside down, television smashed, pictures taken out of the frames, and knickknacks broken to smithereens.

Not surprised, George asked Ryan, "Well, well, what do we have here?"

"I would be willing to bet the 'ugly man' was looking for his drugs. Let's go check the master bedroom," Ryan said.

"Right behind ya, partner." George was smiling. "Now we're getting somewhere."

"Yeah, come on." Ryan entered the hallway.

The first bedroom off the hallway was Emmie's. Everything was neat as a pin. Toys were placed neatly in the toy box or on shelves, the bed was made, the little desk area, where Emmie colored or drew pictures, was even neat.

"This isn't normal for a child her age," Ryan said.

"Well, she isn't normal for a child her age. Did you hear the answers she was giving? She's smart as a whip." George stood there looking around the perfect little room.

"Yeah, I know. It's really kinda sad that she had to be so grown up. Let's go down the hall and check the master bedroom." Ryan wondered why Emmie was so mature when, looking around her bedroom, he could see they encouraged her to be a child. At least, all the toys and stuffed animals made it look like they did. Turning, he walked down the hallway. "Here, right here." Ryan saw the open door to the master bedroom, and it looked like the living room. Everything was turned upside down, the mattress and pillows cut open, pictures destroyed, dresser drawers thrown around, clothing everywhere.

"Do you think they found what they were looking for?" George asked.

"No, I don't think it was here anymore, or they wouldn't have destroyed this place. Emmie told Jade that they always fight. I'll bet he tried to get a little ahead and screwed himself." Ryan stood there, not bothering to move anything.

"You're probably right. Wow, what a mess! I guess maybe he crossed his supplier."

"I have to tell Jade not to bring Emmie here tomorrow. This will scare her pants off."

"Yeah, I agree. Why were they coming here anyway?"

"To get Harry and some of Emmie's belongings, but I wanted to check the place first. Sure am glad I told her to wait."

"Why don't we call her and find out what they need, and we'll get it while we're here," George suggested.

"That's a good idea. I don't want Jade or Emmie anywhere near this place."

"Hey, what's this? Whew, look at her! This isn't Amy." George was drooling over a photo hanging on the hall wall.

"No." Ryan looked at the pretty girl. "What do you want to bet that's Aunt Annie?" Ryan laughed at the thought. 'Oh, she's pretty. Almost as pretty as Jade.' Ryan thought about Emmie's words from earlier. Then a thought hit him, the vision Jade told him of the young dark haired woman. "George, I need to take this photo with me." Ryan wanted to check with Jade.

"Why?" George asked curiously.

"I want to ask Emmie if this is Aunt Annie." He lied, but not very well.

"We're going to meet Annie in the morning." George wasn't letting him off easy.

How was he going to get this photo to Jade to see if this was the girl in her vision? He had to think. "You're right, George. I guess I forgot." Ryan turned from the photo to look at George. It was only a five by seven, so he could stick it in his coat pocket when George wasn't looking. Yeah, he would do that just before they left.

"Look around and see if we missed anything. I'm going to

the living room to recheck it." With that, George walked down the hall. He knew Ryan had another motive for wanting to take the photo, and he wasn't telling him everything. They'd worked together long enough to know, and whatever was going on had to be important enough that Ryan felt he couldn't be up front. It had to be because of Jade, but what about Jade? What wasn't Ryan telling him? He was giving him the opportunity to take the photo and save face. He knew he would find out soon enough. Ryan was a good man, and if it was so important to keep some things to himself, so be it.

They searched the entire house except Emmie's room. Nothing. What were they missing?

"Let's go. We need to catch some sleep before work begins again tomorrow." George was tired; it had been a long day and he knew from experience there were more long days ahead of them.

"Yeah, what time are we meeting to go find Annie?" Ryan couldn't remember since lying was taking up most of his brain at this time. Well, he didn't really lie; he just withheld information.

"Her classes start at nine forty. Do you wanna grab some breakfast first?"

"What, Doris not cooking for you anymore?" Ryan laughed, trying to lighten the mood. He was feeling guilty over the lie.

"Of course she is. I just thought since you had no one, I would take pity on you." George laughed, knowing what Ryan was doing.

"Denny's okay with you?" Ryan was feeling slightly better.

"Sure. Come on, let's get back to the station so you can grab your car." George slapped him on the shoulder. He knew Ryan had the photo in his pocket. He just hoped whatever it was would help him.

7

RYAN got in his car and removed the photo from his coat pocket. Should he call and wake Jade up? Was this an excuse to see her so soon? Shit, he forgot to call from the Linderhoff's. Dammit, now he would need to figure out a way to keep Jade from taking the kid home.

Ryan was already going in the direction of Walt's place. He knew they were onto something. Did James cross his drug supplier? Was the 'ugly man' the supplier or just another thug? Did he take the photo because he believed Jade really had visions? He dialed the phone.

"Hello?" Walt answered the phone sounding very tired.

"Walt, it's Ryan. I need to see Jade right away. Is she still up?"

"Ryan, it's one thirty in the morning. Can't it wait?"

"No, it's important, and I'm on my way."

As Ryan drove to the Hamilton's, questions began to form. What if it was Annie? Why would the suspect try to kill her? Was she into the drug scene too? Maybe he figured she knew where his merchandise was, if indeed theft of drugs was the case. Too many "what ifs". Ryan pulled up and saw the kitchen light. *Good, she's waiting.* That thought gave him a warm fuzzy feeling. He wasn't sure he liked it. Why did his thoughts keep coming back to her? He was falling for her. Just what his hectic life needed... someone who had visions. *Great...*

He knocked lightly on the kitchen window so he wouldn't wake anyone else. Jade was sitting there drinking coffee. She literally jumped out of the chair when she heard the knocking.

Ryan felt a little guilty at that.

Jade opened the back door. "What are you doing back here?"

"I thought if I didn't ring the doorbell, at least someone would be getting some sleep. Sorry to wake you like this, but I have something I need to show you."

"Come on in. Coffee?" She asked, moving aside to allow him entrance.

"No thanks, I'm going to bed after this, and I don't need more caffeine in my body."

Ryan took the photo out and handed it to Jade.

"Where did you find this? This is her, Ryan," Jade said excitedly.

"I knew it. I think this is Aunt Annie," Ryan said.

"Oh no, you can't give Emmie to her, then." Jade was sure that was the plan.

"You said you had this vision tonight. Will it happen tonight?"

"I don't think so. I usually have a day or two to get things together. Why?"

"I would have found her tonight if I needed to," he said.

"Ryan, you're a good man. You can go home and get some sleep. The morning will be fine." Jade reassured him. She was thankful that he was beginning to believe in her gift.

"You're sure?"

"Yes, I'm sure."

"Alright then. I guess I'll call you tomorrow. Get some sleep and I'm sorry I had to wake you up."

"It's okay. This was worth it. I'll sleep better knowing who she is." They stood there in the kitchen just looking at each other, not saying a word.

Finally he broke the spell "Well, okay then, I'll see you tomorrow."

"Be careful driving home. Good night, Ryan." Jade handed the photo back to him.

"G'night, Jade." Ryan took the photo and left.

Jade sat in the kitchen, finishing her cup of coffee, thinking about Ryan and Emmie, and the vision from earlier. Why Annie? She went to bed and considered the vision again. They knew it was Annie, so she didn't have to put herself through recalling the vision. They had to find out what was going on before Ryan made her give Emmie to anyone else.

~

Ryan got home, took a quick shower, and then went to bed. He needed sleep; it was already two forty-five, and he was meeting

George at eight. His mind was going a hundred miles an hour, and he knew they had to get to Annie before the killer did. Was he looking for drugs or money? Who was this drug dealer that had no problem killing to get what he wanted? Was it as simple as James crossing his dealer? *Okay, enough is enough, stop thinking and go to sleep...*Ryan was trying to coax his brain into relaxing. This was going to be hard enough without trying to do things on a mind that was fuzzy from no rest. He needed to be at his best so he could solve this and Jade would be safe. Jade...why did his thoughts keep coming back to her? Ryan lay there picturing her. She was beautiful, smart, caring, and way too trusting. She just went to the park and took a child without really thinking things through. He knew she thought she did the right thing, but anyone in their right mind would not just take a child like that. Not that Jade was crazy, she just took these visions to heart too much. He had to research visions. He needed to know that what he was beginning to believe was real and not just something he wanted to be real. He liked Jade. He knew she wasn't crazy, but he needed to know she wasn't involved in all this and that the information she was giving was really from a vision, not firsthand knowledge.

~

Annie woke up to the alarm ringing and her list of things to do counting themselves off in her head.

She had to call Amy today. She was supposed to keep Emmie for the weekend and needed to find out when Amy was bringing her over. She decided she'd call her as soon as her classes for the day were over. Annie loved spending time with Emmie. They would go to the park since Emmie loved it so much.

Finally, she was up and moving, trying to get her mindset for the classes she hated. Why did she even continue them? She could just take an everyday job like everyone else she knew. Why a degree? Did she think she was actually going to do something with her life? She wanted to be like Amy, get married have children, stay at home...except James—he scared her. He was so nice when he and Amy first dated, married, and had Emmie. Then he got involved in all that drug crap, and why? It boiled down to him being too lazy to work for a living. No! She didn't want to end up like Amy.

Annie let her mind drift over her last conversation with Amy. She'd told Annie about James and the drugs. She said he lost his temper so easily lately. She never left him alone with Emmie anymore. Amy asked her to keep Emmie for the weekend so she could try and talk James into going to rehab. Amy knew

James wouldn't go for it and that they would surely end up fighting; that was why Annie was keeping Emmie for the weekend. It would take at least that long for Amy to reason with James. Amy had told Annie that if James didn't agree, then she was leaving him. She was scared all the time. There were really bad people that he was dealing with, and she didn't want Emmie around that kind of life.

Annie knew that Amy loved James and wanted to at least try to save him before just walking out. "We have a family," she told Annie. "I can't do that to James and Emmie."

Now that she thought about it, Annie was scared for Amy this weekend. Maybe she could talk Amy into staying with her, too, and just reasoning with James by telephone. If he lost his temper that quick, would he try to hurt Amy? No, Annie would talk to Amy and even though she tried to stay out of their business, she wasn't going to let her sister get hurt.

Annie took one last look around her apartment. Everything was nice and neat. She looked in the refrigerator, realizing that she would need to get some things from the store for her and Emmie. She just had to be careful not to get too many sugary items. Amy was very strict on how much sugar Emmie could have.

Annie liked to spoil Emmie, and sometimes she gave her more junk food than she should, but she always reasoned that that's what aunts were for. Emmie never told, so it was their little secret. She'd go pick up some kid's movies, too. They liked to sit around in their nightgowns and eat junk food, watching movies. *Oh well, what Amy didn't know wouldn't hurt her.*

Annie fed her cat, Wally, and left for school.

~

George was waiting for Ryan at Denny's and was already sitting in a booth, drinking coffee, when Ryan arrived. Damn, Ryan looked tired, George thought as he grabbed more sugar for his coffee.

"Morning, George." Ryan dragged himself into the booth.

"Good morning, Ryan."

"Damn, I hate you morning people. Always so chipper."

"Uh-oh, someone didn't get enough sleep. What's the matter, Cinderella?" George asked, laughing.

"Didn't sleep so good, that's all." Ryan glared at his partner.

George wondered what had gotten under his partner's skin. He was lying to him about the picture and about not sleeping well. What the hell was going on? He would get some answers, just not yet. He would choose his time perfectly. He just hoped like hell the kid wasn't in trouble.

They ordered their breakfast and began putting their day in order. First, they would eat, and then they would go to the college and find Annie. Then, depending on what Annie could tell them, they would decide where to go from there.

Ryan had the picture of Annie in his car. He needed to put it back before anyone realized it was gone. Surely Annie would want to go to the house soon. Ryan also had to come up with some way of keeping Emmie from Annie. Until they knew this psycho was in custody and Annie was safe, he couldn't let her have Emmie. Ryan was deep in thought, unaware of his partner watching him intently.

"Hey, did you call Jade last night?" George inquired.

"No, why?" Ryan looked guilty.

"You didn't call and tell her not to take Emmie to the house today?"

"Damn, no, I forgot. I was so tired. I knew I forgot something." Ryan pulled his cell phone out and dialed Walt's number. "Walt, it's Ryan. Do me a favor." He was going to take the easy way out.

"If I can. What's up?"

"Don't let Jade and Emmie go to the Linderhoffs' house today. I'll explain later. Tell them I'll bring Harry to your house. Okay?"

"Okay. Is everything all right?"

"Yes, it's just that I don't know if it's safe to take her there yet. You know what I mean?"

"Alright, I'll take care of it."

"Thanks, Walt, I'll call you later."

George had called Doris to tell her to have a good day and that he would call her later. He hung up almost the same time Ryan did.

"You're going to take Harry over there?" he asked amazed.

"Yeah, why not?" Ryan thought George looked upset.

"I wouldn't put a dog in my car. He's gonna get hair everywhere. Not to mention he'll probably drool over everything," George huffed, pushing his breakfast dishes away and moving his coffee cup closer.

"Poodles don't shed, and they don't usually drool. Don't you know anything about dogs?"

"Yeah, I know, I like cats better," he growled.

"Come on, let's go find Annie Armstrong." Ryan stood, grabbing the check.

"Okay, this time we'll drop my car off at the station and take yours. I'm sick of driving."

"Alright, what happened to you being Mr. Chipper? Was it something I said?" Ryan asked as he paid for breakfast.

"No, you give yourself way too much credit. I'll see you at the station parking lot." George walked out, leaving Ryan to pay for his breakfast, too.

Ryan wanted to have his list of questions for Annie ready when they arrived at the school, so he began to compile the list in his head. He would have George write them down when he got in the car. Neither Jade nor Annie had a criminal history. Were they involved? Did Annie know Amy and James were dead? Did Jade and Annie know each other? Did Annie know about the drugs? Were there really drugs involved? Of course there were. He and George had worked these types of cases way too long not to know what they were dealing with. This was definitely going to be a drug deal gone wrong. They both pulled into the parking lot, and George looked for a parking space.

The department was growing rapidly, and they needed to upgrade the parking lot to accommodate the many officers and workers now employed by St. Joseph's Police Department. George finally found a space and wedged his car in. Cursing, he got out, slamming his door. Ryan sat in his car behind the spot and laughed himself into tears.

"Glad you find my misery so funny," George said, now slamming Ryan's passenger door.

"Hey, hey, watch it. This is a fine piece of machinery," he said, patting the dash.

"Shut up and drive," George spit out.

"Hey, what got your panties in a wad?" Ryan couldn't help laughing and wondering if Harry was the reason George was so upset.

George realized he was acting like an idiot, and he started laughing. "You know no one gets me as pissed off as Doris."

Ryan looked at George. He was serious. "Damn, what'd she do?"

"Oh, you know, the usual. 'What do you want for dinner? When you coming home?' It's the fucking third degree every morning. I don't know why I call her." Veins began pulsing at his temple.

"Wow, she did piss you off. Let it go, man. We're gonna have a great day."

"Yeah, I know. Never mind. Let's go," he said.

The car was silent. No talking, no joking. Then Ryan remembered the questions he wanted George to list. "Hey, do you want to make a list of questions for Annie?"

"No, I don't need a list. Got 'em right here," he said,

pointing to his head.

"Okay then, I'll let you have the lead." Ryan felt relief. George was much better at getting answers. It was a knack that Ryan was still learning.

~

Jade was up and already drinking coffee when her dad came into the kitchen.

"Did you get some sleep, honey?" He looked over to see if she looked rested.

"Yeah, Dad, I slept better than I had for the last few nights. I need to get Emmie over to the house and get Harry for her, though; then I can relax," she said.

"Oh, that reminds me, Ryan called and asked me to tell you not to go over there. He said he would bring Harry here." He took his coffee to the table and sat down.

"Really? Did he say why?" she asked, surprised.

"No, but I'm glad he is. I don't want you there. You never know what'll happen. I wish you hadn't gotten mixed up in all this, even though I know you didn't have much choice. It's just that I worry about you."

"I know, Dad. I didn't mean to get you mixed up in this mess."

"That's not what I meant. I want to know about the vision you had yesterday. Tell me about it before Emmie comes down."

"I wanted to tell you last night. I'm sorry I was so tired when we got back. The vision was the killer and Annie."

"How do you know it was Annie? Do you know her?" he asked, shocked.

"No, that's why Ryan came by so late last night. He and George went to the Linderhoff's house, and he found a picture. He brought it for me to look at and see if it was the girl in my vision. We're assuming she's Annie."

"Is Annie in with the killer?"

"No, he was trying to kill her with a knife. Ryan needs to find her quickly."

"Does he know where she is yet?"

"I don't know. He showed me the picture and then left."

They heard Emmie coming, so they quit discussing the vision. Walt was really worried now. The man obviously had no trouble killing people. He would kill Jade, too, without losing any sleep over it. Walt wouldn't let anything happen to Jade or Emmie. He would be on his toes.

"Hi, Emmie, are you hungry?" Jade asked, plastering a smile on her face.

"No, my tummy hurts," she said, holding her hand across

her stomach.

"Come here." Jade felt Emmie's head. No fever—that was good. She picked Emmie up and sat her in her lap. Emmie laid her head on Jade's shoulder.

Walt warmed up his coffee and then grabbed Jade's cup.

"I don't want anymore."

"Well, girls," Walt said, putting Jade's cup in the sink, "what are we gonna do today?"

Emmie sat up. "We're going to get Harry."

"Emmie, Ryan is going to bring Harry over for you this afternoon."

Emmie looked at Jade and asked, "When am I going home?"

"Soon, honey."

"No!" Emmie jumped down. "I want to go home now!" Emmie ran upstairs. Grabbing her baby doll, she sat on the bedroom floor crying.

"Dad, what am I going to do? I know she misses her mom and dad." Jade felt she was losing control over the situation. She had no idea how to deal with Emmie, yet she couldn't let anyone else have her.

Walt walked over and put an arm around Jade's shoulders. "Just keep stalling her, sweetheart. Ryan will get Annie here soon."

"I can't let Annie have her. That man is looking for Annie. I'm not going to put Emmie in danger."

"You may not have a choice. Ryan will have to give Emmie to her aunt. She's the only relative here." He knew this choice was out of Jade's hands, and she needed to know, too.

"No! I won't do it." She stood up, hands on hips, determination written all over her face.

Walt saw the protectiveness in Jades demeanor. He knew she was in for the fight of her life.

~

Ryan and George went to the front office area of the school. George showed his badge and asked to have Annie Armstrong sent to an area where he and Ryan could talk with her. They were ushered to a small room and told she would be sent for. Ryan and George discussed the situation while they waited for Annie.

"Ryan, I know you're worried about Jade, and I don't want this to end up personal for you." The inner struggle was written all over Ryan's face. George had to set him straight before Annie got there and he made an ass out of himself.

"I know, George. The first rule is not to get personally

involved. But with Jade, I feel something. I know, don't say it."
Giving up trying to figure it out or explain it, he simply said, "I'll
stay in the background until you need me."

"Ryan, that's not what I meant. I just want you tread
carefully. I'm here if you need me." He knew they didn't have time
for full explanations or confessions. He just wanted Ryan to trust
him with the full truth, whatever it was.

"I know that, George. I'm not pushing you out. I just feel
there's some things I have to deal with on my own till I get them
figured out. It isn't anything that will hurt the investigation if I
don't share it right now. It's just I've never kept things from you
before, but this time I have to...at least for a while, anyway." Ryan
felt like he was forced to keep information from his partner, and he
didn't like the feeling. But he knew George was not ready for the
visions thing right now. He would have to let that simmer a while
longer.

Before George could answer, Annie Armstrong, a very
pretty young woman, walked into the office and looked at George
and Ryan with questioning eyes.

"Hello, Annie?" George asked.

"Yes."

"Are you Annie Armstrong?" George asked, though they
both knew she was from the picture.

"Yes, what's this about?" she asked, looking frightened.

"Annie, I'm Detective George Dunleavy and this is
Detective Ryan Douglas. We're with the St. Joseph's Police
Department. We need to ask you a few questions."

"Is Amy all right?" Annie took a step forward.

"Annie, is Amy Linderhoff your sister?" Once again, George
did the questioning.

"Yes, sir. Is she okay?" Annie's heart was pounding.

"Annie, sit down for a minute." George guided Annie to a
chair. Ryan stood by a window. He hated telling people their family
member was dead. He could look out the window instead of at the
frightened and shocked face of Annie Armstrong.

George began, "Annie, when was the last time you talked
with your sister?"

"I guess about a week ago. Why?"

"Did Amy say anything to you that would make you think
someone wanted to hurt her or James?" George didn't want to
blurt out the fact that her sister was dead.

"Is she alright, Detective?" Annie was beginning to think
Amy was hurt.

"No, Annie, and there's no easy way to tell you this, but
your sister and her husband were both killed a few days ago."
George said this as quietly and calmly as he could.

"Oh my God, oh my God!" Annie began to cry.

Ryan kept looking out the window.

Annie jumped up. "Where's Emmie? Their daughter—where is she? Is she okay?"

George grabbed Annie and hugged her. "Emmie is fine. She's with a friend of your sister's."

"What friend? Amy didn't have any friends. James was always running friends off if Amy made any. He didn't want her to have any."

"Do you know Jade?" George asked, looking at Ryan instead of Annie.

"Jade?" Confusion was the most evident emotion on Annie's face.

"Yes, Jade Hamilton."

"No, I've never heard of her. Who is she?"

"She and Amy were friends, and she has Emmie."

"No! She wasn't a friend of Amy's. I would have met her. Oh my God, is Emmie..." Annie began crying again.

Ryan was somewhat relieved now that he knew Jade didn't know Amy and James. That much had been true. But did she know the killer?

George looked over at Ryan. "You did say Jade was friends with Amy, didn't you?"

"Yeah, Jade said they were friends, and Amy asked her to watch Emmie at the park." Ryan answered, knowing this was going to be the hard part.

"Amy took Emmie to the park all the time. But I don't know this Jade person. Amy wouldn't have asked her to watch Emmie. Amy was very leery of people. I'm the only one Amy would leave her with. She wouldn't even leave her with James."

George looked at Ryan again. This time, he saw Ryan was squirming. So Ryan had lied more than once about this case. It was time to get answers. As soon as they were finished with Annie, Ryan was coming clean. George would see to it.

"Annie, is it possible Amy just didn't tell you about Jade?" George tried again.

"No, Amy and I are very tight. I'm the only friend she has."

"I need you to tell me about Amy and James. I need to know what kind of work they did, who they worked for, and other relatives I need to contact. You know—personal information." He would get her mind moving and help her through the immediate shock.

"I'm the only relative here. Our mom lives in California. James' mom lives in New York. James was an only child. Both of our dads are dead. Amy and James didn't work."

"How did they live, then?" George asked.

"James came up with money somehow. But I don't know of any job he held. He didn't want Amy to work. He said her job

~ 80 ~

was taking care of him and Emmie."

"You don't know how James came up with the money they used to pay bills?"

"No. Listen, I just want to go to Emmie; she needs me now. Where is she?"

"We'll take you to Emmie, but first I need to know if your sister or James were doing drugs or anything illegal?"

"What? Amy would never do drugs! James is the one that always tried to get money for doing nothing." She was getting angry.

"Annie, was James selling drugs?"

"Yeah, Amy told me she was scared and wanted out of that lifestyle. She was bringing Emmie to my house this weekend so she could try to talk James into rehab."

"Did Amy ever mention what kind of drugs or who they got them from?"

"She mentioned ecstasy once. She never mentioned anyone. She only said she was scared all the time now."

"Ecstasy, are you sure?"

"Yeah, please take me to Emmie. I know she's scared. She needs me."

"Annie, Emmie doesn't know about Amy or James. Do you want to tell her?"

"They've been dead a few days, and she doesn't know? What's going on here?"

"Get your things together and we'll explain on the way to Emmie." Annie left to get her books and other belongings. George looked over at Ryan. *What are you covering up?* He thought. *You are going to give me answers whether you want to or not. In this partnership we work together, not independently.*

Ryan saw the look and knew George was putting together all the unanswered questions. He knew he would have to come clean. Annie came back, and the three left for Walt's house

8

ANNIE was looking out the window, deep in thought. She didn't even notice how blue the sky was or the way spring was taking over. Flowers were blooming everywhere. The dogwood trees were so beautiful. Tulips of every color that one could possibly imagine were growing and flavoring the areas around them. The trees were so many different shades of green that one could not name them all. Yet all this beauty was lost on Annie, as all she could see were horror pictures of Amy's murder dancing through her mind's eye. Dammit, James! All this was his fault. What did he get them into? What was she going to do with Emmie? Who the hell was this Jade person? She wasn't friends with Amy; that much, Annie knew for sure. Maybe she was friends with James and knew who murdered Amy. Why did she have Emmie, though? What would Annie tell her mom? How would she tell someone her daughter had been murdered? Annie's thoughts were jumping in all directions.

She was numb. The only thing that was working in her entire body was her mind, and she couldn't shut it off. She closed her eyes and cried silently in the back seat. She needed to get a hold of herself before she saw Emmie. They said that she didn't know yet. *Oh my God, how am I going to tell this baby that her mommy and daddy are dead?* She would do it, she knew she had to, but how? "Excuse me, Detective Dunleavy?"

"Yes?" George swiveled to look at Annie.

"How do I tell Emmie? She's only six, you know. She can't possibly understand."

"Annie, it's never easy, but the words will come when you

need them."

"She's just six. How's she going to understand this?"

"We can't even understand things like this. Don't expect Emmie to."

They drove on in silence again. Ryan was thinking about all the information he had withheld from George. George was going to want an explanation at the first opportunity. Ryan couldn't blame him. He'd had no right to deceive him this way. They had been partners for too long now, and the respect was mutual. He would bring it up; he wouldn't make George do that. But how was he going to explain the visions? He had hoped to have time to research them before having to tell George.

Ryan looked over at George as he drove, and when George looked back, Ryan felt all the lies bone deep. George didn't deserve this. What had made Ryan withhold information on this case; what made this case any different than any other they worked? He had never done that.

Jade.

She was the answer to a lot of things lately. But no, he couldn't blame her, either. Ryan himself was the one to blame. Well he would just do what he had to do and get it over with. George would understand.

"Annie, if you need some time to get yourself together, we can stop for coffee and just relax a bit before you see Emmie." George was taking pity on this young lady. He knew how difficult this was going to be.

"No. I need to see her. I need to..."

Annie couldn't even finish her sentence without losing it again. She didn't know what the hell was she going to do with a six-year-old. No one else could take her. Annie would have to raise her. My God, I don't want any kids yet, she thought. Oh Amy, Amy, why? James got them murdered. It was his fault. I hate him! Why are all these thoughts running through my mind? Why can't I shut it off?

George could see the struggle that Annie was going through. He wanted to help her, but he knew it was best to let her deal with it however she saw fit. Maybe he could help by keeping her mind busy with questions. "Annie, had you ever seen James with drugs?"

"No way. Amy wouldn't have allowed him to have them near their home."

"You're sure the only drug talked about was ecstasy? No crack or meth?"

"I've heard meth was cheaper, and James liked the high from it, but I don't think he sold meth. He may have used it though. Hell, at this point I don't know what he did. I just can't believe this is happening."

"Had you noticed a change in James?"

"What kind of change?"

"You know, sick a lot, thinner, irritated, maybe even having open sores? That type of thing."

"Yeah, he'd lost weight, and you could really see it in his face. He used to have sores all the time, like on his face and arms. Amy said he got angry very easily now; that's one of the reasons she was scared of him and wouldn't leave Emmie with him."

"Did you see the sores?"

"Yeah, they were actually like boils."

"Those are meth bumps, usually from missing the vein when shooting up."

"He was shooting up?"

"Probably. I'm sure your sister knew. They almost look like an infection. Did you ever ask her about them?"

"Yeah, she said he was allergic to spiders and they were spider bites. I told her, if they had a problem with spiders, they should have the house sprayed. You know, it's funny; I never once thought to ask why neither she nor Emmie had any. I didn't even notice when he stopped breaking out."

"Well, they say hindsight is twenty-twenty," Ryan said. He was staying quiet for the most part. He knew George was wondering why he hadn't said anything at all. He had been trying to figure out a way to give Jade's friendship with Amy legitimacy without Annie being able to crush it. He would have to get Jade to the side before Annie started in. Maybe, between the two of them, they could come up with a believable story.

"That's a good saying. We use it all the time as detectives." George looked at Ryan, trying to figure him out. He was acting so strange. Not talking much, not really looking at him or Annie, just kind of in his own little world over there. What was going on? George knew Ryan was withholding information but he didn't have to be so blatant.

"Why hadn't someone called me about Amy and James before now? You said they died a few days ago! Has Emmie been with this Jade person all this time?"

"Well, we didn't know about you until yesterday. Then we had to track you down. There are four Annie Armstrongs in the St. Joseph area. We had to get some information from Emmie and make sure we had the right Annie Armstrong, and yes, Jade has had Emmie all along," George said. "You'll like Jade. She's a very nice young woman. They're staying at Jade's dad's house right now. Jade was afraid Emmie was in danger after seeing Amy and James' photos on TV."

"Their photos on TV?" Annie was incredulous over this information.

"Yes, when they were found, there were no IDs on them,

and we didn't know who they were. We had the local news station put their photos on TV and ask for anyone that could identify them. I take it you never saw the report?"

"No, I didn't. I guess I should be thankful for that. How did Jade have Emmie already with her?" Her suspicion was evident.

"She took Emmie from the park that day for Amy."

"No way! Amy would never have allowed her to leave with Emmie."

"Look, Annie, I know you think you knew all of Amy's friends, but obviously you didn't."

"I am telling you, this Jade person was not a friend of Amy's."

George looked over at Ryan. He was staying out of this conversation pretty much altogether. Why? George was beginning to really get annoyed with Ryan and his little secrets. How was he going to get him alone so they could hash this out? "Ryan, why don't you call Walt or Jade and let them know we're on our way over there."

"That's a good idea," Ryan said.

"What? Why give them a heads up? She might take Emmie and run."

"No, Jade's not like that; she has Emmie's best interest in mind. You'll see." George was defending her, and he didn't even know her. That was odd.

Ryan called and told Walt that they were on their way with Annie. He had forgotten Harry again already. Poor Harry—he was likely to die of starvation if Ryan didn't pull his head out of his rear end and start thinking. Anyway, if this went the way Annie wanted it to, he wouldn't need to pick Harry up. He was going to have a hard time keeping Jade from exposing her visions to everyone once Annie tried to take Emmie, but it was not the time to tell all just yet. Maybe Annie would meet Jade and feel comfortable leaving Emmie there. Yeah, right, and they would all live happily ever after, too.

"We'll be there in about five minutes, Annie. You might want to try to get yourself together before seeing Emmie, and please don't cause a scene with Jade. We'll get this all figured out, I promise." George was trying to get Annie in the right frame of mind before getting to the Hamiltons'. He knew this was going to be a sticky situation.

"I won't show my anger, if that's what you're worried about, Detective. I don't want to cause Emmie any more worry or pain than I have to."

"Thanks, Annie. I know this is a tough time for you, and I didn't mean to imply that you would be insensitive to Emmie or her needs."

"I'm sorry. I guess I am pretty touchy right now."

"That's certainly understandable. You're awfully young to have the weight of the world on your shoulders. We'll help you as much as we can."

"I really appreciate that. Truly I do."

"Annie, I know you don't know Jade, but give her a chance, okay?" Ryan turned and was looking at Annie. She could see the genuine caring in his eyes. Did he have a thing with this Jade person? Of course, he probably gave Emmie to Jade, and now he was covering his own ass.

"Detective Douglas, where did you find Emmie?" Maybe she could trick him.

"We didn't find Emmie. Jade's dad, Walt, called us." He looked at her through the rearview mirror. What did she think she was doing?

"So you didn't place Emmie with Jade?" Her voice had a lethal edge to it.

"No, I didn't even really know Jade before yesterday." Ah, so that was her ploy, try to get me to admit something. Good girl, he thought. She was using her head. That was good.

"Well, here we are, guys. Annie, you ready?" George asked.

"Yeah, I'm ready. Do I have black eyes from crying?" She swiped at her cheeks to remove any mascara that may have smeared.

"No, you look fine," George said.

The three of them walked up to the house. Each fighting their own silent struggle, each wrestling with demons that seemed to be everywhere. Walt, always the welcoming host, invited them in and asked if anybody wanted anything to drink.

"No, thank you, Walt. How's Emmie today?" Ryan asked.

"Oh, she's homesick but fine." Smiling at everyone, he waved them into the living room.

"Can I see her please?" Annie was nervous, and she wasn't sure how to pull herself together. What the hell did everyone expect of her? She was scared and doing her best not to fall completely apart. Couldn't they see that?

"Annie, let's sit and talk for awhile. Take time for you to come to grips with what's ahead of you and Emmie. Meet Jade and go into all of this slowly. I don't want Emmie hurt any more than she's going to be." Walt could see the fear in her eyes and knew the longer he could stall, the better their chances were to keep Emmie in his house.

"Mr. Hamilton, I have no intention of hurting my niece any more than I have to. I assure you, sir, I will not cause a scene in front of her." She stiffened her spine and prepared mentally for combat if necessary.

"No, I didn't mean that, Annie. I'm sorry. I guess we're all pretty tightly knotted right now." His eyes showed the empathy he was feeling.

Jade stepped into the room. Hmm, perfect timing, she thought. "Hello, everyone." Jade made her entrance cautiously.

"Jade, this is Emmie's Aunt Annie." Ryan moved to introduce them.

"Annie, I am so sorry to meet you under these circumstances," Jade said as she walked over to shake hands.

"Ms. Hamilton, would you kindly get Emmie for me?" Annie didn't bother to acknowledge the hand outstretched toward her.

"Please call me Jade. I thought maybe we could talk for a few minutes. Give us time to get to know one another."

"Get to know you, Jade? Okay, let's start with this: how did you know my sister?" She might as well jump right to it, Annie thought.

Ryan looked over at Jade with fear in his eyes. He was ready to crack. How did he let this happen without preparing Jade? He knew better. She looked at Ryan, and her eyes told him everything was all right. He stood there looking at her. George watched intently, not missing a thing.

"Amy brought Emmie to the park across the street from where I live. I go over there and just sit, watching people, relaxing, enjoying being outside. Amy and I would sit and talk while Emmie played on the playground."

"You live by the park?" Annie was watching her intently.

"Yes, just across the street."

Ryan began to relax. Jade had everything under control. She was amazing.

"When did you meet my sister?"

"Oh, I don't know. It's been a while though. I'd see her and Emmie, and I'd walk over to talk with her. She was with James sometimes, but usually just her and Emmie."

"You've met James?"

"Yeah, he didn't stick around too often. Usually, it was just Amy and Emmie."

"So the day they died, what happened?"

"I don't know, really. I saw Emmie playing by herself. I walked over and looked around, and I didn't see Amy, so I asked Emmie where her mom was. She couldn't tell me. So, after another look around, I took her home with me."

"You just took her?"

"Well, not took her, exactly. I brought her to my house. Amy knew which house was mine. I figured when she came back, she would know I probably took Emmie home for a drink or to use the potty."

"When did you call the police?"

"I didn't. My dad and Ryan – Detective Douglas – are

~ 88 ~

friends. Dad called Ryan after we saw the photos on TV."

"I see." She had all the answers, Annie thought. Maybe she had met Amy like she said, but wouldn't Amy have mentioned her?

"Would you like to see Emmie now?"

"I would love to, thank you."

"I'll go upstairs and get her. Annie, before I do, though, I would like you to consider...I know this will sound crazy, but I would like to keep Emmie for a while."

"Listen, Jade, I appreciate all you and your dad have done for Emmie, but she belongs with me now."

"Don't you go to school? Who'll be with Emmie while you're in school?"

"I guess I'll just have to quit school. I have responsibilities now that I didn't have."

"You don't have to quit...you can leave her here. You can come see her whenever you want." Jade was desperate now; she couldn't let Emmie go yet.

"No, Jade. I'm taking Emmie with me today." Annie was emphatic. There was no question that she intended to have her niece with her.

"Jade, go on up and get Emmie," Walt said, resigned to the fact that they'd done all they could.

Jade turned, leaving the room. As she went up the stairs, her heart was pounding; her mind was racing. She could just take Emmie and leave. No one would know until it was too late. They still had the cabin at Ivory Bluff. That's what she would do. They could go down the back stairs, into the kitchen, and then out the back door. They could be gone before anyone realized it. Decision made, she went into the bedroom where Emmie was quietly playing. "Emmie, come on. We're going on a little adventure. Grab your stuff and put it in your backpack. I'm going to my room to get my things together. Hurry, honey."

"Jade, where are we going?" Emmie ran behind her.

"Hurry up get your stuff, and I'll tell you all about it when we're in the car." Jade turned her around and pushed her toward her bedroom. Quickly gathering her own things in a small bag, Jade went to get Emmie. Stopping at the top of the stairs, she listened. She could hear them talking. She yelled that they would be down in a minute and then went to Emmie's room. "You ready, Emmie?"

"Yeah, is Walt coming?"

"Not this time, honey. Come on." They went down the back staircase. Emmie started to ask Jade a question, but Jade looked at her, putting her finger to her mouth and showing Emmie she needed to be quiet. Then they were out the back door, running for the car. They got in the car and closed the door quietly. "Hook your seatbelt, Emmie." Jade looked toward the house. She didn't see anyone looking out the window, so she started the engine. "Emmie, we're going back to the cabin."

"No, I wanna go home. I want Harry!" Emmie yelled.

Harry. Jade had forgotten about Harry. "We can go by your house and get Harry first."

"Okay, but what about Mommy and Daddy? Are they coming to the cabin too?"

"I have to explain something to you later, sweetie. Right now, we can only get Harry, okay?"

Emmie nodded her head, and Jade drove to Maggie Lane, wondering if they had realized she was gone yet. If they had, they had no idea where the cabin was. She tried hard to think...did she tell anyone the cabin was in Ivory Bluff? She couldn't think. Well, if she did, they still didn't know where in Ivory Bluff, and right now, she couldn't think about that. She needed to get Harry and get out of town.

Pulling up curbside at the Linderfhoff's was a freaky feeling for Jade. Not knowing why, she sat still in the car for a minute, letting her intuition guide her. After a moment, she got out with Emmie and moved quickly to the gated backyard. "Okay, Emmie, let's get Harry and his food. Where do you keep his food?"

"It's in the kitchen in a plastic trash can. Come on, I'll show you."

The two of them opened the gate to find Harry standing there, growling. Jade looked at Emmie. "Does he bite?" Backing up a bit, she was hesitant to move.

"No, he just growls and barks." Emmie was hugging Harry and laughing.

Jade moved slowly, watching the dog. When she felt safe enough, she went to the back door and saw the glass lying on the ground. Emmie looked at her but didn't say anything. They opened the door and went inside. There was glass on the floor there, too.

"Harry's food is over there." Emmie said, pointing to a plastic trash can in the corner and tugging Harry along beside her.

"Emmie, do you have anything else you want to get before we leave?" Jade began scooping the food into a big plastic container she found in a lower cabinet. The little trash can was a bit too big to carry.

"Yeah, I want some of my clothes and toys. I'll get them." Before Jade could say anything, Emmie was running through the kitchen into the next room. Jade heard her yelling about something being broken. She wasn't sure what Emmie yelled ,so she left the dog food and went to find her.

"Wow, what happened here?" The place was a disaster. Jade felt the need to get out quickly. "Get your things, honey, and let's get going." Jade walked with Emmie into her room. It was clean as a whistle. No one had destroyed this room. Jade helped her to gather a few toys and some outfits and then pushed her out into the hall. This was giving her an eerie feeling, and she knew now why Ryan was going to bring Harry to her dad's.

"Do you have a leash for Harry?"

"Yeah, it's in here." Emmie pulled Jade into the laundry room and opened a drawer. Pulling the leash out, she called Harry. He came running, the sound much like a horse running through the small house.

"Harry, stop it. Jade, help!" Emmie was trying to put the leash on the dog while he was busy licking her. Jade giggled at the two and helped Emmie get the leash on Harry. Grabbing the tub of dog food, they went out the way they came in and headed for the car. They had only been gone for a short time, but surely someone knew they were gone by now.

~

Sitting in the living room and waiting on Jade, George began to wonder what was taking so long. He looked over to see Annie looking in his direction. "Walt, maybe you should go check on Jade and Emmie. It shouldn't be taking this long to go up and get her. Even if Emmie is napping, they could've been back by now." George was beginning to wonder where they were.

"Yeah, you got a point, George." Walt was afraid of what he would find, so, moving slowly up the stairs, he called out, "Jade? Emmie?" When he didn't get an answer, he took the steps two at a time. He knew before he got up there what Jade had done. He looked around, taking his time and buying more time for Jade. Finally, he went downstairs. "Ryan, can I see you for a minute in the kitchen?"

"What's wrong?" Annie asked, standing up. "Where's Emmie?"

"Ryan, now I really need to speak with you. Annie, give me just a minute, okay?" he asked. Looking at her, his eyes were sad.

Ryan looked at George, who was glaring at him. He got up and followed Walt into the kitchen. Dreading what he was about to hear, he asked, "What is it, Walt?"

"They're gone."

"*What?*" Ryan was enraged. "What do you mean, gone?"

"Jade must have gotten spooked when Annie said she was taking Emmie. They had to have left by the back door. They grabbed their things and ran."

"Shit, how am I supposed to explain this?" he asked, slamming his hand on the countertop.

George walked into the kitchen. "Explain what?"

They both turned as George came in. "They left." Ryan said.

"Oh, great...just fucking great." George was pissed but not surprised. He walked back into the living room. Shaking his hanging head, he said, "Jade took Emmie and ran."

"What? Why?" Though she knew something had happened, Annie had hoped for the best. Actually, all things considered, this was better than she had been thinking. With all the crazies on the news, Annie was afraid Jade had locked them both in a bathroom with a gun or something.

"I don't know. Let's get you home, and we'll start looking for them." George was hoping to stop a tantrum he didn't have the patience for right now.

"No. I have to go back to school...I left my car there. Where do you think she took her?"

"I don't know. I promise you, we'll find them. I'll get Emmie back to you soon."

Ryan and Walt walked back into the living room. Ryan was worried about Jade and thinking about how she had just kidnapped Emmie for essentially the second time; he wasn't sure he could keep her from going to jail this time. What the hell was she thinking?

Glaring at his partner as they entered the room, George turned his attention to Walt. "Walt, where did they go?" He was not being a nice guy anymore.

"I don't know, George ,but Jade will call me. That's all I can tell you right now." He knew she was in trouble now. Dammit, what was going on in that mind of hers? He knew she didn't want to turn Emmie over to Annie, but now she was going to catch a kidnapping charge for sure.

"Ryan, where were they going?" Now George was beginning to think Ryan and Jade were in cahoots together. He must be losing his fucking mind.

"You don't seriously think I know, do you?" Ryan asked, shocked.

"Okay, let's get going. We're going to take Annie to the school to get her car, and then we're going to figure this out. This is getting out of hand!" George stormed out of the house.

Ryan and Walt just looked at each other. Annie walked out behind George.

"Walt, where was Jade staying before she came back here? The cabin she talked of, where is it?"

"I don't know. It was a cabin; that's all I know. I didn't even think to ask her."

"Shit, alright, call me as soon as you hear from her." Ryan wrote his cell phone number on the back of a business card and handed it to Walt. "Just in case you forgot it."

"You know why she did it, yeah?"

"Yeah, but it doesn't make it right, Walt."

"You will still try to help her, won't you?"

"I am in so much trouble right now because I have been protecting her. This is how she thanks me. I don't know what more I can do, Walt."

"Ryan, it's for Emmie that she's doing this. She's not thinking clearly."

"Call me, Walt. I gotta go." He turned and walked to the waiting car.

9

JADE was driving too fast. She needed to slow down and think. Were they already on her trail? Surely they knew she was gone by now. Did she ever mention Ivory Bluff?

The same question kept coming back over and over. She would have to call Walt, of course. Would he be angry with her? Would Ryan arrest her now? Sure he would; he was a cop, after all. It was a shame, really, that everything had to get so out of hand. Oh well. The only thing that mattered now was keeping Emmie safe. Annie was probably furious, and she had a right to be. She didn't know that the killer was looking for her. Jade had to figure out a way to get that information to Annie. Ryan knew, but he wouldn't tell her. He probably thought the vision story was really just that: a story.

Jade's thoughts were coming too fast. She couldn't figure anything out at this rate. She needed to get Emmie to the cabin, and then she could slow down and sort through everything.

~

In the car and headed first to drop Annie off and then to the station to form a new game plan, Ryan was lost in thought. Hearing Annie crying again in the back seat was nerve-wracking for him. He felt sorry for her but was helpless to do anything about it.

"Why would she take Emmie again?" Annie was crying, but she had anger in her voice.

"We don't know, Annie, but we will find them," George

tried to reassure her. "Ryan, write down Annie's address and phone number before we get her to the school." At least *he* was still thinking like a cop. He couldn't wait to get Ryan alone.

Ryan pulled his pad and pen from the front pocket of his suit jacket and asked for her home and cell phone numbers. He didn't waste time saying anything to George.

"I don't have a cell phone, but my home number is – here, give that to me, and I'll write it all down." She wrote all of her information, including her address, and handed it back to Ryan.

"You live in Hanes Landing?" Ryan asked.

"Yeah, a second floor apartment. Is that a bad thing?" She looked at him, worried. She didn't know of any crime out there, but who better to ask?

"Nah, they're pretty nice. I was just asking."

They drove , Annie trying to make sense of all the information she'd been given. Amy, oh poor Amy, now what was she suppose to do, Annie asked herself for the hundredth time.

"Where are you parked, Annie?" George asked as they pulled into the college parking lot.

"Over there by Building Two. It's the red Corsica," she directed him. "Yeah, right there."

Pulling up behind her car, George stopped, and Ryan got out, opening the back door. "We'll be in touch as soon as we know something. Try not to worry," he said. George got out of the car too.

"There's more to this than you're telling me, isn't there?" Annie asked, her fear showing in her face as she looked up at him.

Ryan looked at George, not saying a word. George walked over, placing his hand on her lower back and ushering her toward her car, "No, but we'll be in touch soon. Stay home."

Ryan heard what George told her. Home was the last place she needed to be. How was he supposed to tell her not to stay home? He would have to come clean and tell George everything; there was no way around it now. Jade didn't leave him any choice. They both watched as Annie drove out of the lot.

Taking a deep breath and releasing it on a sigh, Ryan said, "George, I have a lot to tell you, and you're going to think I'm crazy. I don't know; maybe I am, but I know that I owe you the courtesy of at least allowing you to decide that on your own." They drove out of the lot.

"Ryan, what the hell is going on? I know you took that picture last night. I gave you time alone so you could. I didn't know why you needed it, but I could tell you did."

"George, I took the photo to show Jade."

"Why?"

"Jade didn't know Amy or James Linderhoff. She took Emmie without anyone's permission." He held up his hand to stop

George from speaking. "I have known Walt for a few years now. I trust him. He's a good man. He called me because he knew Jade was in trouble. He sounded desperate, George." Ryan put his hand to his forehead as if he had a headache coming on. Taking a deep breath, he continued. "I went over there so he could explain to me what kind of trouble. When I got there, he told me something that at first I didn't believe, but the more he talked, the more sense it made, I guess. Do you know anything about ESP or visions?" He turned to watch George now, knowing he was digging the hole deeper, but he didn't have a choice. Ryan had to come clean.

"What, you mean like reading minds or seeing the future?" George snickered.

"Yeah, seeing the future, kind of, I guess."

"Ryan, what the hell are you talking about?" George's humor was gone.

"Well, fuck, here goes, okay? So Walt told me Jade has visions of things, and he gave me some of the most extraordinary instances you can imagine. He told me things that Jade had seen before they happened and then explained how he helped Jade to stop them from happening."

"Ryan, you don't fucking believe what you're saying, do you?" George's face had turned tomato red. He couldn't believe what he was hearing.

"At first, no, I didn't, but I listened. I had only met Jade a couple of times. She had been away at college. I didn't know her very well, just in passing, you know? Well, anyway, I fully expected her to be some crazy lunatic, but she's not. George, you saw her; you talked to her. Did she come across as a lunatic to you?"

"No, but she didn't tell me any fantasies, either."

"George, they're not fantasies. Do you remember about thirteen or fourteen years ago that motorcycle driver that jumped the curb on Main Street and killed himself?"

"I remember something about that. Why?"

"Well, if it hadn't been for Jade, a young woman would have been killed by that motorcycle, too. Jade told Walt about it, and she and Walt kept the woman away until it was over."

"Are you crazy? Are you hearing yourself?" George couldn't believe what he was hearing.

"George, try to keep an open mind while I tell you the rest." Ryan went through the entire thing, watching George as he told the story. He told of Mrs. Hamilton's accident and how at first even Walt didn't believe Jade. Ryan kept explaining, trying to get through to George. He told him that Jade said Emmie would be strangled. "George, how would she know that? We didn't tell the media that Amy and James had been strangled. No one knows that except the killer".

"Maybe she's in it with the drug dealer?"

"You've met her; do you believe that?"

"I've seen weirder."

"Come on, George, this vision thing is possible, isn't it?" Ryan finished up with the last vision about Annie.

"Anything is possible, but this is fucking ridiculous."

"Look, let's go to the Linderhoff house. I bet Jade took Emmie there. They'd go there to get Harry."

"Good idea, and, Ryan, if there is any truth to this story, then Annie's in danger, too, right? Is that why Jade took Emmie and ran again, because we were going to make her hand Emmie over to Annie?"

"Yes, it is, and Annie could be in real danger, if we believe in the vision idea.

"Why did you let me tell her to go home and stay there?"

"What would you have me do, George? Tell her about all this?"

"No, but we're going to have to put an officer on her around the clock for a while."

"Good luck explaining that to the Captain."

"Well then, we'll just have to take turns." George couldn't believe he was beginning to believe any of this.

"You're married. I'll do it."

"No, you can't stay awake all night and work all day. We'll take turns, and Doris will just have to deal with that."

"George?"

"What?"

"I'm sorry I didn't keep you informed on everything, and I know I've made a real mess of things. I just knew you would react the way you did. Same as I would've."

"I'm still not sure I'm buying the vision thing. But I know you're telling me the truth, Ryan. We'll solve this just like we intended to. Don't worry about it, but don't you ever keep shit like this from me again."

"I won't. It's just that Jade has me so fucking twisted I can't think straight." Did he just admit that out loud? He slapped himself in the forehead. "See? I never would've admitted that to you." They laughed as they drove to the Linderhoffs'. It felt good to both of them to be back on track. They were partners, and it was wrong for them to keep anything from one another.

They arrived at the house, and when they walked around back, they knew Harry was already gone.

"Well, you were right. She's been here," George said.

"Yeah, but we're too late, so now what?" Ryan looked around.

"Now we go pick up my car; then we go back to Walt's and wait." George went back to the car and waited while Ryan put the photo of Annie back on the wall. He knew Ryan believed everything he told him. But visions? Could they be real? Well, more than one psychic had helped police solve a crime. Maybe there was something to this...

Ryan was worried about Jade. He was beginning to believe in her visions. He knew George would, eventually. But right now, they had at least one killer on the loose, and Jade was a prime target because she had Emmie with her. They had to find her, and fast.

~

Leaving Ryan's car, they got in George's and drove to Walt's house. They liked trading cars throughout the day. It was something they had always done. It used to be just to break the monotony, but not anymore; the gas crunch had everyone conserving, even the police departments.

George and Ryan arrived at Walt's. He was waiting nervously by the phone for Jade to call. They discussed visions until Ryan and Walt gave up trying to convince George.

"Walt, he'll come around. I didn't believe it at first, either," Ryan chuckled.

"Yeah, but it helped when you talked to Jade. George has already talked to her."

"Yes, but she hasn't talked to George about any of her visions yet. Have faith in her, Walt. I do."

"You're a good man, Ryan."

"Yeah, I keep hearing that a lot lately," Ryan said, laughing.

George was on the front porch, talking to Doris on his cell phone. He came back in, this time with a smile on his face.

"Good conversation this time, I take it." Ryan said, looking George squarely in the eye.

"Yeah, she's had her coffee, which she needs first thing in the morning, so she was nicer." George laughed. "Walt, are you sure Jade will call?"

"Yeah, she'll call me. I know she's trying to figure out what she's going to do. Jade is very intelligent, and she knows she's in trouble. I just wish I had asked where that damn cabin was."

"I'm a detective, and I didn't think to ask. Imagine how stupid I'm feeling right now," Ryan said, trying to lighten the mood.

"Well, do you fellas want some coffee?"

"That sounds good, thank you," George said as he walked behind Walt into the kitchen. "Can I help?"

"No, I got it. Why don't you go make yourself comfortable? We could be here a while."

"You don't think Jade will call soon?"

"I don't know. I thought she would have called by now. It's been almost three hours."

~

Jade and Emmie had arrived back at the cabin. Jade took Emmie and Harry to the kitchen to find a dish for Harry's food. Emmie was playing with Harry and having the time of her life. Jade watched the two of them. She was really in a fix now. What jury in the world would believe her? It's okay, she thought, she would give up her freedom and do time in jail to keep this kid safe. Wow. She was surprised how easy it was to give so much for someone she didn't even really know. Perhaps she'd always known it would be a child that finally did her in. Jade laughed at the thought. Too bad it wouldn't be her own child.

Searching the kitchen cabinets, she finally found the dish she was looking for and filled it with food. She added another dish for water. Harry practically ran over Emmie to get to the food and water. Emmie laughed when Harry knocked her down; she just lay on the floor, watching Harry and laughing.

Jade sat in the kitchen, watching Emmie. She knew in her heart what she was doing was the right thing. She had not realized it till just this moment. Now, she needed to sit and try to figure things out.

Emmie was a precious gift to Jade. As she sat there, watching her lying on the floor and laughing at Harry, Jade knew that in the end, all would be well. She didn't know how she knew it; she just did.

Jade had a lot of thinking to do and needed to be alone, so she told Emmie to stay in the cabin and play with Harry while she went to the front porch and sat down. She listened to the crashing surf and began to relax. She knew she had to call Walt, but that would have to wait until she was able to explain her actions. Walt would understand, but Ryan and George wouldn't. Certainly Annie would not. Jade couldn't worry about any of them right now. Her main concern was Emmie.

She could hear Emmie calling Harry and then hear Harry running around. They were having a great time. She was glad she'd gone to get Harry. At least he was something familiar for Emmie and would help keep her homesickness to a minimum.

Jade knew she was going to have to tell Emmie about her parents. If she had given Emmie to Annie, Annie would have told her, but Annie couldn't keep her safe. Annie wasn't even safe herself, and she didn't even know it.

Jade had to call Walt and make sure they kept Annie safe. Giving up her quiet, relaxing spot on the porch, she went back inside the cabin and picked up the telephone. Taking her time dialing, she tried to figure out what she was going to say. She knew she had put Walt in a bad predicament, but he would just have to understand, as they didn't give her a choice.

"Hello?" Walt answered the phone on the first ring.

"I'm sorry I left, Dad, but I have to keep Emmie with me." Boy, she sounded a little off even to herself. Her voice was flat and monotone.

"I know, honey. Are you alright?"

"Yeah, we're both fine."

"Jade, where are you?"

"I can't tell you that, Dad. I know Ryan is probably there with you, and I need to keep you out of trouble at least as much as I can."

"You don't worry about that. Just tell me where you are."

"No, Dad, please understand that it's better this way."

Ryan and George were listening, and George was getting angrier by the minute. "Walt, tell her I want to talk to her," he demanded.

"Jade?"

"Yeah."

"Will you talk to George?"

"Sure, put him on."

Walt handed the phone to George, the look in his eyes telling George to take it easy with her. Ryan watched the look Walt gave George. He knew that if George screwed this up, they might not have another chance.

"You have to talk to her with respect; don't be demanding," Ryan said. George glared at him like he was stupid.

Jade could hear what her dad and Ryan were saying, and she prayed George would keep an open mind. She guessed they had told him everything.

"Hey, Jade, it's George," he said, trying not to sound demanding.

"Hi, George." She paused. "I just want you to know that I know you've had a lot to deal with and take in, but it's true. All of it, George. You just need to listen to my dad."

"Jade, right now, I want to listen to you." George kept his anger under control and tried to keep his voice calm.

"I know they've filled you in on everything by now. I'm not crazy. I know what I'm doing, and you just have to believe me."

"I do. But you have to tell us where you are."

"I can't right now. Just give me some time to figure this out."

"Emmie has to be given to Annie. We don't have a choice in that."

"I know you don't, but I do. That's why I left. I will take

whatever I have to legally, but I am going to keep this child safe. Period."

"Jade, there are other ways."

"No, there aren't, and you know it."

"Just come back. Or tell us how to get there."

"I promise I will when the time is right. You just have to trust me."

George looked at Ryan. If she felt for Ryan what he knew Ryan felt for her, maybe Ryan could talk some sense into her. "Jade, will you hang on just a second for me?"

A thought occurred to her. Were they tracing her call? Should she hang up?

George waited for Jade to reply. "Jade?"

"I'm still here, George. Are you trying to trace this call?"

"Listen, Jade, I'm not having this call traced. I just want to talk to Ryan for a second. Okay?"

"Okay, go ahead. I'll wait." Jade thought she would give it just a minute, and then she would hang up. She could call back, and they would have to start all over with tracing. If she remembered right, she thought she had to be on the phone for five minutes, but she wasn't sure. She had only been on for about two.

"You try and talk some sense into her, get her back here," George said, handing Ryan the phone.

"Jade?"

"I'm really sorry about this." She felt guilty. She knew she had put Ryan in this mess just as surely she had her dad.

"I know, I am, too," he said quietly.

"I'm going to hang up, but I'll call right back."

Jade hung the phone up before Ryan could say anything. He looked at Walt and said, "She hung up."

"What did she say to you?" Walt asked with concern on his face.

"She just said she would call right back."

"She thinks you're trying to trace the call," Walt said and laughed. He was very proud of his daughter. She was every bit as smart as he gave her credit for. He was still laughing when the telephone rang in Ryan's hand.

"Hello, Jade?" Ryan said as he answered the phone.

"Yeah, Ryan, it's me. I'm sorry; I just have to make sure I don't stay on long enough for you to trace the call. I can't let you know where we are."

"Listen to me. We aren't trying to trace your call. We don't have to know where you are; we just have to know you're both alright."

George was looking at Ryan like he was the crazy one. "Ryan, we *do* have to know where they are." Ryan held up his hand to George.

"Ryan, we're both alright. I'll take very good care of Emmie. I even went and picked up Harry for her."

"We know. We figured that was where you would go, so we went there looking for you."

"Listen, you have to keep Annie safe. I told you what will happen to her."

"Yeah, I told George about the killer and your vision. We'll do what we can to keep her safe, but, Jade, I want you safe, too. Please come back to your dad's."

"Not right now, I can't. Annie will take Emmie, and you can't stop her. Emmie won't be safe with her, Ryan. She's not even safe."

"Yes, she is, because of you."

"Ryan, keep her safe, and I'll bring Emmie back as soon as I know it's safe for her."

"Jade, don't hang up."

"I have to. I'll call Dad soon."

"Jade?" Nothing but dead air on the phone. Ryan set the handset back on the charger and looked at Walt and George. "She's not coming back for a while," he said.

They all three sat there looking at each other. No one said a word.

~

Jade put the phone back and went to check on Emmie. She and Harry had been quiet for a few minutes, and that couldn't be a good thing. Jade walked into the kitchen and stood there staring at the sight. Emmie was curled up in a ball on the kitchen floor, sleeping, while Harry lay right next to her, keeping vigil. Jade quietly walked back out to the porch. Sitting down, she began to sort through this entire mess.

10

WALT sat there for a few minutes, deep in thought. "Ryan, you and George don't have to worry. Jade will be safe, and she won't let anything happen to Emmie. Jade has a good head on her shoulders."

"Look, I know she's your daughter, Walt, but you are going to have to quit protecting her. You need to get her to come home," George began to argue.

"I understand that, George, but I don't control Jade. She has a mind of her own." Walt knew that between him and Ryan, George would eventually come around. In the meantime, Walt had all the faith in the world in Jade, and he would support her, whatever she decided.

"George, Walt's right. We have to wait. We don't have any choice right now. She has a lot on her plate, but I believe she has Emmie's best interests in mind," Ryan said.

George looked at the two men like they had grown horns and tails. "What are you two blabbering about? You guys make it sound like Jade is doing everything legally like she hasn't broken the law. Are you nuts? Especially you, Ryan! What the hell are you thinking?"

"George, hold on a damn minute. Don't you dare start in with me. I know what Jade is doing is technically breaking the law. So what? Isn't she doing her best to keep a kid safe?"

"Yeah, it appears she is, but don't you think Emmie would be safer with us?"

"No. We would've given Emmie to Annie. Then what? The killer could take them both out!"

"We'd be watching that apartment around the clock."

"You know as well as I do: that may not be enough."

"We could stay in the apartment. Annie would let us."

"Yeah, that's what we'll do." Ryan stood up. "We go to Annie's and stay in the apartment. We don't know when the killer's going to try, so we stay until he does."

"Rya, that's a great idea," Walt said.

"Yeah. You have my cell phone number. Give it to Jade when she calls. Tell her to call me." Ryan was walking out of the room.

Shaking hands with Walt at the front door, George said, "Walt, I still don't know what to believe. I know you and your daughter will do your best to keep Emmie safe. I don't doubt that for a minute. But you have to get Jade on the right side of the law."

"I know, George. I'm trying to keep Jade just as safe as Emmie."

"Come on, George," Ryan yelled from the car.

"You better get going. I'll have Jade call. I promise."

"Okay. See you later."

Ryan was waiting in the driver's seat, holding out his hand for the keys. They had brought George's car.

"You don't seriously think I'm going to let you drive my car, do you?"

"Yes. Give me the keys."

"No, get in the other side."

"No, George, I'm driving. Give me the keys."

They stayed there for what seemed like an eternity before George finally relented and gave the car keys to Ryan. He walked around and got in the passenger side. "You better take it easy and drive like an adult."

Ryan started the engine and pulled away from the curb. "George, call Annie and make sure she's home. I don't want to go all the way over there and waste our time if she's not."

"Where did you write her number down?"

"It's in my spiral," Ryan said, handing it to George.

Ryan watched George dig through the notebook until he found the number. He was trying to decide how to get George to let him keep watch on Annie so George could go home to Doris. Ryan knew that George was touchy about being so much older than he was, so maybe if he pissed him off, he could make his point that Doris would totally freak if George spent the night in a younger woman's apartment.

"Annie?" George's voice was deep and resonating in the enclosed space. After a brief conversation, he slapped the cell phone closed and looked over at Ryan, "She's obviously there. We can go on over."

"She thought we'd found Emmie already, didn't she?"

"Yeah, I felt bad. I didn't even think about that. I should have."

"Oh, don't beat yourself up. You're getting up in years and your thought process isn't what it used to be." Ryan figured he may as well get started on his plan to piss George off.

"Hey, what the fuck?"

"Don't get your granddaddy pants in a wad. You know you're a lot older than I am. I should have told you to be careful when you called her."

"What, are you suggesting that I'm too old to think straight?"

"Well, you know when you get to a certain age, your mind starts to slow down. You don't remember things as well, and you get irritated with yourself easier."

"Really, do tell. And while you're at it, bite my ass!"

Ryan started laughing. He knew he was goading George, but he had to piss him off. "You do have a cute ass, partner, but it's a little too old for my taste, not to mention the wrong sex."

"What's up with all this old age bullshit?"

"I know we have lots of things in common. We work great together and usually have the same taste in women when we flirt, but come on, you're my dad's age, George."

"Okay, that's it." George started taking his seat belt off. "Pull over. I'm driving, and you're getting your ass out of my car and walking to Hanes Landing."

"Whoa, partner, you don't mean that. I'm sorry. I know you're touchy about your age. I should have thought before I said anything. Let me make it up to you."

"I don't think you can. You have been lying to me, keeping secrets from me, and now you tell me just how fucking old I am."

"I'll make it up to you. I'll help you keep your marriage a happy one," he said with a twinkle in his eye.

"Oh? How you gonna do that, sleep with Doris?" George was laughing so hard he thought his false teeth would slip. Man, false teeth. He was getting old. That was enough to make him stop laughing and look grimly out the window. Ryan was trying to figure out what made George so unhappy all of a sudden.

"Okay, bud, what you thinking about? You okay? I was just funning, you know," he said seriously.

"Yeah, just thinking, that's all. So what do you have in mind to make my happy marriage go on and on?"

"Well, I figured I would take the first watch at Annie's. That way you could go home to Doris. If she's happy, you're happy right?"

Aha, that's it. George knew Ryan well. "I'll take the first watch. After all, you're too young and need your rest." George thought two could play this game.

"Wait, isn't it supposed to be you who needs your rest, since you're elderly?"

"No, it's for the young, too young!"

"Are you saying I'm a baby?"

"Not a baby, exactly, but you have a lot of growing up to do."

"All right, truce. I was saying all this age crap to make you mad so you'd let me stay at Annie's."

"Why?"

"Because I know how Doris busts your chops all the time, so I thought I would help you out, that's all."

"You let me worry about Doris," he said, smiling.

"You're right. I'll stop aggravating you. I guess I just feel like a lot of this is my fault because I wasn't up front with you on everything."

"Yeah, don't let that happen again. We're partners for a reason. You know?"

"Yeah, I do. I feel like a heel. I'm sorry, man."

"Look, kid, it's not as if you killed anyone."

"I know. But let me take the first watch, okay?"

"Let's see what'll make Annie more comfortable and go from there."

"That's a deal." Ryan was sure Annie would prefer to have him around. After all, he was closer to her age, and they would have more in common. They arrived at Annie's apartment, and Ryan handed the keys to George. Walking up the stairs in silence, they both had time to think.

George had to make sure Annie contacted the coroner's office about Amy and James. He knew Annie was young and had probably never had to deal with something like this before, so he would offer his help. He also had to make sure she contacted both parents, and that was a hard thing to do. George had his mind going in one direction, and Ryan's was going in another.

Ryan was getting impatient for Jade to call. Why hadn't she called him yet? Had she even called Walt? Where was she? Just as they reached Annie's door, he looked at George. "Do you realize we never even checked Jade's house?"

"What are you talking about?"

"Here we are, trying to figure out where she took Emmie, and we haven't even thought to find out where she lives and check there."

"You're right. Guess the mind does go with age. What's your excuse?"

"Haha, very funny. I guess lust works the same way age does." They were both laughing when Annie opened the front door. She looked at them like they had lost their minds. They tried to compose themselves and act professional, but the conversation had been too funny.

"Please come in," she said, stepping back and holding the door open.

"Ms. Armstrong." Ryan tried to put on his serious face but didn't quite make it.

"Hey, Annie." George tried to put her immediately at ease.

The apartment was nicely furnished. The living room had a matching sofa and love seat in earth tones. The carpet was a soft tan. The walls were a beige color with dark woodwork surrounding the floor and ceiling. The art work Annie had picked was African with wooden carvings and masks hanging on the walls.

"This is really nice. Did you decorate it yourself?" George asked.

"Yes, thank you. I'm an art major, in case you couldn't tell."

"Art major, huh?" George asked.

"Yeah. I don't know what a degree in art is going to do for me, but that's what interests me most."

"Well, I like it. You have amazing taste. This is a cozy, warm room," Ryan said, looking around. The three sat down, George and Annie on the sofa and Ryan on the love seat.

"Annie, the reason we came to see you is we believe you may be in danger," George said.

"Why would I be in danger, Detective Dunleavy? I've never dealt with drugs of any kind," Annie said, shocked.

"No, no, I didn't mean to suggest that you did. We believe the killer may be looking for something. We think James took some drugs or something, and that's what got him and your sister killed."

"Why do you think James took something?"

"I take it you haven't been by their house since we left you earlier?"

"No, I came straight home. I didn't even think to go to their house. Why would I? Emmie isn't there."

"I just thought, you know, natural curiosity."

"No, I'm not curious to see my sister's house if she or Emmie aren't there."

"Annie, someone was searching for something. The living room and master bedroom have been ransacked."

"Why? What could James have taken?"

"Drugs, money, it could be anything of value."

"Ms. Armstrong, do you know where Amy or James kept things of value?" Ryan asked.

"Annie, please. Ms. Armstrong is my mother. And no, I have no idea. As far as I know, they didn't have anything of value."

"Annie, they had something, and it was valuable enough to get them killed. We believe whoever killed them lost something worth killing over." Ryan wasn't pulling any punches. He figured she had a right to know.

"You think whoever it was may come here?"

"Yes, we do," George said

"Wow. I never considered myself to be in danger. Emmie! Oh my God! We have to find her even faster now. If I'm in danger, she certainly is."

"The killer would think you knew where it was before she would know. She's just a child."

"Yes, but we have to find her. I don't like not knowing where she is. I know Jade obviously thinks the world of her to put herself in this much trouble, and I'm sure she will take care of Emmie, but I want Emmie with me."

Ryan looked at George, willing him not to mention the visions. He didn't think George would, since he didn't really believe all that nonsense anyway, but...

"Look, Annie." George turned to face her. "One of us will stay around the clock with you. We want to make sure you're safe. The other one will be trying to locate Emmie."

"I don't think you need to stay with me. I don't know any of James' friends or whatever."

"You don't need to know him. He just needs to know you exist. The danger is there." George wanted to make sure she understood.

"Annie, you really need to let one of us stay, or we'll be outside in our car, watching." Ryan was trying to make the point that she was going to be protected one way or another.

Annie sat there looking around her apartment and feeling the goosebumps rise on her arms. What was she supposed to do? The detectives apparently realized she needed time to think because they sat there watching her, not saying a word. They were giving her time to absorb this knowledge and make her own decision. They wouldn't force themselves into her apartment, but they would remain, one way or another.

"Annie, I know you have a lot to think about, but there's more," George said.

"More?"

"Yes. You need to contact the coroner's office and also call your family and tell them about Amy and James, if you haven't already."

"Oh, I know. I've called our mother. She's trying to get flight information now. She told me she would call James' mom. I haven't had time yet to call the coroner's office. I have to go to Amy's and see if they had insurance. I just haven't been able to make myself do it."

"Ryan's going to stay here with you. I can go by there and look for the paperwork if you'd like me to."

Ryan was amazed. He thought they were going to let Annie decide which of them would stay. George was probably realizing the Doris thing was the truth and that he would need time to explain before he just didn't come home for the night. Ryan almost wished he had someone to worry about him if he didn't come home. Whoa, where did that come from?

"That would be a big help, but I can't ask you to do that."

"You didn't ask. I offered," George said.

"George, we need to go get my car, and I have to pick up a few things from my apartment," Ryan said, standing.

"Annie, do you need us to bring you anything?" George was feeling protective of this kid. He was a cop, not a delivery boy. What the hell was he thinking?

"No, thank you. I still don't think it's necessary for either of you to stay here."

"Guess I really do need my car since I'll be staying in it throughout the night." Ryan tried to lighten the mood.

"You're young. You won't be too sore tomorrow." George got a jab in that made him feel good.

"Detective Douglas, you don't have to sleep in your car. You can sleep on the couch if you're that insistent on staying." Annie tried to smile.

"Thank you, Annie." Ryan smiled back.

"Okay then, come on, Ryan, I'll take you to get your car; then you can run by your apartment. I'll go by the Linderhoffs' and check on the insurance."

"Guys, you're a big help. I'm sorry I was such a bitch earlier." Annie looked down at her feet.

"Don't talk about yourself like that, Annie," George said.

"I'll be back in about an hour. Annie, try to stay on the phone with a friend or go visit someone until I can get back," Ryan jumped in.

"I don't feel much like visiting with anyone. I'll just sit here and wait for you."

Ryan and George both knew she shouldn't be alone in the apartment. George tried again. "Annie, why don't you go out and get some fresh air, then? Maybe take a walk. You don't need to sit here by yourself. You and Ryan can come back up together so you won't just be sitting here with time to think."

"Really, guys, I'll be alright alone. I'm used to it."

The two detectives gave up. They stood and went to the door. Annie walked behind them.

"Annie, do you want us to search the apartment before we leave?" George didn't want to leave her there.

"No, really, I'm fine, but thanks." Annie opened the door and stood to the side of it. She smiled goodbye to them. Ryan looked at George, and they walked out, not saying another word.

"Ryan, hurry and get your ass back here as quick as you can."

"Why didn't we bring both cars?" Ryan asked. "That way, you could have stayed until I got back."

"Once again, we're just not thinking," George said.

"Yeah, we really need to get our shit together," Ryan laughed.

They rode in silence, George driving this time and Ryan watching out the window. Both had their minds going over things that still needed to be taken care of. They would solve this; they always did. That's why they were partners. They worked well together, and their results showed it. That was one of the reasons they had been given this case. Captain Mallory told them the morning he assigned the case to them that they were his best team. It was true, and they both knew it.

The age difference never came up before, and George was still trying to decide if it was becoming a problem for Ryan. Maybe he wanted a partner his own age. One he could go hang out with. He and Ryan went for a beer occasionally. They played pool together once in awhile. He would watch Ryan for signs that he was ready for a younger partner. If George found any, he would bow out gracefully and save Ryan the embarrassment of having to actually say it.

"What are you thinking about that's causing those frown lines, George?" Ryan had been studying his partner, and the look on George's face concerned him.

"Not much, just thinking about how young Annie is and all she has to deal with."

"Don't worry. I'll take good care of her."

"I know that. I'm not worried. I mean, it's not like she's my daughter or anything."

"Yeah, but I saw the protective way you're handling her."

"It's crazy, isn't it? I mean, I feel responsible for her, and I don't know why."

"Because she's trying so hard to be responsible, quitting school to take care of Emmie, calling the parents, making funeral arrangements. You know how hard she's trying, and that's touched you. Nothing wrong with being human, partner."

"Human. Yeah, that's it. I guess I'm not so hardhearted after all these years."

"We do get hardhearted in this job, that's for sure. But we're still human, and we can still feel."

"Do you think she'll be alright while she's waiting for you to get back?"

"Yeah. I was wondering, though, how did it end up that I was staying? I thought Annie was going to decide that."

"That just slipped out. I don't know. You don't have to if you have other plans or something."

"No, I was just wondering, that's all."

They drove the rest of the way in silence. Ryan needed to call Walt. Not hearing from Jade was driving him nuts. She would have to bring Emmie back for the funeral; he hoped she realized that. He would have to make sure he brought that up in their next conversation.

George was thinking he would go back to Annie's and wait in the car until Ryan made it back there. He wouldn't forgive himself if the killer got to Annie. They had to protect her. Wow, was he beginning to believe in that crap? Visions. Yeah, right.

They pulled up to Ryan's car in the parking lot.

"Ryan, I'm going to Annie's. I'll wait in the car outside her apartment until you can get your things and get back. I just don't want her alone there."

"I agree. I'll hurry," Ryan said, getting out of the car.

"Later." George nodded and drove off.

Ryan got in his car and pulled his cell phone out. No missed calls. He dialed Walt's telephone number and waited.

"Hello?"

"Walt, it's Ryan. Have you heard from Jade yet?"

"No, and I'm getting worried."

"She'll call, Walt. I just thought I might have missed her call, that's all."

"Are you staying with Annie tonight?"

"Yeah."

"I'm glad you guys are going to be staying with her until this nut is caught."

"Me too, Walt"

"I'll call you if Jade doesn't; that way you won't just be waiting."

"Walt, where does Jade live?"

"She lives on Fox Hollow. Why?"

"We haven't looked at her place for her."

"She isn't there, or she would have told me."

"Probably, but it won't hurt to check it out. Do you know the numerics on Fox Hollow?"

After getting what he needed, he ended the call with Walt. He was getting worried. Jade should have called by now. What was she doing? He'd call George and let him know he was going by Jade's house before going to Annie's. Fox Hollow. Wow! That was a nice area. Walt had a nice house, but he was retired. He would have to find out what kind of work Jade did.

Ryan called George and then drove to his apartment. He quickly grabbed an overnight bag and the few things he would need in it. He would have to come home before going to work, so he didn't worry about his shaving kit or an outfit.

He listened to his messages and made a mental note to call his mom. She had called yesterday and again today. Maybe he would even try to get out and visit her soon. He rifled through his mail, then locked up.

As he drove by Jade's, he kept thinking about her. He loved her smile, and he would have to make her use it more. Her eyes were enough to make a man melt. He thought about what it would feel like to run his hands through her silky hair. Smiling to himself made him realize he could be a goner if he wasn't careful.

The house was a big, two story, light brown brick with a big porch. The porch had two chairs and a swing. The lights were off except for a small light in an upstairs window. She probably left that on to make people think she was home. The landscaping was professional. Palm trees were placed strategically with birds of paradise and some type of lily-looking flowering shrub for filler. It really was a great looking place. He wanted to see inside, but that would have to wait. He'd get the chance, though. He'd make sure of that. Bet the bed is big, too, he thought.

He drove past and looked over at the park. Not too many people out this time of the evening. The air was a little cool, and it was a school night. He decided to head for Annie's and let George get home.

11

BACK in Ivory Bluff, Jade was watching Emmie play in the bathtub. Harry lay on the floor near the door. He was never too far from Emmie if he could help it. She was playing with the bubbles, making a Napoleon-type hat. She laughed and dunked herself to remove the hat.

After a while, Jade decided to wash Emmie's hair and get her moving toward bed. "Sweetie. let's get your hair washed," she said, reaching for the shampoo.

"I can do it." Emmie sat up and took the bottle.

"All by yourself? You don't want help?"

"You can help if you want to."

"Okay. I want to." Jade laughed at the look on Emmie's face. She had made herself a moustache with the bubbles and was crossing her eyes.

Jade took the baby shampoo and squeezed some into Emmie's hand.

"Don't get it in your eyes," she cautioned.

"I won't." Emmie splattered the shampoo on her head and began to rub it around. More bubbles were forming, and she was having fun playing with the soft soap. "Will you wipe my face with that worsh rag?"

"Worsh rag? You mean this wash cloth?" Jade held it up.

"Wash cloth?" Emmie asked, scrunching her little face up.

"Yes, Emmie, this is a wash cloth. If it was a rag, we would use it for chores."

"Mommy always called it a worsh rag."

"What is 'worsh'?" Jade was laughing again.

"It's what we do with our bodies and things, isn't it?"

"I don't know what you do with your body, but I wash mine." She took the cloth and gently wiped Emmie's face. "There, that looks better. Oh, you're so pretty!" she said, tweaking the child's nose.

"Thank you. So are you."

They finished the bath, and Emmie got into her pajamas. Sliding into bed and covering up, she asked Jade if Harry could sleep with her. Harry took that as a cue and jumped up on the bed, lying across her legs and feet.

"You're heavy, Harry," Emmie laughed.

Jade shoved Harry over so he lay next to Emmie, not on her.

"Thanks."

"You're welcome, sweetie. Good night."

"Night!"

Jade left the room and went to the living room. Sitting down, she realized that her feet were hurting. Rubbing them and looking at the telephone, she knew she needed to call her dad, but she wouldn't just yet. She needed to sit in the quiet for a few minutes and give Emmie time to go to sleep. She would have to go pay a few more days' rent on the cabin tomorrow.

She also needed to find out if anyone was watching over Annie. Surely Ryan would be.

It had been a long day, and Jade felt her eyelids getting heavy. She thought she'd better call her dad before she fell asleep in the chair. She dialed her dad's number and waited for him to answer, which he did immediately.

"Hi, Dad."

"Jade, thank God. I was beginning to wonder if you were going to call back."

" I had to wait until Emmie went to bed."

"Jade, where's the cabin?"

"We've been over this. The less you know...."

"I'll take care of myself. Tell me where you are."

"No, Dad, I won't."

"Ryan went to your house tonight to see if you were there."

"Why would he think that?"

"I don't know. I guess he just had to check it out. You know cops."

"Dad, I have to tell Emmie about her parents."

"Yes, you do. Since you took her again, you'll have to deal with that."

"I guess I'll tell her tomorrow. I don't look forward to that at all."

"Jade, Ryan wants you to call him"

"Why?"

"I don't know. He didn't say. Maybe he's just worried about you."

"Yeah, right, he's not worried about me. He wants Emmie brought back."

"You will call him, won't you?"

"Sure, I'll call him."

"I have his number here. Let me know when you're ready to copy it."

"Go ahead. I have a pen and paper right here." Jade wrote the number down and pushed it to the side. "Dad, I know this has been hard on you, and I'm sorry."

"Don't worry about your old man; I'm just fine, other than worrying about you and Emmie."

"Emmie is doing a lot better since we picked Harry up." She paused and stated, "Well, I'm getting tired; I think I'll call Ryan real quick, and then I'm going to bed."

"Alright, honey. Call me tomorrow?"

"I will."

"Promise?"

"Yes, I promise. I love you, Dad."

"I love you too, pumpkin."

"Good night."

"Sweet dreams, honey."

They hung up, and Jade looked at the number she wrote down. Why did Ryan want her to call him? She would call him, she knew. She hardly knew him, and yet... she missed him. How strange. She dialed the number and waited to hear his voice.

"Detective Douglas," he said with a slight Texas drawl.

"Ryan, it's Jade."

"Jade, are you alright?" He held the phone so tight his knuckles went white.

"Of course I am, why?"

"I talked to Walt a while ago, and he was worried to death over you. What took you so long to call your dad?" he asked angrily.

"Are you going to chastise me, Ryan?"

"No. But you would deserve it."

"I know. Why did you want me to call you?"

"I was worried about you. I even went by your house."

"So I heard."

"You heard?"

"Yeah, Dad told me you were going to."

"Oh."

"Is someone watching Annie?"

"Yeah, George is there right now, and I'm on my way. I'm going to stay the night."

"Really, inside or out?"

"What?"

"Are you staying inside or outside?"

"Does it matter?" Ryan's heart was fluttering. Did she care? Was she jealous? Maybe she was feeling it, too.

"No, it doesn't matter. I just want to make sure you can see all the way around her apartment because I don't know how the killer gets in."

"Oh, that's all?" He felt deflated.

"I just wanted to know."

"I'm staying inside, Jade, on the couch," he felt compelled to add.

"You don't owe me any explanations."

"I know that, and I know you won't tell me where you are, but will you at least give me your number so if I need to get hold of you, I can?"

"Uh-uh, if I give you the number here, you'll know the area I'm in."

"Is that so bad?"

"Yes. I don't want anyone to know where we are just yet. Can you understand that?"

"No, I can't, Jade. I want you to come home."

"Not yet, but hopefully soon."

"What about the funeral? Are you going to make Emmie miss her parents' funeral?"

"No, of course not. When is it?"

"I don't know yet, probably in a couple of days. Annie is waiting for her mom to get here and to give James' mom time to fly in."

"You'll let me know, right?"

"Yeah, I'll tell you as soon as I know anything. You know you won't be able to sneak off with Emmie again."

"We'll see, won't we? I'm a very resourceful woman, Ryan."

"Jade, what are you running from?"

"Uh, hello, there's a killer loose!"

"That's not true. The killer doesn't even know about you."

"No, but he does know about Emmie."

"I don't think he'll bother with Emmie. He just wants what's his."

"I'm going to bed, Ryan. I'll call you tomorrow, maybe even let Emmie say hi to Annie."

"That would be nice of you. Sweet dreams. I'll wait to hear from you."

"Bye."

"Bye." Ryan drove to Annie's and parked in front of the complex. He could see George sitting in his car just across the parking lot. George was waving at him. Ryan waved back. He got out and grabbed the overnight bag. Locking his car, he headed toward George.

"Thanks, George. I got it from here."

"Okay, buddy, see you bright and early in the AM."

"Yep. Anything going on I need to know about?"

"Nope, just quiet as can be. I hope for your sake it stays this way."

"Yeah, me too. Tell Doris hi for me."

"Will do. Good night."

"G'night." Ryan walked across the parking lot, looking all around and trying to see if anything or anyone looked out of place. He could see a van sitting in the parking lot – not in a space, just parked by a curb area – and someone sitting in the passenger seat. He stopped and stared for a minute, trying to get a reaction out of the person. It was a white male who looked as if he didn't have a care in the world. He was reading the newspaper. It was twilight and difficult to read the paper.

Ryan decided to walk over and have a talk with the subject. As he approached the passenger side of the van, he saw the man fold the newspaper and roll the window down. "Hey, guy, what you doing out here?"

"Just waiting on a buddy of mine."

"Oh yeah? Where's your buddy now?"

"He's in his girl's apartment. Why?"

"So you don't live here?"

"No."

"What apartment is he in?"

"What's it to you?"

"I don't like people I don't know hanging around my parking lot."

"Your parking lot?"

"That's right. What apartment is he in?"

"I don't know, pal. Why don't you just let it go?"

"No. Why don't you collect your friend and move on?"

"Look, I don't want any trouble. Just go on."

Ryan was sizing this guy up and making a mental note of the license plate so he could run it later. He wanted a good look at the guy's right hand. The guy had put both hands in his pockets, and Ryan had no reason to make him remove them without giving up the fact that he was a cop. He stood there, staring, hoping to make the guy nervous enough to try something stupid.

Finally, it worked. The man took the folded newspaper off his lap and laid it on the dash. Reaching over to open the door, he said, "Look, fella, I haven't done anything to you. Why don't you just go? We don't like strangers hanging around here. Get your friend and leave. Then we'll have no problem."

Hearing a door open behind him, Ryan maneuvered himself slightly so he could see who was coming out of the building. George was still there in his car, watching and waiting. Ryan saw a young man of about twenty-five walking toward him. As the new man approached Ryan, George moved his car closer.

"Hey, what're you doing?" the new man asked.

"Is this your van?"

"Yeah, what about it?"

"I was just talking to your friend here, telling him he needed to get moving." Ryan gestured at the man in the van.

"Who put you in charge? We'll leave when we're ready."

"I think you're ready."

George got out of his car and walked up to Ryan. Ryan looked at George, and both knew what the other was thinking. It came from working together a long time; it was one of the things that made them a good team. The young man walked to the driver side and got in. He said something smart to his friend, and they both laughed. The engine started, and the driver backed the van enough to make a U-turn, then flipped Ryan and George off and drove away.

"Well, so much for it being quiet," Ryan said.

"It is if you leave people alone," George laughed.

Once again, they said good night, and George went home. Ryan went to Annie's apartment to get settled in for the night.

"Hey, Detective, welcome back," she said, smiling and welcoming him in.

"Annie, I'll stay out of your way as much as I can. I want to do a quick walk through and make sure no one has snuck in. Just kind of familiarize myself with the place; then I'll be as quiet as a church mouse."

"Make yourself at home. I'm just making a cup of tea. Would you like some?"

"Tea? No, thank you."

"Would you prefer coffee? I have some. I just don't drink it at night, but I can make a pot for you."

"No, thanks, though. I'll put this bag in the living room and check the apartment, then settle on the couch, if that's okay."

"Whatever," she said, walking back to her tiny kitchen.

Ryan walked through the apartment, checking closets, behind doors, under the bed, any space that looked big enough for a small person to hide. The cat was in the tub behind the shower curtain and scared the daylights out of Ryan when he jumped out.

After he was satisfied there wasn't anyone besides him and Annie in the apartment, he walked to the living room and sat on the couch. Annie was in the kitchen getting her tea and humming to herself. This was going to be a long night, Ryan thought. It was only the beginning of many long nights if they didn't catch this nut pretty soon.

The TV was on, and Ryan tried to concentrate on the program, but thoughts of Jade kept creeping back into his mind. He could see her face, hear her voice. He needed to get back on track. He was in Annie's apartment, and he needed to stay focused. He would deal with Jade and lustful thoughts later; right now wasn't the time. Annie walked into the living room, carrying a cup of tea and a plate of cookies.

"I didn't know you had a cat."

"Oh, that's Wally, I'm sorry. I just didn't think. Was he in the tub?"

"Yeah, he jumped out just as I opened the shower curtain. Took about ten years off my life, I think," Ryan said, smiling.

"He does that to me sometimes, too. Sorry."

"No biggie. I was just surprised." Then Jade's vision struck hard. *A cat jumped out from somewhere and tripped him.*

"Do you want some cookies? I'm kind of a junk food junky," she said, smiling.

"That's okay. I have my moments, too. Chocolate is my downfall."

"Mine, too. I guess I need to get it under control before Emmie gets here. I have to make sure she has a good diet. Not a bunch of sugar."

"Yeah, kids are tough. So you think you'll raise her, then?"

"I don't see where I have a choice. I'm the one Amy would want to take her."

"Did you find out when your mom will be here?"

"Yeah, she'll be here tomorrow evening. I guess we'll schedule the funerals for the next day or so. George hasn't made it back yet, so I don't know about the insurance or money situation. I'll just do what I have to, and Mom and Mrs. Linderhoff will have to help out."

"I spoke with Jade a little while ago. She told me she would bring Emmie back for the funerals. You know Jade's a pretty good person; she's just scared for Emmie."

"Why?"

"There's a killer on the loose, Annie, and Emmie is James' daughter. The killer might think the kid has the goods somewhere. Who knows what these psychos think?"

"Does Jade think I can't take care of Emmie?" she asked, a little offended.

"No, I don't believe she's thinking clearly right now. You have a lot to deal with, and so does she."

"What does she have to do with all this, Ryan?"

"I guess because she took Emmie from the park that day and now she knows Emmie's parents are dead, she feels obligated. I don't know. Just try to be patient with her."

"I still don't get why she took Emmie."

"Well, she said she could see Emmie playing from her house. She looked around and didn't see Amy or James. Jade said they never left Emmie alone like that. So she walked over there and asked Emmie where her mom was. Emmie told her she was 'in the parking lot,' so Jade walked to the parking lot. Still not seeing Amy, she went back to Emmie. She told Emmie to come with her, and they went to her house to wait for Amy. Then Jade saw the report on Amy and James and went to Walt's house."

"That's when Walt called you?"

"Yeah."

"Why did Jade take Emmie this afternoon, though? I mean, I am her aunt, but it's like she doesn't trust me or something."

"Jade's not thinking straight, I guess. I don't know why she would run with Emmie." Ryan looked uncomfortable and was beginning to squirm. He never had been a good liar. Surely Annie could see he was lying. Maybe he should tell her about Jade's visions. No, not yet. "Jade said she would call tomorrow and let you talk to Emmie."

"That would be great. Has she told Emmie yet about Amy and James?"

"No, I don't think so, but she'll have to before she brings her to the funerals."

Annie didn't say anything, and her eyes began to mist up. Ryan sat there trying to look away and give her some privacy to cry if she wanted to. He looked around the room at the different art objects and didn't make any comments that she would feel obligated to answer.

With his back to her, he could hear her sniffling and trying to get herself under control. He hated that. She should just let it go. It was natural to cry when hurt. "Annie?"

"What?" she sniffled.

"Go ahead and cry. There's nothing wrong with that. Stop trying to be so damned in control. You don't have to."

"I do have to! I can't fall apart. I have to think of Emmie."

"Look, Emmie's not here." He walked over and bent down in front of her. "You need to let it out."

"No. I can't." Sniffle, sniffle.

"Okay, whatever you think is best. I'll leave you alone. I'm going to walk the grounds and check things out. I'll be back in a few."

Annie sat back and tried to watch TV.

Ryan walked to the parking lot and looked around, then did a complete perimeter check of Annie's building. There were about fifteen buildings in all, but he only had to focus on hers. He went back to the parking lot and noticed another vehicle that looked out of place. He walked over to it and looked in the windows. No one was in the vehicle. He looked around and saw no one. Hmmm...

He sat down on the curb and decided he would give Annie some time to herself.

12

JADE was sitting on her bed and running through different ways to tell Emmie about her parents. This would be harder than she had thought. She would do it in the morning.

She wasn't going to get much sleep, she already knew. She got up and went to Emmie's room to check on her. The girl was sound asleep. Harry hadn't moved an inch. Jade quietly walked over and grabbed Harry by the collar. She may as well let him out to potty before she called it a night. Taking Harry to the front door and opening it was enough invitation for him. He ran out into the yard and did his thing. Jade stood in the open door and waited for him. He ran around the yard, exploring things. Deciding everything was as it should be, he went directly back to Emmie's bed and lay down to sleep again in comfort. Jade wondered if he slept with Emmie every night. He had certainly missed his little mistress; that was evident. She closed the door partially and went back to lock the front door. Looking out into the still night, hearing the water not far away, she decided to open her bedroom window, and maybe the surf would lull her to sleep. She closed and double locked the door, then went to her bedroom. Opening the window, she breathed deeply of the tangy, salty air.

Lying down on the bed, she concentrated on the sound of the crashing surf. She lay there for quite some time before finally drifting into the wonderful darkness of sleep.

~

He stood in the hallway, knife in hand, watching her drink from her cup. She was just as stupid as the rest of them. She didn't even know he was there. He started to creep slowly toward her. Quietly he walked, keeping his eyes trained on her, waiting for her to turn and see him.

Then something jumped in front of his feet. Losing his balance, he fell, keeping the knife away from his own body. It was a damn cat.

Annie heard his body hit the floor and the groan that escaped his lips. Turning, she saw him and the gleaming blade still in his hand. As she ran for the door, she began screaming.

He got up slowly, the pain in his left ankle slowing him down. He had to get her before she opened the door. He grabbed for her hair; it was swinging behind her. He got a fistful; it stopped her in her tracks.

Annie began sobbing, asking him, "Why are you doing this?"

He heard someone running up the stairs. Should he stay and finish what he came for? Maybe the person was going to another apartment.

Then he heard the door knob turning.

"Annie, are you okay? Open the door!" Ryan was yelling.

The man let go and ran back to the rear of the apartment, back through the window he had scurried through. Ryan came through the front door, practically knocking it off the hinges. He saw Annie lying on the floor, rolled into a fetal position. Ryan ran to her.

"Annie, are you okay?" he asked, out of breath.

"He's here. Oh my God. He has a knife. He, he went down the hallway," Stuttering, she tried to tell Ryan what he needed to know.

Ryan told her to stay there as he went after the killer. The window in the bathroom had been pried open, and the screen was gone. Ryan tried to go that way, but he was too broad to get through. He ran back to the front door and down the stairs. Gun in hand, he went to the side of the building that the bathroom window was on. He looked around and ran to the parking lot. No one, damn it! He went back to the side of the building where he'd started and began looking around. He could see small indentions in the grass where the weight of the person who had jumped had landed. Not a big person at all. The grass was thick, and no shoe prints had been left.

Ryan called George. "He was here. The son of a bitch was here, George."

"What?" Now fully awake, George sprang up in his bed. "Did we get him?"

Doris sat up now, too. "Who? What? George! Is that Ryan?" George waved at Doris to wait a minute.

"No, I was outside. He came in through the bathroom window. I came in before he hurt Annie, but I missed him, George. The fucker got away."

"It's okay. You stopped him from hurting her. That's what you were there for."

"Yeah, I know, but he was here." Ryan was holding his head in his hand. "Damn it."

"Hey, stop it. You know we don't always get the bad guy the first time around. Did you get a look at him or his vehicle?"

"Vehicle!" Ryan remembered the car in the parking lot. "Hang on, George, let me look at something." Ryan walked around to the parking lot. The vehicle was still there. "I saw a car earlier and was keeping an eye on it. It's still here. Let me call you back. I want to run the plate real quick. It could be his and he just didn't have time to get it."

"Okay, call me back. I'll be waiting."

Ryan called dispatch and told them to run a "28" – a license plate check – for him. He was giving the plate – Zebra, 2, 6, Nora, Frank, 7 – when a subject came out of another building and walked over to the vehicle. Ryan watched him open the driver side door and get in. He was a big burly type. No way he was the suspect. Ryan told the dispatcher to disregard and hung up. He called George back.

"False alarm," he said when George answered.

"What happened?"

"He came in through the bathroom window. I was checking things outside. I don't know how I missed him. I need to go back up stairs and check on Annie. She's pretty freaked out. Just wanted to let you know."

"Do you want me to come out?"

"No, go back to sleep. This was our chance, and I blew it."

"We'll have more. Don't sweat it. I'll see you in the morning. Call if you need anything, okay?"

"Yeah, bye." Ryan went back upstairs. Annie was still rolled into a ball on the floor. Ryan walked over and began helping her up. She was sobbing uncontrollably. Wally wanted to get in the middle of things. Ryan pushed the cat away and got Annie onto the sofa, softly talking to her the whole time.

It hit him then. Jade had been right. Good God, she was right! The visions, they were real. Holy shit...

Ryan let go of Annie and stood straight up. The shock of realization hit him full force.

Annie sat back against the sofa and tried to calm down. She was still sobbing and hiccuping for air, but at least she was aware of it and trying to get herself under control. Ryan draped an arm around her shoulders as he sat down next to her.

"It's okay, Annie. I'm sorry I left you alone. I was checking outside. I don't know how he got in here without me seeing him."

Annie shook her head. She couldn't talk just yet. She didn't blame Ryan. He had to know that.

Thank God for Wally. She had almost made it out the door, but if Ryan had not come in when he did, the man would have killed her, too.

Shaking badly, she reached for Wally. He jumped into her lap. She petted him without thought and let Ryan soothe her.

"Annie, are you going to be okay?"

"Yes, thanks to you." Her words were slurred as she continued to cry.

Ryan pulled her closer and let her. This was what she needed to do anyway.

He was really feeling like a heel. It had been too close a call. How the hell did the killer get up and into that window? After Annie was calmed and okay, he would go back outside and try to figure this out. She was on the second floor. There were no stairs or fire escapes. It was just a brick wall with windows.

He couldn't wait to see George in the morning. Jade had been right. How was George going to feel about the visions now? Ryan was relieved he no longer had to be skeptical of them himself. He knew he believed her before, but then he still had his doubts. Not anymore. She was amazing. He couldn't wait to talk to her again. She had saved Annie's life. Now, maybe, he could tell

Annie about her. But no, he should wait and think it through a little more.

Ryan got up and went to the kitchen. He made Annie another cup of tea to help calm her. Carrying the cup to her, he said, "Here, Annie. Drink this. It'll help calm your nerves."

"Thanks," Annie said, taking the cup. She was still shaking like a leaf.

Ryan sat down next to her again and took Wally from her lap. He started to pet Wally and praise him for saving her life. Annie looked at him and asked, "How did you know Wally jumped in front of that maniac?"

Ryan was taken aback. He forgot to wait until she told him. "I'll explain later. Right now, you need to drink your tea and calm down."

Annie looked at Ryan. She could see he was worried about something, but right now, she didn't care. She leaned back and closed her eyes. Breathing deeply, she was able to stop her sobbing and the chattering of her teeth. She had been shaking and her teeth chattering like she was freezing. But she wasn't cold, just scared to death. She would get some answers soon. Right now, she just wanted to relax and get herself under control.

Ryan went to his car and grabbed his tool box that he kept in case of emergency. This was definitely an emergency. He walked back upstairs and took a look at the damage he had done to Annie's front door. He had bent both the top and middle hinges. They looked fixable if he could bend them back into shape. Two of the screws in the top hinge were still in the jamb; he had knocked it completely loose without moving the screws. He closed the door as well as he could, then went to Annie.

"Where do you keep your throw blankets?"

"The linen closet in the hallway."

He found a blanket, and bringing it back, he covered Annie so she wouldn't get cold while the door was open. "Keep this around you while I fix the door," he told her.

"Ryan, thank you. If you hadn't been here...." The tears started flowing again.

"I know, Annie, but I was. It's okay now."

Ryan went to the door and opened it wide. He removed the screws from all three hinges and then laid the door against the outside wall. He then removed the top and middle hinges. Laying the top hinge on the concrete walkway, he began hammering it back into shape. He did the same thing with the middle hinge. He then checked the door jamb. It hadn't even cracked. It was a pretty strong jamb.

Putting the hinges back on the door, he then re-hung it, walked inside, and closed the door to make sure it still fit properly. Not a difficult job, he thought. He walked over and sat down across from Annie. She appeared to be doing much better.

They sat quietly for a few minutes, neither feeling the need to fill the quiet with unwanted chatter.

The TV was still on, and no one was paying attention to the show that was now almost over.

"Annie, I know you've got to be beat. Try to go get some sleep. He won't be back now that he knows I'm here."

"I couldn't sleep now, Ryan. I need to sit here a while longer. If I'm keeping you awake, you can turn the TV and lights off. I don't mind." She pulled the blanket tighter about her.

"No, I'm not tired. I was thinking you were. You look beat."

"Jeez, thanks a lot."

"You know what I mean."

They both laughed.

"Ryan?"

"Yeah."

"How did you know Wally tripped that guy?"

"Annie, that is a long story and one I really don't want to go into just yet. It's been a hell of a long day, and I'm tired."

"See? I thought so. But this whole situation is so out there."

"Yeah, it is, and you only know part of it. Wait till you hear it all."

"See, that's what I mean. You're keeping things from me, and that's not fair."

"All in good time, Annie. There's a lot going on, and I'm probably not the best one to explain it."

"So who is?"

"I would have to say Jade."

"Jade?"

"Yep, Jade's the one you need to talk to. I will get her here tomorrow. When she calls, I'll explain what happened tonight, and I know she'll come back."

"Ryan, you guys have my mind going in circles. Nothing makes sense to me anymore."

"I know, Annie. It's not going to make sense to anyone until this guy is caught."

"Why would he want to kill me?"

"I don't know. I guess he thinks you know where his stuff is."

"What stuff? You keep talking about his stuff. I don't know what stuff."

"Don't exactly know, but it's whatever got your sister and her husband killed." Ryan grabbed the remote control and turned on the late show. He then went to the bathroom and changed into some sweat pants and a t-shirt. He went to the linen closet and grabbed linens and a thin blanket to make his bed on the couch. Annie had moved to the love seat and sat watching him. He lay down between the sheets and threw the blanket over him. "Does your TV have a timer?"

"Yes, here." Annie took the remote control. "What time do you want it to turn off?"

"I don't know, maybe one."

Annie set the timer, then sat back for a minute. "Ryan?"

"Yeah."

"Did you see him?"

"No."

"How did he get in here?"

"I know he came in through the bathroom window. How he got there, I don't know, but once it's light outside, I'm going to find out."

"I think I'll sleep on this love seat. Do you mind?"

"No, go ahead. This is your place."

Annie got up and went into her bedroom and closed the door. Opening her dresser drawer, she pulled out a pair of footy pajamas. She liked the footy kind because she always had cold feet. Getting into her pajamas, she kept looking around, feeling like someone was there. Of course, no one was, but she had had a close call tonight, and it would take a while before she was comfortable being alone again. Did Ryan think she was a sissy because she was going to sleep in there? Then she thought, what do I care what he thinks? This is my apartment. Pulling the comforter off her bed and taking one of her pillows, she padded back to the living room. Ryan was watching the show he had put on. Annie made her bed quietly and then snuggled into it. "Good night, Ryan."

"Sleep tight, Annie." He smiled at her.

"Ryan... Thanks for being here tonight."

"No problem. It's my job, Annie. I'm glad I was here." They both turned their attention back to the TV. Eventually, Annie fell asleep. Ryan noticed Wally sneak up there with her. He practically wrapped himself around her head. Ryan walked over and pulled the comforter up around her shoulders.

Realizing tomorrow would be another long day, he turned the TV off and turned over to sleep. He had to find out if Annie got a good look at the killer. He knew she needed to calm down before he started questioning her. Tomorrow would be soon enough.

Jade heard Emmie creep into her bedroom and could hear Harry following right behind. The next thing she knew, Emmie was crawling into her bed and cuddling against her. She pretended to be asleep and threw her arm around the child. Harry waited until they had settled, then, with a jump and hard landing, he settled on the end of the bed. Jade wanted to laugh, but she knew if she did Emmie would know she was awake. She just lay there with a smile on her face and warm thoughts running through her mind as she drifted off to sleep again.

George rolled over and put his arm around Doris. He sure was glad he had come home and left Ryan at Annie's. After being married as long as he had, he had gotten used to being in bed with someone, and without her, sleep didn't come easy. He smiled. As old as he was, God knew how much he needed his sleep. He slowly drifted back off again, and Doris cuddled closer.

Walt slept fitfully through the night. Knowing that Jade and Emmie were safe was good enough for him. He also knew that Annie would have either Ryan or George with her for the night, so she was safe, too. Walt said his prayers and went to sleep.

~

The killer was sitting in his bedroom, soaking his ankle in hot water and epsom salts to take the pain and swelling away. What the hell happened? Who was that guy? He couldn't believe he had jumped from the second story window after already hurting his ankle. He was lucky it wasn't broken. Parking his car on the side street was smart.

Why the hell did Linderhoff have to fuck him over? He should have made him talk before he killed him. That stupid bitch of a wife wouldn't have known anything, so killing her quickly was fine. He thought they had a good working relationship; after all, didn't he keep Linderhoff supplied with meth? As long as he had sold the ecstasy like he was supposed to, everything would have been good. The killer should have known better than to give him so much at once. When James told him he needed two thousand pills at twenty five dollars a pop, the killer should have kept his head instead of seeing all those dollar signs. That son of a bitch was going to take his dope, make himself some good money, then run. The man should have seen it. All he wanted was his dope back. No one else had to die. He didn't like killing people; it was just part of the job. A thief was worse than snail shit. They're the worst scum around. The killer just sold dope, though, and that didn't make him a bad guy, did it? Hell no, he said to himself, it didn't.

Drying off his foot, he decided to get some sleep and figure out how to get to the sister later. Maybe he should just try for the kid. Hey, if he took the kid, then the sister would surely give his dope back to him, wouldn't she? He would have to do some heavy thinking.

~

Jade woke up with a headache. Today was the day she would have to break Emmie's little heart. Emmie lay there sound asleep, and Harry was still on the bed, too. Jade got up and went to the medicine cabinet. She had Excedrin on hand all the time. If she didn't keep on top of her headaches, they would turn to migraines. She took two of the tablets and grabbed a couple cold washcloths. Getting back into bed, she placed one washcloth behind her neck and the other over her eyes. In a few minutes, she would be good as new. As she laid there, her head pounding and her mind running over the different ways to tell Emmie about her parents, thoughts of Ryan intruded. He seemed to enter her mind a lot lately. She wished all this could be over with.

After a while, Jade remembered Emmie hadn't mentioned

her angel lately, and Jade wondered about that. She thought maybe her dad was right that Emmie already knew about her mom and dad but didn't know how to say it. Why would she put that knowledge into the form of an angel, though? How did Emmie know Jade was coming to get her if there weren't an angel? Jade lay there clearing her mind of thoughts so the headache would subside. Then she felt the vision coming.

The funeral was about to begin. Emmie was sitting between both her grandmothers, in the front pew. Annie was next to her mom. The two caskets were covered with flower blankets, and photographs of both Amy and James were on stands next to the caskets. The music was calming. Ryan and George were sitting with her and Walt. The little chapel was almost empty.

The killer was standing outside -- waiting. Jade knew he was going to take Emmie. He was smoking a cigarette, and the tattoo was sticking out like a diamond in sunlight. She could hear his thoughts. He had to get the kid. He just wanted his dope back. He would kill if he had to, but he really didn't want to.'

Jade sat in the chapel, unable to speak. She could feel his presence. She needed to tell Ryan, but she couldn't move. She sat there, helpless, frozen. If Emmie walked out that door, he would snatch her.

Everyone was praying now; the service was almost over. They were all going to the grave site.

The killer was getting antsy. This was too close for comfort, he decided, and this would not be the best time to grab the kid.

The vision ended. Jade sat straight up in bed, flinging the wash cloth from her eyes as she sprang up. She was breathing heavy. This vision was not right. Why was she hearing his thoughts? Why couldn't she speak? What was going on?

She had never had one change while she was still seeing it. She had actually heard the killer's thoughts. She had to call her dad. She got up, careful now not to wake Emmie. Jade tiptoed to the living room and dialed Walt's number. "Dad," she said quietly.

"Good morning, honey."

"Dad, I just had another vision. The killer is setting his sights on Emmie. But that's not all. Dad, my vision changed as I was having it." Her voice held panic that she couldn't quite control.

"Whoa, slow down. What are you talking about, Jade?"

Jade went through the whole thing with him, explaining how she could hear the killer's thoughts but couldn't move or speak. The she explained how the killer began changing his mind.

"So are you saying it won't happen?" Walt asked.

"I don't know. I've never had this happen before. Maybe I shouldn't bring Emmie back for the funeral."

"Jade, I want you to call Ryan. Tell him what you just told me and get advice from him. Then call me back."

"I will." It was the smart thing to do. She hung up and dialed Ryan's cell phone.

"Detective Douglas," he said in a sleepy, raspy, sexy voice.

"Ryan, it's Jade. I need you to wake up and listen to me."

"I'm awake. What's wrong?"

"I'm not sure. I just had another vision, but it doesn't make sense."

"What do you mean?"

Jade went through her explanation again. She was worried now. If she couldn't depend on her visions, then how was she going to keep Emmie safe? Ryan was sitting up on the sofa. He was listening to Jade and scratching his head. He was still too fuzzy to grasp what she was saying. He needed to shake the cobwebs. "Jade, hang on a sec."

"What? Oh, okay."

Ryan got up and went to the kitchen. Getting a glass of ice water, he drank slowly and splashed some of the cold water on his face. Using a dish towel, he dried his face and went back to his phone.

"Okay, Jade, try again. I think I'm awake enough now."

Jade was frustrated. "Ryan, you need to listen to me."

"I am, Jade. I was just sleeping when you called. It takes me a minute. Go ahead."

Jade began again. Every time she said it, it scared her more. Once she completely ran through the entire vision, she waited to see what Ryan would say.

"Are you telling me that this won't happen, then?" he asked, confused.

"No, Ryan, I'm telling you I don't know what's going to happen. He changed mid-stride on this one. I've never had that happen before."

"But you are saying that Annie isn't the target anymore; it's now Emmie?"

"I don't know." Jade was scared and knew she wasn't making sense. "Dad told me to call you," she said.

"I see. Where's Emmie now?"

"Still asleep."

"Alright, the funeral will probably be tomorrow. You need to bring Emmie back here."

"No."

"Are you serious? You're not bringing her for the funerals now?" Ryan was getting loud, and Annie sat up.

"Ryan, is that Jade?" Annie asked.

"Oh, I'm sorry. I didn't know you were in Annie's bedroom." Jade hesitated. "I'll call you later." Jade hung up. He was in her bedroom. Had they slept together? Of course they did. That was obvious, wasn't it? Jade sat there feeling numb. What right did she have to get upset if Ryan and Annie slept together? He wasn't her property. They were two consenting adults. This was too much to process this early in the morning. If she didn't sit back and breathe in and out slowly, her headache would be a bang. Jade laid the telephone down put her head on the back of the chair and began concentrating on her breathing. No thoughts. She wouldn't allow any thoughts. She would keep her mind blank.

~

"Damn it," Ryan said, slamming his cell phone closed.

"Was that Jade?" Annie asked again.

"'Was' is the key word. She hung up."

"Did she tell you she wasn't bringing Emmie back for the funeral?"

"I don't know what she was saying, Annie. I'm confused right now; give me a few." He got up and went to the bathroom. Closing the door, he leaned against it. What the hell just happened? He couldn't make sense of the conversation. What was Jade saying about another vision? The killer was going to take Emmie? No, he changed his mind. Would he take her or not? Jade, call me back, Ryan pleaded silently.

She must have thought he and Annie had slept together. He couldn't believe it, but he liked the effect it apparently had on her. Was she hurt, angry, what? He didn't know, but boy, was he going to use it to his advantage if she ever called him again. She would. He knew she would.

He looked around the quaint little bathroom in which everything matched. Annie really had a flair for decorating. Maybe when this was all over, he would see if she wanted to decorate his apartment. She could take something and make it feel both homey and classy. He liked that. She would need a job to take care of her and Emmie anyway; maybe this was the answer. He would suggest it to her later.

Ryan went back to the living room to clean up his bedding mess. Annie was in the kitchen. He hoped she was making coffee. He went to the kitchen. "Can I help you with anything?" he asked.

"No, I'm just getting a pot of coffee on. Do you usually eat breakfast?"

"Yeah, but not at home. I go to Denny's a lot."

"I can cook us a couple omelets if you'd like."

"Really? Pretty and can cook?" He laughed.

Annie laughed and started pulling the fixings for breakfast out of the refrigerator. "Do you like just plain cheese or cheese and meat?"

"Whatever you want is fine with me," he said, heading back to the living room. "Hey, where do you want this bedding I slept on?" he yelled from the other room.

"Just leave it. I'll take care of it. Can you tell me what Jade said now?"

"No. I'm still not sure myself. But don't worry, she'll have Emmie here in plenty of time for the funeral service." He hoped.

Deciding not to push too hard yet, Annie yelled back, "Alright, Ryan, I'm gonna trust you on this. You and George have been too good to me so far, and I have to believe you know what's best."

"I won't let you down, and she'll be back," Ryan called.

Jade was jealous, he thought, and for some unknown reason, he was ecstatic. Today was going to be a good day.

13

JADE called her dad back. "Did you talk to Ryan?" Walt asked.

"Kinda. He was a little busy."

"What do you mean? What could be more important?"

Jade paused again. "Annie."

"What?" He asked, confused.

"He was with Annie, and I think I interrupted something, so I hung up."

"Oh, I see." He was smiling to himself. Annie, huh?

"I was embarrassed. So I just hung up on him."

Walt could tell by her voice that it wasn't just embarrassment, but something else, too. "Ryan's a young man with needs. It doesn't mean there's really anything special between them."

"Dad, I would hope he wouldn't just be using Annie at a time like this. That's horrible!"

"Maybe he wasn't using her. Maybe she was using him."

"Whatever. I really don't care one way or another."

"Okay, if you say so." Walt decided to let her off the hook. They had more important things to worry about right now.

"Where's George? Do you know?"

"I'm sure he's home asleep. It's not even eight o'clock yet."

"I know. Did I wake you, too?"

"No, I'm an early riser; you know that. I was just sitting here drinking coffee and reading the paper."

"Good. Dad, since I don't know what the killer is doing, I don't think it's safe to bring Emmie back there."

"Honey, you can't allow that child to miss her parents' funeral. That would be wrong. Between you, me, Ryan, George, and Annie, I think we can keep her safe, don't you?"

"While we're all together, yes, but when I bring her back here, what if we're followed?"

"That's simple. Don't go back there. Stay here."

"I have a lot of thinking to do, and I'm going to have to tell Emmie about her parents this morning. I guess I need to go. I'll call you later."

"Jade, come home."

As he hung up, he thought it was good to know she was upset with Ryan. This could be good. Very good indeed.

~

Jade hung up and went to make a pot of coffee. Caffeine: just what her headache needed. Oh well, her morning called for it. Caffeine it was.

She was piddling around in the kitchen when she heard Emmie calling Harry. Jade walked into the living room and watched Emmie standing at the door, holding her baby doll and blowing kisses, trying to get Harry to come back in.

"Morning, little one, did you let Harry out to potty?"

"Yep, and he won't come in. He's bad this morning."

"Oh, it's alright. Let him run for a bit. We don't have neighbors that will complain."

"But I don't want him to lose himself."

"You mean run away?"

"You know, where I can't find him."

"Don't you worry, kiddo. As big as Harry is, I don't think we could lose him." Jade walked back into the kitchen. She was glad that Emmie had Harry and her baby doll. The poor kid she would need both to get through this day. Jade got a cup of coffee and then started frying some bacon. She could still hear Emmie yelling at Harry. She needed to find out about Emmie's angel too. What a day. Too much to do, and none of it good.

Emmie and Harry came running into the kitchen. Poor Harry couldn't get any traction to stop and slid into the cabinet. Stepping back and shaking his head, he looked at Jade. Poor Harry, Jade thought, laughing. He had hit the cabinet door hard. He sat there, still looking at Jade.

"What? Are you hungry, Harry?" Jade asked. She poured dog food into his dish and gave him fresh water.

"Emmie, sit down, honey. You need to eat, too," she said.

Emmie crawled up onto the chair and scooted herself to the table. Smiling, Jade finished putting the food on the table.

Picking up her glass of milk, Emmie asked, "Are we going home today?"

"I'm not sure yet. Why? Do you want to?"

"Yeah. I wanna see Walt and Ryan."

Jade noticed there was no mention of her mom and dad this time. "We'll see. Do you want eggs and toast with your bacon?"

"Yes please."

They ate in silence. Jade was going to talk to Emmie just as soon as dishes were done. Emmie took a piece of bacon off her plate and looked over at Jade. Jade pretended not to see as Emmie gave the bacon to Harry. Jade thought that was one of the cutest things she had ever seen. Emmie sure loved Harry, and Harry sure loved Emmie. They were so cute together. Harry was a playmate for Emmie as well as a protector. She wondered now if Emmie had any friends. Of course, there were always kids at the park, but Jade didn't know if they played with Emmie. She thought again how mature this child was and wondered at the baby talk used occasionally. She was a well balanced kid. Amy must've been a very strong woman to do so well with her daughter and also to deal with her husband's obvious drug problems. She must have kept Emmie shielded through it all. Of course, this was all speculation on Jade's part, and all this thinking wasn't helping her headache.

They finished eating, and Jade sent Emmie to get dressed while she cleaned the kitchen. Maybe she should call Annie and ask if she wanted to tell Emmie about her parents. After all, she would have been the one to tell her – and rightly so if Jade hadn't run away with her. She didn't know Annie's telephone number, but Emmie might. If not, she sure as hell wasn't calling Ryan to get it. No way!

"Emmie, come here please," Jade called.

Emmie came running in to the kitchen again. "What?" she asked, looking up with her face scrunched.

"Do you know a telephone number for your Aunt Annie?"

"Nope." Emmie stood there staring at Jade. She was holding her baby doll again. This time, she was fully dressed and her hair needed to be brushed.

"Okay, just thought I would ask. Have you brushed your teeth, young lady?"

"Nope."

"Well, skedaddle and get it done, then come here with your hair brush, and I'll fix you up."

"Okay!" Emmie ran back to the bathroom.

Jade could hear her in there, rummaging around and talking to Harry.

"Wanna race, Harry?" Emmie asked the dog. "Come on then, let's go!" They came running together, Harry trying hard not to trip Emmie. Once again, Emmie stopped but Harry just kept going. His head banged into the cabinet once more.

"Uh-oh! You silly dog," Emmie laughed at him.

"You two should not be running through the house, Emmie," Jade said, trying to look stern.

"Harry's the one running into things, not me!" she said, trying to pout but not quite pulling it off.

"Well, he wouldn't run into things if you weren't running, would he?"

"Prolly not," Emmie said, pronouncing 'probably' like a baby would.

Jade just laughed and took the hair brush from Emmie. Sitting Emmie between her legs, she combed her hair into two pigtails, then sent her back to the bathroom with the brush. Jade went to the living room and sat down. After waiting a few minutes, she called out to Emmie.

She came into the living room.

"Sit down here with me for a few minutes. I think we need to talk. Okay?"

"Okay. What about?"

"You."

"Can Harry listen too?"

"Sure."

Emmie patted her hand on her leg. Blowing fake kisses again, she got Harry to come to her. "Lay down, Harry!" Emmie ordered. Harry complied. Jade just laughed.

"Emmie, you haven't talked about your angel anymore. Does she still come to see you?"

"Yep."

"You haven't told me lately. Why?"

"Because she said not to tell you."

"Really? Why?"

"She said you were gonna break my heart. But I shouldn't hate you. She said you were really sad about it. You gonna break my heart, Jade?"

Jade looked at her. Tears were already welling up in her eyes. Yes, damn it, she was going to break this child's heart. Jade grabbed Emmie and hugged her tight. "Yes, baby, I think I might."

"Why, Jade?"

"I don't want to, honey, but I have to tell you some really sad things, and you're gonna get hurt. I am so sorry, baby."

"Just don't tell me, then."

"I wish I didn't have to, but I do. Are you ready?"

"Because... you have to?"

"Yes."

"I'm ready," she said, hugging onto Harry.

"No, you're not, but here goes. Do you know why you're here with me?"

"My mommy told you to take me?"

"No, she didn't, honey. I took you to keep you safe. Do you know where your mommy and daddy are?"

"No. Are they lost?"

"No, baby, your mommy and daddy aren't coming back anymore." Watching her take this information in, Jade continued, "They died, honey."

Emmie didn't say anything. She just sat there holding onto Harry and looking at her. Did she understand 'died'? Did she hear what Jade just said? Come on, some reaction, please. "Sweetie, do you know what 'died' means?" she asked carefully.

Emmie nodded her head yes but didn't say a word. She stood up, grabbing Harry's collar, and walked out of the room. Jade sat there. What now? She wasn't sure if she should go after her or give her some space. Emmie's bedroom door slammed shut. Jade listened intently. Not another sound. She got up and walked down the hallway, stopping to listen at Emmie's door. Not a sound. After a minute, Jade knocked on the door. "Emmie?" Nothing. Not a word. Jade walked outside and around to Emmie's bedroom window and looked inside. She could see Emmie on the floor. Harry was lying next to her. Emmie had her little arms wrapped around Harry, and Jade could tell she was crying by the movement of her little body. Jade walked back around the house.

Sitting on the porch, she decided to give Emmie time to cry. Emmie would come back when she was ready to hear more.

~

Ryan was getting his things together to leave Annie's. He was going to call George and see if he wanted to meet him somewhere. George would, of course, choose Denny's, which would be fine with Ryan. He could always drink more coffee.

"George, are you awake? We gotta talk." He spoke quickly when the phone was answered.

"I'm awake. What's up?"

"Can you meet me?"

"Are you still at Annie's?"

"Yeah, but I'm ready to leave. Just tell me where to meet you, and I'll be there."

"Yeahm alright." Thinking for a minute, George said, "Denny's okay with you?"

"Sounds good. See you there." It was nice to know some things would never change. Grabbing his overnight bag, he walked into the kitchen, where Annie was still cleaning dishes. He watched her for a few minutes, wondering if she was safe now. He knew he would be back later this morning to check on her and find out what time her mother would be in. Once her mom was here, it would be safer for her. He just needed to keep her safe until then.

The kitchen was a sunny room in the morning. He liked that it made everything seem cheerful. He walked over to Annie and tapped her lightly on the shoulder. She jumped, drawing a quick breath, and she struck him. Her eyes were wide with surprise and embarrassment.

"Shit, Ryan, why did you do that?" Annie asked, still breathless.

"Sorry. I didn't mean to scare you. I just wanted to let you know I was leaving, but I'll be back in a couple hours." He felt bad knowing he upset her. She didn't need that.

"Oh, okay, sure." She stood there composing herself. "Do you know what time you'll be back? I don't know yet what time my mom is coming in, and I'll have to go get her from the airport. I'll also have to pick up Mrs. Linderhoff when she gets in." Her words rushed out. She was still not quite settled.

"Well, I plan to be back by midmorning, and if you need to leave before then, would you call me and let me know?" Ryan wrote his cell phone number on a business card for her.

"I may already have your number. Do you want me to go look?"

"No, just take this card and keep it with you. I'll be with George, so you can call either one of us." Ryan handed her the card.

"Ryan, is Jade coming back today?" she asked, worry written all over her face. "My mom will expect to see Emmie as soon as she gets here, and I'm sure Mrs. Linderhoff will, too."

Ryan shook his head back and forth as if to clear it. He wasn't sure what to tell her. He knew what she needed to hear, but could he give her that? What if it was a lie? Could she take that?

Looking her in the eye, he said, "I promise to do everything I can to get them back here today, Annie. I don't want you to worry about that. You just get your mom taken care of and let me and George do the rest, okay?" He hoped she wouldn't question anything else.

"Ryan, I need to know what's going on."

"Annie, I promise I'll tell you everything as soon as I can. You just have to trust that we know what we're doing, okay?"

Nothing more to say, Annie walked him to the door. She opened the door, wondering what he was hiding. He walked out, not bothering to look at her. She watched him walk down the stairs, and when he turned back, she waved goodbye.

Closing and locking the door, she went back to the kitchen. Seeing the clock, she thought she'd better telephone her mother. Annie laid the dish towel on the end of the table and picked up the cordless telephone, dialing her mother's number as she sat down.

"Hello," Nora Armstrong said.

"Hey, Mom, it's me, Annie." Why did she say that? It wasn't like her mom was expecting her sister to call.

"I was just going to call you. Are you alright?"

"Yes, Mom, I was just calling to find out when you'd get here."

"I'll get in at five twenty-six this evening. Do you have a pen and paper handy to write the flight number down?"

"Sure do. Go ahead."

Nora Armstrong gave her daughter the flight information, then proceeded to do the same with Donna Linderhoff's. "Donna arrives on Aces High a little after six," she said.

"Donna? You mean Mrs. Linderhoff?"

"Yes. You can call her Donna, Annie. Will you be able to pick us both up?"

"Yes, I'll be there. I know you're staying with me, but what about Mrs. Linderhoff?"

"Donna asked me to stay with her at the kids' house, but I just don't know what I'm going to do yet. I don't know if I can stay there without Amy. Have you been there since..." She trailed off.

"No, I haven't had any reason to. I have a lot to explain to you. I need to ask the detectives if we can even go to the house yet."

"Why couldn't we, Annie? You did say they died near the park, not in their house, right?"

"Yes, Mom, but there's an ongoing investigation. The police may want to go through the house for clues or something, I don't know."

"Well, you may want to contact them and find out for us. I don't know where poor Donna will go if she can't stay there. I guess we could go to a motel together."

Annie knew her mother was trying to make her feel guilty and get her to say that Mrs. Linderhoff could stay at her place. Annie refused to be treated like this. After all, she wasn't a child. Annie really didn't want Mrs. Linderhoff to stay at her apartment ,so why should she pretend? This was a hard enough time, and she shouldn't have to be put out, too.

No one had said anything yet about Emmie and where the poor child was going to end up. Annie knew she would get her, and that was just fine with her. She would gladly take Amy's baby. She had already decided that if Mrs. Linderhoff wanted to fight about where Emmie would go, then she was ready for that, too.

"Mom, please don't expect me to invite Mrs. Linderhoff to stay here."

"Annie, would it be so difficult?"

"Yes."

"Annie, she's Emmie's grandmother, and you know she just lost her only child."

"I just lost my only sibling, too, but I'm not putting anyone out over it."

"Annie, call the police and find out about the house. I'll stay there with Donna, and then you won't be put out. I'm sorry, honey, I would rather be with you right now, but I know Donna has no one."

"Oh, right, Mom, I forgot I have so many people I can turn to. You're right. Stay with her. I'll be at the airport to pick you both up and then drop you both off on Maggie Lane. If you can stay there. I'll have an answer for you when I see you. Be careful, Mom."

"Annie, try to understand. I love you too. See you soon."

"Bye, Mom." Annie hung up. Why did she and her mom always have to argue? Amy used to tell her that it was because they were so much alike. Annie just couldn't see it. Life was going to be so hard without Amy there to run interference for her.

Annie wondered if she was going to be able to do a good enough job raising Emmie. After all, she didn't have any experience with kids other than Emmie.

She went to the bathroom and started a bubble bath. She would sit in the tub filled with bubbles and lavender aroma to help her relax. She could even light a few candles and turn off the lights. No noise, no telephones, just hot water and bubbles. She went to her bedroom and found her outfit for the day. It was a periwinkle blue blouse with off-white casual pants. As she bent down to pick a pair of shoes, the telephone rang.

"Hello?"

"You were lucky last night, but you won't be next time." The voice was raspy, whispery, deep. "I'm coming for you."

"What? Who is this?" Annie stopped looking for shoes and froze.

"You know who this is, little sister, and I'm coming for you." He made his point and hung up.

Annie was shaking now. She ran to the kitchen to get the business card off the counter. She tried to dial Ryan's cell phone, but she was shaking so badly she kept hitting two numbers at a time, then dropped the phone. She stopped. She tried to get herself under control, breathing deeply and talking to herself. "Come on, girl, get a grip. You need to call Ryan. Nice and steady, that's it." The deep breaths had the calming effect she had hoped for. She bent down, picking the telephone up. Giving herself a mental shake, she dialed the number on the card. The phone began to ring.

"Detective Douglas," Ryan said as he answered the phone.

"Ryan? Oh, thank God. I need you to come back right away."

"Annie?"

"Ryan, he called," she said shakily.

"Who called?"

"He did. The killer, I think."

"What? Are you sure?"

"Yes. He said he was coming for me," she all but screamed into the phone.

"Alright, make sure your doors and windows are all locked. I'm on my way."

~

Ryan hung up and called George. He hadn't made it to the restaurant yet, but George might have. Ryan just hoped he could reach him. After explaining the latest events to George, they both drove at breakneck speeds to get to Annie's place. Ryan pulled into the parking lot, tires squealing. Two people standing in the parking lot and talking stopped to see what the commotion was. As he parked his car, George came flying in right behind him. They both jumped out of their cars and took the stairs two at a time. Ryan pounded on Annie's door. "Annie, open the door," he said.

The door flung open, and Annie stood there crying. Stepping back, she allowed both detectives to enter, but she didn't say anything. She was still holding the telephone.

~ 148 ~

"What did he say?" George asked.

"He said I was lucky last night and that he was coming for me." She set the telephone on the coffee table and picked up Wally.

"Annie, did you get a good look at him last night?" Ryan asked.

"No, he had a black stocking cap pulled down over his face."

"Did he use your name at all last night or just now on the phone?" George asked.

"No, but he called me 'little sister' on the phone."

"'Sister' like a gangster would or 'sister' like you're Amy's sister?" George asked.

"Like I'm Amy's sister." She walked in circles, unable to calm down enough to sit. Ryan and George stood there looking at her. No sitting, relaxing, or taking this lightly.

"Annie, what did he sound like?" Ryan asked. "Was he young, old, what did you notice?"

"I don't know. His voice was evil."

"Evil?" Ryan asked.

"Yeah, you know, deep, raspy like. I don't know."

"Have you ever heard that voice before?" George asked this time.

"No. He sounded angry. He's coming to get me. Maybe Jade was right to take Emmie." Annie began crying harder now. Ryan walked over and stopped her walking in circles. He sat down with her on the love seat and put his arm around her shoulder to try to comfort her. George watched and felts his guts twisting at the fear etched on her face.

"Ryan, I'm going to take a look around you. Stay here with Annie."

"George, I still need to find out how he got in the bathroom window last night. I couldn't see out there very well in the dark. Take a look at the side of the building where that window is and see if I missed anything last night." Ryan watched his partner leave.

~

George went down the stairs slowly. Why would he call her, except maybe to see if she were alone and maybe to keep her in fear? He didn't know, but he was going to find out. This son of a bitch was getting braver by the minute. He walked around the side of the building and searched the ground for footprints or signs of the killer. Looking up, he noticed a thick ledge that went the whole length of the side, and walking around the corner of the building, he could see it went around the back side. The killer could have walked on that ledge, but from where? He walked back to the side where the window was located. Standing there and looking up, he noticed the window in the apartment next to Annie's didn't have any window covering and that the screen was gone. He walked back around to the front of the building and up the stairs.

He looked in the windows of the apartment next door. It was empty. George tried the door knob and the door opened. He walked in, and looking around, he went to the back of the apartment. The killer had definitely been here a while. There were fast food wrappers on the floor where he apparently sat and ate his dinner, just waiting. Was he in here when George and Ryan were talking to Annie yesterday evening? Was he watching her place? Then why didn't he know Ryan was there? Maybe he did and waited for Ryan to go outside. That slick son of a bitch. He was a step ahead of them. George left and went back to Annie's apartment.

"Did you find anything?" Ryan asked.

"Yeah, the apartment next door is empty. He used that and got on the ledge outside, then walked to her window."

"What? You're kidding, right?" Ryan asked with a look of disbelief on his face.

"Oh, yeah, I forgot that apartment was empty," Annie said.

"Okay, so now we know how he got in, but he jumped out of the second story window and took off running. He has to be in pretty good shape to do that," Ryan said. "How long had he been there? How did he get in there without us seeing him?" Ryan stood up and began to pace the floor, thinking.

"Well, all I can figure is he must have been in there while we were here with Annie yesterday evening," George said.

"So do you think he was in there when we left her here alone?" Ryan asked.

"Yes, I think he was just waiting for it to get dark," George answered.

Ryan walked over and picked up the telephone to look at the caller ID. 'Private' was all that showed up. He set the phone back on the table. "Annie, you can't stay here. Get some of your things together," Ryan ordered.

"Wait just a minute. This is my home. I don't have anywhere to go. You can't expect me to stay on the streets," Annie blasted.

"You can stay at my place if you have to, but you're not staying here. It's not safe," Ryan said.

Annie looked at Ryan, then at George. "My mother is coming here tonight. She'll be expecting to stay with me."

"We will deal with it as we go. Get some of your stuff packed. Let's get out of here," Ryan said sternly. Taking charge was what he did best when he was under stress.

Annie went into her bedroom, closing the door. Standing there, she thought, who does he think he is, ordering me around like I'm a child or something?

George walked over to Ryan and patted his back. "Let's take Annie to Walt's house and wait for Jade to call. Then we can try to figure this mess out," he suggested.

"That sounds like a good idea. I'm going to call Walt and tell him to make a pot of coffee."

Ryan picked up the telephone and dialed Walt's number. After explaining some of what had taken place, Ryan advised him they would be there shortly. Walt agreed to have coffee ready and was eager to learn the rest of what had happened.

Annie came out of the room with a small suitcase. Still fuming, she looked at George. "I am not staying at his house. It's not right."

"We'll figure something out, Annie. I know you don't want to stay with me, and I can understand that. I apologize for my anger and telling you what you're going to do. Set your suitcase down, and we'll go to Walt's for a while to see if we can find out when Jade and Emmie will be back. Then we'll figure out a place for all of you to stay that'll be safe," Ryan said.

Annie put the suitcase down, and, petting Wally, she smiled toward George and didn't say a word. George smiled back and walked over to stand next to Ryan. "We need to try to get along," he said like a parent chastising his children.

As they walked to the door, she took one last look around, making sure the coffee pot was turned off, the lights were off, the

TV... Everything was fine. She double locked her door and walked down the steps. Ryan and George walked behind her, Ryan thought women were such strange creatures. He looked at George, who shook his head. They each went to their own vehicle. George told Annie to follow them, and she agreed. They drove to Walt's house, each in their own world of thought.

14

RYAN was thinking about Jade and her reaction this morning. He wanted her to call him. He was glad after all that she had taken Emmie yesterday. Annie was glad, too, he thought. He wondered if George had put two and two together yet. Did he realize that Jade's vision of Annie's apartment had happened just like she said it would? He would ask him about it at Walt's place. Annie was going to hear the whole story now. He still needed to find out about the vision that Jade said she had this morning. Did Walt understand it? Maybe he could shed some light on this newest vision. Ryan's cell phone began ringing.

"Detective Douglas."

"Ryan, it's Mom."

"Mom, is everything alright?"

"You tell me, Mr. I-Don't-Call-My-Mom anymore." Agitation dripped from her voice.

"I was going to call you today, Mom. I've been extremely busy. I'm sorry."

"Uh-huh, so, anything new I should know about?"

"No, just the usual work, sleep, eat. What about you?"

"The usual sleep, eat, worry about my son. No new women in your life?"

"No, Mom, just work. I know, I know, don't even start."

"What? You wound me. I just wanted to check on my son. Is that so wrong?"

"No, but please don't give me another lecture on finding a good girl, getting married, blah, blah, blah."

"Blah, blah, blah? Is that what I sound like to you?"

"No, it's just a repetitive conversation, that's all. I didn't mean to hurt your feelings. I'm sorry."

"I don't mean to lecture you, son. I just called to check on you and see if you wanted to come home for dinner this weekend."

"I can't this weekend, Mom. We're working on a pretty tough case right now, but soon, okay?

"Alright, Ryan, I won't harp. I know you're busy. I just miss seeing my son. You haven't been home for a while, so I thought maybe you could tear yourself away. Call soon, okay?"

"I will, Mom. I know it's been a while, and I'll get myself home soon. I promise."

"I love you, Ryan."

"I love you too, Mom." As he hung up, he thought, what was it with his mom? Did she want him to marry the first girl to come along? Maybe her instinct told her about Jade. No, that was too farfetched. Laughing to himself, he drove on.

~

Jade decided she had left Emmie alone long enough to deal with the news of her parents. Jade got up and walked into the house, listening as she went and not hearing a thing. She dreaded going into Emmie's room. What was she going to do with this kid? She had no clue how to deal with this situation. Maybe she should call her dad. Walt would know what to do. What to do.... She decided to try and handle this on her own. She walked down the hallway to Emmie's door. She still heard nothing. Taking a deep breath, she opened the door. Emmie lay on her bed, arms still wrapped around Harry, with the baby doll squished between the two of them. She didn't turn to look at her. Harry just barely lifted his head, then laid it back down on Emmie's shoulder.

"Emmie?"

Emmie buried her head deeper into Harry's fur.

"Emmie, I know you're upset, honey. I wish I knew how to make you feel better. I won't bother you. I just need to know you're okay." Jade walked further into the room. Hesitating next to the bed, she looked down at the sad picture the child and her dog made. Jade stood there for a few minutes, then sat next to Emmie on the bed. Harry growled low, letting Jade know that was far enough. Jade didn't move to touch Emmie. "Baby, I'm going to leave you alone. If you need me, I'll be in the living room. Do you want anything before I go?" Jade waited a moment, but when Emmie didn't bother to answer, she stood and walked from the room.

~

George, Ryan, and Annie all arrived at Walt's house. Walt was getting a tray with coffee cups, cream, and sugar together when the doorbell rang. He left the tray on the counter and headed for the door.

The smiles were hesitant when the door opened.

"Any word from Jade?" Ryan asked.

"No, not for a while. I expect she'll be calling any time now."

"Boy, the coffee sure smells great," George said.

"Thanks. You guys make yourselves comfortable. I was just putting a tray together. I'll be right back." Walt went to the kitchen to finish his task.

"George, do you want to fill Walt in on all that's happened, or do you want me to do it?" Ryan sat down on the single chair and waited for George's reply.

Annie sat down next to George on the sofa. George, deep in thought, was trying to put his thoughts in order about Jade's visions. Walt came in with the tray and set it on the coffee table. Removing cups and plates of cookies, he looked at Ryan.

"What's wrong? You guys are being too quiet. Did I miss something?" he asked, looking first at Ryan, then at George.

"You can have the honors, Ryan," George said, looking at Ryan.

"Wow. Where to begin?" Annie didn't know about Jade's visions yet. "Walt, before I fill you in, I think you should explain Jade's gift to Annie."

Walt looked at Ryan, surprised and questioning. Ryan just looked back and nodded his head to go ahead. Deciding to just jump right in, Walt asked, "Annie, do you know anything about visions?"

"Visions? What do you mean? Like ESP?" Annie, looking fearful and somewhat confused, stared at Walt.

"Kind of, yeah. You know people who can see things before they happen?"

"You mean like psychics? No, I've only heard of that on TV. Why?"

"Jade has the gift. She has since she was ten. They're not hard to prove since they always happen after she tells them."

"You mean to tell me you expect me to believe that Jade can see the future?"

"Yes. Well, kind of. She sees things that are going to happen and sometimes stops them from happening. Other times, she helps them to happen. It just depends on the circumstances of the vision and the outcome."

"Okay, so what does this have to do with anything?"

"Ryan, you take it from here."

"Annie, Jade warned us about the killer breaking into your apartment last night. That's why we were there. She saw it all happen, and that's the reason she couldn't let you take Emmie home with you. She knew you weren't safe; therefore, Emmie wouldn't be safe."

"What? You knew the killer was going to try to get me and you didn't even tell me?" Annie was angry. She stood up, hands on her hips.

"Annie, take it easy. We knew he would try, and we were hoping to catch him there. At first, we didn't know it was you because we didn't know you existed. Jade just saw him with a knife in his hand in the home of a female. She saw the cat trip him and the female scream and try to run for help. She saw all that. Then we found your picture at the Linderhoffs' house, and I took it to show Jade. She confirmed you were the female in her vision." Ryan, trying to explain things to Annie and calm her down, talked softly. Annie sat down, confusion plain on her face. Walt and George sat there quietly, letting Ryan handle the situation.

"So she knows who this killer is. I need to talk to Jade," Annie said. "She needs to bring Emmie home today."

"No, she doesn't. She can't see his face, only a tattoo," Ryan said.

"Annie, where do you suppose your mom and Mrs. Linderhoff plan to stay?" George asked.

"I was supposed to ask you if they were allowed to stay at Amy's. I think they would like to be there if they can."

"You'll probably want to go there and straighten things up first. Someone made quite a mess of the place. But yeah, they can stay there. It would probably be a good idea for you to stay there, too," George suggested.

"Yeah, maybe I should, since I've become a target," Annie reasoned.

"What happened to the killer?" Walt looked at everyone.

"The killer broke into Annie's apartment last night. I was outside checking the area when he went in through the bathroom window. I missed him."

"I see. Annie, how did you escape?"

"Ryan came in and scared him away. He jumped out a window, and Ryan lost him."

The four of them sat there, each thinking their own thoughts. The telephone rang, and Walt went to answer it.

"Hello?"

"Hi, Dad, how is everything on the home front?" Jade asked.

"Jade, baby, how are you? How is Emmie?"

"Not so good, Dad. I told her about her parents, and she hasn't said a word to me since. She went to her bedroom at least two hours ago, and she's still in there."

"Have you tried to talk to her?"

"Yeah, but she has made it very plain she doesn't want to talk to me."

"She just needs time, honey."

"Dad, do you know how to get hold of Annie?"

"Yes, she's here now. Do you want to talk to her?"

"Yeah, thanks."

"Annie, Jade wants to talk to you."

Taking the phone from Walt, Annie tried to smile. "Thanks, Walt. Hello, Jade. How's Emmie?"

"Not good, Annie. I told her about her parents, and she won't talk now."

"Where is she?"

"In her bedroom with Harry. Do you think she would talk to you?"

"I hope so. Tell her I'm on the phone."

"Great, hang on." Jade laid the phone down and went to Emmie's room.

"Emmie?" No answer. Jade opened the door. "Emmie, your Aunt Annie is on the phone, and she would like to talk to you." Emmie lay there not moving. Jade walked over and rolled her over. The girl stared up at Jade, her eyes red and still teary. Jade held her arms out, and Emmie crawled into them. Jade sat there holding her tight, and Emmie held tightly to Jade. The silent crying tore at Jade. "I know, baby, I know. It hurts so much, but I promise it gets better. Will you talk to your Aunt Annie?" The only answer was a nod of Emmie's little head.

Jade carried her to the living room. Sitting down, she kept her in her lap. Harry followed and sat down next to their chair. Jade thought it was endearing how Harry protected his little mistress. Handing the phone to Emmie, Jade sat back and stroked her hair.

"Hello?" Emmie said, sniffling.

"Emmie, it's Aunt Annie. Baby, are you okay?"

"Yeah. Where you at, Aunt Annie?"

"I'm at Walt's house. Where are you?"

"I'm at the cabin. Harry's here too."

"I know. I love you, baby. Do you want to come and stay with me?"

"Where's my mommy?"

"Don't worry about your mommy right now, honey. I'm going to take good care of you, I promise."

"I love you, Aunt Annie."

"Love you too. Put Jade back on the phone, sweetie."

"Annie?" Jade was thrilled Emmie was talking again.

"Jade, bring her home."

"I'm not sure that's a good idea just yet."

"Jade, the killer already broke into my apartment."

"He did?"

"Yeah, last night"

"Annie, are Ryan and George with you?"

"Yeah, we're all here. Please bring Emmie back. We'll work something out that you're comfortable with. I won't fight you."

"When are you going to have the funeral, Annie?"

"I think tomorrow, maybe. I don't know exactly. I'm waiting on my mom."

"Okay. Tell Dad we'll be there in a few hours. We all need to sit down and talk. See if we can't figure this out."

"Thanks, Jade."

"You're welcome." Jade hung up. Looking at Emmie, she asked, "Do you want to go back?"

"I wanna see Aunt Annie and Walt and Ryan."

"Okay, go get your things together."

"Come on, Harry. We have to get our stuff." She pulled Harry by the collar so he would follow her. He would have followed even without the extra encouragement.

Jade went to her room and began getting her things together. She would stop and turn the keys to the cabin in – she wouldn't need them, after all. It would be good to get back to her normal life. She needed to contact her new boss and let him know she couldn't start work as scheduled. She would need some extra time. She hoped they would give it to her. If not, she would go back to job hunting again. She could not go to work now and let Emmie down.

She had to get some time to herself this afternoon to try to recall her vision. She really needed to try and make sense out of it. She had been looking forward to seeing Ryan again, but now, since he and Annie... well, she didn't have time for those thoughts now. She would deal with that later. After all, he didn't make any promises to her. Finished packing, she called to Emmie. "Are you all packed?"

"Yep, be there in a minute. I have to let Harry go potty first," she yelled, opening the door.

"Good thinking. I'll start putting our stuff in the car. You should go potty before we leave, too." Jade grabbed her suitcase and went to get Emmie's. The baby doll was lying on the bed, crumpled up. Jade walked over and picked the doll up. She was a pretty doll, very realistic in look and feel and heavy like an actual baby would be. Jade took the suitcases to the car. Taking a long look around the cabin, she remembered Harry's dog food container. Going to the kitchen, she grabbed the container and went looking for Emmie. Jade found her in the bathroom. She told Emmie to get her baby doll and meet her outside.

Starting the car, she loaded Harry in the back seat, knowing Emmie would want him in the back with her. Emmie came to the car, holding her baby doll hugged close to her. She always carried her doll like a real baby. "Emmie, does your baby have a name?"

"Her name is Molly."

"That sure is a pretty name. How long have you had Molly?"

"Daddy just got her for me. He said I should keep her with me always."

"That was nice of your daddy." Closing the car door, Jade went to lock the cabin door. She knew she would miss it. The tranquility the cabin provided was a luxury she would have to take the time to enjoy again.

She hoped she was doing the right thing, taking Emmie back. Surely between all of them they would be able to keep this child safe. She turned and walked back to the car. "Well, here we go. You excited to see your Aunt Annie?"

"Yep, I want to see everyone."

"Yeah, me too."

Jade stopped at the Ivory Bluff office and dropped the keys off, thanking the agent for turning everything on for her and now making sure all would be turned off. She explained what a delight it was to have such a service available and that she was sure she would use it again. The agent and Jade shook hands, and then she left.

Once again in the car and heading home, her thoughts turned to Ryan. It hurt her even though she didn't want to admit it, not even to herself. She should wish Annie and Ryan well, but she couldn't. Was there something between them, or had she only thought there was?

There had been something between her and Ryan; she knew there had been, and she knew he had felt it, too. Ryan was sweet, and she would still do whatever she could to help them catch this killer.

~

Annie told everyone that Jade and Emmie were coming home. Ryan was excited to see them again, especially Jade. He had to keep himself under control and not show too much emotion. George, of course, could see it, but that was because he knew him so well.

George smiled to himself. Walt saw it, too. Walt knew Ryan was going to have his hands full, since Jade thought he and Annie had had a thing last night. His daughter could have quite the temper when she felt the need for one.

"I guess I should go to Amy's and get things straight before I take Emmie there," Annie said.

"Annie, you don't know me very well, but if you need help getting the place together, I'd like to help," Walt offered.

"George and I have to get to work, or we would help out, too," Ryan said.

"I appreciate all of you. Walt, that is very sweet, but I don't know what kind of mess I may be dealing with, and it could take quite a while. You should be here when Jade gets back."

"I could leave Jade a note telling her where I am and the telephone number to Amy's. She could call when she gets here."

"Well, I'm sure I could use the help if you're sure."

"Great. It's settled then. I just need to clean this coffee mess up, and then we can be on our way." Walt got up and began collecting cups and plates. Carrying them back to the kitchen, he felt good offering to help Annie.

George was making notes on his pad, trying to put the day into perspective. He and Ryan were going to be quite busy.

Ryan stood up and went to look out the window. He knew the killer didn't know about Jade, but he wanted to make sure no one was out there watching Walt's place. The killer could have been watching Annie and followed them here this morning. Nothing seemed out of place; he couldn't see anyone sitting in a vehicle or standing around. "Annie, before you go to Amy's, why don't you go back to your place and get whatever you want to take with you to Amy's? We can go with you and make sure you're not followed," Ryan suggested. He wanted to make sure the killer didn't know where she and Emmie were.

"I have to get Wally and my suitcase. Should I forward my telephone calls?"

"Definitely. If the killer calls again, we want him to be able to reach you," George said.

"The killer called Annie when?" Walt asked, coming back into the room.

"He told her he was coming for her. He called this morning right after I left her apartment. That's why I don't want her going there alone. He could be watching. I just checked the street to see if anyone or anything looked out of place. I want to make sure he didn't follow her here," Ryan said.

"He said he was coming for you, Annie?" Walt was concerned.

"Yes. He said I was lucky last night." She shivered as she said it.

"Ryan, you need to give her around-the-clock protection. This guy isn't scared of anything if he let her see him and hear his voice."

"She didn't see him. He was wearing a mask. But we'll keep tabs on her as much as possible. Tonight she won't be alone. She'll have her mom and James' mom there with her and Emmie," George put in.

Walt didn't like this one bit. He knew the killer was getting braver. He had to do some thinking.

"I'm ready when you are, Annie," he said, grabbing a light jacket.

Annie walked toward the front door. "So, to my apartment first, right?" she asked.

"Yeah, we're right behind you. George, do you want to take your car or mine?" Ryan asked.

"We'll take yours this time. Walt, can we leave my car here?"

"Sure. I think I'll ride with you, Annie, if you don't mind."

"That would be fine with me," she said. "I have plenty of room."

"Oh, hold up, I need the telephone number to Amy's house for Jade." Walt wrote the number down as Annie gave it and left the note on the kitchen counter for Jade. They all walked out, and Walt locked the door. Turning, he watched Ryan and George get in Ryan's car. Annie stood next to the driver's door of her car and waited for Walt. He walked out, looking around, trying to see everything at once. He wasn't a cop, but he knew his neighborhood.

"We'll follow you, Annie," Ryan told her.

"Walt, I can't thank you enough for offering to help me. I really didn't want to go to Amy's by myself. This is going to be so weird."

"I didn't want you going by yourself. I know I won't be much help, but at least I'll be there if you need me."

"I'm so scared. What if I can't keep Emmie safe?"

"You're not in this alone. We'll all be there to keep Emmie safe."

Annie didn't know Walt or Jade very well, but she knew deep in her heart they were good people. She couldn't understand why someone would get involved in something like this if they could avoid it. A murder, for goodness sake! No, a double murder! Yet they didn't hold back. This was going to be a lifelong friendship, she knew. Surely Emmie was getting attached to Jade. The poor baby. She had no idea what her life would be like now. Annie had to make sure she did things right, take her time, and most of all, keep her safe.

15

GEORGE and Ryan were driving to Annie's apartment.

"Ryan, when we get there, I'll stay outside and talk to Walt. You go up with Annie. I don't want her there alone," George said.

"I already planned on that one, partner."

"Damn. I sure wish we had more to go on. This psycho has all the cards in his favor right now. We need a break." George was even more on edge than he normally was at this point in an investigation. He knew that if they didn't catch this guy soon, they could lose someone else. "We need to get a crime scene team over to that empty apartment today. Actually this morning."

"We take it a step at a time, George. We're not new at this. We're going to get him. Just hang in there." Ryan could feel the strain his partner was experiencing. Then again, he wasn't sure if he was trying to convince George or himself, but it sounded good.

~

Jade was driving and keeping her eyes on Emmie. The poor child ever so quietly would start crying again, then stop and start again. Jade knew the hurt and fear the child felt. She was only ten when her own mother died, but she still had her dad.

Whatever happened from now on, she knew Emmie would always be a part of her life.

Harry had his head in Emmie's lap, trying his best to comfort her. He was a very smart dog and loved Emmie. He would do whatever he needed to protect her.

They drove in silence, except for the occasional whimper from Emmie. After driving quite a while and being deep in her own thoughts, Jade barely heard Emmie say she needed to go potty. Jade began looking for a gas station. The stretch of highway they were on didn't yield much hope, but surely they would find one soon. There was a small country store coming up; she could see if they had a restroom. They would be at her dad's soon, but Emmie was so small she probably couldn't hold it another thirty or forty minutes.

"Emmie, I'm going to stop at this store. Do you want something to drink or snack on?"

"Maybe, but first, I hafta pee."

Laughing, Jade pulled into the parking lot and sat there for a minute. No cars had been behind her, but she wanted to give it a minute just to make sure. After a few minutes, she got out and started for the store, but realizing she didn't want to leave Emmie even for a minute, she went back and opened Emmie's door. "Honey, we have to leave Harry in the car."

"I know, but I'll hurry because he'll miss me."

Harry didn't like being left in the car and showed his displeasure by barking. As they approached the door, Jade saw a man sitting alone in a vehicle way off to the side of the store. She kept her eyes on the man to see if they appeared to be of interest to him. She didn't see the man even look up. Feeling somewhat comfortable that he was not interested, Jade led Emmie inside the store.

"Excuse me, sir?" Jade went to the clerk behind the counter. "Do you have a restroom we can use?"

"Back there by the soda cooler," he replied.

They walked together to the door in the rear of the store. "Emmie, I'll wait right here," Jade told her as Emmie tried to get to the toilet in time.

Jade stood outside the door like an overprotective mother. Once Emmie came out, they went to look for drinks and a snack, then returned to the car.

"Emmie, where's Harry's leash? He probably needs to go to the bathroom while we're here."

"I put it in the back seat. I'll get it." She opened the door, and Harry jumped out. He ran behind the building, and they both ran after him, calling to him, but he kept running. They came around the side of the building, and Harry was just finishing his business.

"Emmie, call him and run to the car. I think he'll follow you," Jade said with hope.

Emmie began yelling for Harry and then ran as fast as her little legs would carry her to the car. Harry was right behind her. Once they were all loaded, they took off again. The man in the parked vehicle was still just sitting there when they left.

He watched them when they went in and watched them leave. His luck was getting better and better.

Emmie was sharing her chips with Harry. She was laughing and having fun for the first time today. Jade didn't want the food all over the car, but she decided to just let them have fun.

~

Annie and Ryan went up the stairs to her apartment. Annie was making a mental note of everything she would need. Poor Wally. He didn't like going outside. He would make a fuss, she was sure, but she couldn't leave him here. She opened the door and started to walk in.

The place was a disaster. "Oh my God," Annie screamed.

"You stay out here," Ryan ordered, pulling his gun and pushing her aside.

George came up the stairs. "What's the matter?"

"He's been here. Look at my place. Wally, oh, Wally," Annie cried.

George went inside with Ryan. They methodically checked the apartment. Wally was laying in the tub. His throat had been slit. There was blood everywhere.

The killer hadn't left anything in its normal place. He had made a total mess of the apartment.

Ryan looked at George. "Tell Annie to go back downstairs. We need to get a crime scene team out here now."

"Yeah. I'll tell her about Wally, too." George turned to walk out. "Annie, you need to go back downstairs. I'll explain things in just a minute. I have to call for a crime scene team first."

"Where's Wally, George?"

"Go on, honey, give me a minute."

Walt was out of the car and standing at the steps when they came down. Annie was white as a ghost. Walt reached out and took her in his arms, then walked her to the parking lot. They stood there and waited for George to complete his telephone call. George hung up and walked over to Annie. She was still standing with Walt's arms around her, fearing the worst.

"Annie, your apartment has been completely ransacked. I'm sorry to tell you, but Wally is gone."

"Gone? But he doesn't like being outside. He doesn't have claws to protect himself." Pushing away from Walt, her instinct was to start looking for Wally.

"Annie, I didn't mean he was outside somewhere. The bastard killed Wally. I am so sorry," George said, reaching for her arm.

Annie turned back and buried her head on Walt's shoulder, crying. This wasn't fair. What did she or Wally do to deserve this? Poor Wally, he had nowhere to go to get away from this fiend. She would tear the bastard apart with her bare hands when he was caught! How could he have done this?

Walt watched George as he furiously made notes. Walt was more concerned now. He was going to have to do something to keep this maniac away from the girls.

"So what happens now, George?" he asked.

"Ryan and I will wait for the crime scene team. Why don't you two go ahead to Amy's?"

"What about my suitcase?" Annie asked, still crying.

"We can get that later, Annie. Right now, I don't want anyone else in there until the team has completely gone through the apartment."

"Come on, Annie. If you want, I'll drive," Walt said.

"Yes, thank you, Walt," Annie said, handing over the keys.

They walked to Annie's car. Walt helped her in and then went around to the driver's side. "I don't know where they lived."

"Do you know where Maggie Lane is?"

"Yeah."

~ 168 ~

"It's on Maggie Lane. I'll point out the house to you."
Trying to compose herself, she looked out the side window as Walt
pulled out. "I just can't believe this. Why would he kill Wally?"

"I don't know. He's sick."

"Poor Wally, he had nowhere to run. I should have been
there."

"No, it's a good thing you weren't. He would have killed
you, too. Then where would Emmie be?"

"I know. Walt, I'm not sure I can keep her safe. I mean,
look at me. I'm a mess. I can't even think straight anymore. I had
no idea he would come back so soon."

"None of us did. It's not your fault. We'll all help you keep
Emmie safe."

"How?"

"I don't know, honey, but we will." They drove on in
silence, except for Annie's crying. Walt had to help them get this
figured out. This guy wasn't going to stop. What could be so
important to him?

Ryan and George stood on the walkway outside the front
door, waiting for the team to arrive. They both knew that they were
dealing with someone more dangerous than either knew at first.
Yes, he had killed James and Amy, but it wasn't unusual for a
drug dealer to kill the person responsible for ripping him off. But
now this one was breaking into apartments of people that logically
had nothing to do with the situation and even killing animals and
leaving threatening messages. He wasn't in control of himself, and
that made for a dangerous situation. They were going to have to
work faster and be more productive.

"George, let's have another look around while we wait. I
can't help feeling like we're missing something," Ryan said.

"Okay, but we can't start letting our feelings for these
people get in the way."

"What are you talking about?"

"I know Annie is a sweet girl and that you have feelings for
Jade, but this is still an investigation, and we're going to work it as
such. Not something personal."

"I can't believe you just said that to me. Why would you
think I would handle this any different than any other case?"

"You did tell Annie we would help her clean Amy's house if
we didn't have to get back to work, didn't you?"

"Yeah, but that was just being polite."

"Are you sure?"

"Yes! Damn it, George, I know what I'm doing. I just felt we should come across as caring, that's all." Why did he feel he had to explain himself?

"Okay, take it easy, Ryan. I was just making a point."

They walked back inside the apartment and began looking around, not touching anything, just looking. The answering machine on the kitchen counter had a flashing light. Ryan noticed it immediately. "Do you think we should listen?"

"This thing shows five messages. Maybe he called to make sure there wasn't anyone here before he came back," George said.

"You want a pair of gloves? I'm going to my car to get me a pair."

"Yeah, bring me some," George said, looking around.

Ryan ran down to the car and opened the trunk, and taking out his camera and two pairs of gloves, he went back upstairs.

"Here." He handed a pair of gloves to George and pulled his own on. Careful not to make any smudges where prints were possible, he pushed the play button on the answering machine with the tip of his pen.

The machine began to play. "Annie, it's Mom. Don't forget to pick me up tonight. My flight number is 877 Golden Pen Airways at five twenty-six. I guess we could grab a quick bite to eat, then pick Donna up at six ten. Okay? Okay, see you then, honey. I love you."

The second message was also from Annie's mother. "Annie, it's Mom again. Sorry, but I forgot to tell you if those police agree that we can stay at Amy's, I was thinking you should stay there, too. Give it some thought. Okay, bye."

The third message was from the vet. He wanted to remind Annie of Wally's appointment on Wednesday.

The fourth message was not so normal. "Hey, little sister. It's me again. Miss me?" The voice on the machine laughed. "I'm coming to get you!"

The fifth message was more of the same. "Little sister, I killed your fucking cat. Guess he won't trip me next time, will he? Aww, don't cry. You can see him soon if you don't help me get my shit back, bitch! See you soon, little sister."

"He's taunting her, that sick son of a bitch!" Ryan was outraged.

"Yeah, did you hear that sinister laugh? He's really getting off on this. Wish I knew what shit he was referring to. It's gotta be drugs."

"Well, he obviously hasn't found it yet. Where would James have hidden drugs he was planning on dealing but had to wait for the deal to be done?" Ryan thought aloud.

"I don't know, but James didn't leave it here or at his own house, so what's left?"

"Does Emmie have any personal effects with her, do you know?" Ryan's mind was starting to work like it should. Maybe it had been getting jumbled with thoughts of Jade. He would keep his mind clear until they solved this thing.

"Do you think James gave it to the kid?" George was seeing where Ryan was going now.

"Surely not, but what's left?"

They walked through the apartment again, looking closely at the places the killer went through more thoroughly.

"It would help if we knew what kind of drugs we were looking for and the amount. Then we would know what type of places he could have hidden them," Ryan said.

"Look here." George pointed out a shoebox. "It can't be that much if he thought it would fit in this."

"Or it's not powder. What's smaller and valuable enough to kill for?" Ryan was racking his brain.

"Hello, anyone here?" The voice came from the front door.

Ryan and George came out of the bedroom and saw Victor Young standing there. Vic was with the crime scene division.

"Hey, Vic, come on in," George said.

"What do we have here, guys?" Vic asked.

"We're working a double homicide, and this is one of the victim's sister's apartment. This ransacking happened this morning. See what you can find for us." George stepped back, allowing the team members' entrance. "We'll get out of your hair. Let me know if you find anything. Oh, Vic, the empty apartment next door. You need to check that thoroughly, too. He was there for a while."

"Sure thing, detective," Vic said.

"Oh, and, Vic, there's a dead cat in the tub. Put him in a bag for the owner, please. Take some good photos of the cut throat and anything else you find we might need later." George knew they wouldn't clean the bloody mess up it wasn't part of their job. He would have to let Annie know that before she came back in here. He was sure she would want to bury Wally, though, so bagging him was the best he could do right now.

"Ryan, let's head over to Amy and James' place. Oh, Vic? Take the answering machine tape for evidence, too." George walked out, following Ryan down the stairs.

"Man, how much more do you think this family can take?"

"Oh, it's gonna get worse before it gets better. We just need to make sure they understand that."

"Yeah."

~

Walt and Annie arrived at Amy's. Walt automatically took the lead into the house, looking around. The mess was shocking. It was going to take some work to clean, but at least Annie wasn't alone. This guy was ridiculous the way he just tore people's homes up and didn't give it another thought. "Come on in, Annie," Walt told her.

She followed him in. "Wow, look at this mess. Amy would have a fit. She kept things so nice and neat."

"What do you suppose he's looking for?" Walt asked.

"I don't know, but I wish I knew where it was," Annie said, looking around.

"Annie, instead of cleaning this mess, why don't you all stay with me and Jade at my house? I have plenty of room, and that way Jade and I can help with Emmie."

"Oh, Walt, that is so sweet of you, but we couldn't put you out like that. No, I couldn't do that."

"Yes, you could. Look at this place. The killer doesn't even know about me and Jade. You'd be safer there."

"That's four people you're not used to and hardly know. No, we'll be fine. You're a sweet man, and I thank you from the bottom of my heart for even thinking about it." Annie hugged him.

"Alright, but know that the offer is open." Deciding not push the point, Walt let it go for now. They walked around the small house, assessing the damage. The mess was just in the living room and master bedroom areas.

"Well, where do we begin?" Annie was stepping over things and looking around.

"Why don't you go take care of the bedroom, and I'll start in here?" Walt suggested.

"That would be great. I guess we could stuff the cushions again and then throw a sheet over the whole thing to make it look presentable. What do you think?"

"It's either that or buy new furniture, and we don't have time for that."

"Let's just do what we can. I'll head to the bedroom. Yell if you need anything. Walt, don't worry about making it perfect, just livable. Emmie's the one that will have the hardest time with this, but I'll get her through it." Annie left and walked down the short hallway. Looking in the master bedroom, she just wanted to throw her hands up and say forget it. But she didn't have a choice. She began picking up the photographs and putting them back in the frames, hanging them on the wall and setting them on the dressers. Then she folded the clothes and put them away, seeing to every little detail.

Walt was trying to do the same. He had no idea what this room looked like before, but he would do what he could. This was going to take a while.

~

When Jade and Emmie arrived at Walt's, the front door was locked, and after walking around to the back of the house, they found the back door was also locked. Jade got the keys from under the mat and unlocked the back door. They went inside. She saw the note on the counter and went to read it. At Amy's? Why? She and Emmie went out the front door and got Harry out of the car. They all went inside, and Jade called her dad.

"Hello?" Annie answered.

"Annie, it's Jade."

"Hey, Jade, you made it back safely, great! We're over here at Amy's trying to get the place cleaned up for us to stay here."

"Why?"

"Our parents will be here this evening. They want to stay here, and I guess Emmie and I will be staying here with them."

"Is my dad there?"

"Yeah, hang on a second." Jade heard Annie yell into the other room.

Walt came in. Taking the phone and giving Annie an assuring smile, he answered, "Hey, honey, you made it home."

"Yeah. What are you doing there?"

"Thought I'd help Annie out. We're going to be here a while. I want you to stay there; don't come over here. I have a lot to tell you. Is Emmie okay?"

"Yes, she's fine. How long you gonna be there?"

"Maybe a couple more hours. Why don't you two get something to eat and then relax for a bit?"

"Okay." Apprehensively, she hung up.

~

Ryan and George were on their way to the Linderhoff residence, brainstorming as they went.

"Okay, so we know it has to be a small drug. But what could it be?" George said.

"Some type of pill maybe?" Ryan suggested.

"Yeah, but what would bring a lot of money per pill?"

"Well, we start with a list of all the pill-type narcotics and then go from there. When we get done here, we can go to the station and get with one of the guys from the drug task force. We need to see how much ecstasy is going for per pill these days. They have a lot more knowledge about this than we do."

"That's a good idea," George said. "Why do you think he killed Wally?" George was still bothered by the senseless killing.

"I don't know. From the sound of his voice on the machine, I would say he was pissed at the cat for tripping him."

"Yeah! What a reason to slit his throat. I guess it doesn't take much to push this bastard's buttons. I just wish he would give me the chance to push a button or two."

"You and me both, partner," Ryan said, shaking his head.

They rode a ways in silence, both thinking of things that needed to be checked out. Ryan was playing that voice over and over in his head when it occurred to him what Ms. Armstrong said in her message. "Shit, George, he knows Annie will be at the airport. He even has the flight info."

"Oh, man, you're right. I didn't even think about that."

"Well, maybe we can be one step ahead, and hopefully the creep will try something there."

"This could be the break we've been waiting for."

"We have to get with Captain Mallory and see if he'll give us some extra men."

"Yeah, when we get back to the station, we'll go see him and explain what's going on."

George once again began making notes in his pad. This case was finally coming together.

Ryan was thinking about Jade again. He wondered if she was back yet. He couldn't wait to see her again. He decided that when this case was over, he was going to pursue a relationship with Jade. He couldn't wait to see where it was going. This case had to end pretty soon. He had hoped she would call his cell phone and tell him she was back.

Every time he thought about her, he got anxious for this case to wrap up. She was something very special, and he knew that when he laid eyes on her in the backyard.

~

Jade rattled around the kitchen, trying to decide what to do. Emmie and Harry were playing in the backyard, and Jade could see them through the window. Maybe she should go out there with them. She picked up the phone to call Mr. Croft, her boss. She had forgotten she needed to call him today. Calling quickly and explaining her predicament, Jade was relieved when the conversation ended. Okay, that was done. Whew! Jade was surprised to realize she was worth waiting for. Who would have known?

Jade sat on the back porch watching Emmie and Harry run around each other, Emmie laughing and Harry barking. They had so much energy! Jade sat there, not meaning to, but thinking about Ryan. He popped into her head more often than he should have. Especially now that she knew they weren't going anywhere. Surely Annie was the one he wanted, or he wouldn't have slept with her. He was too nice a man to sleep with her at a time like this and not have any intentions. Guess we weren't meant to be, she thought.

"Emmie, be careful you don't kick Harry when you swing."

"Okay."

Jade would probably go back to her house tonight. After all, Emmie would be with Annie, so there would be no reason she couldn't go home. That would be nice. She missed her own bed. Living on a roller coaster was too up and down for her. She was usually very organized and together; this way of life was for the birds.

16

ANNIE and Walt were making lots of headway. The place was shaping up quite nicely. As Annie walked into the living room to check on Walt, she saw he was almost done. What a difference he had made.

"Annie, hey, just in time. Where's the vacuum?"

"I think it's in that closet over there. Wow, this looks great!"

"Yeah, not too shabby. Thanks. I think I had the easy room."

"I see you found the sheets okay. That doesn't look bad. I think this just might work."

"How are you coming in there?"

"Oh, it's coming along. Actually, I'm almost finished too."

"Great, then we should be out of here in no time."

"Yep. I still have three hours till I need to be at the airport to pick my mom up, so we're making good time."

"Well, let's get back to it then."

"Walt? Thanks again. I couldn't have done this without you."

"Hey, don't give it another thought."

They continued cleaning. The place was looking like a home again: not Amy's spotless, efficient home, but a home nonetheless. It wouldn't take much more time. Annie couldn't wait to see Emmie.

Ryan and George arrived at the Linderhoff home finally. Ryan was making a mental note to get the answering machine tape from here as well. He was trying to decide if he should listen to it here because he might not need the tape after all. "I think we should listen to the answering machine tape while we're here. What do you think?"

"I had already planned on that. You seemed so into your own thoughts I didn't want to interrupt you." He was always one step or thought ahead. Experience was priceless.

"What's that supposed to mean?" Ryan asked offended.

"Just what I said. What were you thinking about, anyhow? Or should I say 'who'?"

"Yeah, you should." Ryan knew George was having fun, and it wasn't going to stop anytime soon.

"That's what I thought." George was laughing, enjoying himself too much.

"Yeah, go ahead and laugh at my expense. I'll have the last laugh, buddy." Ryan was laughing, too.

They got out and walked up to the front door. Ryan could see Walt through the window. He waved at him, and Walt waved back.

"Annie, Ryan and George are here."

Annie hurried to the front door. "Hey, guys."

"Hi, Annie, how's the cleanup going?" George asked.

"Great, actually. How's my apartment?" She didn't have the heart to ask outright what they did with Wally.

"You're gonna have quite a mess, but all in all, not as bad as this place was."

"Oh. Thank you. I know this is horrible, all things considered, but I just want you both to know how grateful I am that I didn't have to see Wally like that."

"Annie, there is something I need to tell you, though."

"What now, George? I don't know how much more I can take."

"I understand. I just wanted you to know that the team doesn't clean anything up. I told them to put Wally in a bag for you, but that is the most they'll do."

"Thank you. I didn't think they would clean up. That's fine." She was doing her best not to picture her beloved cat. He didn't deserve this. Damn, this whole thing was just a nightmare, and she prayed she would wake up soon.

"You do know there will be blood all over your bathroom, right?" Picturing the countless scenes in his mind, he dreaded her return home.

"All over the bathroom?" she asked.

"Well, maybe not all over, but there is a lot of blood."

"I'll deal with what I have to. Thanks for trying to prepare me."

"Annie, if you want, I'll go back later and clean it up," Ryan said.

"No, Ryan, it's sweet of you to offer, but I'll take care of it. You guys have done enough. All of you have." She thought to herself that maybe this would give her some type of closure. She knew she would miss Wally fervently. The loss of her beloved cat was a pain she was eager to have subside.

"How much longer are you two going to be here?" Ryan wanted to know.

"Not long, then we're going to Walt's house."

"Walt, have you heard from Jade yet?"

"Yeah, she's there. She called about an hour ago."

"Oh, she did?" Ryan was disappointed.

"Ryan, is everything okay?" Walt had heard the disappointment in Ryan's voice.

"Sure. I just thought maybe she would call and let me know she was back."

"I see," Walt said, walking away and smiling to himself. This was really going to get good!

"Wow, this room looks great! How's the bedroom coming along?" George walked in and looked around. He had to move so Ryan wouldn't see his smile.

They each went their own way in the house. Ryan went to the answering machine and checked the message counter. The light was not lit, but that didn't mean there weren't any messages. George was in the bedroom doing the same thing. Neither knew there were two answering machines. They each took the tape and put it in their pocket, each thinking they could use the tape to laugh at the other when they got in the car. They did truly think too much alike. The microtapes were the only thing that either saw in the house that they might want to take a look at.

"George, we should get going," Ryan yelled down the hallway.

"Yeah, I was just coming. Hey, guys, see you at Walt's house in a little while," George said, smiling.

"Okay. I'll get Annie going here shortly. We'll see you two there."

"Later," Ryan said, walking out the door. He saw Walt and George laughing. Did they think he was stupid? He would show them he knew what he was doing. Time would show them. Jade should have called him, though. He wondered why she didn't. Was she still angry with him for this morning? Surely she didn't really think he had slept with Annie. He would get her to the side later and let her know that, if nothing else, he was trustworthy.

~

Jade was getting impatient, waiting for her dad to get home. Emmie was still swinging on the tire swing and squealing in delight every time Harry jumped and licked her when she swung past him. Jade went back inside to get Amy's phone number. As she walked back out, she thought about Ryan and dialed the phone.

"Emmie, what are you doing?" Jade dropped the phone as Emmie turned to face her. She had a piece of rope wrapped around her neck. Running frantically to Emmie, Jade looked around wildly. She didn't see anyone. She opened the gate and looked down the alley. No one.

"Emmie, where did that come from?" Jade pulled on the rope.

"The ugly man gave it to me. He said it was my new necklace."

"Where did he go, Emmie?" Jade was shaking.

"He took off when you opened the door."

"Why did you come back here to him? He could have hurt you, Emmie!" Jade had to stop herself. She was letting her fear turn to anger, and it wasn't Emmie's fault.

"He called me back here. He said to hurry and that he had something for me."

"Emmie, you are never to go near him again, do you hear me?" Jade grabbed hold of Emmie's shoulders, slightly shaking her. The rope around Emmie's neck was a frightening thing. She needed to call Ryan. Pulling Emmie with her, she went into the house. Harry ran behind them.

Jade got them inside and looked at Harry. "Why didn't you bark when that bad man came here, Harry? Bad dog, Harry, bad dog!"

"Jade, why are you so mad at me and Harry?"

"Emmie, that man is bad, and he will hurt you. I don't ever want you to go near him again!"

Jade, get a grip, you're yelling at the poor child and repeating yourself, and she doesn't even know what she did wrong, Jade though. She locked the door and dialed the telephone.

"Detective Douglas."

"Ryan, oh thank God. I need you now!"

"Jade?"

"Ryan, can you come to Dad's right away?"

"Jade, what's wrong? Emmie? Is she okay?"

"Yes, she's okay, just please get here as soon as you can." She couldn't keep the panic out of her voice, and she felt silly.

"I'm on my way, honey." Ryan hung up and looked at George. "We're running code. Something's happened. I think Jade's in trouble."

"What's going on?"

"I don't know, but she's freaking out." Turning on the overhead emergency lights and siren, Ryan began running red lights, stop signs, and everything else that got in his way. He had the only investigator car that had overhead lights. Most of them had to put those silly bubbles on top and pray that the public saw the lights in time to get out of the way.

"She didn't say anything to indicate what was going on?" George was peeved.

"No, she just asked that we get there quickly, but she sounded panicky."

"Jade isn't the type to panic unless something is really wrong. You're right. Step it up!"

"Call Walt and tell him to get home. We should all be there if she needs us."

"Alright, but you know he'll panic if we can't give him some information on what happened."

"He'll be alright. Just call him."

"Okay." George got Ryan's cell phone and tried to look up the number to Amy's. Not finding it there, he got Ryan's spiral tablet. He looked through it but still didn't find the number.

"Ryan, do you have the telephone number to the Linderhoffs'?"

"No, why?"

"Well, that's where Walt is."

"Shit, you're right. Call Walt's house and get the number from Jade."

"Okay." He dialed Walt's number. He spoke briefly with Jade, but she wouldn't tell him anything more about what had happened. She said it was something he would simply have to see for himself. Then she gave him the Linderhoffs' number.

George called Walt. He told him to get home, but without details, George knew Walt was upset. Nothing he could do about it. Walt wanted to know why the siren was going, and George could only tell him they were on their way to his house. He told Walt he had talked to Jade and that she was scared but okay.

~

Walt hung up and told Annie to wrap it up; they had to leave now. Annie came into the room with a questioning look.

"What's wrong?"

"I don't know. George just said that Jade called, upset over something that happened, and they want us on our way. I could hear sirens in the background."

"Emmie! Is Emmie alright?"

"Annie, I believe everyone is alright, but I really don't know what's going on."

"Okay, let's go. I'll lock up."

Walt was at the car waiting for Annie. Finally, after checking all the windows and both doors, she came outside.

"I'm driving. Get in," he said. She didn't argue.

They drove off at a higher rate of speed than they should have, but Walt was anxious to get home. Annie was worried, too. What could have possibly happened to make Jade call Ryan like that?

Jade set Emmie down on the couch and looked at the piece of rope. How did he tie it on her little neck that quickly? She had only stepped in the house for a minute. Damn it, why did she leave Emmie in the backyard by herself? He could have killed her.

Jade's shaking got worse, and her bones felt like Jell-o. She had to sit down before she fell down. Emmie sat there with the sweetest look on her little face. Jade began to cry, and Emmie reached over and touched her cheek.

"Jade, why you crying?"

"I'm sorry, Emmie, I just got scared, that's all."

"Jade, I won't talk to the ugly man anymore. I'm sorry."

"No, no, sweetie, you didn't do anything wrong. You didn't know. It's okay."

Ryan and George came running through the front door like two bulls. "Jade?" Ryan yelled.

"We're in here," Jade answered.

Entering the living room and seeing both of them sitting on the couch, Ryan's heartbeat tripped and he gave a silent prayer of thanks. They both saw the piece of rope around Emmie's neck at the same time. They walked over to take a closer look.

"Where did this come from?" Ryan asked, touching the rope.

"The ugly man gave it to me," Emmie said.

"The ugly man? When did you see him?" Ryan asked.

"Out back, just a minute ago," Emmie answered.

"Jade, are you okay?" Ryan bent down in front of her, a very worried look on his face.

"Ryan, he could have killed her," Jade said, still crying. "I just came in for a minute."

"It's okay, she's fine." Ryan reached out and put his arm around her.

"George, why don't you take Emmie into the kitchen and get her a drink or something?"

"Come on, kiddo, let's go raid the kitchen."

They walked out of the room, and Ryan slid next to Jade on the couch, putting both arms around her and pulling her close.

~ 182 ~

"Honey, get a hold of yourself. You didn't do anything wrong. You stepped in the house for a minute."

"He could have killed her, Ryan."

"Yes, but he didn't."

"Why is he doing this? How the hell did he find her?"

"I don't know. He's really gearing up. You should see what he's done to Annie's apartment and cat."

"Cat?"

"Yeah, Wally... He slit his throat."

"What? Oh my God. Ryan, we have to do something."

"We are, Jade. The sick bastard is getting to the point where he likes to spread fear, then sit back and watch everyone fall apart. We're not going to give him that satisfaction."

Walt and Annie came in. "Jade?" he was yelling now.

"I'm in here, Dad."

"What's going on?" He grabbed hold of Jade, checking her out for injury.

"Dad, I'm fine. It's Emmie."

"What? Where's Emmie?" Annie began freaking out.

"Oh, Annie, Emmie's okay. It's just – that creep came here, and he left a piece of rope around Emmie's neck."

"What?" Annie turned white.

"Annie, Emmie is fine. She's in the kitchen with George. We need to keep calm. She doesn't know what's going on." Ryan gave her a thoughtful pat on the arm.

"Who is this son of a bitch?" Annie asked.

"We don't know his name. Emmie refers to him as the ugly man. She said James called him Mickey," Ryan explained. "Have you ever heard your sister or James mention him?"

"Mickey?" Annie was completely lost.

"Yes, have you ever heard your sister or James talk about Mickey?"

"No. Why does Emmie call him the ugly man?"

"She said he's ugly, and every time he cameound, her mommy and daddy would fight." Jade answered.

"So this is the killer?" Annie was turning whiter by the second.

"We believe so, yes," Ryan told her.

Annie ran to the kitchen. Emmie turned and saw her aunt coming through the door and squealed with delight, running to Annie and jumping on her.

"Aunt Annie!" she yelled, delighted.

"Hi, precious, how are you?" Annie set Emmie down and looked her over. The rope was still intact around the child's neck. Annie took it off, throwing it across the room.

"I'm okay. Hey, that was my new necklace! Why did you throw it?" Emmie asked.

"I'm sorry, baby, but I don't ever want to see rope around your neck! Never, do you hear me?" Annie needed to calm down.

"Annie, she's okay. You need to get control of yourself," George chastised her.

"George, how could this happen? How the hell did he get that close? Stop telling me to get control of myself and find him, damn it!"

"Hey, it's okay," he said, leaning down to touch her head like he was pacifying a child, "but you need to calm down. You're going to scare Emmie."

Annie looked at Emmie, whose big bright eyes absorbed everything that was being said and the way it was being said.

"What did I do wrong? Why are you and Jade yelling? It must be the ugly man, but what did he do? He only gave me a necklace. Mommy just said I shouldn't take things from strangers, but the ugly man's not a stranger. I know him. What did I do wrong?" She was looking so innocent.

"Sweetie, I'm sorry. You didn't do anything wrong. You know the ugly man? I don't want you to ever talk to him again, okay?" Annie had calmed down enough to handle this the right way.

"Okay, I won't."

"Em, why do you call him the ugly man?"

"Because he's ugly."

"That's not very nice, you know that, right?"

"I'm sorry, Aunt Annie. I just don't like him."

"Is he a friend of your daddy's?"

"I guess."

"Don't worry about it, sweetie, just don't go near him again, okay?"

"Jade told me that, too. Am I in trouble?"

"No, baby. We just don't want you to get hurt. So listen, no more ugly guy, okay?"

"Okay."

"Do you wanna go to the airport with me and get your nanny and your grammy?"

"Yeah, let's go!" The ugly man was forgotten.

"Not just yet, but pretty soon. They'll be coming in tonigh,t and we'll all be staying at your house." Emmie looked at Annie. Not saying a word, she turned and walked out of the room.

"What did I say?" Annie asked George.

"I don't know. Maybe she isn't ready to go home."

"Jeez, I didn't think about that. God, I'm stupid. Of course that would be very hard for her."

"Emmie!" Annie went after her. "We don't have to go to your house, honey. If you don't want to, we'll stay somewhere else."

"Really, Aunt Annie?"

"Really, sweetie."

"Goody! Because I don't wanna go back there."

"Then it's settled. We won't."

"Let's go get my nanny and grammy. Let's go now!" She pulled on Annie's shirt.

"We still have about half an hour, kiddo, so hold your horses." Annie was laughing now. Boy, Emmie looked good. Jade had indeed taken good care of her. She would have to remember to thank Jade.

"Annie, do you want something to drink?" Walt asked, walking into the dining room where Annie and Emmie were.

"That would be wonderful, Walt. Thanks."

"Me too, me too!" Emmie said.

Laughing, Walt said, "Sure thing, short stack."

Walt saw that Ryan was still sitting on the couch with Jade. She had pulled herself together somewhat, but Walt figured she needed a drink, and he wasn't getting her a soda.

"Jade, are you feeling better?" Ryan asked, looking into her eyes.

"Yes, thank you, Ryan. Your being here is a big help, but don't you think you should move over a little so Annie doesn't get upset with us?"

"Why on earth would Annie get upset?"

"Gosh, are you that ignorant?" she asked, surprised.

"What? Am I missing something here? Why on earth would Annie get upset with us?"

"You can't be serious?"

"Serious is exactly what I am. I don't understand."

"You know, Ryan, when you sleep with a woman, we don't just take it in stride like men do. It means something to us."

"Sleep with a woman?"

"Yes. You know, make love, have sex, or whatever term you call it."

"Oh, I see." Laughing, he got up and walked out of the room. Annie was just coming into the living room, and seeing the big smile on Ryan's face made her smile.

"Jade, are you alright? I know you had a heck of a scare. How did he get close enough to Emmie to put that rope around her neck?"

"Annie, I'm so sorry. I just stepped into the kitchen for a minute. I came back outside, and he had already put the rope around her neck and left."

"Jade, I'm not mad at you. I appreciate you taking such good care of Emmie. She looks great. He could've gotten to her if she had been with me, just like he did with you. I'm not blaming you; I'm just asking."

"I know, I'm sorry. This has been a horrible day from the start. I'm sorry I took Emmie and ran with her but..."

"Hey, I understand. The guys have filled me in on quite a lot of information, and actually, I'm glad you had her with you. I mean, if she had been with me at the apartment when that sicko came in, I don't know what would have happened."

"Yeah, I heard. I'm really sorry about your cat."

"Wally. I don't know why he had to kill him."

"We don't know why he had to kill anyone. This man has to be stopped, and soon."

"I'm taking Emmie with me in a few minutes to the airport. My mom and Emmie's other grandmother are both flying in."

"So you're going to take her with you?"

"Well, yes, I think she should stay with me. I'll be careful and not do anything to put her in danger, and I want you to know you can see her whenever you want to."

"Thanks, that means a lot. That kid and I have gotten quite attached to one another," Jade said with a warm smile.

"Yes, she's adorable and very easy to love. I just hope I can do right by her."

"You're gonna do great by her. It's obvious that you love her and she loves you. It's not going to be as hard as you think. Besides, now you have us too. We can be one big happy family, kinda." They both started laughing.

"I'm not sure where we're going to stay. I had planned on staying at Amy's; that's why your dad and I cleaned the place up. But Emmie doesn't want to go there."

"Hey, I have a great idea. I have a big house. Why don't you guys come and stay with me for a while? Let all this calm down."

"Jade, that's sweet. Your dad even offered his house, but I just don't feel right about that."

"Why not? It's perfect."

"It's a lot to ask of someone to open their home to four people they're not used to and don't know all that well, not to mention a huge dog."

"Okay, first of all, you didn't ask, and second of all, I know you and Emmie."

"Can I call you after talking to Mom?"

"You bet. I'll be here for a while, then if I leave, Dad can give you my number."

"You've been great. All of you have. I don't know how to thank you all for all that you've done." The tears were beginning to swim in Annie's eyes yet again. Jade squeezed her hand.

Emmie and Harry were running around the living room. Harry was tugging on her shirt, and Emmie trying to pull away. They were making a racket.

"Emmie, calm down. You and Harry need to respect Walt's house. This is not the way to act, young lady," Annie chastised.

"I'm sorry, Aunt Annie. We're just having fun. Harry likes to play tug-of-war with me because I'm strong." She held her little arm up, showing her little bicep.

Ryan and George sauntered into the room. The sight of Emmie and Harry made them laugh. Ryan noticed how chummy Jade and Annie appeared to be getting. Good, he thought, maybe now she'll find out we didn't sleep together.

Walt walked in with drinks for everyone. Handing the Pepsi to Annie and a smaller glass of Pepsi to Emmie, he smiled. Then he went to Jade and, handing her a smaller glass with a couple ice cubes and some amber liquid, said, "Drink this, and don't argue with me."

Jade took the glass and sniffed it, then she gave her dad a look that said 'yuck'. She wrinkled her nose and took a small drink. Everyone laughed when she started coughing and choking. Annie leaned over and patted her back, smiling.

"I would be drinking something stronger, too, if I didn't have to drive to the airport," she said.

"The airport! I sure am glad you mentioned that, Annie." George walked over to Annie and whispered in her ear, "Come to the kitchen for a minute." She followed him to the kitchen.

"What is it?" She knew he was concerned about something.

"The airport may be a problem we need to talk about. Do you have a minute?"

"Sure."

"Annie, the killer left you another couple messages on your answering machine. Your mother left a couple, too. But the thing is, if he listened to the messages, or if he was there when your mom called, then he knows her flight number, the time she's coming in, and also the info for Mrs. Linderhoff's flight. We don't think it's a good idea for you to go alone."

"What do you want me to do?"

"Well, we were going to talk to the Captain about some extra men, but time has gotten away from us, so Ryan and I want to go with you to the airport."

"Oh."

"We'll be out of the way. We don't want him to know we're there."

"Okay."

"We want you and Emmie to go just as planned. Emmie doesn't even need to know we're there. Just go about your business as if we weren't tagging along. We'll be in our car, just keeping a watch for you."

"Alright, if that's what you and Ryan want to do, then I don't have a problem with it."

"Also, he knows your mom and Mrs. Linderhoff are staying at your sister's place and that your mom wants you to think about staying there, too."

"I didn't tell mom I was thinking about that."

"No. One of her messages said she wants you to think about it."

"Oh, so now what?"

"It's not a good idea, that's all."

"Emmie doesn't want to stay there."

"Good."

"I don't know where we're going to stay. Both Walt and Jade have offered their homes to us."

"Yeah, they're good people. You should consider staying here and talking Jade into it, too."

"I guess there's safety in numbers, huh?"

"Yep. Hell of an idea that all of you should stay here. Walt?" George yelled from the kitchen.

"What?" Walt asked as George came flying into the room. He moved fast to be as big a man as he was. It was amazing to watch.

"I think you should keep everyone here. That was a good idea. It'll make our job easier," he said, slapping Walt on the back.

"What? I don't know what you're talking about." Confusion was plain on Walt's face.

"Having Annie and her family, as well as Jade, stay here: great idea," he said as he slapped Walt on the back yet again.

"Oh, yeah, it was, but Annie said no thanks."

"She's reconsidered."

"Good. I'll get the spare rooms made up while you're at the airport then, Annie."

"Walt, you're too nice. Don't bother. We can do that when we get back; you've done enough."

"It's no problem. I'm glad to do it, but you better get going," he said, looking at his watch.

"You're right, Walt." Turning, she asked George, "Are you and Ryan ready?"

"We're right behind you."

"Emmie, come on, honey, we're off to the airport."

"Can Harry come?"

"Uh..."

"Annie, you can leave Harry here with us."

"Thanks, Walt, you're a lifesaver."

Emmie walked over and kissed Harry on the nose. "You be good boy," she said.

~

After they left, the house was very quiet. Even Harry went over by the fireplace and lay on the floor to sleep. Jade was kicked back on the sofa, and Walt was laid out in a recliner chair.

"Ah, the peace and quiet," Walt mused.

"Yep, don't get used to it, Dad. Sounds like you're gonna have a houseful," she said, giggling.

"It will be great, Jade. I'm glad you're staying, too."

"No, Dad, I'm not. I plan to go home."

"No, you're not. George says you need to stay here, too."

"I'm sorry, but he isn't my boss, and I'm ready to go home."

"Please stay, Jade. I won't have to worry about you if you're here."

"Dad, I have things I need to do. I have a job to prepare for."

"That can wait. You're not safe at home."

"I can't get my visions clear with all the commotion of everyone being around."

"You'll have your own bedroom. Go lock yourself in and have visions all day. I don't care. I want you here!"

"Let's just sit here and relax, and I'll think about it, okay?"

"Good enough." He knew he had her now.

They both just kicked back and enjoyed the quiet for a while. Walt decided he would rest for a few minutes before going upstairs and getting the guest rooms and bathrooms ready.

Jade knew she needed to try and get a better understanding of her vision she had had earlier, but right now, she just wanted to relax.

17

RYAN and George were staying about four cars behind Annie's car. They didn't want anyone to know they were traveling with her. Ryan was thinking about his short conversation with Jade concerning women and sex. He wanted to laugh out loud, but then he would have to explain to George what was amusing him. She truly believed he had slept with Annie. He decided he would let her stew for a while longer.

George was trying to figure out how the killer knew where Emmie was. "How did he find her to put that rope around her neck? What message is he trying to send to us? He could have taken her right then if that had been his intention," he reasoned.

"I know, it doesn't make sense. I'm thinking maybe we should head back to the station and talk to the drug guys. Fill the captain in on everything that's happened, except the visions, and see what his take is on all this. After we get them back to Walt's safely."

Ryan's cell phone rang. He looked at the number but didn't recognize it. "Detective Douglas," he answered.

"Hey, detective, this is Vic."

"Hi, Vic, what'd you guys find?"

"Actually, we lifted some pretty good prints. This guy didn't bother with hiding his identity. The food wrapper's where we got them. I used magnetic powder, and it was easy to get the prints from the papers."

"Great, did you run the prints through AFIS?"

"No, not yet. We just got back to the station, and I thought I'd call you and let you know we found something to work with. I bagged the cat like Detective Dunleavy asked, and I even cleaned up the blood. I don't usually do that, but I got the feeling this was something special to you guys."

"Damn, guy, thanks. That was above and beyond, and we both appreciate that. Let me know if I can do anything for you."

"Yep, will do. Meanwhile, I'll get these prints running and see if we can come up with anything."

"Good deal. We'll be on our way to the station shortly; just let me know what, if anything, you get."

"Alright, see you soon."

"Yeah, later, Vic, and thanks."

"Well, what did they find?" George was sitting on the edge of his seat.

"They got some good prints. He said he's going to run them through AFIS for us."

"Really?" George was surprised. This guy had been on top of his game. Why leave prints?

"Yeah, he said the idiot didn't worry about prints on the food wrappers."

"Hmmm. Maybe we'll know who he is tonight. This airport is pretty busy...Do you think we should go inside to keep a better eye on the girls?"

"Yeah, I do. With this crowd, it's going to be too hard to keep a good lookout. Annie is parking over there, and we'll go over here." He pointed in the opposite direction.

"Right, don't get too close to them."

"I won't. Oh, and Vic said he cleaned the blood up, too. We owe him, you know."

"Man, that was above and beyond."

"That's what I said. He figured it was personal for us."

They parked and went in the terminal, going in a different door than Annie and Emmie. Annie was looking around and didn't notice them. She looked like she was looking for the killer, not Ryan and George. Her face showed the fear that George knew she was feeling, but he had the feeling that she was looking for them. He wanted to put her mind at ease, but he couldn't get her attention without drawing attention to himself and Ryan. They didn't want anyone to know they were there with her. They walked to the gate area and waited in the crowd. Annie was constantly looking around her.

Emmie stood there with an excited look on her face, holding Annie's hand. It had been a while since she had seen either one of her grandmothers. Emmie loved her nanny Nora; she was funny. When she visited, they would have tea parties and play a lot. Grammy Donna was fun, too, just not as much fun as nanny Nora. Emmie wondered if she would have to move and live with one of her grandmothers. She hoped not. She wanted to stay here with her Aunt Annie and Jade. Emmie knew there was something special about Jade; she just didn't know what it was. She was a smart kid for six years old.

The plane was already on the ground, and the group was excitedly awaiting their loved ones. Ryan and George were acting like they were waiting for someone to come off the plane, but they were nonchalantly watching the crowd. They knew he wasn't a very big guy and that he had a tattoo on his right hand, but that was all they knew about him - not a lot to go on.

"As soon as Annie gets both women and walks back to her car, we'll get her attention and let her know we'll follow them to Walt's, but then we have to go to the station and get some information on this case," Ryan told George quietly.

"Yeah we have a lot to look up and run by the Captain. Do you think we should call and ask him to hang out for a while?"

"No, he always works late. He'll be there," Ryan said knowingly.

They stood watching, not seeing anyone that seemed out of place. Would he really come to the airport? Probably not; it was way too public. He could be sitting in his car waiting to follow them.

"Maybe we should be in the parking lot." Ryan felt uneasy.

"I was just thinking the same thing. But if we go out there, walking around and looking in cars, he'll take off for sure if he's here."

"Maybe. Did he get a good look at you last night?" George asked hopefully, but knew the answer.

"No, I don't think he saw me at all, but then we don't know how long he was in that apartment next door."

"That's okay. He's the one being hunted, and we're the hunters," Ryan said with a gleam in his eyes.

"I like that idea. He's gonna get caught, too."

"Yep, it's just a matter of time."

"Here they come. Keep your eyes open." George didn't have to stand on tiptoe; he could look well over the heads of the people lingering around them.

They watched every person that came out and who they were meeting. They watched Annie greet her mom. Mrs. Armstrong hugged Annie, then bent down and picked Emmie up, hugging her tightly and kissing her cheek.

"Wait just a minute. Give them time to get a little ways away," George said, watching them over the crowd of people lingering.

"They're supposed to go get a bite to eat. We could get Annie's attention that way. We'll just walk in there and sit down, letting her see us."

"Yeah, but we don't want Emmie to come over to us or yell to us."

"Hopefully, Annie will have already had a talk with her about that." Ryan felt sure Annie would take care of that so Emmie wouldn't point or wave at them.

~

Annie, her mom, and Emmie walked to the baggage claim area. Annie was talking to her mom and keeping a tight hold on Emmie's hand. They looked like a typical family catching up on news.

"Aunt Annie, let go of me," they heard Emmie say.

"Why, Emmie? Where do you want to go?"

"I want to stand next to Nanny."

Annie bent down and quietly talked to Emmie. "Ryan and George are here, but we have to pretend we don't know them," she whispered.

"Why?"

"Because, honey, we don't know the man that killed your mommy and daddy, and he may try to hurt us. So we have our own police officers to protect us, but we don't want the bad man to know they're here, okay?"

"Aunt Annie, did the ugly man kill my mommy and daddy?" The look on her little face was heartbreaking.

Ms. Armstrong stood there watching Annie deal with the child. Annie looked like a pro. It made Ms. Armstrong feel proud.

"We think he did, but we don't know for sure yet. That's why I don't want you talking to him or going near him."

"I'll stay right here. I just want to hold Nanny's hand."

"Okay, sweetie." Annie released Emmie's hand and stood up straight.

Emmie walked over to her grandmother and reached up to take her hand. Then Emmie started looking for Ryan and George. She liked them. This was kind of a game to her; it was like they were playing hide-and-seek because she didn't know where they were. She kept looking and sometimes standing on her tiptoes.

Ryan and George were watching her, but she couldn't even see them. They stood off to the side of everyone, talking quietly, but never allowing the three out of their sight. The baggage claim area was swarming with people. Everyone looked normal, but then Ryan knew looks could be deceiving. He stood there sizing everyone up. Thoughts of Jade kept trying to creep in, but he kept them at bay. The luggage began to drop onto the conveyor belt, and people grabbed theirs as it came around. Ryan and George were watching for someone that wasn't interested in luggage. Too many people to keep an eye on, Ryan thought. They stood there, watching, waiting. Ready.

~

Walt looked over and found Jade sound asleep. He got up and went up the stairs to get the rooms prepared. He walked down the hallway to the linen closet, taking out a set of sheets, pillows, pillow cases, blanket, and comforter.

Walking into the first guest room, he stopped, looked around the room, and tried to decide if he should make up Jade's room also. He set the bedding on the trunk at the end of the bed, then went back to the linen closet to get the bedding for the other guest room. That room had twin beds in it. He should have asked Annie if she and Emmie wanted the big bed or the twin beds. It didn't matter; he'd let them decide that once everyone was here.

Taking the bedding into the room, he set it on the dresser. He looked around that room and then reached for the first twin bed's set of sheets. Making the beds up quickly, he remembered he needed to get fresh towels for the bathrooms. He finished the rooms and then took care of the bathrooms.

Going downstairs again, he was quiet, not wanting to wake Jade. He forgot he was going to make her bed up, too, and turned to go back up stairs.

Jade was awake already, but Walt didn't know that. She lay there thinking about going upstairs to help her dad. Should she stay here or go home? She could go to her room to get in touch with her visions, so that wasn't an excuse to go home. She would be safer here. She could be with Emmie if she stayed here. Maybe she should start separating herself from Emmie, though, she thought. She had become too attached to the child. But no, Annie had said she could see her anytime she wanted to.

Jade got up and went upstairs; noticing that the guest rooms were already finished, she went to her room. Walt was there putting sheets on the bed.

"Dad, I can do this; you've done enough already."

"It's going to be so nice to have you home again."

"It's just temporary, but yeah, it'll be nice for me, too."

"This house will seem alive again. It was meant to have children in it. You know I keep waiting for you to get married and settle down, giving me some grandbabies."

"I know. Someday, hopefully."

"Don't rush it, honey. I don't mean to put pressure on you. I'm just a silly old man talking, that's all."

"You're not a silly old man. I would love to get married and have kids."

"Maybe you and Ryan..."

"No, it's Annie and Ryan, Dad."

"Jade, Ryan and Annie aren't an item."

"He slept with her. That makes them an item."

"You don't know that. You're just assuming."

"Well, when he and I talked earlier, he didn't deny it."

"Did he admit it?"

"Well, no..."

"There you go, then."

"I don't have time to worry about that right now, Dad. Emmie is the most important worry I have."

"Don't worry about it. Just let it happen."

"Yeah, I agree. Don't worry about it." Her smile was strained.

"Honey, really, I believe you and Ryan like each other, and that's a good start."

"Yeah, sure, we'll see, Dad." She walked out of her room and went to the guest bathroom. She was going to put fresh towels and soap in there, but it was already done. The glass doors of the shower were sparkling clear. The mirror looked freshly cleaned. The royal blue bath towels hanging on the wall racks matched perfectly with the hand towel on the ring. There was plenty of toilet paper. She opened the top sink drawer and found brand new toothbrushes and toothpaste, as well as floss, lying neatly inside. She closed the drawer and opened the next one. Inside this drawer were small bottles of lotion and face creams. Jade wondered how Walt knew what lotion and creams to buy. She shook her head and walked out.

Going to the first guest room, she stood in the doorway and took in the color scheme. A pretty lilac lacy comforter rested on the bed. The curtains were the same lilac with a deeper purple running through them. The bed was a dark cherry wood sleigh bed with a matching dresser, mirror, and chest of drawers. This was a pretty room.

She went out and walked to the other guest room. This room was more for a child. The twin beds had matching sage green comforters with two chests of drawers. The small vanity in the corner was a place Jade had spent much time as a child, trying out different shades of eye shadow, new hairstyles, and her mother's costume jewelry. She could remember sitting for hours playing at that vanity. Walt always knew where to find her.

He'd offered to give her the vanity when she got her own place, but she declined, saying it wouldn't be the same if not in her childhood home. She tried to picture her own little girl sitting there playing one day. Jade could almost see her. Sighing, she walked back to her bedroom, where Walt was still making the bed.

"Where did you go?" he asked.

"I was just doing a walk-through. I was going to help you, but you seem to have everything under control."

"Yeah, I started while you were asleep."

Jade stood there watching her dad. He was in his fifties now and still in great shape. She never took the time to worry about his health or what she would do if he died. Now with Emmie losing both of her parents, Jade began to think what she would do if Walt up and died on her. She couldn't imagine life without him. He had always been there for her.

She missed her mother, but Walt was such a good and loving father that she never wanted for anything physically or emotionally. Jade shook the thoughts from her mind and watched as Walt finished the room. She realized what a good-looking man her father was. He was tall and still slim. He stood six feet and one inch, and he had silvering hair with dark skin. It was like he had a perpetual tan. He had the same brown eyes as Jade and a perfect smile. He was strong and protective, always there. She wanted a man just like her dad.

She wondered why he never remarried and decided she would ask him sometime. Walt was finished. He asked if she was ready to go back downstairs, and she smiled and nodded. They walked down the stairs with their arms around each other. Walt had always provided a good home for Jade, and she had nothing but good memories. She only hoped she could do half as good for her own children one day.

"Jade, how do you think the killer found Emmie today?" he wondered.

"I don't know. I tried to keep a close eye out for anyone that could be following us."

"You know, if he is half as ugly as Emmie makes out, then he should stick out like a sore thumb."

"Yeah, maybe I should quit looking for someone ugly and start looking for someone mean."

"That's not a bad idea. Sometimes children mistake mean for ugly."

They stopped talking and both began thinking through that thought. Ugly could mean: not nice looking, wicked, mean...anything a child related to not being nice. How many times had they heard a parent tell their child 'don't be ugly'?

~

Ryan and George were sitting in a small diner at the airport, drinking coffee and appearing to have a deep conversation with someone who didn't know any better. Annie, her mom, and

Emmie sat across the diner, eating dinner. Emmie appeared elated to have her grandmother there. She would smile and laugh when someone would say something to her. She looked as if she didn't have a care in the world. Annie, on the other hand, looked as if she carried the weight of the world on her shoulders.

Ms. Armstrong was a small woman with dark hair and a pretty smile. She had kind eyes. They seemed to twinkle when she looked at her daughter or granddaughter. The three made a pretty sight. You could tell they were all related.

Ryan wondered what Mrs. Linderhoff would look like. They didn't have too much time left to wait for her; she would be there soon. He was sure that the killer was lurking somewhere close, so he kept looking around inconspicuously but not seeing anyone that looked suspicious.

George watched Ryan deep in thought and assumed he was thinking about Jade again. It did his heart good to know the two would be a good match. He had always hoped his partner would find a good woman, and in his opinion, they just didn't come any better than Jade Hamilton.

The group across the diner got up and walked by them. Emmie smiled at Ryan and waved her little hand hello. Both Ryan and George smiled back at her. After the three exited the diner, Ryan and George paid their bill and followed.

Emmie was walking between Annie and her grandma, holding both their hands. Ryan didn't know how much Annie could tell her mom with Emmie sitting there, but apparently, she was able to tell her enough. They were being very protective of Emmie.

Ms. Armstrong pulled a suitcase behind her on wheels. The suitcase was medium size, and Ryan figured that meant that Ms. Armstrong did not plan on staying long.

"Ryan, let's just go to the car and wait on them."

"Are you getting tired?"

"No, I want to get a look at the parking lot."

"Okay, let's roll."

They walked out, looking in all directions. Taking their time, they made their way to their car. No one appeared to be sitting in any of the vehicles they passed or just standing around. What a waste of time, George was thinking. Soon they would go to the station, and then they could begin collecting the information they needed. The drug thing was coming together for them. He thought they were onto something with the pill idea. They should find out what personal effects Emmie had with her when Jade took her. If she had anything, then it was possible James gave her the drugs. What didn't make sense was that surely James knew he was putting her in danger by doing that. Then again, maybe he thought he would be there to protect her. George thought about it, then asked, "Do you believe James would have put the drugs in something he gave to Emmie, thinking he would have been around to protect his little girl?"

"Yeah, right now, I think anything is possible. But what I can't figure out is why he would give it to Emmie instead of hiding the stuff in a good place."

"He might not have realized what a mistake he had made until it was too late."

"Whatever. There is no way you can convince me that he didn't know he was playing a deadly game, taking the drugs and cheating his supplier."

"Well, you know these people aren't in jail and prison because they're intelligent," George said, laughing.

"Yeah, but don't you think he would have wanted to keep his family out of it?"

"Of course that's what I want to think, but maybe he was a selfish bastard!"

"From the sounds of it, he didn't do a lot for Amy or Emmie. Maybe the drugs blurred his vision and thoughts because it appears to me he had a great little family. Annie talks like Amy did everything for Emmie, and James wasn't bothered by the fact that he didn't provide a good life for them."

"Yeah, what a shame. Emmie is a great kid, and if Amy was anything like her sister, then she had to be pretty damn great herself." George was shaking his head. "What a waste it all is," he said.

They sat there quietly for a few minutes, just looking around the area and trying to keep an eye on the building, waiting for Annie and her family to come out. Each man tried but wasn't able to understand someone like James, someone who appeared to have everything but didn't give a damn. How could any man have had a family like that and not taken good care of them?

Neither of them would have been surprised to know they were thinking pretty much the same thing.

Ryan decided to get out of the car and pretend to stretch his legs. Looking around the parking garage and the street in front of the airline terminal, he searched for the killer.

George knew Ryan was getting a good look outside the vehicle, so he sat there, still stewing in his thoughts about James. He realized that life wasn't fair when it came to who was blessed with children. He and Doris would have been great parents, but they weren't given the chance. Sure, Amy was a good mom by all accounts, except her taste in a chosen father for her children. Life had too many unfair ideas that made absolutely no sense to George. Of course, he gave up trying to figure that out a long time ago. Still, he didn't have to accept this kind of thing. The door opened and Ryan got back in.

"There they are. Annie spotted me, and I let her know we were going to follow them," he said, using the same hand signal he used to give information to Annie.

"Great. Let's get moving. We still have a lot to do tonight." George was trying to get his anger under control. Every time he thought about children being given to worthless, undeserving people, he got angry.

Ryan looked over at his partner, not understanding the sudden anger. He figured it was due to the killer not showing up. They had hoped to catch him here.

~

Pulling out of the airport, Annie felt the need for general conversation, so she asked, "Mrs. Linderhoff, did you have any difficulties getting here?" She had been quiet and didn't want Donna to think she was angry with her for any reason. They all had a hard time to get through, and it would be so much easier if they were considerate of each other.

"No, everything has gone pretty smoothly so far, considering," Donna said.

"We have a tough time coming up, and we'll help each other through this, Donna," Nora said.

"Yes, it will be hell. But just knowing our children are gone is hell." Donna started to tear up.

"Grammy?" Emmie was sitting in the rear with Donna.

"Yes, baby?" Donna tried to control the tears as she looked at Emmie.

"Don't cry, Grammy." Emmie leaned over to hug her grandmother. The seatbelt didn't allow a lot of movement, but she did her best. They all laughed. Emmie, the one who lost the most, was the one worrying about the adults. Just like her mom, Nora thought.

Annie turned the music up, and the car got quiet, except for the tunes on the radio. No talking was probably better right now, she thought. As she drove, she watched for Ryan and George. She could see them about three cars behind hers. She wondered who was in those three cars that separated them. Did she miss anything she should have seen? She wished she had paid better attention since leaving the airport. She wasn't really thinking about the killer following, since she knew Ryan and George were there to protect them.

Plus, there was the excitement of her mom and Donna being here. Well,it would be excitement if it were for a different reason. Her sister was gone, and the idea still hadn't hit her completely yet. She knew it and was trying to understand, but she could not fathom the entire situation. She knew she needed to explain where they were staying and why, so she decided she might as well get on with that.

"Mom, Donna, I forgot to tell you. We won't be staying at Amy and James' house," she began.

"Why not, Annie?" Her mom asked with a frown puckering her forehead.

"Annie, honey, I don't understand. That's where I want to stay," Donna said.

"I know, but just hear me out. Emmie, honey, I'm sorry, but you're going to hear things I had hoped you wouldn't have to hear," Annie said, looking at Emmie through the rearview mirror.

"Annie, what is it? What's going on?" her mom asked.

"To start with, the killer broke into my apartment last night and then again today. He killed my cat today." She began to tear up but kept explaining. "While I was at Amy's today trying to straighten up for you two, the police were at my apartment. Apparently, Mom, you left both Donna's flight information and yours on my answering machine, as well as the fact that you were staying at Amy's and wanted me to also. The killer was at my apartment, and the police don't know if he was there when you called. He may have that information." Annie watched the expressions on both her mom's and Donna's faces as she explained. "The police don't want us to stay there now for fear the killer will try something. We have some really great new friends, and they have offered all of us a place to stay while we try to sort all this out and take care of the funeral and such."

"What friends?" Donna asked.

"Jade and her dad Walt have offered to let us stay with them. Walt has this beautiful Victorian home with plenty of room for all of us. I have accepted on behalf of the two of you, as well as Emmie and I. The police think this is the best idea for now." She stopped and waited for comments.

"Annie, don't you think that's asking too much of these people?" her mom asked.

"At first I did, but Walt insists it isn't. Jade and Emmie have gotten pretty close, and I think the more support Emmie has, the easier this is going to be for her," Annie stated.

"The house is so big, and Walt, he's very nice," Emmie said.

Donna patted Emmie's knee and smiled. No one said anything else. They rode in silence as Nora and Donna each thought it out. Annie was glad no one really put up too much of an argument, as she was tired and really didn't want to argue.

18

WALT was sipping on a soda, and Jade was sipping on the drink he'd brought her earlier, a bit watered down, but that was good. Both were still enjoying the quiet that was going to end soon. Harry was sitting next to Walt's chair. Walt rubbed Harry's head absently while sipping on his soda. The house was very quiet, no TV or radio. There was no talking, no barking. Just blissful quiet. They sat there in their own thoughts when the loud noise and shattering glass caught their attention. Harry ran to the kitchen barking, and Walt grabbed Jade by the arm, stopping her from running to the kitchen.

"No, stay here," he commanded.

"Dad, wait!" Jade didn't want him to go alone.

Walt went to the hallway closet opened the door and pulled a Colt .45 off the shelf. Jade stopped dead in her tracks, looking at the weapon with surprise on her face. "When did you start keeping a gun in the house?" she asked him.

Pulling the slide back and making sure a bullet was in the chamber, he answered "I've always had one; you just didn't know about it." He started for the kitchen, Jade right behind him. Walt cautiously walked into the kitchen and looked around. The picture window behind the table was completely shattered. The glass lay everywhere. On the table was a rock with paper wrapped around it. Walt went to get the rock when Jade stopped him.

"Dad, don't touch that!" she yelled.

"What?" Walt turned to look at her, his arm out stretched toward the rock.

"Prints, Dad. Maybe they can get prints off that."

"Damn it, you're right, sweetheart. Man, this guy is pissing me off. You stay here. I'm going to look around outside." Walt went to the door.

Jade picked up the telephone and dialed Ryan.

"Detective Douglas," his usual answer rang in her ears.

"Ryan, Dad just had a rock thrown through the kitchen window," Jade practically yelled in the phone.

"Are you guys alright?" Ryan was shaken to the core by the fear he could hear in her voice.

"Yeah we were in the living room when it happened. Dad's outside looking around now."

"Did you say a rock?"

"Yes, and it's got paper wrapped around it. I think it's a note."

"Have you or Walt touched it?"

"No, of course not."

"Good, don't. We're on our way back there now."

"Dad's outside, Ryan. I'm really worried about him. He has a gun, and I didn't even know he had one."

"That's good, Jade. He should have a gun. Don't worry about your dad; he knows what he's doing."

"I know, just hurry, Ryan!" Jade said and hung up the phone.

Going to the door, she looked for Walt; not seeing him, she ventured out on the back porch. Straining to see in the dark, she looked around; spotting him by the back fence, she went out there.

"Do you see him?" she asked.

"No, he's long gone. Damn, I don't know how or even why he knows about us." Walt was angry. He felt like he should have been on his toes and not let his guard down.

"He must have followed me earlier. I just don't know how. I was so careful." Jade was apologetic.

"Honey, you did what you could. Don't worry, he doesn't want to come here messing around with my girls. I'll shoot him." Walt said this with finality, realizing he meant it.

"I called Ryan. They're on their way back. He said not to touch anything."

"Alright, come on, let's get back inside."

They went in the back door. Glass was everywhere. Walt and Jade stood there looking around. The rock was big enough to take the entire picture window out. There was a big gouge in the table where the rock had landed. Walt was past anger; he was enraged. That table had been in his family for years. His mother gave it to him, and he didn't know how long she had had the table before that. He knew it was at least fifty years old. He could remember eating his meals as a child at that table. He would have to have the damage fixed.

They walked into the hallway leading to the living room and found the front door wide open. Walt stopped Jade. "Stay here!" he said.

Jade backed up; standing with her back against the wall, she watched Walt move toward the door. "Dad, is he here?" she whispered.

"I don't know. Stay there and let me check the house out," he said quietly.

Walt walked to the door and closed it. He looked around the living room and in the closet, then went up the stairs. Jade stood quietly, listening. She could hear the floorboards squeak occasionally as Walt walked around upstairs. She kept watch on the rear stairs in the kitchen.

What would she do if the killer came flying down those stairs? Her mind was racing. Should she go get a kitchen knife? No, that would put her right in his path if he came down. She would just stay right here where her dad told her to stay. She hated girls in horror movies that went searching through dark houses or tried to act brave and ended up doing something really stupid. She waited.

Ryan filled George in on the broken window and told him about Walt's gun.

"Good for him," George said.

"Yeah, that's pretty much what I told Jade. She seemed really upset that Walt even had a gun."

"I'm glad he does. So many people are opposed to having one in their home, not realizing the bad guy always has one. You just need to be responsible, and then there's no reason you shouldn't have one. I just hope he's careful with it," George said finally.

"He will be. If Walt is anything, it's careful and responsible. I just wish Annie would pick her speed up a little bit."

"We're not that far away now. We'll be there in a minute."

"I know. I just hate Jade being scared, and she sounded terrified."

~

Annie, of course, had no idea what had happened. They were still enjoying the tunes and really not talking a lot. She couldn't wait for her mom to meet Walt. He was such a nice man. Annie looked in the mirror at Emmie; she was dozing, and her little head was hanging in a painful looking way.

"Donna, could you move Emmie a little so she's leaning on you? I'm afraid she'll get a sore neck, the way she's holding her head," Annie said.

"Oh my goodness, I'm sorry, I didn't even know she went to sleep. Here, baby," Donna said to Emmie as she moved her slightly. Emmie didn't even open her eyes.

The poor child she has had so much going on she must be completely worn out, Annie thought as she watched in the mirror. Donna got Emmie readjusted and then smiled at Annie. Nora was thinking about Emmie and wondering if Annie was ready to raise a child. She figured that Emmie would go with Annie, no question. But they really hadn't discussed that. She wondered if Donna would want Emmie. Nora knew she herself was too old and in no way prepared to take Emmie home with her. Of course, she would if it came to that, but... This family had so much they needed to work through, and she only hoped that Donna and Annie would cooperate with her. She sat there mentally making note of all that needed to be done.

Of course they needed to catch the killer before anyone would feel safe again, but that was what the police were supposed to take care of. She would try to guide Annie on the rest.

"We're here," Annie said, parking the car.

"Wow, this is a really nice, upscale neighborhood!" Nora said, looking around.

"Yes, it is. Your friends must be wealthy," Donna commented.

"I don't know about all that. I do know they're caring and giving people. They're not at all snobby," Annie said, shutting off the engine. She could see Ryan parking down the street a ways.

~

Jade was still standing in the hallway when she saw Walt come down the back stairs. Dad, did he go up stairs?" she asked, fear showing in every line of her face.

"No, I don't think so. I think he's playing with us." Walt walked back to the front of the house, opening the front door he peered out.

Annie got out of the car and waved at Walt. He noticed now that everyone was back. He waved to her, then turned to Jade. "They're here," he said.

Jade looked out. Annie was getting Emmie out of the back seat. Ryan and George were helping with the luggage. She couldn't hear what they were saying.

"Annie, before we go in, I should tell you the suspect was here while we were at the airport," George told her.

"What?" Annie spun around to look at George. "He was here?"

"Yeah, Jade called Ryan and said something about a rock being thrown through the kitchen window. We need everyone to stay calm. We're going to help get everyone and the luggage into the house, then take a look around," he said. "Just act normal and don't overreact."

Annie just nodded her head and started up the side walk to the porch with Emmie still half asleep in her arms.

Walt stood on the porch, the gun in his hand. He was smiling and trying to keep everyone at ease. Jade was standing next to him.

Annie walked up on the porch, and Jade reached her arms out to take Emmie. Annie gladly handed her over. Her arms were beginning to feel like lead. Jade hugged Emmie tightly to her;

squirming slightly, the girl stayed asleep. Jade walked into the house with her and was going into the sitting room to lay her on the small settee when Annie came in behind her.

"Jade, what happened while we were gone?"

Laying Emmie down, Jade turned toward Annie, putting a finger to her lips and pointing to the door. Once they were out of the room Jade explained what happened.

"Oh my God!" Annie exclaimed.

"My dad has a gun that I didn't even know he had. He checked the house and the outside area thoroughly," Jade said.

"Walt keeps a gun in the house?" Annie asked, surprised.

"Yeah, he still has it in his hand. Didn't you see it?" Jade was surprised.

"No, I was so thankful to hand Emmie over to you, I didn't notice anything else."

"Well, come on, let's go make sure everyone's inside and see what's going on," Jade suggested. They walked toward the living room where everyone was standing around. Walt and Nora had begun introducing everyone, and the conversation was becoming a whirlwind.

"Walt, Ryan and I are going to look at that window and the rock. Can you keep everyone in here for a while?" George was saying as the girls entered the room.

"Sure, you go ahead." Walt turned back to talk to Nora. George and Ryan walked out of the room, heading for the kitchen.

"Walt, it was very considerate of you to open your home to all of us," Nora said.

"It is my pleasure. I love having the house full; I'm just sorry for the reason for it. Ladies, please accept my sincere sorrow for your losses," Walt said as he touched Nora's hand.

"Ladies, this is my daughter Jade." He turned, pulling Jade in the room. "Jade, this is Nora Armstrong and Donna Linderhoff," he said, stepping back to clear a path of sight between all the women.

Walt was surprised by Nora's loveliness. She was a very attractive woman. He didn't realize how lonely he had been until now. What a time to be thinking about that, he thought.

"Jade, I was just telling your father how grateful we are to you both," Nora said, walking over to Jade.

Jade stepped around her dad, and instead of taking the outstretched hand Nora offered, she impulsively grabbed her into a hug. "My dad is a very thoughtful person, Ms. Armstrong, and I know he is glad to do this for you and your family," Jade said as the two continued to hug each other.

"Jade, this is Donna Linderhoff, James' mom," Nora said, stepping back.

"Mrs. Linderhoff, we are glad to have you here," Jade said as she stepped toward the woman who had remained very quiet since arriving.

"It's a pleasure to meet you," Donna said as she lightly hugged Jade.

"Please, everyone, have a seat. What can I get you to drink?" Walt asked, looking at each woman individually.

George and Ryan were looking at the window glass laying everywhere and the rock in the middle of the table.

"I'll go get gloves out of my car again. Do you want a pair, too?" Ryan asked, looking at George. He was feeling like an errand boy, always running to the car for this that or whatever.

"No, I don't need any," George said, shaking his head at this newest incident.

Ryan turned and walked out, almost running into Walt in the hallway. "Whoa, sorry," he said.

"Hey." Walt stopped short. "Is it alright if I go in and get the ladies some drinks?"

"Sure, just don't touch the rock," Ryan said, shaking his head and smiling.

"No problem." Walt continued into the kitchen and Ryan to the front door.

"Hey, George, Ryan said I could come in and get drinks for the ladies."

"Sure, no problemo," George smarted off.

"Can you believe this shit?" he said to George, pointing to the rock on the table.

"No. We thought he would be at the airport. We're really sorry about all this, man."

"It's not your fault. I just want to get my hands on this asshole. The table makes me angrier than the window. That table belonged to my mother."

"Man, I'm sorry, Walt. We'll catch this son of a bitch one way or another." George meant dead or alive. Frankly, it didn't matter much either way to him.

"I know. Trust me, I would like to be the one to get him first." Walt smiled at the thought. "Oh, well shit, I better get those drinks. Are you all going to read that note?"

"Yeah, Ryan just went to the car to get some gloves."

"Great. If you don't mind, I'd like to know what it says."

"We'll see, Walt. I'll let you know."

"Thanks." Walt started pouring soda into glasses of ice; he placed all the glasses on a tray and walked back to the living room. He was wondering what kind of message was left by the killer this time. Walt wasn't afraid; he was actually anxious to catch the guy. He was tired of worrying about Jade, Annie, and Emmie. Now he had two more females to worry about.

Walking first to Nora, he handed her a glass, then to each of the others while taking one glass for himself as he sat down in his recliner.

"Walt, you are quite the gracious host," Nora said, taking a sip of her soda.

"With guests like you, it's easy and pleasurable," Walt said, smiling at Nora.

Jade and Annie sat there, both just looking at the two and then at each other. Jade smiled and winked at Annie; Annie smiled back then turned her head.

Ryan poked his head into the living room on his way back into the kitchen. "Everyone doing alright?" he asked in general, but he was staring at Jade.

"Yeah, we're just hanging out, waiting on you guys to tell us what that note said," Walt said.

"We should know here in a minute or so. Will let you know, if we can, what it says," he said, once again looking at Jade. Jade just smiled at him, so he smiled and winked at her, and then he was gone. Annie noticed the smile and wink as she looked over at Jade.

"Is there something going on there I need to know about?" Annie asked with a smile on her own face.

"No, he's all yours," Jade replied.

"What?" Annie asked, looking surprised.

"I won't get in your way, Annie. I know Ryan and you have a thing, and I think that's great," Jade said.

"A thing?" Annie asked, still surprised.

"Yeah, you know." Leaning over to whisper in Annie's ear, Jade said, "Yeah, I know you two spent the night together last night. I think that's wonderful," she lied.

"Whoa, what are you talking about?" Annie asked, backing up from Jade.

"What? You look surprised that I know. It's okay. Ryan is single and free to do whatever he wants," Jade said.

"Well, yeah, but he and I don't have a thing going. Where on earth would you get an idea like that?" she asked.

"Maybe we should take this conversation to another room where we'll have some privacy," Jade said.

"I don't need privacy. Jade, just what are you thinking?"

"I'm not just going to blurt it out here in front of everyone."

Walt and the women were watching the exchange between Jade and Annie. Walt knew what was coming, but Nora and Donna had no idea what was going on. Walt wanted to crack up laughing, but the situation was not funny to anyone but him at this point.

"Blurt what out? I swear I have no idea what you are talking about," Annie said.

"Annie, is it true or is it not true that you and Ryan spent the night together last night?" Jade asked, thinking 'if you want everyone to know, then so be it.'

"Well, yes, it's true. So what?" Annie answered.

"That didn't mean anything to you?" Jade asked with her eyes wide in shock. Maybe Ryan was right. Maybe she was making too much out of this. Maybe her dad was right. Maybe Annie used Ryan.

"What? That Ryan was in my apartment last night to keep me safe? Sure, that meant something, and I thanked him repeatedly for it," Annie said, confused.

"Well, sure, but what about....?" Jade could not come right out and say it.

"About what?" Annie was persistent.

"Sex, damn it. Didn't the sex mean anything to you?" Jade blushed as she said it.

Annie jumped up off the sofa. "What the hell are you talking about?" She was furious.

~

Ryan and George could hear the yelling now coming from the living room. George looked over at Ryan with a questioning look.

"Shit, Jade must have asked Annie about last night," Ryan said, looking at George.

"Last night?" George was lost.

"Yeah, she thinks I slept with Annie." Ryan was laughing.

"Why would she think that?" George was getting a bad feeling.

"Because she has a good imagination, and I didn't correct her when she accused me of it."

"What? You let her believe that you slept with Annie?"

"I didn't deny it. Shit, why should I when she comes right out and accuses me undeservingly?" Ryan said with a big smile on his face.

"I don't know if you are stupid or brave," George said.

~

Annie was staring at Jade "Sex? I don't know what you're talking about, Jade."

Nora was watching the girls, and when she looked over at Walt, she saw the amusement on his face and knew something was going on. She decided to sit back and keep her mouth shut. Donna just looked over at Nora and smiled.

"You don't know what I'm talking about?" Jade looked at Annie with disbelief in her eyes.

"We didn't have sex, if that's what you're getting at, Jade." Annie stood her ground.

"You didn't?" Jade asked, still disbelieving Annie.

"No! Where did you get an idea like that?" Annie demanded.

"From Ryan," she said.

"Ryan told you we slept together?" Annie asked.

"Well, yeah," Jade said.

Ryan walked into the room and heard what Jade said.

"I did not tell you that; you assumed that all on your own." Ryan wasn't laughing anymore.

"You did too," Jade accused.

"Ryan, you told Jade we slept together?" Annie was appalled.

"No, Annie, I didn't. Jade assumed we had, and she wouldn't listen to me, so I just gave up and let her think whatever she wanted to think." Ryan wasn't giving an inch.

"Ryan, didn't I tell you to move over so that Annie wouldn't get upset at us earlier, and you played it off like it was nothing?"

"I tried to let you know I didn't know what you were talking about, but you insisted I did, so I just left it alone."

"Oh, I see, you're going to blame all this on me?" Jade looked at Ryan with hurt eyes.

"Jade, I never said Annie and I slept together!"

"Not in so many words, but you let me believe you did." Jade wasn't backing down to look like the idiot. She refused, even though she realized what had happened. He let her believe it, and she wasn't letting him off the hook.

"Not in any words. You thought we did, and no matter what I said, you just thought I was taking it lightly. I thought you and Annie talked earlier when I left the room and she came in."

"We did talk, but not about you. You are so arrogant!" Jade stood up and walked past him.

"Where are you going? Come back here so we can get this straightened out!" Ryan told her as she took the stairs two at a time.

"I have you figured out. You do whatever the hell you want to and just leave me out of it!" Jade yelled back down.

Ryan turned to look at everyone staring at him.

"What?" he said, then turned and walked back to the kitchen. George turned and followed Ryan. He had walked into the hallway so he could hear the conversation in the living room. He had thought things were getting intense between Ryan and Jade, and now he knew they were.

Ryan pulled his gloves on and walked over to the rock. He removed the note and read it. George was standing behind him looking over his shoulder. The note said:

I want my drugs back. No one else has to get hurt. I don't care what it takes. I will get them back. Heed this warning, girlie, and heed it well: I will kill again if I have to. I don't want to hurt you, but I will!!! The kid knows more than she's telling you. Find my drugs, and I will leave everyone alone. If you don't return my drugs, you are as good as dead already!!! This is not a threat. This is a promise. Did you see how easy I can get into your house? Think about it!!! The cops can't help you either!!! You're not safe!!!

Ryan placed the note in a plastic bag, then filled the item tag out. George stood there watching as Ryan processed the scene. Ryan put the rock in a brown paper bag. Even though prints couldn't be taken from the rock, he would log both into evidence when he got to the station.

Ryan turned to see George watching him. "What?" he said.

"Nothing, I'm just watching you process the evidence," George retorted.

Ryan picked up the plastic bag and the paper bag and turned to walk out. Walt was just walking in. George told Walt what the note said.

"So the message was for Jade?" Walt was scared and furious.

"It would appear so," George answered.

Ryan went out and put the evidence in his patrol trunk. He needed some fresh air. He could not believe the way Jade reacted in the living room. Maybe he should have straightened her out earlier, but he let her squirm. After all, she hung up on him and then wouldn't let him explain. Women. He stood out there breathing in the fresh air and not feeling the slightest bit guilty, just angry.

He needed to talk to Emmie, and he wondered if she was awake yet. He would go back inside soon and talk to Emmie, then he and George would go to the station to get this case moving. He wanted nothing more right now than to solve this case and get his life back on track.

If Jade thought he would come after her, then she didn't know him at all. He would not chase her.

He locked his trunk and went back in the house. Emmie was in the living room, sitting on Mrs. Linderhoff's lap.

"Emmie can I talk with you a minute?" Ryan asked her, smiling.

"Yep, sure," Emmie said, and she began to climb off her grandmother's lap.

George was sitting in the living room with everyone. Everyone, that is, except Jade, Ryan noticed. "We'll be back in a few," Ryan told everyone. He walked Emmie into the sitting room, and George followed. "Emmie, did you have anything with you when Jade picked you up?"

"When Jade picked me up?" She looked confused.

"At the park, the day your Mommy and Daddy didn't come back."

"Oh yeah." She squiggled onto the settee.

"What did you have, honey?" Ryan squatted down in front of her.

"A backpack, of course."

"Where is it now?"

"I don't know. I guess Jade has it. Why?"

"What's in the back pack?"

"A jacket"

"Oh, just a jacket?" Ryan was sure the drugs wouldn't be in Emmie's jacket.

"Yep."

"Okay, sweetie, thank you for being so brave and answering all of my questions. You can go back in there with your family now." Ryan stood up and patted the top of her head.

"Ryan, are you okay?" Emmie asked, looking up at him. She looked so serious.

"Yeah, why?" he laughed.

"Because I heard you and Jade yelling at each other, and you're mad." She put her hands on her hips as if she were scolding him.

"We weren't yelling. We were talking loudly. We forgot you were asleep."

"That's okay, but why are you mad?" She was too smart sometimes.

"Not mad, sweetie, just confused." He gave her a little shove toward the doorway. She walked out of the sitting room, and Ryan turned to look at George. "We should go to the station now and get this moving." Shaking his head, he turned to leave the room.

"You're right. Let's go say goodbye." George was not going to suggest that he talk to Jade first.

When George and Ryan walked into the living room, everyone was talking and laughing, and Emmie was back in her grandmother's lap. Jade still had not made an appearance. Ryan thought about trying to talk to her before leaving, but he decided to give her some cool down time, as well as time to calm himself down. He knew he owed her an apology, but at the same time, he felt she owed him one, too. He would deal with that later; right now, he had a double homicide to solve, and he needed to get his head in the game and get it done. Priorities, he told himself.

"Walt, we appreciate all you've done, but we have a lot of work to get to, so we're gonna head out," George said.

"Guys, we appreciate all you're doing too. We know you have work to do, and we'll be fine. I'll keep all these women inside and safe until we hear from you," Walt said, smiling.

"Walt, I'm sorry for any trouble I've caused. It wasn't my intention to upset anyone, but that daughter of yours has a mind of her own, and you can't tell her anything." Ryan was red-faced and not very happy. He hated having to look like an idiot.

"You don't owe me an apology. Jade is stubborn, but that's a quality I like. You two will both calm down and talk it out. I'm not worried. Call her later," he suggested.

"I might call her, but it'll be a while. I have a lot to get done, and I think she needs some time."

"I wouldn't worry about this a lot. It will work itself out. You get your mind on this murder investigation and get that maniac behind bars," Walt said.

"We'll get him." George said, nodding "We just need to get to the station to get some information and clarify a few things. We've been spending so much time chasing this creep that we're behind schedule."

"Detectives, it was good to meet you both, and I can't thank you enough for watching over my Annie and Emmie for me." Nora stood up to shake their hands.

"Ms. Armstrong, these girls are sweet, and it was our pleasure to watch over them," George said, shaking her hand.

"I wish we would've all met under different circumstances, ma'am," Ryan said as he took her hand.

Donna sat across the room and smiled at both men. She was a woman of few words. But she watched everything and heard everything. That was one of the reasons she stayed quiet. She could learn so much more that way. Both men told her goodbye, then hugged Emmie.

As they left, Emmie was yelling at Harry to quit tugging on her dolly. They played tug-of-war a lot, but she didn't like him trying to take Molly away from her.

"Harry, lay down," Annie ordered the dog. Harry stopped tugging on Molly and walked over next to Walt's chair. He walked in circles three or four times, then lay down, tucking his head between his paws. Harry knew he was in trouble. "He is so smart," Annie said.

Emmie was hugging Molly. She was afraid that Harry would chew Molly up. Molly was the last thing her Daddy gave her, and she would treasure her always.

Mrs. Linderhoff was still holding Emmie on her lap, and she leaned forward, putting both arms around Emmie. "Your baby is alright, honey," she told Emmie.

"I know, but my daddy gave me Molly, and I don't want Harry to eat her."

Walt was sitting there listening to the two. Emmie was surely enjoying her grandmothers. The child was due some happiness, and he was glad he was getting to be a part of this, even though the circumstances were horrendous. He decided he would go upstairs and check on Jade. She had been up there long enough to get herself in check. He knew Jade, and she was not the type to pout. He wanted to make sure she was all right. As he got up, he looked over at Nora. She was watching him and smiling. He liked her. She was an interesting woman.

~

"I'm going upstairs to check on Jade. I'll be back in a minute. You all help yourself to whatever you want. There's plenty of soda and snacks in the kitchen."

19

WALT walked up the stairs thinking about Jade and worrying about her pride. She was going to have a hard time coming back down with everyone; he knew that she was embarrassed. As he approached her door, he had the thought that maybe he shouldn't interrupt her. Maybe she was trying to see her vision. He stood there for a moment, then decided to knock.

"Come in," Jade said clearly.

Walt opened the door and saw Jade lying on her bed. "Are you okay?"

"I was lying here considering my vision. I know now why he changed mid-stride."

"You do?"

"Yeah. He's focusing on me now."

"Why do you say that?"

"Because I let the vision come to me, and it was slightly different this time. He's getting angry and impatient. He wants his drugs back."

"What was your vision, Jade? Did you hear his thoughts again?"

"No, he's talking to me. It's like he knows I have a gift."

"How?"

"I don't know that he knows; I'm just saying it's *like* he does."

"Well, do you want to talk about it?"

"I want to know what the note said."

"It pretty much said what you just did. He wants his drugs back, or he'll kill you."

"Did he use my name?"

"No, he called you 'girlie,' I believe."

"That's good. I was afraid he had somehow found out my name."

"Are you going to tell me about your vision?"

"I saw him, or, I should say, his form. He was wearing a black coat with a hood and black gloves. He was standing outside of the Linderhoffs' home. Or, I believe it was their home. He was talking about his drugs, saying he just wanted his drugs back; he didn't want to hurt anyone else, but he would. He would even kill again if it came to that. He believes Emmie has some information that she's not giving us. He said he would stop at nothing to get his drugs, and then he laughed, saying that he didn't like to hurt people, but it was part of the deal. I saw him standing there, just talking to himself and saying all these things. That's why I believe he knows I can see him and hear him. I do know he finds it very easy to kill. Life has no value for him. He's cold, evil feeling."

"I'm worried about you. He did get in here earlier, but I couldn't find him. I don't believe he just opened the door and then walked away."

"He did just that. He didn't come into the house. He wants us to know he can come in whenever he wants. He wants us to feel unsafe." She said all of this without feeling, staring off into space.

"How do you know that?"

"Because my vision wasn't a future vision. It was the note information and the incident leading up to the note. That's why I wanted to know what was in the note. It's weird, like my visions are evolving or something."

"I see... So you weren't up here pouting." He tried to lighten her mood.

"Dad, you know I don't pout."

"I know. I was hoping you were trying your vision again, but you were so upset, I wasn't sure what to think."

"This guy has my visions all screwed up. I'd never had one like the last two."

~ 222 ~

"Maybe your visions are evolving into more? We know that most gifted people have more than one gift, and it's been fourteen years, Jade."

"I don't need visions that tell me what's already happened. I need them to tell me what to expect."

"Yes and yes. You do need the ones that are going to happen, but I think the ones for the present are important, too. I mean, you didn't know what was in that note, and if we weren't on good terms with Ryan and George, we may not have been told what was in it."

"You're right. He has no idea that the detectives are friends of yours. Maybe he's trying to contact me, and he has this all figured out."

"I don't see how that would be possible."

"Me either. I'm just guessing here."

"Jade, I want you to take this a step at a time. I want you to get back on track. Take all the time you need. We'll be downstairs keeping things under control, so you don't have to worry about anything except information."

"Alright, I'll try. Did Ryan leave yet?" She was sure he had, but hope still lingered.

"Yeah, they had to get to the station."

"I'm sorry about the scene downstairs. I don't know why he did that to me."

"Honey, I don't think he did anything to you. I think you let your imagination run away, and when it all came out, you got embarrassed."

"Gee, thanks for your understanding."

"Think about what happened. I believe you'll see what I'm talking about."

"Point taken."

"Just think about it, Jade."

"I will. I may have taken things out of context, but Ryan allowed me to continue instead of taking the time to set me straight."

"Yeah, maybe you both owe each other an apology."

Always the peacemaker, Walt walked out, closing the door. He hoped she would think about what he had said. He knew they were both wrong. He also knew they would make an excellent couple. He would still encourage both of them down the path he knew they should be on. He even thought about calling Ryan and having the same talk with him.

Annie was talking about getting a snack when Walt came back into the living room. "I think popcorn sounds good. Anyone else interested?" She looked around, hopeful.

"Popcorn with butter...I would love some. What about you, Donna?" Nora asked.

"No, thank you, I'm fine."

"Walt, do you like popcorn with butter?" Nora asked.

"Is there any other way to eat it? Annie, sit. I'll get it."

"No, you've done enough. You sit, and I'll get it." Annie went to the kitchen.

Walt went to the kitchen to show her where the popcorn was, but she already had it on the counter and was locating a pan. He helped her with the pan, then went back to the living room.

"Would you ladies like to watch a movie?" Walt asked.

"What do you have, Walt?" Nora asked.

"I have a variety. Jade and I like all kinds of movies. We don't watch horror movies, but we have thrillers, comedies, chick flicks, sappy and sad... You name it."

"Wow, a man that watches chick flicks that are sappy and sad?" Donna was intrigued now.

"Sure, I'm a man of many interests. I don't like the fights, but I do like sports. I don't like horrors that make you want to heave, but I do like thrillers that make you sit on the edge of your seat."

"Well, I'll watch whatever you choose. I like just about anything, too," Nora said.

"Emmie, would you like to watch a movie with us, or is it your bed time?" Walt was asking when Annie came in with the popcorn.

"Emmie has to go to bed pretty soon. She can stay up and have some popcorn and maybe some of a movie, but I don't think she'll be up long enough for a whole movie," Annie answered for her.

"I took a nap, Aunt Annie, so I'm not tired now," Emmie whined.

"I know you did; that's why you can stay up for a little while longer."

"Do you guys want to watch a kids' movie? Jade and I have been collecting them for years."

"Whatever you have appropriate would be great," Annie answered again.

Walt walked over to the wooden cabinet. Opening the lower left door, he began looking through the movie collection. After pulling out four or five DVDs and handing them to Annie, he closed the door to the cabinet and went to the DVD player. He checked the connections to make sure it was hooked up right. He had just bought a new DVD player and had installed it in a hurry. Annie walked over and handed a movie to Walt.

"This one would be great," Annie stated. "What are you doing?"

"It's new, and I've never used this player. I just wanted to make sure my cleaning lady didn't unplug it or anything. She does that sometimes." Walt took the movie and put it in the DVD player.

Annie, Emmie, and Nora were sitting on the sofa, munching on the popcorn.

Donna was sitting in a chair and wasn't interested in the popcorn or the movie. She was in deep thought about James. She was suffering greatly and trying hard not to show her pain. What she really wanted right now was to go to her room and lie down.

Walt sat down and started the movie. As the credits began to scroll down the TV, he looked over at Nora. She was a very interesting woman to him. He planned to get to know her better.

He looked over at Donna and realized she wasn't watching the TV. As he watched her, he noticed that her chin was quivering. Realizing she probably needed some alone time, he decided to give her the space he thought she wanted. He said, "Annie, while you guys watch the movie, I think I'll take your luggage upstairs. Would you and Emmie be more comfortable in the room with the twin beds or share the big bed?"

"Mom, do you and Donna want the twin beds?"

"That would be wonderful, honey, if you don't mind sleeping with Emmie."

"Not at all. Emmie and I will take the room with the big bed."

"Good. I'll get these suitcases upstairs then, and if any of you want to rest, you'll know which room is yours." Walt got up and went to the entry hall. Grabbing both Nora's and Donna's suitcases, he went up the stairs. Going into the pretty sage colored room, he set both suitcases on the floor. He made sure there were plenty of hangers in the closet and opened the chest of drawers to make sure they were empty. Satisfied that all was well, he went back downstairs. "Annie, where's your luggage?" he asked.

"I left it in my trunk. I'll get it in a minute."

"No, I don't want any of you going outside. Where are your keys?"

"In my purse." She got up and went to the table in the entry hall, took her keys out of her purse, and handed them to Walt. "Do you want me to go with you?"

"No, you go enjoy the movie." Walt unlocked both locks on the door and stepped out onto the front porch, looking around. Everything looked normal; he didn't see anyone. He walked to Annie's car, opened the trunk, and removed the suitcase. Walking back to the house, he strained his ears and eyes for anything out of the ordinary. All seemed quiet. Walt went in and locked the doors. Going back into the living room, he asked if any of the women were ready for bed.

"I would love to go to my room now, if you don't mind," Donna said quietly.

"Sure. I'll show you where your room is. I hope you and Nora don't mind sharing a room," he said.

"No, not at all. I'm sure Nora is every bit as thankful as I am that we have such a nice place to stay."

Walt led the way up the stairs. He opened the sage room door and showed Donna in.   He explained where the bathroom was, as well as extra blankets, towels, whatever they might need. Donna thanked him, and he walked out, closing the door behind him. He knew she wanted to be alone.

He walked down the hall to Jade's door. The room was quiet and dark. He walked in and watched Jade sleep. He knew she'd had a rough couple of days, so he covered her up and closed the door. Going back downstairs, he could hear the movie playing. He decided to go to the kitchen to clean up the glass and find something to cover the window with until tomorrow. Grabbing the broom and dustpan, he began clearing away the big shards of glass.

Once that was done, he went to the garage for some plastic he thought he had kept. Looking around the garage, he found a huge blue tarp and decided it would be good enough for tonight. Using the tarp and his staple gun, he quickly had the opening covered.

He went back to the living room, and, once again sitting down in his chair, he relaxed and watched the movie.

~

George and Ryan were back at the station. The Captain was still there, so they decided now was the time to fill him in.

"George, you talk to Captain Mallory. I want to find Vic and see what, if anything, came of the prints he found earlier," Ryan said.

"Alright, I'll find you when I'm done." George walked to the Captain's office.

Ryan went to the crime scene lab to find Vic. When he walked in, he was surprised to see so many of the investigators still there. Vic was in the back corner looking through a microscope.

"Vic," Ryan said as he approached.

"Oh, hey, detective, I was hoping to have better news for you, but I don't think we're any closer now than we were before."

"Nothing came back on the prints?"

"Oh, yeah, the prints were good, but they belong to an employee of the fast food place. The suspect must have been wearing gloves."

"Damn. When are we going to get a fucking break?"

"We will, detective. Hang in there. I'm looking at some carpet fibers we found in the empty apartment that didn't come from there. I think it's going to be carpet fibers from a vehicle. I was just trying to get some characteristics from the fibers."

"Well, here are some more items for you to go over. Apparently he wanted to give us a message. This is a rock that was thrown through the window and a note that was tied around the rock," Ryan said, handing his evidence over to Vic.

"Good, I'll get right on this. You know I can't print the rock, right?" Vic said, looking at Ryan with a weary look.

"Yeah, we know that, but we brought it anyway."

"Okay, give me a few minutes."

Ryan stood back and gave Vic room to work. He was going to wait for any results.

George was explaining everything to Captain Mallory. The Captain sat quietly behind his desk and took in all the information being given to him.

"So what you're saying, Dunleavy, is that we still don't know who this guy is."

"That's right, but it's not from a lack of trying, Captain. Douglas and I have been working practically nonstop. This guy is getting braver and braver. He'll make a mistake. Douglas is talking to the crime scene guys right now. Maybe they'll give us some good news."

"Well, I appreciate the work you two are doing, and I'm not sorry I gave this case to you guys, but we really need to get this asshole. You guys are my best team," Captain Mallory said, sitting back.

"Thanks, Captain. We will catch him," George said. Then he left the office and went to find Ryan, who was still in the crime scene lab.

~

Vic was busily working on fingerprinting the note. George watched as Vic sprinkled magnetic fingerprint dust on the note; then, taking his magnet pen, he began lifting the dust back off. "No prints," Vic said, turning to look at Ryan.

Both Ryan and George shook their heads. "Okay. Thanks for getting to it so quickly, Vic," Ryan said. "Why don't you go home and get some rest?"

Vic just nodded and put the note back into the baggie.

"Come on, Ryan, let's go find the drug guys and see what we can find out," George said, walking away. "Thanks, Vic, I appreciate you," he called over his shoulder.

"I'm going to get a cup of coffee. You want one?" Ryan asked, catching up with George.

"Yeah, thanks," George replied. While he waited for Ryan, he decided to call Doris to explain it would be a long night and not to wait up for him.

Ryan went to the break room and fixed their coffee. It was so strong he could smell it from the hallway. This was going to be helpful in keeping them awake. As Ryan walked back to George, he saw that his partner was on the phone, so he slowed his pace, giving George time to see him coming. George hung the phone up and smiled at Ryan. "That was Doris," he said.

"Here you go." Ryan handed a cup to George.

"Thanks, I really need this."

"Yeah me too. It's going to be a long night."

They walked to the drug task force office to see if any of the guys were still around. As they rounded the corner, Ryan could see Danny Miller was still there. Danny had been a part of the task force for a while. Surely he would be able to help them out.

"Hey, Danny, how's it going?" Ryan asked as they walked up.

"Hi, Ryan, George. What's up?" Danny asked.

"You may know we're working a double homicide, and we need some help with some drug information," Ryan said.

"What kind of drugs?" Danny stopped what he was doing and listened to the detectives.

"We don't know. That's where you come in," George said.

"Okay, I'm lost." Danny was looking at the two detectives like they had lost their minds.

"We need to know a drug on the market right now that would be small and valuable," Ryan said.

"Wow, that doesn't narrow it down very much."

"Okay, let me explain what we're looking for." Ryan and George went into detail about the case and what they needed.

Danny stood there for a minute thinking, then said, "Ecstasy would be small enough and valuable enough. I think you're on the right track with that drug."

"How much are they getting per pill these days?" Ryan asked.

"Usually twenty five dollars a pill," Danny said.

"So if he took two thousand pills, he would have fifty grand worth, right?" Ryan asked.

"Yeah," Danny answered.

"I'd be willing to bet that's what we're looking for." Ryan turned to George.

"Yeah, I think you're right." George was beginning to see it wouldn't take a lot of space for the drugs to be hidden.

"We need to talk to Jade and see if she has any idea where Emmie could have these pills," Ryan said.

"I think that's a great idea. The sooner we find the drugs, the better off the family is going to be." George was thinking now. He knew the pills could be anywhere. It was no wonder the killer was getting angry. He had no idea where to look, and that was a lot of money he was losing.

"I'm going to our office to call Walt." Ryan walked away. "Thanks, Danny, you've been a big help." George thanked him and shook hands, then followed Ryan to their office.

20

EMMIE was getting bored with the movie and with sitting still. She got down and went to get Molly, her baby doll. Harry was alert to her every move. She walked over to the chair where she had left Molly, and as she picked her up, Harry jumped up and grabbed one of Molly's legs. Emmie began tugging and pulling, and Harry pulled too.

"Harry, don't tug on her! You're gonna break her!" Emmie yelled.

But Harry kept pulling. Annie got up to help Emmie. She was so tiny next to Harry, and she was struggling. Before Annie got across the room to Emmie, Harry pulled Molly's leg off. Emmie started crying, and small blue pills came pouring out of Molly. "What in the world?" Annie was startled.

Walt got up and walked over. At first, he thought the doll was a Beanie Baby, but as he got closer, he could see little symbols on the pills. He stooped to pick up a pill and knew these weren't beans of any kind.

"My daddy gave Molly to me, and now Harry broke her," Emmie wailed.

Nora was up now, too, and all three adults were looking at the pills and at each other.

"I have to call Ryan," Walt said as he walked to the telephone. Before he could pick it up and dial, it started ringing. Startled, he answered.

"Hello?"

"Walt, is Jade where I can talk to her?" Ryan asked.

"Oh, Ryan, thank God. I was just going to call you. No,

Jade is asleep, but I think you need to come over right away."

"Why? What's happened?"

"Harry just broke Emmie's doll, and it's filled with blue pills."

"What? Tell me exactly what they look like." He was excited. Yes, yes, yes, this is what they needed.

"They're blue and very small. They have symbols on them. Some are different from others, but they're symbols nonetheless."

"We're on our way. Don't do anything till we get there." He hung up and smiled at George. "We got 'em!"

"No shit?" They both ran for their cars.

~

"I think these will be the drugs the killer's looking for," Walt told Annie and Nora. "We need to leave everything where it is. The guys are on their way back now."

"Oh my God, he put them in her baby doll." Annie scooped Emmie up and held her while she cried. "It's okay, honey. We can fix your baby," Annie said to her.

"Daddy gave her to me. Bad Harry!" Emmie said, looking at the dog. Harry walked over and sat on the floor next to Walt's chair once again.

"Why don't you take Emmie and Harry upstairs to the bedroom, Annie?" Walt suggested.

"That's a good idea. Emmie, it's bedtime, and you can take Harry with you." Annie sat Emmie down.

"I don't wanna go to bed. I want Molly fixed," Emmie complained.

"Not tonight, young lady. You're going to bed. Come on, Harry, you're going, too." Annie took Emmie's hand and started up the stairs. Midway up, she realized Harry wasn't following. "Harry, come on." That got him up and moving. "We'll fix Molly in the morning," she assured Emmie.

"Walt, do you really think these are drugs?" Nora asked, visibly shaken.

"Yes, I do." Walt was looking in the doll to see how many more were in there. The whole doll had been stuffed with the blue pills.

"Put your pajamas on, Emmie, and brush your teeth. I'll wait right here for you." Annie sat down on the bed. Harry was already on the bed waiting for Emmie.

Emmie put her pajamas on, then went to the bathroom. When she came back, she looked at Annie. "Aunt Annie, do you think you can fix my Molly?" She still had tears in her eyes.

"Yes, honey, I'll have her good as new for you." Annie brushed Emmie's hair, then put her in the bed and covered her up. "Sweet dreams, little one," Annie said as she kissed Emmie's forehead.

Annie went to Jade's room and knocked on the door. When she didn't hear anything, she opened the door and walked in. Jade was asleep. Annie walked over and shook her shoulder.

"Jade, wake up," Annie said.

"What?" Jade looked up and saw Annie. "What's wrong, Annie?" Jade sat up.

"You should get up and come downstairs. We think we found the drugs."

"What? Where?" Jade got up and looked for her robe.

"You're not going to believe this. That bastard put them inside the baby doll he gave to his daughter." Annie was furious.

"What? Are you kidding me?" Jade was astonished.

"No, I wish I were. Come on." Annie turned and left the room.

Jade put her robe on and went down the stairs right behind Annie. They walked into the living room to find Walt and Nora sitting there looking at all the pills on the floor.

"Dad, have you called Ryan?" Jade asked.

"Yeah, they're on their way here. I can't believe the drugs were with Emmie the whole time." Walt was pissed off.

"Why would James do that? Didn't he know he was putting Emmie in danger?" Nora was angry now.

"Of course he knew. You know he only thought of himself, Mom." Annie was angry too.

"He probably thought he would be there to take care of her. Aren't you guys being a little hard on him?" Jade asked.

"You didn't know James. He wouldn't get a normal job. Amy was always begging him to get a job and stop all this drug nonsense," Annie huffed. "He was too lazy and always tried to take the easy way out."

"What kind of drugs are these?" Jade asked, picking up one of the pills.

"I don't know," Walt answered.

"Well, they don't look very valuable to me," Annie said.

"How many do you think there are?" Nora asked.

"I'd say a couple thousand at least," Walt answered.

"Well, let's pick them up and count them," Jade said.

"No, Ryan said to leave them just where they are," Walt said.

They all sat down looking at all the pills spread over the floor "There are still a good many inside the doll," Walt said.

"I promised Emmie I could make the doll as good as new. I hope Harry didn't damage the leg," Annie said, looking at the doll laying there.

Walt got up and went to the DVD player; taking the movie

out, he turned the TV off. The last thing they needed was more noise. No one really said anything. They just sat there waiting for the detectives to arrive.

Walt was thinking he should teach Jade to shoot his gun. Maybe he should teach Annie, too. He would suggest it later. Right now, they just needed some down time. Too much excitement was not good. Lord knew they all had had enough for now.

The doorbell rang, and Walt went to answer it.

"Hey, guys, come on in. We're in the living room." Walt pointed.

George and Ryan went into the living room. They walked over to the pills on the floor. Picking them up, Ryan looked at George. "These are definitely ecstasy," he said.

"Yep, that they are. Man, how many do you think there are?" George was excited.

"Damn, I don't know. Let's get to counting." They both reached down, grabbing pills by the handful. Walt went to get a big bowl. He gave the bowl to George.

"Thanks, Walt."

"Sure thing. Do you want help counting all those?" Walt asked.

"Yeah, let's get them all picked up, and then we'll separate them into piles of a hundred," George said.

After all the pills on the floor were picked up, Ryan grabbed the doll and shook her over the bowl. Pills fell out for what seemed like hours. Ryan couldn't believe the number of pills that were there. "I think there's a few thousand pills here," Ryan said excitedly.

"Yeah, I think you're right," George said, smiling.

They went to the table in the kitchen, and all six of them sat down and began counting pills and putting them into piles of one hundred. After what seemed like half the night, they all got up to stretch their backs and looked at all the piles laying on the table and counter tops.

"Okay, let's see how many we have." George began counting the piles.

Ryan stood back with Walt and all the women. He looked at Jade and could see the excitement in her eyes. He had no idea the drugs had been with her and Emmie. He realized now how lucky they had been. The killer was just getting around to thinking Emmie had the drugs, and that was a good thing. If he had realized it earlier, he would have done something horrible to them. Ryan couldn't keep the thought process from going in that direction. He couldn't fathom something happening to Jade. He walked over to her and put his arm around her shoulders. She turned to look at him. Neither said anything, but she leaned into his embrace. He would protect her with his life if necessary, he knew. He would make sure she knew that, too. This case was not going to stand in his way anymore. Not now that he had realized how easily he could have lost her for good already. No way, he decided. The time was right tonight, and he would tell her so as soon as they got the drugs counted and tagged properly. He would let George know he was going to be busy for a little while.

George finished counting the stacks and turned to look at Ryan. "There are forty stacks here," he said in awe.

"Forty?" Annie was amazed.

"Yeah, that means four thousand pills. That's one hundred thousand dollars," George said, still in awe.

"Holy shit!" Ryan exclaimed.

"Go to the car and get me a brown bag to tag this for evidence," George said to Ryan.

"You got it. I'll be right back." Ryan went to the car once again for evidence bags, but this time he didn't mind.

"Good Lord Almighty, one hundred thousand dollars worth of drugs in my kitchen." Walt couldn't believe what he saw laid out in front of him.

"Yeah, now we know why he's been so desperate to get it back," George said.

"How do we let him know we have it?" Walt asked.

"We don't," George said.

"What? Why not? That could get him off our backs," Walt said, looking directly at George.

"Let us handle this, Walt. We know what we're doing." Looking at Walt, George couldn't believe he thought they would just hand the drugs over to not only a drug dealer, but a murderer. "Do you think we're gonna give the drugs back to him?" he asked incredulously.

"No, I meant to lure him in. Do I look like a damn idiot to you?" Now Walt was taking offense.

"Oh, I get it. Good God, I thought you wanted us to give the shit to him so he would leave y'all alone." Laughing, George slapped Walt on the back. "We will lure him, Walt, just not like you mean."

"Jade, first thing in the morning, I'm going to teach you how to shoot my gun. Annie, you can learn, too, if you want to," Walt said.

"Let's not get carried away, Walt. We're not going to leave you all in danger," George said.

"Well, I want to learn to shoot anyway." Jade was interested and thought it may even be fun.

"Yeah, me too," Annie put in.

"Good. We'll leave Emmie with Nora and Donna, and I'll take you two to the range right after breakfast." Walt was making sure George understood what his intentions were.

"Here you go, partner," Ryan said, walking back in with a big brown paper bag.

"Thanks." George filled out the form on the front of the bag, putting the information concerning the evidence in the proper spaces, then filled the bag with the dope.

"George, I need to talk to you a minute outside," Ryan said once the bag was taped closed.

"Okay, let's step out on the back porch," George suggested, and both detectives walked out the back door.

"What is it?" George asked.

"Look, since we have the drugs now, you can log them into an evidence locker by yourself, right?" Ryan asked.

"Sure, why?"

"I need to talk to Jade, and I'm not sure how long it's going to take."

"Oh, I see." He'd go easy on the kid. This was all new to him, George thought to himself.

"I have to do this now, George. It can't wait."

"Okay, no problem. You do what you need to do."

"Thanks." Ryan was thankful there wasn't any teasing involved.

When they went back into the kitchen, they locked the back door. George picked up the bag, and they went to join the group in the living room.

"I have to go get this stuff logged into evidence. I'll see you all tomorrow," George said to the entire group. He wanted to call it a night. He was tired, and now he couldn't pawn logging the pills into evidence on Ryan, so he was going to do it simple and fast himself.

"George, I'm not looking to cause trouble, you know, about the gun thing. I just think it's important, and the time seems right," Walt said.

"I know. You just be careful, that's all," George said, smiling.

"We will." Walt walked him to the door.

~

"Jade, we need to talk," Ryan said, looking at her.

"I agree we should talk." From his tone, she was feeling apprehensive.

"Some place private."

"Uh, we can go to my room if you want," Jade said.

"That's fine." Ryan followed her upstairs to her room.

Going up to her room, Jade's mind was running in a direction she didn't want to accept.

"What is it, Ryan?" Was he going to tell her now that they

had what they needed; she and the rest were on their own? She gave herself a mental shake.

"I have a lot to tell you, and I didn't want to do it in front of everyone," he began.

Hesitantly, she said, "Okay, so go ahead." She sat on the bed and looked at him. She could see the look in his eyes and feel the butterflies starting to churn in her stomach. No, he wasn't leaving her.

"Jade, I'm not sure where to begin. I just want you to know that tonight, when I realized you and Emmie had the drugs with you the whole time and what could have happened if the killer had realized that, I felt such a gut-wrenching fear. I need to tell you that I know there's something between us, and I would like to find out what it is. I mean, I have these feelings for you, and I think you're feeling them, too."

"I know we have something churning between us. I do feel it too. I just don't want to do anything that will take your mind out of the place it needs to be right now. I don't know that this is the time to act on these feelings, Ryan," Jade said, standing up and feeling excited but confused. She continued, "I guess what I'm trying to say is, I know you need to concentrate and get this case resolved, and I don't want you worrying about me and not focusing on what you need to.

Ryan pulled her into the circle of his arms and tipped her chin up so she was looking him in the eyes. "Honey, did it ever occur to you that I can multitask?" Then, without another thought, he brushed his lips lightly across hers, savoring the taste that was her. Feeling her response, he invaded deeper, the moan that left his throat mingling with the moan leaving hers. She felt so wonderful in his arms, and he decided that was where he wanted her. He also vowed to take it slow with her but wrap the case up quickly.

Jade felt the butterflies taking off and flying now. The kiss was remarkable. She couldn't get enough. He was a wonderful kisser. She knew they had to explore and find out what this was between them. She couldn't let her fear get in the way. They would just have to move slow and take their time. She would make sure of it.

Ryan pulled away and held her at arm's length. "Now, that's what I'm talking about," he said, panting.

Jade took a step back. She had never been kissed like that, and her heart was still skipping beats. "I won't get in the way of this case, but you have to promise once it's over, we'll make time to explore this." Giving a sexy smile, she tugged at his jacket collar.

"Bet on it." He was smiling a wicked smile. "We are going to continue this, I assure you, but we have to think it through. All the dangers right now make it more exciting, but we both know it's more than that."

"The danger is exciting, but you're right. It is more. I'm glad we had this talk. I was feeling like a loser earlier. I know I should've asked instead of assuming, but you could've stopped me from making an ass out of myself, and you didn't." She wanted to clear the air of what happened earlier, but she wasn't willing to take full blame. She was letting him know she took responsibility, but she also expected him to.

"You're right. I could have, but the blame game isn't going to work for us, so let's put that behind us. Move on. Get this case behind us. See what happens." Laughing, he asked, "Is that enough clichés for you?"

Slugging his arm, she said, "Let's go back downstairs before they get suspicious and come looking for us."

He pulled her by the hand, and they walked downstairs and into the living room holding hands. Walt looked up and smiled when he saw them. Jade was beaming.

"I'm leaving, but I'll be back in the morning," he said, squeezing her hand.

"Be careful. Do you still have to go to the station tonight?" she asked.

"No, I'm going home. George is taking care of the evidence. I'll call before I come back in the morning."

They talked like no one else was in the room. Walt decided to break the magic and speak up. "I'm taking Jade and Annie to learn to shoot after breakfast. We're going to the range, and you're welcome to come along."

"What range are you going to?"

"The one on Westmoreland. I have a membership there."

"What time did you say?" He couldn't remember if the time was mentioned. Confusion was becoming second nature to him.

"I figure about eight-thirty." Walt wanted to laugh.

"Great! I'll just meet you guys there." Looking around the room, Ryan suggested they all call it a night. It had been a long day, and tomorrow would be, too.

Saying goodnight to everyone, he pulled Jade to the front door with him, which was fine with her. She wanted another of those delicious kisses. The kiss was sweet, tender, and quicker than the one upstairs. Even though they were alone in the foyer, he was keeping it light. When he ended the kiss, he cupped her chin. "See you in the morning, Jade." Then he sailed out the door.

Ryan strode like the cat that ate the canary. A little spring in his step, he thought as he reached the sidewalk. Laughing to himself, he got in his car and pulled away, heading for home.

"Yes, you will," Jade guaranteed him even though he couldn't hear her.

21

AFTER Ryan left, Jade stood there for a few minutes, trying to pull herself together. She knew she would have that just kissed look, and she wasn't ready for all the questions. She decided to go to her room and avoid everyone. Walking to the stairs, she yelled into the living room, "Good night! I'll see you all in the morning."

Back in her room, she sat on the bed and licked her lips; she could still taste Ryan and feel the tingling sensation on her lips. She was going to have a hard time going to sleep tonight. She decided to see if she could get a vision of what was to come. Lying there in the dark, she concentrated on Emmie, but nothing happened no matter how hard she concentrated. Finally, she gave up and turned over to go to sleep. The house was quiet, which meant everyone had retired for the night.

Laying there, she pictured Ryan with his beautiful blue eyes and sexy lips calling her 'honey.' It was her last thought as she fell asleep.

~

Emmie woke up screaming, jolting Annie awake.

"What is it, sweetie?" Annie asked.

"The angel said my daddy is mad at me," Emmie cried.

"What angel, honey? It was just a dream," Annie soothed.

"No, the angel that told me mommy and daddy weren't coming back, the one that told me to go with Jade," she cried.

"Emmie, I don't know what you're talking about." Annie was confused.

"I have dreams about the angel. She tells me things."

"Oh, I see. Well, honey, I think your angel is wrong. I just don't see your daddy being angry with you." Annie figured Emmie had heard that Jade has visions and was confused between dreaming and visions. She would talk with her about it later.

"You don't?" Emmie asked hopefully.

"No, I don't. Your daddy loved you more than anything. It would be very hard for him to get mad at you."

"Really? Even though Harry broke Molly and Daddy told me to keep her with me always?"

"Yes, even though." Annie lay down next to Emmie and held her while she went back to sleep.

So James had told her to keep the doll with her always, huh? He knew exactly what he was doing. At that moment, Annie hated James. She didn't much care for him most of the time anyway, with the way he treated her sister, but this took the cake. She hoped she could hold her tongue and not cause Donna any more heartache but, after all, Donna did raise him.

~

The next morning, Jade and Walt made pancakes and bacon for breakfast. Nora was the first to enter the kitchen.

"Do you drink coffee, Nora?" Walt asked.

"Yes, thank you."

"What do you take in it?" he asked, reaching for a cup.

"Just cream, thank you," she said as she sat down at the table. "I'll bet this room is beautiful very early in the morning, with the sun beaming through that big window."

"Yes, it is. Hopefully you can get the full effect tomorrow," Walt told her, turning to flip a pancake.

"Here's your coffee." Jade set the cup on the table in front of Nora.

"Thank you, Jade. Can I help you two?" she asked, beginning to rise.

"No, sit, we've got this," Walt answered.

Nora sat there watching father and daughter. They worked together beautifully. She was so comfortable here. She hated the idea of going back home all by herself again. Maybe she should make a move. She did only have Annie and Emmie left; why not live near them and enjoy what time they had together? She would have to think this through. California was a nice place to live, but she was so lonely there. She could live here just as easily.

Annie and Emmie came strolling in with Harry tagging behind. "Emmie, why don't you let Harry out in the backyard?" Annie suggested.

"Okay." Emmie walked over and opened the back door. Harry went running as soon as the door was open wide enough. Emmie laughed and closed the door. "I didn't even hafta tell him," she giggled.

"No, you didn't. He needed out bad, I guess," Walt said with a smile. "How did you ladies sleep?"

"We slept just fine, thank you," Annie said as she picked Emmie up and put her in a chair.

"Mmm, something smells good," Emmie said. "My tummy is hungry."

Everyone laughed.

"Well, you can have the first plate, sweetie," Jade said, poking Emmie's tummy.

"Goody!" Emmie giggled.

"Have any of you seen Donna?" Annie asked.

"No, not yet. Maybe she sleeps late," Walt suggested.

"I don't know. Maybe I should go back up and check on her," Nora said.

"I'll do it," Jade said.

"You don't mind?" Nora asked.

"No, not at all. I'll be right back." Jade left the kitchen, going up the back stairs.

"Annie, do you drink coffee, or would you prefer juice?" Walt asked, setting a glass of orange juice in front of Emmie.

"Coffee, please."

"What do you take in it?"

"Nothing, thank you."

"A girl with guts. I like that," Walt said, laughing.

The kitchen was bright even with the tarp over the window. The different shaped glass bottles above the cabinets were filled with brightly colored liquid, and the sun coming through the two smaller windows had colored shadows dancing on the ceiling. The day was going to be another beautiful day. Annie was sipping her coffee and didn't want thoughts of what had to be done to ruin her morning. She wasn't much of a morning person, but she would learn to be, since Emmie apparently was.

"Annie, I've been thinking that we shouldn't have a funeral. Maybe just a memorial service and cremation. What do you think?" Nora asked.

"Why, Mom? I mean, what made you think that?"

"Because it's been so long since... well, you know, and so I think it will be easier on Emmie."

"I wanted to suggest that, but I thought you and Donna would throw a fit."

"Well, I haven't really talked to Donna yet, but you said the kids didn't really have any friends, and I can't see putting Emmie through a viewing and such."

"I agree. I hope Donna will, too."

"Donna will what?" she asked, walking into the kitchen.

"Morning, Donna. We were just talking about what to do with Amy and James."

"What do you mean, what to do with them?" she asked, feeling her head begin to pound. She hadn't slept well and was not in the mood for people to make choices for her.

"Well, we were thinking it might be easier on Emmie if we just have a memorial service and cremation."

"Absolutely not! James will not be cremated!" Donna all but shouted.

"Donna, I didn't mean to upset you. We're trying to do this the quickest, best way possible. Don't forget Emmie is sitting here. We can discuss this and reach some kind of compromise, I'm sure." Deliberately keeping her voice calm, Nora continued, "May I ask, why not cremation?"

"We don't believe in cremation," Donna said through clenched teeth.

Jade walked over to Emmie, and, sliding the chair back, she said, "Emmie and I are going to go swing. Let us know when breakfast is ready." She then led Emmie out the back door. What were these people thinking, she thought as she headed for the tire swing.

Nora waited for the door to close, then continued. "Oh, I see. Well, what do you suggest, then? This is really taking a toll on Emmie," Nora stated.

"Don't you think she would like it better if she had a grave site to visit her daddy and mommy, especially when she becomes a teenager and needs someone to talk to?" Donna asked.

"No, I believe she will have us to talk to. She won't need to sit in a cemetery talking to the air. Her parents won't be there, and it's not healthy to allow her to think otherwise," Nora said calmly.

"I believe we have a lot to discuss, and I would like to have my coffee first." Donna didn't care to discuss this now and made that very clear.

"We need to contact a funeral home today if you want to have a funeral. We're going to have to find plots and pick out caskets, clothing, flowers, someone to give the service…. The list is endless, Donna." Nora was making her point clear.

"Annie, dear, you could take care of all that, couldn't you?" Donna asked in a sickeningly sweet voice.

~ 242 ~

"To be honest, Donna, I don't have the time. I think Mom's idea is the best way to go."

"I see." Donna was not happy with the idea. She poured a cup of coffee and sat down. Seething quietly and not really feeling like doing battle first thing in the morning, she decided to state her case plainly. "Well, I suppose you can do whatever you like with Amy, but I intend to see James buried properly." Standing, she planned to leave the room.

"Donna, I don't see any reason for you to get that kind of attitude. It was a suggestion. If you want to bury James, then we'll do the same for Amy. We can both work together on this while Annie is learning to shoot today," Nora said, feeling the tension in the room thicken.

"Learning to shoot?" She sounded appalled.

"Yes, Walt is taking Jade and Annie to the gun range and teaching them to shoot."

"Why ever for?" Donna was truly surprised.

"Safety reasons, Donna. There is a killer loose, and he is a threat to this entire family." Nora was beginning to get irritated with Donna.

"Well, I don't know about you, but where I come from, women don't carry guns."

"They're not going to carry guns, Donna; they're going to become familiar with the weapon so if they need to use one, they'll know how." Walt put his two cents in.

"Nora, did the kids have insurance, do you know?" Donna asked, pointedly ignoring Walt's comment.

"No, I don't believe they did. Annie, did you find any papers when you were at their house?" Nora asked sweetly.

"No, I don't think they got that far in life. They were young and probably hadn't thought about it," Annie said.

"Well, I guess we'll just have to absorb the cost ourselves, then," Donna said.

"You and I will. Annie doesn't have any extra; besides, now that she'll have Emmie, she'll need all she can get her hands on," Nora said, figuring they may as well get everything out in the open.

"What do you mean, now that she'll have Emmie? I haven't been asked a thing by either one of you. Don't take me for granted, Nora," Donna warned.

"Let's discuss this like adults, Donna. My intention was not to get you angry nor take you for granted, whatever that's supposed to mean," Nora said.

"I just feel like you and Annie are calling all the shots. He was my son, you know."

"Yes, and your son is the one that brought this danger to our family!" Now Nora was pissed.

"Wait just a damn minute! Don't you blame James for

this! How dare you!"

"James was the druggie, not Amy," Annie said.

"James had his faults, but this is..." Donna couldn't finish; she just began crying.

"Okay, ladies, I know it's not my place, but I am going to make a few suggestions here," Walt said, holding his hand up to stop the arguing.

"Walt, this is your home, and your generosity has been exceptional. Any input you want to give will be welcomed," Annie said.

"Why don't Nora and Donna plan the funeral while we're out this morning, then after the burial, the three of you can sit down and talk about Emmie and where she should go?"

"We don't know anything about this area. Walt, we wouldn't know a good cemetery just by looking in the phonebook," Nora said.

"I won't go this morning, Mom. I'll stay, and we'll get all these details worked out," Annie said.

"I want you to know how to take care of yourself. You and Emmie are all I have left, Annie," Nora said.

"I'll take her later, Nora, and make sure she knows how to shoot. I promise," Walt said.

Nora got up and walked over to Donna. Placing her hand on Donna's shoulder, she said, "I'm sorry, Donna. We'll get through this together. I don't know what came over me."

Donna reached back and put her hand over Nora's. "I know, Nora. We are all under great strain right now. I know James had a drug problem, and I'm sorry, too."

Walt went to the back door and called Jade and Emmie back in. "Come on in, Jade, so Emmie can get her tummy full," Walt shouted out the door.

Jade and Emmie, along with Harry, came running through the back door. "I won, I won!" Emmie yelled as she slid to a stop.

"Yes, you did, brat. Here, get up here and eat your breakfast," Jade said, laughing and putting Emmie on the chair. Breathless, she flopped in a chair herself.

"You need to get ready to go, honey. I don't know how much time we'll have, but it's almost eight, and I told Ryan to meet us at eight-thirty," Walt said, looking at Jade.

"Oh, alright, I'll get up and get moving, slave driver," she said with a grunt, and she pulled herself back up and went upstairs to get her shoes and a light jacket. Walt went to get his gun and some extra ammunition.

Emmie finished her breakfast, then laid her head on the table with a sigh.

"What's wrong, Em?" Annie asked.

"Nothing. I'm just bored," she said.

"We'll go play on the swing in a little while, okay?"

"Sure," Emmie said with another sigh.

"Do you want to go watch cartoons?" Annie walked over and picked up Emmie's hand.

"Okay, Aunt Annie." Emmie grabbed Harry's collar, and they walked to the living room. Annie followed and helped Emmie pick out a good cartoon. Then Annie went back to the kitchen.

"We're ready to go. Do you need anything before we leave?" Jade asked no one in particular.

"Honey, hang on. I wanna call George to see if he can be here while I'm gone," Walt said. He looked through his junk drawer in the kitchen to find the card that George had given him. Once he found it, he dialed George's cell phone.

After a brief exchange with George, it was decided he would come and stay with the ladies until Walt's return. They agreed it would be best not to leave the family alone. "Okay, he'll be here in about fifteen minutes," Walt told everyone.

"Thank you, Walt. You're too kind," Nora said.

"Hey, you don't have to thank me. We're all like family now, and I will do whatever it takes to keep all of you safe," Walt said, smiling.

~

Ryan was trying to hurry. He had been up getting ready for some time now. He was actually wearing cologne today, though he never wore cologne. He laughed to himself. God, it felt good to be alive today. He couldn't wait to see Jade. He planned on teaching her to shoot himself. Walt could teach Annie, but Jade was his. He finished getting ready and then checked himself. Shaved, showered, dressed, cologne, boots for the range, what was he forgetting... Oh, the gun. He went to his master closet and took out a Beretta .45 and two magazines. He got the extra ammo and a case for the gun. He was giving this to Jade today. He would make sure she knew the weapon inside and out. Taking a deep breath, he checked to make sure everything was turned off, grabbed his to-go cup of coffee, and walked out, locking the door.

During his drive to the range, he replayed his kisses with Jade in his head. That woman could curl his toes. He knew they would be good together, but this was better than good. Yep, she was going to be fun. He would take his time with her, and they would enjoy every minute they could get together. He knew his work was very demanding, but he'd never had a problem with that before. After this case was over, he planned on taking some time off. He wanted some time to get to know Jade. He hoped she was ready for him because he was not letting her slip away. He felt like she had knocked his socks off last night, and that's what his mom had told him would happen when he found the right one. He couldn't quit smiling, and he liked the way that felt. He was becoming sappy like one of those chick flicks. He laughed again.

~

"George is here. I'll let him in. Jade, why don't you offer him some coffee? Then we'll go meet Ryan," Walt said.

"Sure, Dad." Jade was getting a cup out of the cabinet.

"Good morning, Walt," George greeted him when he opened the door.

"Good morning. Come on in. Everyone is in the kitchen." He thought about giving him a warning on the attitudes that were prevalent but decided he'd let him deal with that however he wanted.

"Hey, George, how are you this morning?" Jade cheerfully asked.

"Good, and you?" He smiled at her sunny disposition this morning. Man, Ryan must've done something right last night, he thought.

"Great, thank you. Can I get you a cup of coffee?"

"Absolutely. Cream and sugar, please."

"You bet." Jade made the cup and brought it to him.

"We're gonna go now," Walt said. "Everyone good to go?"

"Yeah, take your time. We'll be fine," Nora said.

When Walt and Jade left the house, Walt had everything they would need: safety glasses, ammunition, weapons, ear plugs, targets, and a staple gun. He was proud of Jade for her willingness to learn to shoot. He thought she would fight him over this.

Jade wasn't thinking about shooting; she was thinking about seeing Ryan. That kiss last night had been the best kiss she had ever experienced, and she planned to have that experience over and over. She hoped Ryan still felt the same way this morning. She was excited to see him.

She wore a pretty outfit for him, not something she would normally think to wear to a gun range. She hoped he noticed.

Now that Annie wasn't going, Walt planned to take Jade and give everything to Ryan, then leave her there with him. He would teach her everything she needed to know; Walt had faith in the boy. He hoped they wouldn't try to keep him there because he wasn't staying.

"Dad, did you talk to Ryan this morning?"

"No, why?"

"I just hope he doesn't forget, that's all." Jade sat there biting her lip.

"I don't think he will, honey."

"I hope not." Now she worried that he may still be asleep or at work or something.

They both sat quietly in the car. Walt was letting her stew a little over Ryan. He knew Ryan wouldn't forget any more than Jade would have.

Ryan was already at the range. He had everything laid out on the table and was hanging a target when Walt's car pulled in.

The gun range was an outdoor range with about ten target holders in front of a dirt hill. The hill was there to stop the bullets from leaving the range area. The target holders were made of steel and wood, making it easy to affix the paper targets as needed. Firing lines were marked on either side by a sign stating how many feet from the target the shooter was standing. The range was empty this morning, and Ryan stood stapling a target to one of the holders.

Walt parked the car, and Jade jumped out. He shook his head and laughed, but neither Jade nor Ryan noticed. Walt took his time getting all the equipment out of the vehicle.

Jade walked up to Ryan, and, smiling, she said, "Well, good morning, handsome."

"Back at you," Ryan said with a huge smile of his own. He finished hanging the target, then turned toward her. Walt was still at the car, so Ryan grabbed Jade, giving her another sweet kiss, and then he released her.

"Wow, a quickie, huh?" she asked laughing.

"Your dad's here, and I don't want to make you or him uncomfortable. I thought we would ease into this in front of everyone for your sake."

"Ease into it? Ryan, I don't care what anyone thinks. I can't stand not touching you."

"Good, but isn't that something I should say?" He laughed.

"Oh, are we going to be the perfect girl-boy relationship?"

"God, I hope not!"

"Good, because in case you haven't noticed, I'm very outspoken and have been known to be aggressive. Are you scared?" She was laughing at the face he made.

"I have handled meaner than you, Jade Hamilton. You don't know what you're dealing with." Ryan grabbed her up and really laid one on her.

"Uh, hello?" Walt said, walking up to the couple.

"Hey, Walt" Ryan said, still holding onto Jade.

"Dad, you have to excuse his manners. He obviously doesn't have any," Jade said, laughing and pushing Ryan away.

"Wait just a minute. Jade, you're the one that said..."

Jade stopped him with a look. "I said I don't care who sees us together. I didn't mean you could stick your tongue down my throat in front of my dad." Jade started laughing at the horrified

~ 247 ~

look on Ryan's face.

"I did not stick my tongue down your throat."

"Well, guys, I don't care who did what. I'm glad to see that the two of you have come to your senses." Walt laughed and turned around, looking at the table with everything Ryan had lay out. Walt turned and looked at him.

"I have a weapon I want to teach Jade on, and then she can keep it as long as she wants to," Ryan rushed to explain.

"You seem to have everything under control." Walt turned, facing his car. His smile was so big he couldn't hope to hide it, so he simply turned away.

"I hope you don't mind, Walt. I just figured this way she would have a gun in her possession, and..." Finally, he shut up, knowing he was babbling. What the hell was wrong with him?

"No, not at all. It looks like you have everything here. I guess I'll put mine back in the car."

"Dad, I'll use yours," Jade rushed out.

"No, if he has one you can keep for a while, it's better to use that one. That way you'll be familiar with it if you need it."

Ryan relaxed a little.

Walt took all of his stuff back to the car, then came back to say goodbye.

"Ryan, take your time with her, and make sure she's comfortable enough to pull it and use it," Walt said.

"I thought you were going to teach me, Dad."

"Well, I thought Ryan could teach you and I would teach Annie, but since she didn't come with us, I'm going to say goodbye." Walt smiled a knowing smile at Ryan, then hugged Jade. "You listen to him," he ordered.

"I will, Dad, but you don't have to go."

"Yeah, I do. I need to get back so George can go to work."

"George is at your house?" Ryan asked, shocked.

"Yeah, he's looking after the ladies for me."

"Wow, no shit." Ryan had not even considered leaving them alone and the consequences that could bring.

"We won't be long, Dad," Jade said.

"Take as long as you need. There's no hurry. Since you're with Ryan, I won't worry." He waved as he walked away.

"See? There. I have his permission to do anything I think is necessary." Ryan's eyes gleamed with mischief.

"Watch yourself, buddy." Jade giggled.

"I'm just playing, Jade. We need to get serious before picking up the weapon and using it." Ryan put on a serious face.

"I know, and I'm ready whenever you are." Jade stood there smiling at him.

Ryan picked up a magazine and a box of bullets. "This is called a magazine; it's where the bullets go." Ryan began to walk her through it step by step.

"Ryan, I know what a magazine is. I know some about weapons. I don't think we need to start from the very beginning."

It was endearing to Jade that he wanted her to know every inch of the weapon and its use.

"Oh, well, okay, why don't you show me what you know, and we'll go from there." He spread his arms wide at the table and stepped back.

"Okay, this is the slide," she said, pulling the slide back and locking it in place. "This is the trigger, this is..." Jade went through the weapon, showing Ryan what she knew. He was pleased. He handed her the box of bullets. "Load the magazine, and I'll check the target." He walked toward the firing line.

"How many magazines do you want me to load?"

"Just one."

Jade stood there loading the magazine. She was excited about shooting. It had been a long time since she'd shot a gun. She liked the feeling of power when holding and firing one. She was never a great shot, but she could hit her target.

Ryan finished double checking the target he had hung earlier. He was going slowly, giving Jade time to load the magazine. He knew sometimes women had difficulty loading the bullets in the magazine. He thought that if he tried to help her load the bullets, she would get angry, so he gave her some space.

She looked up to see what he was doing and what was taking so long, and she saw that he was watching her. He was leaning against the target stand with his arms crossed over his chest and legs crossed at the ankles.

"What?" she asked.

"Nothing, can't I just look at you?"

"Well, yeah, I guess. Come here."

He walked back to where she was standing. The sun was glinting off her hair, making it look like warm honey. Her smile was so bright, she looked almost like she was glowing.

"What do you want?" he asked, stopping a few feet away and smiling.

"I'm finished."

"Are you ready?" he asked, taking a step closer.

"Yep. Where do you want to start?" she answered, taking a step closer to him.

"On the firing line would be good." He smiled at her and pointed to the area he was referring to.

"Let's do this." She began walking past him with the magazine in her hand.

"Hey! You're gonna need this, too." Ryan picked up the pistol and held it up.

"Well, I thought you would carry something," she said

flippantly.

They walked to the firing line; she carried the magazine full of bullets, and he carried the pistol. Stopping for a quick kiss, he grabbed both sides of her face and held her there while he kissed her. The pistol was held dangling from his third finger away from her head and forgotten.

She stood there breathing in all that she could. He smelled so good clean and fresh. She didn't want this morning to end. Right now, there was nothing but her and Ryan. No killer, no child in need, no danger, no arguing or pain. Just bliss.

"Alright, have you ever shot a gun before?" Ryan broke the spell.

"No, never. I just study the nomenclature of a weapon for fun," she said saucily.

"Okay, Miss Smartypants, are you comfortable with one?"

"For the most part. I mean, I don't want to have to shoot anyone, but I would."

"You think you could?"

"If the killer comes for Emmie, I don't have any doubt."

"What if Emmie isn't there; it's just you?"

"Well, I hope I would, but I guess it would depend."

"On what, Jade?" He didn't like the sound of that.

"I don't know. I mean, I know I could shoot him if I was defending someone, but if it were just me, I don't know." The smile left her face and she looked like she was a million miles away.

"Hey, where'd you go?" Ryan was worried she became so serious so quickly. He stood there watching the expression on her face and her eyes staring at the sky.

"Jade?" He wasn't sure she could hear him anymore. She stood there not moving. "Jade, honey, can you hear me?" Still nothing. She was frozen in this place and time, but she wasn't really there.

22

He stood there panting and holding the gleaming knife. The shadowy face still unseen, Jade felt the panic rise and held her breath. Nowhere to run, she stood still, staring at the dark figure a few feet in front of her. With the street light broken, the moon just a sliver, and no light available, Jade couldn't see anything but an outlined figure.

"Well, well, what do we have here?" he taunted her.

Jade could see her car but knew she couldn't reach it in time. "What do you want from me?" she asked in a shaky voice.

"I want the kid, bitch, and you can deliver her to me." He snarled as he spoke.

"Why? What did she ever do to you? You can't have her!" Jade felt like her knees were buckling.

"Oh, I will have her, and you will deliver her to me." He stood unmoving.

"I won't!" Jade yelled at him.

Laughing, he took a step closer. Jade tried to retreat, but the building she had just come out of was at her back, and the door was locked. Crying, she crumpled to the ground. This was it, she thought. I'm going to die right here. He reached down and grabbed her by the arm. Yanking her hard, he pulled her to her feet. His breath smelled bad, like rotten meat. His eyes glowed red, and no features could be seen.

"Go! Before I change my mind," he growled at her.

~

"Jade." Ryan was still trying to get her to answer him. She stood there blinking. She could tell now that she wasn't in danger but with Ryan.

Ryan, standing there looking worried, had a fierce grip on her arm. "Jade, where did you go just now?"

"Ryan." She dropped the magazine and held on to Ryan.

"Honey, it's okay. I'm here." He talked soothingly to her. Trying to stop her body from shaking so badly, he held on tight. "Did you just have a vision?"

"Yes, and I was so scared. I thought he was going to kill me," Jade said, crying.

"It's okay, baby, you're right here with me. You don't have to be scared anymore. I will keep him away from you," he vowed.

"You can't. I just saw it."

Ryan stepped back and got a full view of her sickly pale face. "What did he look like? Did you get to see his face this time?"

"He was wearing a hooded jacket, and it covered his face. I still didn't see him." She was calming down but still held on.

"It's okay, honey, I'm here." Ryan tried to comfort her.

They stood there for a while just holding each other, Ryan giving her the time she needed to get herself under control.

"I saw him on a dark street, and he had a knife. I don't know where I was, Ryan, but I was alone."

"What was he doing?"

"I don't know. The vision started there. I was coming out of a building, and I locked the door; when I turned, he was there."

"Go ahead. What happened next?"

"He told me to deliver Emmie to him." Jade related the whole vision to him. They talked long enough to calm her down. Jade answered what questions she could, and the two went over the vision several times.

Jade was ready to shoot the gun; she needed to feel it in her hands. "I'm ready to practice." Jade took the gun from Ryan's hand and picked up the magazine. They walked the rest of the way to the firing line. The shaking had subsided, and her coloring was almost completely back. She put the magazine in the pistol, the ear plugs in her ears, and the safety glasses on.

Ryan stood back and let her handle the situation the way she needed to. He didn't need to show her step-by-step to make himself feel good. He was very proud of the way she just took over. He knew she could have fallen apart, but she was too strong for that. If she needed to start shooting to feel better, then so be it. He put his ear plugs in and stood back, watching her. Jade pulled the slide back, injecting a round into the barrel. She aimed and fired. The first shot seemed to take her by surprise, but she recuperated quickly and fired again. Ryan was amazed at the calm and precise way Jade held her weapon and fired repeatedly.

After she finished the magazine, Ryan took her by the arm and walked her to the target to take a look. Ryan counted the shots and realized she had hit the target with everyone. They were spread out, and not a good set of groupings were found, but she had hit every time. "You know what you're doing, so what are we doing here?" he asked, laughing.

"I've never shot a .45 before, but I told you, I have shot before." Jade smiled too.

"Honey, I don't think I have to worry about you. You did great."

"Let's shoot some more. I want to feel comfortable with this gun, since it will be the one I'll be keeping with me."

"This isn't the one you're going to keep with you. This is my duty weapon. Wait just a second," he said as he turned toward his car.

Ryan dug around the front seat and came out with a small black box. Walking to the table where she waited to load more magazines, he handed her the box.

"What's this?" Jade opened the box.

"This is yours." Ryan stood back smiling.

"Ryan, I don't plan to keep your gun...."

"It's yours," he said simply.

"This is very nice. I love the fit of it in my hand," Jade said, holding the small .380 caliber. The magazines were even small. "I could hide this anywhere." Jade was amazed.

"That's the idea. Also, you won't have the recoil when you shoot it. Come on, let's try this one." He handed her another box of ammo. This time, they stood there together and loaded all three magazines.

Jade put her safety gear back on and got ready to shoot the new gun. "Alright, now we're talking." Jade was in love with the feel of the small handgun. After emptying the magazines, she removed her earplugs. "Whew! This is so light and easy to shoot," she drawled.

"Look at that shooting! Wow!" Ryan was in awe. "This is great!" He was smiling when he grabbed Jade up off the ground and swung her around.

"Whoa, put me down. I'll get sick going around in circles, Ryan." Jade was pushing at his shoulders.

Ryan was surprised at how small she was and how easy she was to pick up. She was so tiny...It brought out a new protectiveness in him he didn't even know existed. "Sorry, you go ahead and load the gun and shoot the whole box of ammo." He stepped back. "With this one, you have to be up close and personal, so I wanna make sure you're comfortable with it."

Jade smiled at him and began loading the clips she'd just emptied. They spent a few hours at the range, just getting her used to the gun.

~

Walt got back and let George leave for work. The kitchen, breakfast dishes, and broken window area were gleaming from being cleaned. Walt walked over to Nora. "You guys didn't have to clean all this," he said, touched.

"Yes, we did. We've also called a window man to install a new window for you."

"What?" he asked, surprised.

"Donna and I are paying for it. We figure if you didn't try to help our family out, you wouldn't be in this mess."

"Nora, I can't let you do that; after all, it was my daughter that got us involved."

"Speaking of your daughter, Walt, I think I believed Annie when she told me that Jade has visions of things." Nora stood there looking at Walt and wondering what an exceptionally handsome man he was and why someone had not snatched him up after his wife died.

"Thank you for not making us explain. People have a hard time with Jade's gift. She is my masterpiece, and I thank God every day for her." Walt was looking down at Nora and smiling with such pride.

"Donna and I insist on paying for the window, and did you see the damage the rock did to your lovely table?" she asked, walking over and running her hand across the missing chunk of wood.

"Yes. That, I think, makes me angrier than the window. I know a good guy that can fix that for me, and I'll call him when this is all over."

"We'll pay for that as well. Where's Jade? Didn't she come back with you?"

"I left her with Ryan at the range. I wanted to get back here so George could go to work. I didn't want to hold him up too long."

"Oh, I understand. Okay, well, I have some more details to work out with Annie and Donna on the funeral, so if you don't mind, I guess we should get at it." Nora waited, hoping Walt would say he wanted to whisk her away from all of this. What was she thinking? Where had that come from? She shook her head slightly and turned away from him, going back to sit down and finish the funeral business.

"I'll go outside with Emmie. Surely she's sick of cartoons by now. If you all need any help, just call." Walt went to the living room to get Emmie. A few minutes later, he, Emmie, and Harry were going out the back door.

"Annie, where were we?" Nora asked.

"Let's see, we have the funeral home called and moving on preparations, we have plots picked out, and flowers ordered. I guess we need to go by the house and get their clothes, then to the funeral home to pick out caskets and finalize everything."

"Wow, we've accomplished a lot in a short amount of time." Nora turned to Donna, who was still sitting quietly. Now that Nora thought about it, Donna really had not said too much about the funerals.

"Donna, are you alright?" Nora asked, concerned.

"Yes, I just can't believe any of this yet. I feel like I am watching all of this take place instead of being here and being an actual part of it."

"I know. I can't believe any of this either, but we have to finish what we started and get this done."

"Mom, if you and Donna want me to, I'll finish this, and you two can try to come to grips with it. We have a lot done, so it won't take too long." Annie was worried about Donna. She just didn't seem too together.

Nora looked at Donna to see what her reaction was; after all, earlier she was the one wanting a funeral. "Donna, I don't think we should stick this on Annie, so are you ready to go?"

"I'm as ready as I can be."

Annie got up and went to the back door. "Walt, we're finished in here but have to run a few errands. Would you have Emmie come on in so I can get her ready?"

"Where are you going?" Walt wasn't letting them out of his sight.

"We have to go by Amy's house for their clothing, then the funeral home."

"I'm coming with you. I don't want you all out there by yourselves." Walt called to Emmie and had her running to the porch. Then he told Annie, "We can leave Harry out here. I'll get his food and water dishes while you get Emmie washed up."

"Walt, we can't keep monopolizing your time. You have a life of your own, and we have already put you out enough." Annie was worried.

"Nonsense. You need to have Nora call the window place and reschedule the repairs." Walt walked right past Annie. Picking up the dishes for Harry, he went back to the porch and set them down where Harry would see them. Harry was lounging in the cool grass, not a care in the world.

"Aunt Annie, where are we going now? I was playing good," Emmie said, coming through the door.

"I know, sweetie, but we still have a few things we need to take care of, and you have to come with us."

Hanging her head, Emmie dropped her shoulders. "Okay."

Nora and Donna were still sitting at the table. "Donna, I'm curious as to when James got involved in all this drug stuff." She knew her son-in-law had had a drug problem, but she'd tried to stay out of the kids' business unless asked for advice. She knew Amy had taken exceptional care of Emmie, so she left it alone, but now she wanted answers.

"Oh, I guess he first got hooked on painkillers. You remember when he fell off that ladder while hanging the Christmas lights?"

"Yes, I do. Amy was worried he had broken his back." Memories flitted through her mind.

"Well, he did. If you remember, it just was a break that you couldn't do anything about. They said he didn't need surgery or a brace, just time to heal. They gave him painkillers for about ten weeks, I think. He told me he wasn't taking the pain pills anymore, but I knew he was lying. I just prayed all the time that God would heal my baby." She shook her head, fighting back the tears. "Next thing I knew, he was taking whatever he could get his hands on. He even told me once that he'd tried cocaine." Donna remembered the conversation she'd had with her son and continued, "I begged him to go to rehab, but he refused. He downplayed the addiction on the phone, and I know it was for my benefit, but what could I do? Amy was the one that had the power to get him help, not me!" She changed quickly, turning the blame on Amy.

Nora was a mother, too, and understood the guilt that Donna was feeling, but she was not about to let her lay the blame on Amy.

"Well, I understand what you are saying, for sure, but we both know the only one that had the power to make a difference was James. It isn't going to do anyone any good to sit here and do the 'what if' game or to blame someone that was not at fault just to make ourselves feel better." Nora felt that she had taken the high road on this one. Everyone was stressed enough, and no one needed to endure another argument.

Annie washed Emmie's face and hands, then turned to look at her mom. Everyone was tired; this all needed to end soon. "Are we ready?" Annie put her hand on Nora's shoulder. She was proud of the way her mother had just handled Donna.

"Yes, I just need to grab my purse. Donna?" Nora inquired.

"Right behind you." She had to admire the way Nora had just manipulated her. She smiled to herself.

All of them were walking to the front door when the telephone rang. "I'll get that and then meet you at the car," Walt said, turning toward the living room.

"Hello?"

"Mr. Hamilton?" The voice on the phone was pleasantly

inquiring. "I'm Cathy with Seasonal Windows. We need to set up a time with you for your broken window replacement."

"Oh, yes, of course. I'm going to have to say later this afternoon sometime."

"Is four o'clock alright with you, sir?"

"Yes, I believe that will work."

"We'll see you then, Mr. Hamilton."

Walt hung up, set the alarm system, then went to the car.

"Is everything alright, Walt?" Nora asked.

"Yes, that was the glass place. They'll be here at four this afternoon."

"Oh, dang, I was supposed to call them with the time after you got home. I forgot to ask when a good time was." Nora began laughing like a silly schoolgirl.

Everyone got in the car, and Annie drove to the Linderhoff house. No one talked much during the ride. Walt felt very sorry for Donna. He knew she was having a hard time, and he had no idea how to help her. Of course, he knew from experience that words didn't help, and neither did hugging. He just sat quiet and thought about how blessed he was that he still had Jade.

~

George was talking to Danny Miller about the drugs they had found in Molly. "Can you believe that son of a bitch put the drugs in the doll he gave to his little girl?" George was still fuming.

"Hey, I've seen worse, believe it or not." Danny said, shaking his head.

"Yeah, but she is so young and sweet...How the hell could a daddy do that?"

"Who knows why these people do what they do? If you ask me, none of it makes sense. I have to tell you, though, that was a hell of a find, as there were four thousand pills! He really was pretty stupid. Any one of the drug dealers I know would kill for that amount. Did this guy really expect to get away with it?" He was dumbfounded. Criminals were infamous for stupidity, but this really took the cake.

"I don't know. I guess so. He obviously was not the brightest bulb in the lamp." George was still amazed at the amount of ecstasy James had stolen.

"So how do you and Douglas plan to pursue this?" Danny asked.

"I don't think we've put that together yet. Any ideas?"

"Why don't you use the kid for bait?"

"What?" George was incredulous at this suggestion.

"You know, stick her out there and have her flash the doll around until he puts two and two together."

"Are you crazy? She's only six."

"I'm not saying leave her alone. I'm saying to use her and be there to protect her."

"I don't think the family would allow that."

"Don't tell them."

"Man, you are one hard son of a bitch. Would you really use the kid?"

"Sure would. I have faith in my ability to protect her."

"I don't know." George turned to walk out.

"Hey, if you guys need anything, let me know," Danny yelled at George's back. George just waved his hand in answer. He was thinking now that they could do that. Would Ryan go for it? They didn't have to tell anyone what they were doing. This was going to need some thought and planning before he approached Ryan with it.

~

Ryan and Jade were picking up the spent shells on the range. Ryan could not believe how Jade took to the gun. She was completely at ease with the whole thing. He had never met a woman, other than policewomen, who was comfortable with handguns. He was proud of her and had told her repeatedly.

He could smell her perfume every time she moved and the wind blew. He loved that scent. He could still see her fiery expression when she thought he had slept with Annie. She was going to be jealous, and that was supposed to be hard to deal with, but he kind of liked it.

"Hey, are you gonna help pick these up or what?" Jade asked when she saw he was daydreaming.

"I am helping. What are you talking about?"

"Oh, I don't know. You seemed a million miles away."

"Well, I'm not. I was just thinking we should hurry so I can get to work," he lied.

"I think we're about finished. Do you have to go to work?" She sounded disappointed.

"Well, only if I want to eat and have a roof over my head." He started laughing.

"Are you always so cocky?" she asked, jabbing him in the ribs.

"Ouch! Yep, better get used to it," he said, faking injury.

"Come on, sissy boy, you can take me home and then go to work," she teased.

~

Arriving at the Linderhoffs' house and seeing it for the first time since hearing about James was even harder on Donna. She sucked in a little air at the sight of the house.

"Grammy, you okay?" Emmie asked.

"Yes, baby. I just haven't been here in a while, and I guess I forgot how pretty the flowers in the front yard are," Donna lied, trying to keep herself intact.

"My mommy plants flowers every year," Emmie said with a smile.

"Do you all want to wait here while I go grab some things?" Annie asked.

Nora looked at Donna. "Can you do this?"

"I don't know." Donna was shaking.

"Ladies, I'll go in and help Annie. Why don't you both stay here with Emmie?" Walt said, getting out of the car.

"We're asking way too much of him," Nora said to Donna after Annie and Walt disappeared into the house.

"I know. I'm sorry, Nora. I knew this was going to be difficult, but I had no idea how difficult. I guess I'm weak." Donna hung her head and studied her hands.

"Hey, this is very hard on both of us, but we know it has to be done, and we will pull together and get it done." Nora looked at Donna. "You're not in this alone, Donna. We're all going to get through it." She hoped she could continue to appear to have the strength that she didn't feel.

"I know, Nora, and I also know I've been overbearing and bitchy. I'm sorry. I'll try harder to do my best. It's just..." The crying started again, and this time, she didn't try to control it. "Poor baby. I love you so much," Donna said, grabbing Emmie up into her lap. She just needed to hug her for a few minutes.

Emmie hugged back and held on tight. She knew Grammy missed Mommy and Daddy, too.

Nora looked around at the parked cars and the cars passing by. The thought occurred that the killer could be watching. It sent shivers up and down her spine. She wished Annie and Walt would hurry. Reaching over, she pushed the lock button, hearing all the doors lock at the same time. Donna looked up and saw the fear etched in Nora's face. Without scaring Emmie by saying anything, she just looked at Nora for answers. Nora looked around the car with animation, showing Donna what she was thinking. Donna caught on and began looking herself. Nothing seemed out of place or suspicious to either of them, but they kept their guard up. Donna held Emmie in a tight embrace, and Emmie was getting fidgety. Donna released Emmie, sitting her back on the seat, and replaced her seatbelt.

Annie and Walt came out of the house. Annie was carrying the clothes they had thought would be appropriate. Opening the trunk, she placed the outfits in there. Nora popped the locks to allow them access.

"Mom, is everything alright?" Annie asked as she and Walt climbed in.

"Yes, dear. Donna and I were just being cautious."

Annie looked at Walt in the mirror and saw he was thinking the same thing. Had something happened while they were in the house?

"Did you find a suit for James?" Donna asked, changing the subject.

"Yes, and a very pretty dress for Amy," Annie answered.

"Good, that will make things easier. I was afraid we would have to buy something for them to wear, and I had no idea what size James would wear now," Donna stressed.

"No need to stress about that now; everything is going as planned." Annie smiled at Donna.

As they drove on to the funeral home, Annie began to worry about Emmie. Emmie had never been to a place like this before. Had Amy explained anything at all to Emmie about death? Annie wanted to ask, but she wasn't sure how. Everyone was being so quiet. Maybe she would just let it ride and just answer questions as Emmie asked them. That way, she wouldn't feel like the bearer of bad news. As Annie drove on, her mind whirled and body stressed at the thought of seeing Amy in a casket. Wow. How was Emmie going to deal with that? Maybe they should have closed caskets. She would have to remember to talk to her mom and Donna about that.

23

RYAN pulled up outside of Walt's house. He looked around and didn't see Annie's car. "Where did Annie go?" he asked.

"What?" Jade was taken by surprise.

"I said, where did Annie go? Her car isn't here."

"Oh, I don't know. Let's go find out." She got out of the car and headed for the front door. She could hear the alarm going off and turned to look at Ryan.

"You stay here, Jade," Ryan said as he ran past her. When he reached the front door he found it unlocked. Pushing it open, he went in.

Jade ran back to the car and got her gun. Loading magazines and running to the house, she mentally prepared herself for the worst. Going inside, she could see the house was empty. That gave her a great flood of relief. She followed Ryan up the stairs. When she reached the top, she could see Ryan standing in her bedroom doorway. He did not move his body; he just turned his head to look at her.

"What?" she asked, moving toward him.

"I think he's gone already," Ryan said, moving to the side and giving her a view of the room. All of the baby dolls that Jade had had as a child were hung by the neck and swinging from the ceiling fan in her room. One had a missing leg and a note attached.

Hey, girlie. I finally figured out where that thieving bastard put my dope. Get the doll from the brat and bring it to me tonight. You are to come alone with the doll. Will wait for you at sister's place. If you bring the cops, I will have my partner kill your dad.

"Oh my God." Jade was shaking.

Ryan was on his cell phone calling George. "It's okay, Jade. We'll handle this." He tried to put his arm around her, but she backed away, shaking her head.

"No, you can't. He'll kill Dad if you do."

"No, he won't, babe. You're going to have to trust me. Do you trust me?"

Nodding her head yes, she sat down on the floor. Holding her head in her hands, she began to cry harder. Why had she gotten involved in this? Why couldn't she learn to just walk away?

As if in a dense fog, she heard Ryan talking, but it sounded like he was miles away from her. Then she was standing there...

"You are a lovely creature indeed." He stepped out of the shadows and into her line of vision. The dark figure cloaked in the hooded jacket laughed wickedly. The knife gleamed in the light cast from the car headlights that were now blinding her.

Whose car, she wondered. Feeling the building at her back and knowing she had nowhere to go, she watched him walk slowly toward her. "I'm not afraid of you!" she yelled.

"Yes, you are," he sneered. "I can smell your fear." He stopped and watched her squirm. "Can you guess what I want to do to you, girlie?" he asked, his voice getting raspier.

"What do you want from me?" she asked, barely able to form the words. He stepped closer, the evil mouth curved into a smile of crooked, broken teeth, his breath unbearably horrible. She tried to move backwards, but the building held its ground.

He laughed the wicked laugh again and reached out to touch a lock of her hair. "You smell good." He loved watching her squirm. Oh, the things he wanted to do to her. Scenes of his fantasy flitted across his mind's eye, and he leaned in for a taste.

Jade dropped to the ground, folding her body like a piece of cloth. She couldn't bear his touch or the rancid smell that permeated from him.

Staying as still and quiet as she could, she prayed for someone to help her. He quit touching her, and she could no longer smell him. Looking up, she realized he was gone.

Looking around her, she only saw the bright lights of the car headlights and wondered yet again: whose car? Standing, she walked toward the car. It was her car...

Jade felt herself being shaken. She opened her eyes to see Ryan with a face full of concern.

"Jade, oh, thank God, are you alright?"

"Yes, I think so. I had another vision. I don't know why they're so close together."

Ryan was reeling. How did this guy get in? Why did he want to meet Jade? What the hell was going on? He grabbed Jade in a tight embrace. "Everything's going to be okay, honey. George and I are going to put an end to all of this. I promise." He could feel her body shaking. "I'm not going to allow you to meet him, either," he said with finality.

"If I don't go to meet him, how are you going to protect us? Wait a minute. What do you mean, you're not going to allow it?" She pushed away from him, demanding an explanation.

"Hey, hey, wait just a minute. He said he would have his partner kill your dad. What partner?" Ryan pushed the explanation aside; changing the subject would stop the fight that was inevitable after a statement like that.

"I don't know... No partner has ever been mentioned before."

"He's playing games with us. I don't believe he has a partner and that it's a scare tactic. He feeds on fear."

"How do you know that?"

"He's just trying to keep you scared and under control. I have to call George, so give me a minute, and then I want full details on this last vision."

"I thought you just called him," she said, bewildered.

"I was calling him until you zoned out. You scared the shit out of me. I'm not used to that."

Ryan turned away and dialed George's number. As he waited for George to answer, thought after thought ran through his mind. He had to keep these people safe no matter what. During his brief telephone talk with George, he agreed he and Jade would meet George at the station. "Come on, Jade, we gotta go, and you can explain that vision," he stated.

"Go? Go where, Ryan? I'm not leaving. I have to clean this up before everyone gets back." She wasn't budging. He was becoming extremely bossy, and she wasn't one to follow; she was her own person.

"Jade, George can't come over here right now. He's in the middle of something. I need to fill him in and log this evidence," he said, lifting a small bag to put the note in.

"That's fine, go ahead. I have things I have to do and can't keep running around with you, not being productive."

"Being productive?" What the hell was she talking about? He wasn't sure what was happening, but he didn't like it.

"Yeah, you know, getting things done." She was standing with her hands on her hips and a very defiant look in her eyes.

"You have plenty of time to do whatever you need to do, but right now, you're coming with me to see George. I want his take on all of this, and I want vision details."

"Ryan, I appreciate that you have a job to do. You should also appreciate that I have a job to do. I don't mean actual employment type job, but a job to do nonetheless." She waved her hand around at the dolls still hanging on the fan.

"I am not leaving you alone. We'll get back as soon as we can and clean this up."

"No! I need to take those dolls down and straighten my room so Dad doesn't know this happened. This has all been too much for him; he's stressing way too much. I'm afraid he isn't showing what this is doing to him. It's all my fault I got us into this."

"I understand your concern for your dad, and I'll help you take those dolls down. Your dad is a strong, healthy man, Jade. Don't worry about him." Ryan stepped into the room again. "Come on. Let's get this done. We really have to meet George."

"I'll make a deal with you. We take them down and this isn't mentioned to my dad; then I'll agree to go with you to see George."

"Deal. I need to get some photos first and then tag the letter for evidence." Ryan went to his car and got his camera, film, and gloves. When he came back to Jade's room she was standing there looking around. "Jade, are you alright?"

"Yeah, I just don't like the idea of that maniac being in my dad's house, let alone in my bedroom."

Ryan knew exactly what she meant. He loaded the camera with the film and began taking the photographs. Then, carefully, he put his gloves on and bagged the letter for possible fingerprints. He knew they wouldn't find any, but he still had to do it the right way.

He looked over at Jade and nodded. They began taking the dolls down and putting them back in their rightful places on the shelves. The room was put back the way it looked before the man intruded on her space. Once they were finished, Ryan stepped back and watched all the emotions playing on Jade's face as she stood looking at what had been her private space for the majority of her life. Not wanting to rush her but knowing there was work to be done, he asked, "Are you ready, Jade?"

Taking a long last look around, she said on a sigh, "As ready as I can be." She turned to look at him and saw the concern in his eyes. Deciding *he* wasn't going to ruin her day, she smiled brightly and put some spring in her step. "Let's go, sexy."

After checking everything and resetting the alarm, they left.

~

He sat in the attic quietly. His plan was coming together now. They would never think to look in the attic. He was so smart. He quietly laughed to himself. He would have his drugs back in no time. He would just stay there as long as it took. He wished he had a better vantage point, but this was as good as it was going to get. He would just have to try to hear what was going on and take it a step at a time. Now that he was in, he could come and go by the rose trellis, and no one would be the wiser. He knew she wouldn't meet him, but he figured it a nice touch.

~

Annie pulled up to the funeral home. Still wondering about Emmie's reaction to the events that were going to take place, she made a decision to talk with her quietly before going in.

"Mom, why don't you all go ahead? I want to talk with Emmie for a few minutes alone."

"I think that's a good idea, honey." They left Annie to deal with Emmie.

She had her hands full and no experience in dealing with any of this, but she had common sense and a tender heart. If she was going to raise this little girl alone, she may as well do it right from the beginning, not expecting anyone to always be there to guide her through each trial and tribulation. She wasn't a parent by choice but by circumstance, and she was going to be the best damn parent she could be.

"Emmie, I know you don't understand a lot of what is going on, but I want you to know that I'm here if you have questions or you're afraid. I'm here, honey."

"Aunt Annie, are my mommy and daddy in there?" She pointed to the building.

"Look, Emmie, this is not easy, and I can only hope I explain this where you understand what I'm trying to say." Annie looked at Emmie with sadness and hoped that she could talk to her without crying, but before she could continue, Emmie asked, "Aunt Annie, I know they're dead. Can we go in now?" She looked bored and not bothered by anything.

"I know you know that, but do you know what that means?"

"Yeah, they can't come home with me, but I can see them."

"Honey, you need to know a little more than that. Will you sit here with me and give me a chance to help you understand what's going to happen and why?"

"Okay, but hurry. I really want to see my mommy." Emmie was excited.

Annie had no idea how to start this conversation and knew that Emmie would still not understand when she was finished, but she wasn't able to take her time, either, since Emmie thought they were in there waiting for her. "Emmie, when someone dies, do you know what happens to them?"

"Yeah, they go to heaven."

"Okay, that's a good start. Do you know that they cannot talk to you or walk with you or hug you or anything?"

"Why can't they? I thought I could talk to them."

"Well, sweetie, you can talk to them, and you can see them, too, but they won't look like you want them to." Taking a deep breathm she continued, "They will be lying in a box-like container, and they will have on nice clothes and look like they're sleeping."

"We can wake them up so I can talk to them."

"No, baby, we can't wake them up because they aren't really sleeping." Annie prayed to God for strength. She didn't know how to bring this up right. "Emmie, when you die, you never come back. Your body is here, but your spirit..."

No, that was too adult. What the hell was she supposed to say? Annie sat there struggling for the right words.

"Aunt Annie, I know Mommy and Daddy will make everything alright. Let's just go see them."

"Emmie, you're not going to see them right now. You will see them at the funeral. We are here to pick some things out that are needed for the funeral. Then we're going back to Walt's house. Maybe your grandmothers can explain this better." So much for doing this on her own.

"So mommy and daddy aren't here?" She began to cry. "When can I see them?" she wailed.

"Soon, baby, I promise." Annie picked her up and held her, allowing for time to cry, Annie decided to just hold Emmie and give her all the love and all the time she needed.

After some time, Emmie didn't say anything; she just let go of Annie and sat there. "Come on, honey, let's get this over with." Annie opened the door and stepped out. Taking Emmie's hand, she walked into the funeral home.

Nora and Donna were sitting in a room with the funeral director and talking quietly. Walt was standing outside the door. waiting for Annie and Emmie. He walked over to Annie when she came through the door. Annie stopped to talk with him, and Emmie beelined into the room with her grandmothers.

"You okay?" Walt looked at Annie's pale face and crestfallen look.

"No, I'm not sure we will ever be okay again."

"What can I do to help?"

"Nothing, Walt. I'm sorry for being so mean. I just can't get Emmie to understand any of this, and it's killing me."

"Hey, quit trying so hard. You're not in this alone. We're all here to help. Let us help."

"I would gladly let you all help, but I think it's too overwhelming for Emmie, and the more we tell her, the more confused she is. I thought if I could get her alone and talk to her, she would grasp it easier, but I was wrong. I don't know what else to say or how to say it." She took a deep, steadying breath. She couldn't start crying again, not now.

"Look, Emmie is a smart child, and she knows more than you think she does. I think you're not giving her enough credit."

"I know she's smart, Walt, but she has no idea about death and what all it entails."

"She knows more than she's letting on. I think she is enjoying the attention."

"What a horrible thing to say!" Annie was appalled.

"Hey, hold on a minute. That's not what I mean. The harsh reality is, I believe she knows what death is, and I believe she knew Amy and James were dead, and *that's* why she created the angel."

Emmie was standing in the room with her grandmothers, and at Walt's raised voice, she looked out at them. Annie smiled at Emmie, letting her know everything was okay.

"What are you talking about, Walt?"

"You know about the angel, don't you?"

"It was mentioned briefly. What do you mean, you think she knew they were dead?"

"Children know more than we give them credit for, but in this particular case, I believe she could tell us what we don't know."

"Walt, you're not making any sense."

"I know. It's just a feeling I have. When Jade mentioned the angel to me, I told her then that I believe that was the way a six-year-old was trying to tell her she already knew."

"I think you're wrong. I know my niece, and she's not conniving."

"No, honey, that's not what I meant. I just mean I think she is more in touch with what's going on than any of us are giving her credit for."

"So are you saying that I shouldn't try to explain to her what's happening?"

"No, I'm saying don't try to explain unless she asks."

Annie stood there thinking through what Walt had said. Was he right? Was she making too much of this? How was she supposed to know? She had never raised a child before, had never had to know what to say and when to say it. She'd talk to her mother and get some advice. Walt had raised a child and spoke with wisdom. Her mother would have that same wisdom.

She said, "Walt, you're right. I'll just wait and let this happen as it happens. Thanks for the advice."

"I know I was too much to the point, but I can help. Annie, remember I went through loss and dealing with my little girl." He took her hand and gave a squeeze.

Donna and Nora were answering all the questions and making all the decisions. Walt and Annie stood back and let them handle everything. Emmie stood by very quietly, absorbing everything.

~

Ryan and Jade pulled into the station parking lot. Ryan had been thinking about the killer wanting to meet Jade at Annie's tonight. He didn't want her in harm's way and would not allow her to meet the killer. He would talk to George and try to be impartial where Jade was concerned, but his mind was made up: she wouldn't be meeting anyone.

"What are you thinking about?" Jade was looking at Ryan and the frown lines between his eyes.

"The whole thing: the killer, the visions, everything," he answered honestly.

"What about the killer?"

"You know, the note he left wanting to meet you tonight, the fact he broke into your dad's house, the fact you seem to be his new target. All of it."

"Are you thinking I should meet him?"

"I don't know what I'm thinking. I just know we need to take our time with this and not miss an opportunity." He lied, not wanting to start another argument.

"I'll do whatever you think I should. I trust you, Ryan."

"Thanks, honey. I won't put you in danger. I promise. I have to tell George about the note."

"Of course you do. If you don't, then we could be giving up a chance to catch this guy."

Ryan shuddered inwardly. He would not let that fucker within a mile of Jade. No ifs, ands, or buts about it.

They got out and went in to find George. He was sitting in the office, looking over the note from the rock that sailed through Walt's window. The fingerprints were not identifiable, and so once again, they were back to square one. He looked up to see Ryan and Jade walk in. Setting aside the note, he got up from his desk and walked over to the window. He didn't want to see her face when he told her. "Fingerprints were not identifiable. I'm sorry, Jade. Looks like we're back to square one."

"George, it's okay. We got another chance!" Ryan said, pulling out the evidence bag with the latest note in it.

George turned around and saw the paper in Ryan's hand. "What's that?"

"It's another note from the killer."

"What?" George moved quickly to see it.

"You did preserve it for prints, wearing gloves, right?" he asked, anger turning his face red.

"Yep" was all Ryan answered.

"Okay, explain. Where the hell did this one come from?"

"He broke into Walt's house and left this note in Jade's bedroom. He wants to meet her tonight at Annie's place. Read the note." He tossed the baggie in George's direction. "This is what I was trying to explain on the phone earlier when you send you couldn't leave here."

George took the note and read it. "You're not seriously thinking about letting Jade meet him, are you?"

"Of course not. I wanted to talk to you first and hash it out at every angle. So let's get to it." Ryan pulled a chair out for Jade, then took one himself. He looked at George, waiting for him to take a chair so they could get started.

"So he's figured out where the drugs were. Interesting! I guess he's seen Emmie carrying her doll around. Ain't that some shit." Shaking his head back and forth, he decided it was time to get this son of a bitch once and for all. "Alright, let's hear what you're thinking."

"Um, guys, before we get started, I just want to say thank you to both of you. You've been a big help through all of this, and I trust you with my life. I will do whatever you two think is best, but if you should decide I should meet with him, Dad can't know about it, or I won't do it."

"Jade, we can't do this behind Walt's back," Ryan said.

"Then I won't do it."

"Jade, listen to yourself. If something happens, Walt has a right to know about it. I respect him too much to do this, or anything, for that matter, behind his back." Ryan stood up, looking down at Jade.

"Okay, hang on a second." George would run interference. "Jade, why would you ask us to keep this from Walt?" George asked, trying to avoid a fight.

"Because I think this is getting to him. I'm worried about his health."

"Why? Has something happened we don't know about?" Ryan asked.

"No, I just don't want anything to happen. Ny dad isn't young, you know."

Laughing, George said, "What, is he all of fifty-five, fifty-seven?"

"Don't make light of my feelings, George. I know you're older, too, but this is my dad. He's all I've had most of my life."

"Point is, Jade, he's not unhealthy, and he's not that old. Give him some credit, kiddo." George used the term on purpose.

Jade sat there feeling like they thought she didn't have any faith in her dad, when all she wanted was to protect him. That wasn't so wrong, was it? Cops could be arrogant, and these two were for sure, so flippantly, she said, "Fine, I'll sit here quietly and listen to the pros and see what you can come up with. If it works for me, good; if it doesn't, too bad." She crossed her arms over her chest and looked at them like a spoiled child might.

Ryan sat back down. "We are blowing this all out of proportion here. Everyone take a deep breath, and let's think before we jump to conclusions." Taking a deep breath, he continued. "Okay, so the note said he wants Jade to come to Annie's apartment alone. No cops, or Walt dies at the hand of his partner."

"Who the hell is the partner, anyway, and since when does he have a partner?" George asked.

"I don't believe he does. That's one point. I think he's grasping at straws because he's at a dead end and needs his dope to keep his boss happy," Ryan said.

"Okay, we know he got the drugs from somewhere, we know James took them from him, and we know we now have the drugs. So he's getting desperate," George reasoned.

"Right, so why should we deal with him at all?" Ryan asked, having a light come on. Brainstorming was one of his best attributes. "He's the one that needs us now."

"We still need to catch him, so what we need to decide is how." George loved this cat and mouse game. He lived for it.

"We've had the chance to get fingerprints, and that didn't work. We've had the chance to catch him in Annie's apartment, and that didn't work. We've gotten a description and possible tattoo, so we went through mug shots, and that didn't work. What are we missing?" Ryan, trying to tear it apart and break it down, looked at George.

"We aren't missing anything. We just haven't caught him yet. He keeps getting into Walt's house. How? The doors are locked and the alarm system is set, yet he gets in and leaves his mark without getting caught. He seems one step ahead. Always one step ahead," George said.

Jade sat there watching the two go back and forth. Everything they were saying was true. What were they missing? They were missing something, even though George stated otherwise.

"I don't think he's one step ahead. I think he watches and picks his timing very well." Ryan smiled as a thought occurred to him. "What if we give him something to really watch?"

"What do you have in mind?" George was curious now.

"I think Jade should ignore this chance to meet with him. He'll be watching to see if she's going to go, and when she doesn't, he'll be pissed. He'll watch her to see what she's going to do and then try again."

"Yeah, so what?"

"Well, we give him the chance to try and communicate with her when he thinks she's alone."

"What do you have in mind, Ryan?" Jade's arms covered with goose bumps.

"I think you should give me the keys to your house when we leave here. You and George go to Walt's house. He'll be out there somewhere, watching and waiting. After a good, long wait, you get in your car and drive home alone. I'll be there waiting in the dark. He won't know it."

"I think I'm following you here! Then, when he tries to come in to get to me, you're there." Jade was getting excited. "It would be like using me for bait."

"Well, yeah, kinda," Ryan said with a straight face. "But I'll be there to protect you."

George sat there thinking it through. "Don't you think he'll wonder where you are?"

"I could make an appearance, then leave."

"No, that's too obvious. We need someone else to be at Jade's house waiting. Someone he doesn't know."

"I don't want someone else there. I am not taking any chances with Jade." Ryan was emphatic on this point.

"I have my gun, Ryan. I can take care of myself." The visions popped into her mind. She really didn't want to be alone.

"No, absolutely not! You are not going to deal with him by yourself." Ryan was getting angry.

"Okay, okay, hang on, let's think some more." George tried to calm everyone down. The three sat, each thinking their own thoughts, no one saying anything.

"Hey, Ryan, you know Danny Miller? He 's kind of built like you." George was pumped.

"Yeah, so what?"

"We take him to Walt's with us, that is, Jade and me, and he pretends to be you. Then you can already be at Jade's house, and the killer won't think twice about it."

"That could work. Call Danny and see if he can come up here."

George put the call in. "He's on his way."

"This could work, George. Jade, you would have me there to protect you, and Walt will know what's going on but will have no problem with it since he knows I would lay my own life down to protect yours." Ryan smiled.

"Give me a break. You are such a moron sometimes, Ryan. I still don't want my dad to know about all of this."

"I told you, I'm not keeping anything from Walt," Ryan said.

"George, would you want your daughter doing what you guys want me to do?"

"I don't have a daughter, Jade."

"I'm speaking hypothetically."

"I don't know. I mean, if Ryan is there, it would make me feel better."

"So you have no problem with this if Ryan is there, but you think I can't protect myself, right?" Jade was getting red-faced and pissed. She wasn't a little girl. She knew things and saw things these two could only read about. No, she wasn't going to do this their way. They were going to do this her way.

"Honey, you're getting bent out of shape for nothing." Ryan tried to placate her.

"Bite me." She walked to the window. "You guys don't know me very well if you think I can't handle myself."

"No one is saying you can't handle yourself, Jade, but you have to realize this isn't just some Joe Blow. This is a killer who would not hesitate to murder you." Ryan slapped his hand on the table.

George stood up. "We can't fight about this. Jade, it's not going to happen unless you are completely safe."

"Alright, fine, I'll let Ryan be the big hero and protect me. I just want you to know I'm not scared and will do whatever needs to be done to get this maniac. I just want to say I'm not a bimbo. I can protect myself." For some reason, she felt better saying it.

"Hello? Am I interrupting anything?" Danny asked as he stood in the doorway.

"Hey, Danny, come on in, have a seat." George walked over to shake his hand.

After all four sat down again and they put their anger aside, the conversation went on without a hitch. It was agreed that Danny would accompany George and Jade to Walt's house. Ryan would wait about an hour and then go to Jade's to wait. This could work, Ryan thought again. Maybe finally this will all be over.

Danny was told that Ryan and Jade were seeing each other, and since the killer might know this information, he was to act as Ryan would: like a boyfriend.

George was going to explain things to Walt so nothing was being done behind his back, and George would handle whatever reaction Walt had.

Jade was to be confident in Ryan's ability to handle what was to come, and she was to stay out of the way of danger. Jade agreed, but not easily. She knew Walt would be surprised at her giving Ryan the upper hand, but if it helped him not to stress, then she could pull it off. Ryan just didn't know her well enough to know she would never stand back and let someone else fight her battles.

After everything was laid out to perfection, Jade gave Ryan a key to her back door. She would enter from the front, just like always. Jade would leave Walt's house at approximately nine o'clock and head home alone. She would, of course, act like she was watching for anything out of the ordinary, just like she had been. George and Danny would leave at approximately nine thirty and drive to the station. They would see if they were being scrutinized as they believed they had been.

24

WALT put the key in and opened the door. He could hear the beeping of the alarm system and realized everything was still intact. The alarm had not been set off, and everything was as it should be. Without another thought, he showed the women into the house.

"What time is the window guy supposed to be here, Walt?" Nora asked.

"At four o'clock, and it's ten till," he answered.

"As soon as he leaves, I'll start some dinner. Do you know when Jade will be home?" she asked.

"I would have thought she and Ryan would be here. I guess I'd better call her." Walt went into the living room and called Ryan's cell phone.

Caller ID was a wonderful thing, Ryan thought. "Hi, Walt, we're on our way."

"I was just checking. Hadn't heard from you."

"I know. That was pretty thoughtless of me, and I'm sorry."

The doorbell rang, and Walt, needing to cut the conversation short, said, "Gotta go. The guy is here to hang my new window. See you when you get here." Walt hung up and opened the door. Seeing two men standing on his porch, he asked "Can I help you?"

"We're here to replace a broken window," the older one said.

"Let me show you where it is, and then we'll get out of your way." Walt walked the two men to the kitchen. Explaining to the women who they were, he walked over and removed the tarp. "Will you need the table moved?"

"No, sir, we'll be working from the outside mostly."

"Okay, if you need anything, we'll be in the living room."

The men went to work on the window and the rest went to the living room to discuss the day's events.

"You are so lucky that you don't worry about small, petty things, Walt, I could never leave workers in the kitchen like that and go sit in the living room where they couldn't be seen," Nora said.

"Really? Why?"

"I don't know. I'm just funny that way. I mean, I've never had a bad experience or anything. It's just, you know, strangers in my home." She laughed at herself, knowing she sounded paranoid.

"I don't worry about things that often. I just let life be life and try to go with it."

"You are an amazing man, Walt Hamilton. I don't think I've ever met anyone quite like you before."

"Thank you, I think." He wasn't sure if that was a good thing.

"Yes, it was a compliment, and you're welcome."

Smiling, he said, "Ladies, I know you still have a lot to discuss for tomorrow, so how about I take Emmie outside to play on the tire swing and let you all get to it?"

"Walt, you sure you don't mind? I mean, you have already been so helpful and gracious. I feel like we're putting you out." Annie looked at Walt with such sincere appreciation that he blushed.

"Annie, you are the ones that I should be thanking. You have all filled my home with family again. You have no idea how much that means to me."

"Yay! I wanna play on the swing!" Emmie yelled, jumping up off the floor.

"Well, let's go, short stack, and leave the ladies to the hard work." He smiled at Nora and followed Emmie out of the room.

"Well, I can't think of anything else we need to do for tomorrow." Annie was getting anxious to have the funerals over so she could get back to her life. School was important, and she was missing way too much.

"Annie, I think Donna and I covered most everything that you didn't. You've been a big help, and I know you have other things you should be dealing with. I just want you to know how much I appreciate all you have done."

"Me too, Annie. I know this is hard on you, honey, and I want to take the time to thank you, too." Donna spoke quietly.

"This is a difficult time for all of us, and I don't think it's quite over yet," Annie said sadly.

"What do you mean?" Donna asked.

"We still have to talk about Emmie." Annie threw it out there. She prayed they would all agree that she take Emmie.

"I believe Emmie will be better off with you, Annie. Donna, what do you think?"

"I was hoping to take Emmie away from here. You know, back to New York. A new beginning for her." Donna sat straight up, realizing that she might be in for a fight.

"Donna, you can't be serious! Don't you think taking a six-year-old to raise at this time in your life would be too much?" Nora was ready.

"No, not at all. I did raise James, you know, and he turned out alright."

"Hold it a minute. I didn't mean to start an argument. We are three grown women, and what we want is not the issue. Emmie is." Annie stood up, hoping to stop any comment her mom was going to make about James turning out alright. What was Donna thinking? Didn't she realize he was the reason Amy was dead?

"Well, maybe we should ask Emmie where she wants to live," Donna suggested.

"No, absolutely not. That child has been through enough already, and tomorrow is going to be bad. I won't let you put her in the middle of this." Annie was getting red-faced.

"You won't let me?" Donna was standing now.

The men working on the window stopped to listen. The women were getting loud, and they wanted to see what was going on. Walt heard the yelling when the men quit pounding the rest of the broken glass out. He walked up on the porch slowly, trying to listen, too. "What's going on in there?" he asked the men.

"Don't know, sir, just heard some yelling, so we quit making noise. You know, hoping not to add to the anger," the younger man said.

"Uh-huh," Walt replied. Turning to Emmie, Walt waved at her. She was fine, swinging like a champ. He turned back to listen.

"Donna, you need to stop and think about the life Emmie would have living with you. You're her grandmother. Annie is young enough to be her mother."

"Yes, but she's not." Donna sat back down. Thinking that she'd made her point, she relaxed.

"Okay, listen. We're not asking Emmie, so why don't you tell us why you want her to live with you, and we'll see if we agree?" Annie decided to show Donna she was the better person to have Emmie.

"Well, we have good schools in New York, and I have plenty of income to see that she is comfortable and wants for nothing. I have lots of time to spend with her and teach her things, and I'm not going to be getting remarried, so I won't have to put her through a lot of change."

"I think you're too old. I'm not trying to be mean or unkind. I'm too old, too. Annie is young and has a whole life to spend with Emmie. Hopefully, she will be getting married sometime in the future, but that could be good for Emmie. Annie will spend lots of time with her and be there when she wakes up crying for her mommy and daddy. You can see her whenever you want, Donna. We would never keep her from you." Nora was trying to get Donna to understand that the age difference could be a problem for Emmie and to reassure her that Emmie wouldn't disappear from her life.

"Donna, I want Emmie. I love that child with my whole heart. She has lived here by me her whole life and has friends here. I would give her a good, stable home. Mom is right; we would never keep her from you. Please give this some thought," Annie pleaded.

"Alright, guys, I think we've heard enough. Let's stop eavesdropping." Walt went back out to the swing, where Emmie was twisting round and round.

The two work men just looked at each other and went back to work.

"I will give it some more thought, but I want you to know I have been thinking about this since I got on the airplane to come here. I think James would have wanted me to get Emmie." Donna didn't realize what a stupid comment she had just made.

Annie walked over to stand in front of Donna. She had tried to be the bigger person, to take the high road as her parents had taught her, but enough was enough. She took her time before saying anything. She didn't want to hurt Donna any more than she had to, but the lady needed a reality check.

"Donna, at this point, I hate to say this, but I don't give a damn what James would have wanted. You do realize that he is the reason my sister is dead, don't you?"

Nora sat back. She had been proud of Annie for keeping quiet as long as she had. This was Annie's fight, and Nora was going to let her have it.

Shocked and appalled that Annie would say such a thing, Donna stumbled through a response. "Well, I never... I can't believe you would say such a thing to me!"

"I wouldn't have, had you not been so pushy, but I have had my fill, and I am at the point where I don't care anymore."

"I'm sorry you feel that way. I just don't see how you can justify saying that my son, who, I may remind you, was murdered too, is at fault for your sister's murder."

"Listen, Donna. Your son was into drugs. He stole drugs from his supplier and hid them, of all places, in a baby doll! Then he had the nerve to give it to Emmie, his own daughter, as a gift, and furthermore, he told her to keep it with her always. This is the idiot you so proudly call son." Annie started to cry. She was never hurtful, and this was so out of her nature. The only thing she could think of right now was Emmie, and if it took hurting Donna to keep Emmie safe and give her a good life, then damn it, she would do just that.

Donna sat there staring at Annie, the tears having no effect on her anger now. What a little bitch to say her son was the reason for this horrible situation! Her heart was broken with the loss of her only child, and now they were trying to take her only grandchild, too. She got up and walked out of the room, leaving Nora looking at Annie, who was standing there in tears. She would pack her bags and go to a motel. She didn't belong here anymore. She needed to be alone. Her head was reeling right now. Was this the way everyone here thought? That James was at fault?

She didn't need this. Going to her room, she got the suitcase she had unpacked and began filling it up with all of the items she'd brought with her. She would get a phonebook, make a reservation somewhere, then call for a cab. Why didn't she see all of this before? How could she have been so blind to their hatred? What did she mean, he'd put drugs in the doll he gave to Emmie? Had they all lost their minds?

"Mom, I'm so sorry. I would never have hurt Donna." Annie was still crying.

Nora calmly got up and went to embrace the only child she had left. Holding Annie, she encouraged her to cry, to get it all out. Annie just clung to Nora. She had been holding this anger in for too long.

~

"Jade, you need to get going, and I need to get to your house." Ryan stood up. "We were supposed to leave a half an hour ago," he said, reflecting back on his phone call with Walt. "The details are worked out, so I say let's get this show on the road."

"You're right, Ryan. I think we're done here. It may take some explaining; I don't think Walt is going to be an easy obstacle to get by," George stated.

"He'll be fine with it. I've known Walt a while now, and he knows he can trust me, not to mention his feisty daughter here." Ryan looked at Jade and smiled.

"Don't try to placate me now." Jade smiled at Ryan.

"I just want everyone to know: I am the innocent one here," Danny said with a laugh.

George stood up, and that was the cue for Jade and Danny.

"I'm going to wait here for another hour or so, and then I'll head out," Ryan said, giving Jade a quick kiss.

"Help yourself to whatever you want from the fridge when you get there." She liked his kisses, even his quick kisses.

"Lucky man, lucky man," Danny said, shaking his head.

The three went out the front door, leaving Ryan to stand back and watch as Danny nonchalantly put his arm around Jade's shoulder. Ryan didn't like the feeling in the pit of his stomach. It made him feel left out and alone - not to mention he really didn't like another man putting his arm around Jade, even though he had agreed that Danny would pretend to be him.

George directed everyone to his car. Once they were all situated, he smiled at Jade. He didn't know if she was aware of it, but he noticed the look on Ryan's face.

"So, let's go get us a killer." Danny was making small talk, not quite comfortable after seeing the reaction Ryan had when they left. He'd known Ryan long enough to know he wasn't happy right now and hoped Ryan remembered this was just roleplaying.

"Yeah, that's what we're hoping," George answered.

"Maybe this will be the end of it all," Jade said, hope filling her voice.

"When we get there, let me explain this to your dad, Jade, okay?" George wasn't looking forward to telling Walt about the plan.

"George, believe it or not, I can be quiet and nice," Jade said with a smile on her face.

"I know. I just don't want to get off on the wrong foot with your dad. I think this is going to be difficult enough."

"He'll be okay with it. Don't sweat the small stuff, George," Jade said, laughing.

"So what makes you all think the killer will strike tonight?" Danny asked. He hadn't been given a lot of the details.

"He left Jade a note telling her to meet him tonight, but she's not going to. He obviously has been keeping his eye on all of us because he stays a step ahead. We're hoping he will see that she went home and try to get to her that way," George explained.

~

Ryan was sitting at his desk, going over the file of information compiled on the case so far. He couldn't believe that with all the chances they'd had, they still did not have an identity on this guy. He left lots of things to fingerprint, yet no prints. He was smarter than he had been given credit in the beginning, but he wasn't going to outsmart them.

Ryan made it a point to say a prayer and ask that Jade was kept safe. He couldn't believe how much he cared for her in such a short amount of time. Thinking about all of that, he decided to call his mother. He did tell her he would call, and he hadn't done it yet. He closed the file and picked up the telephone. Dialing her number, he put his thoughts into perspective so he didn't give her any false hope too soon.

"Hello?"

"Mom?"

"Hi, baby."

"Sorry it took so long for me to call you back. I've been busy, but I wanted to touch base with you. Everything good at home?" he asked.

"Yes, except you not being here. Your brother and Sandy are expecting their first baby. He said he tried to call you, but your line was incessantly busy." This was said nonchalantly.

"Wow, really? A baby! Man, he has it all. I am so happy for him. How is Sandy?" Ryan was excited. He was going to be an uncle. He loved kids.

"You know, morning sickness and all, but she's doing well. They are really excited. You should call him."

"Oh, hell yeah, I will. How are you. Grandma?" he asked, laughing.

"I know! Exciting, huh?" Now she put the excitement in her voice.

"A grandma for the first time, wow. I'll try to get home soon. Just trying to finish up a case that's been very difficult, but George and I will close it soon."

"Always working a case. You need a life, son. So, anything new your way?" Hope dripped from this question.

"Well, actually, yeah," he said, laughing "I' m seeing someone, and I don't want you to blow this out of proportion, but I really like her."

"Good, it's about time. Dish some details."

"Dish some details?"

"Yeah, you know, give me more!"

"What more?" he asked, laughing.

"Well, a name. What she's like? What does she like to do? That kind of thing."

"Her name is Jade."

"Oh, what a lovely name."

"What a lovely woman. She likes me. You'll have to wait to find out the rest when you meet her."

"When I meet her? You like her enough to bring her home?" The sound of awe in her voice had Ryan laughing.

"Yeah, Mom, I like her enough to bring her home. Let's just hope she likes me enough not to leave me after meeting my family." He laughed again.

"Hey, wait a minute, what's wrong with your family, young man?"

"Nothing, Mom. I was joking. Tell Billy I'll call him soon."

"So you're hanging up now?"

"Mom, I'm a little busy. Just wanted you to know I was thinking about you."

"Alright, honey, I know when I'm being dismissed. I miss you. Do you know when you're coming home?"

"Soon, Mom, I promise." He couldn't wait for her to meet Jade. "Oh, and by the way, I would never dismiss my mother."

"I know, talk to you soon, then. Love you."

"Love you too, Mom. Bye."

After they hung up, he wondered why he called and told her he was bringing Jade home. Wow, and Billy was going to be a daddy! How cool. He would have to call his brother tomorrow. Now he couldn't wait to share the news with Jade. She didn't know his family, of course, but he wanted her to. What the heck! He would call Billy now. He still had time to waste and nothing else to do. The file on the case, not worth looking at, lay forgotten on his desk. He picked up the phone and dialed his brother.

"Hey, what's up?" Ryan asked when Billy answered the phone.

"Hi, been dying to talk to you, bro. Have you talked to Mom?"

"Yep, just hung up." He could keep the smile out of his voice.

"So she blew it. She told you, didn't she?" he asked, deflated slightly.

"Well, hell yes."

"So what do you think?"

"I think it's fucking fantastic. How's Sandy?"

"Doing good, actually. She's had some morning sickness and is pretty tired, but she's dealing with it like an angel."

"Good, glad to hear it. Man, you're gonna be a daddy, wow!"

"I know. I don't think it's quite sunk in yet. But we are both so excited."

"Mom is, that's for sure. You know Grandma is her thing. She is so excited about the baby, she forgot to harp on me. Thanks, I owe you." Laughing was such a good feeling. This is what he needed: something to take his mind off Danny touching Jade.

"So what's new with you, little brother?"

"Oh, just working a case. You know, the usual."

"When you coming home?"

"I was just telling Mom I should be able to come home as soon as we finish this case we're working."

"What kind of case are you working now?"

"Double homicide."

"Cool, what's it about?"

"Drug deal gone bad. You know, typical bullshit for this area, except this one has a kid involved and quite an interesting female."

"Oh? You can't leave off with that. Come on, details, little brother, details."

"Well, the female, as it turns out, is now dating me. Can you believe that?"

"Really? Is that wise? I mean, what role does she play in this murder deal?"

"She's kind of an outsider. It's really complicated, but yeah, it's all good. She's something, though, I gotta tell you."

"Sounds like my little brother may have been bitten by the love bug."

"I wouldn't go that far, not yet, anyway." He snickered.

"Well, you will let me know when I can go that far, right?" Billy was enjoying the fact that his brother was a goner. It was evident to everyone but Ryan.

"Will do. Listen, give Sandy my love, and I'll talk to you soon."

"Yep, take care."

"Congrats, bro." Ryan checked his watch. Another few minutes, and he would be able to leave. He sat there wondering what Jade was doing. Was she at Walt's yet? She should be in a few minutes. Well, he would see her soon enough, and the great thing about that was that it would be just the two of them. At least for a while, he hoped.

25

ANNIE sat quietly reflecting on her choice of words with Donna. She wondered what Donna was doing upstairs. She felt bad about the way the conversation had ended, but Donna couldn't live in a dream world. While sitting there quietly thinking, Annie heard footsteps and a scraping noise coming down the stairs. She got up to see what the noise was. Donna was slowly coming down the stairs, dragging a suitcase behind her. "What are you doing, Donna?"

"I'm leaving, Annie. I think it's best for everyone if I stay in a motel."

"Donna, please don't do that. I didn't mean to hurt or upset you."

"You made your feelings clear, and I won't say you're not entitled to your opinion, but I can't stay here knowing how you all feel."

"Donna, let's talk this out. Don't leave. Tomorrow is going to be hard on all of us, and I don't want you to be alone."

"I need to be alone, Annie. I have some things I need to figure out. I'll let you know what I decide about Emmie at the earliest possible time."

Nora and Walt were coming in, and Annie could hear Emmie with them. "Donna, please don't make a scene in front of Emmie. I'm sorry, but I don't know what else you want me to say."

"Do you know where Walt keeps his phonebook?"

"No."

"Where are you going, Donna?" Walt noticed the luggage and the strained look on Annie's face.

"Walt, I need a phonebook, please."

"Why?"

"I feel I need some time alone. I am going to call for a taxi and make a reservation at a local motel."

"You don't need to do that, Donna. There is plenty of room for you to be alone here." Walt knew he shouldn't interfere, but no one was safe with the killer out running around.

"I know, and I appreciate all of your hospitality; however, right now, I need to go."

"Donna, you're making too much of this," Nora put in.

"This is my decision, and it's made." She stood her ground.

"Alright, I just hope you know what you're doing." Nora turned and took Emmie by the hand and walked back toward the kitchen.

"Why is Grammy leaving?" Emmie wanted to know.

"She is really sad right now, honey, and she wants to be alone. You can understand that, right?"

"Nanny, are you leaving, too?"

"Not yet, sweetie. I want to spend some more time with you." Nora watched Walt take the telephone book out of a kitchen drawer, then turn to look at her. She wasn't sure what the look was. Concern, anger, what? She watched him walk back to the hallway. Sitting Emmie down, Nora began looking for something she could make for dinner. Emmie was looking out the new window, watching the two men finish their job. They were waving at her through the glass and smiling. Nora turned back to the refrigerator.

Jade came through the front door, and Emmie heard her voice. "Nanny, I'm going to see Jade, okay?" she said, jumping down.

"Alright, just be careful. Don't fall." Nora's heart faltered a bit when Emmie leaped out of the chair.

"Jade!" Emmie shouted, running to see her.

"Hey, little one," Jade said, leaning down for a hug.

"Grammy is leaving, Jade. She wants to be alone." Emmie rushed the words out.

"She does?" Jade stood up and looked at her dad.

"Where have you been? I called over an hour ago." That was about as much chastising as Walt did.

"I know, Dad, I'm sorry. Dad, this is Danny Miller. Danny's an investigator." Jade turned in Danny's direction.

"Hello, Mr. Miller." Walt extended his hand. He had not even noticed the stranger until Jade introduced him. He thought it had been Ryan standing there.

"Danny, please," he said, taking the offered hand. A firm grip was always on his mind when he shook hands.

"George," Walt acknowledged.

"Hey, Walt, what's up."

"So where's Ryan?"

"We need to talk, but I see you're a little busy right now. It'll wait."

"I'll get with you in a few. I have to see that Donna is taken care of first." Walt rolled his eyes.

"Sure, is she alright?" George watched the woman on the telephone.

"I'll explain when I can."

Annie stood in the living room. Jade looked over to see the worry etched in her face. Not moving any closer, Jade quietly mouthed to Annie, asking if she was okay. Annie numbly nodded back that she was. Jade went to the kitchen and found Nora.

"Nora, what's going on?" she asked, hoping for details.

"Donna and Annie had an argument, and now Donna is acting like an imbecile and leaving."

"She shouldn't be alone, Nora. Doesn't she know the killer has probably been watching us?"

"I don't think she cares right now, Jade."

"Well, someone has to stop her."

"I don't think that's a good idea."

"Where will she go?"

"She said to a motel for the night."

Walt waited for Donna to hang up. As he waited, he tried to explain to George what was going on to the best of his knowledge, but that was lacking some. Annie began to fill in the blanks for George, and Jade walked in too late to hear the whole story. Donna hung the telephone up, and George decided he needed to step in.

"Mrs. Linderhoff?"

"Donna, please."

"Okay, Donna, I wish you wouldn't leave. It's not safe for you on your own yet."

"I will be alright, detective. I just need some space. Please understand. I can't stay here anymore."

"Donna, did I do something to make you uneasy?" Walt asked.

"Certainly not, Walt. You have been very gracious. I just need some breathing space. I need to have privacy to grieve. I'm sure you understand."

"Of course I do, but you have to understand that there's a killer out there, and you're not safe alone."

"I will be fine. Please don't worry. I will see you all tomorrow at the funeral."

Donna went to the living room and sat quietly, waiting for the taxi to arrive. Annie just shook her head. She felt like such an ass. How could she blow up like that?

Danny stood back and watched the people around him. He didn't have a lot of details about this case, but he did have some knowledge. The woman named Annie looked about ready to have a breakdown. He felt for her but said nothing. Emmie was a cutie. She went into the living room and hugged her grandmother. The woman latched onto the child, and Danny thought she would start crying, so he turned away. Women's tears always hit home with him. He couldn't stand to see one cry. He made a point of looking around to see if any windows were revealing the outside world. All were covered with heavy curtains. No one was going to get a look inside unless the people inside wanted them too. Walt appeared to be a strong, masculine man with a lot of interesting women running around his house. Danny was glad he had the chance to meet these people. He was so often stuck with the dregs of society, the druggies. He really should consider a department change, he thought. Nice, normal people would be a refreshing change for him.

The telephone ringing interrupted his thoughts. He watched Annie go to the phone and pick it up. "Hello?"

"Hey, Annie?"

"Yes, just a sec." She turned. "Jade, it's Ryan." Annie handed Jade the telephone.

"Ryan?"

"Hey, babe. I see you made it okay."

"Yeah, are you getting ready to leave?"

"Yes, just wanted to make sure you were there before I left."

"Be careful. I'll talk to you soon. Something is going on here, and I'm trying to get information. I'll fill you in when I can, okay?"

"Everything alright?" He was worried.

"I think so. Don't really know, though. Donna is leaving, and I don't know what's up yet."

"Leaving? What do you mean, leaving?"

"I don't know yet. Something about an argument, and she wants to leave. I'll fill you in when I can."

"Jade, you have to stop her. She needs to understand the danger is real."

"I know, Ryan, I'll do what I can, but it appears there's no talking her out of this."

"Damn, alright, I'll see you in a few."

Emmie ran to the phone before Jade could hang it up and yelled "Bye, Ryan!" Everyone smiled at the face she made when she knew he didn't hear her.

Now Ryan was confused. Donna was leaving? Where the hell was she going? The funeral wasn't until tomorrow; surely she wasn't going home. Oh well. He would wait and see what Jade could tell him when he saw her. He cleared off his desk and left the station.

The taxi arrived and beeped its horn. Donna stood up and went to Walt. "I can't thank you enough for all you have done. Truly, I thank you," she said sincerely.

"Donna, please reconsider," Walt said as he gave Donna a hug.

She shook her head and turned to find Emmie. "Emmie, sweetie, come say goodbye to Grammy," she said, holding her arms out. Emmie walked over to her, and Donna bent down. "Love you, sweetie. You be good, and I will see you tomorrow." Then she leaned even closer and whispered in Emmie's ear, "Remember your daddy in your prayers, baby."

"I will Grammy." Emmie said squeezing tightly. "I love you too."

Donna let go. Grabbing her suitcase, she started for the door.

"I'll get that, Donna." Walt said, taking the luggage from her.

The taxi driver was standing next to the car on the sidewalk. "Good evening," he said.

"Good evening. Could you put this in the trunk please?" Donna said to him.

"Donna, are you sure about this?" Walt was trying one last time.

"Yes, Walt, thanks again." Donna turned and opened the back door of the taxi. Smiling at Walt, she got in and closed the door. She didn't want anyone to know which motel she'd selected, so she waited for the driver to get in before she gave the address.

The driver closed the trunk and tipped his hat at Walt. Going to the driver side door, he climbed in. "Where to, ma'am?" he asked.

"The Savory Palms Inn, please," she said, almost too quietly for him to hear.

Walt was still standing on the sidewalk. She turned and smiled at him as the car pulled away. Waving, he turned to go back into the house and said a silent prayer that God would watch over her and protect her.

"Walt, you couldn't make her stay. She'll have to watch out for herself. She made this choice," George tried to reassure Walt.

"I know. It just seems so foolish."

"It is," George said.

"What did you want to talk with me about? Is Ryan okay?" Walt remembered that they showed up without Ryan and that George wanted to talk to him.

"Yeah, the kid's fine. Where can we talk in private?"

"Let's go in here." Walt walked into the sunroom and closed the French doors.

"I need you to listen to me and to keep an open mind."

Walt didn't like where this was going. "I'll try, go ahead." He leaned against the door and listened.

George explained the break-in to Walt's home, then walked him through the plan that had been discussed and well thought out. He kept watching Walt's face for any sign that he was going to disagree. So far, so good, George thought. He explained Danny's role and the reason he was there, then explained that Walt needed to let Jade go to her house for the night and the fact that Ryan was already there waiting. After going through every detail and not seeing any reaction from Walt, George thought this was a go without problems.

Then Walt hit him with the hammer, metaphorically, of course. "I understand what you've said, George, and I can appreciate the thought that went into this plan. However, if you think I'll let Jade be used as bait, then you and Ryan are both insane." Walt moved to leave the room.

"Wait just a minute, Walt. We need to talk this out. Don't just leave."

"I've said what I have to say. What else is there to discuss?"

"Look, Walt, I don't have children, so I won't pretend that I know what you're thinking or feeling right now, but I do know that if I did, I sure as hell wouldn't want to worry for days and days whether my kid would be alright. Work with me here."

"George, as a parent, you worry every day. This is more than worry. It's a nightmare. I want Jade out of it, not smack dab in the middle."

"I know, Walt. We want Jade out of it, too, but he's fixated on her, and right now, like it or not, she's our best chance to get him."

"No!"

"Jade will do this without your permission. Don't make her have to do that. What can I say or do to make this easier for you?"

Walt turned and glared at George. He knew George was right. He knew Jade would do this whether he wanted her to or not. He walked over and sat down. Putting his head in his hands, he said, "George, you're right. She'll do it anyway, so tell me again the plan, and don't leave anything out."

George went through the plan again, then sat back and watched the emotions play across Walt's face. He knew this was hard on him, but he knew now that Walt wouldn't stand in the way.

"Just one question."

"What's that?"

"How do you know Jade will make it safely to her house and then safely inside?"

"Good question. Jade won't stop anywhere for anything. She will be walked to her car by Danny, so the killer will think its Ryan. Then she'll drive directly home."

"He's going to be angry with her for not showing up at Annie's, but how do you know he will come back here to watch her?"

"So far, he's been one step ahead of us. That tells us he's watching. He'll be here watching to see if she goes to Annie's, not there waiting for her."

"I hope you're right about all of this. I don't take chances with my daughter, and if I thought there was any way of talking her out of this, I would."

"I know. I'm sorry, but you gotta trust us, Walt."

"I don't have a choice, do I?"

"No."

Walt got up and left the room. George sat there for a few minutes. That had been worse than he thought it would be.

Nora was in the kitchen cooking; she decided on chicken breast with potatoes and broccoli. Walt must have liked all of those dishes, or he wouldn't have had them in his kitchen, so she felt safe deciding on the meal. Annie was setting the table in the dining room. Seven places were set. Jade told her and Nora that George and Danny would be staying for dinner. Jade simply explained that Ryan was still at work and would not be there this evening. No one questioned her further.

Jade was sitting in the living room with Danny, watching Emmie play with Harry. Poor Harry! After he broke Emmie's doll, Jade didn't think he would ever be treated well again. Apparently Emmie was over that; she played with Harry just like she always had. They were lying on the floor, and Harry was half on and half off her little body. Emmie was scratching him and laughing at his hind leg rapidly hitting the floor. Harry was in heaven. He didn't care that the only reason she was scratching him was so he would move his leg like that; he just wanted her to be near him. He was good with Emmie. Danny sat back to watch the spectacle. No one was talking. The only sounds were Emmie's laughing and Harry's leg banging.

26

RYAN arrived at Jade's house and looked around before getting out of his car. Parking in front of a house down the street, he locked the car up tightly.

He sauntered down the sidewalk, acting as if he didn't have a care in the world. Slipping down the side of Jade's house, Ryan entered the backyard. She had a wooden fence that was decorative and provided privacy. The gate wasn't locked, and he had no problem getting in without being seen. He walked around the backyard, looking at everything before going to the back door.

He noticed the flowers that were planted in the flowerbeds, the small set of table and chairs on the patio, the gleaming water of the pool with its slate rocks that stacked up to make a beautiful waterfall that splashed into the pool. It was like a small paradise that he was sure Jade had created. He could see touches that he knew she'd made with her own hands. Even though he hadn't known her that long, he still saw her personality in this creation.

A refreshing swim would help him stay alert and break the monotony and worry. He decided he would after a quick check of the house. He opened the back door and heard the beeping of her alarm system. Shit, she didn't give him a code; hell, she didn't even mention an alarm system. He dialed Walt's house quickly, and Jade answered the phone. "Hey, your alarm is going to go off. I need your code."

"What? Oh, I forgot. It's one, two, three, four."

"You're going to have to change that, you know." He pushed the numbers quickly, then pressed 'off'. The beeping stopped. "I can't believe that's your code. What were you thinking? A child could have figured that out."

"You didn't," she said through a smile.

"I didn't try. People who commit burglaries always try the easy ones first."

"Point taken. I'll change it. So you made it alright?"

"Did you think I would get lost?"

"No, just making a comment. We're getting ready to eat. Make sure you get something, too."

"I will. Haven't had a chance to look around yet, so I want to do that first."

"Look around?"

"Yeah, you know, so I won't fall over things in the dark."

"Oh, good point. I have some lights on timers, so don't freak when they come on."

"No prob. See you in a couple hours." He didn't want to waste any more daylight.

"Alright, make yourself at home. I'll see you soon."

He went back to close the door. The house was so quiet, he could hear a clock ticking from somewhere. Walking through the house was a delight. Jade had very good, expensive taste.

Ryan wondered again where all the money came from that provided this place and all that came with it. He knew she was waiting to start a job, but that didn't pay for this. He would make it a point to find out.

He went into the kitchen where the granite countertops had a light coat of dust. The house smelled of freshness, even though it had been closed up for days. Opening the refrigerator, he decided on a ham and cheese sandwich. That would be easy and hardly any mess. He made the sandwich quickly, then ate it while he toured the rest of the house, noting where pieces of furniture and items that were large enough to trip him later were. A beautiful grandfather clock sat in one corner of the foyer. That must have been the clock he heard ticking.

The color scheme throughout was neutral and soft. He could imagine Jade kicked back on the sofa, wearing something soft and comfortable, leafing through magazines while drinking a glass of wine. He smiled to himself.

After checking the house and eating the sandwich, he grabbed a beer and headed for the pool. Taking a towel with him, he stripped down and slid in. "Oh, cold." He knew it would be chilly, but he didn't expect it to be this cold. He set the beer on the concrete next to the pool and swam a few quick laps. He had a smooth, muscle-toned body that men and women alike admired. He spent hours in the gym lifting and toning.

His body quickly adjusted to the water's coolness. He slowly moved back to the side and took a long drink from the beer. Leaning against the side, looking over the pool, he knew he could get used to this.

Finishing the bottle of beer, he climbed out and dried off. Pulling his pants and shirt back on, he went inside. Retrieving the playing cards from the kitchen drawer he went through earlier looking for a knife to make his sandwich, Ryan set up a game of solitaire on the coffee table in the living room. He would play until it was too dark to see the cards.

~

He had watched the cab pull away from the curb. Where was she going? He couldn't hear where she had called. It was a motel, but which one?

It didn't really matter. He wanted the young, golden-haired beauty. Girlie, oh yeah, she would help him in so many ways. He smiled grimly as he sat back and listened to everyone else in the house.

~

Annie called everyone into dinner; as they all found a seat and sat down, Nora brought dishes in. The smell filled the dining room, and comments of delight were coming from every direction. Nora laughed and took a seat herself.

Looking over at Walt, she commented, "It sure is nice to have a houseful to cook for again. I see your point on the houseful of family."

"Isn't it wonderful?" He smiled at her.

The feeling in the dining room was one of family. Everyone was at ease with each other, and the food smelled wonderful. Of course, they were still worrying about Donna. Walt was thinking about Donna and Jade being targets for this killer. Nora was thinking about Amy and how she would never share another family dinner with her. She had been trying so hard to keep her grieving under control for everyone else, but she could feel it slipping. Going on as if nothing had happened was taking its toll. She was going to do her best to maintain it for a few more days. Once she was home, she would allow herself the freedom to cry, break down, melt down, whatever she wanted. But for now, she would continue as she has been for Annie and Emmie.

Walt wondered how it had all happened. This mess needed to be over with. It had been taking its toll on all of them. Would he really try something tonight? Walt shook his head to clear it. He couldn't dwell on any of that right now. Lifting a bowl of potatoes, he spooned some onto his plate, then passed the bowl to George. Everyone filled their plates.

After the plates were full, Walt reached out and grabbed George and Nora's hands. "It's time for grace before we all dig into this delicious meal," he said.

Once everyone around the table was holding the hand of the person next to them and making the circle complete, Walt said the prayer. Nora closed her eyes and listened to the words that fell so easily from Walt. Her heart fluttered at the ease he had in speaking to God. The prayer was all-inclusive, not just about the food, but everyone's safety and well-being.

With an amen from everyone, the prayer was finished, and the eating began. Talk was flowing from across the table and down the table. Everyone participated freely and with ease.

Danny thought this was a phenomenal family. He could not believe that with everything these people had been through and were still going through, they still found reason to be thankful. Sitting back, eating, and listening, he learned a lot about each person at the table.

Dinner was going great, and everyone seemed able to act a little normal through the entire meal. It amazed Walt that they were all together under these circumstances, and yet it felt right. He kept thinking about the plan for tonight. He was having a difficult time swallowing what they expected him to accept. He would, he knew, but still he didn't have to like it.

"Why don't we all go sit in the living room for a while and let our food settle, then I'll clean up and occupy my mind while Jade is held out for bait?" Walt looked directly at George.

"Dad, I'll be fine." Jade had caught the look and the meaning behind it.

George didn't say anything as everyone got up and walked toward the living room. Annie and Nora exchanged quick glances at each other, wondering what he was talking about. Quietly, they followed everyone into the living room. Nora felt she should speak out on Walt's behalf. This was happening because of her daughter and her son-in-law. What were the police planning? Jade as bait? What was that supposed to mean?

Everyone seated in the room was quiet, except for Emmie and Harry. They played together nicely on the floor. Tonight, there was no running or acting foolishly.

Nora looked over and saw the concern on Walt's face as he looked at his daughter. Deciding she would help him with the dinner cleanup and could then pump him for information helped put her at ease. Not finding the words to express how she felt, she decided to keep her mouth shut for now.

~

Donna sat in the small motel room. Twiddling her fingers, going over the conversation in her mind again, she still could not understand what had made everyone so against her James. She knew there was more going on than she was aware of, but what could have happened that she didn't know about? Sitting there for what seemed an eternity, she started crying again.

"James, oh, my baby James." She cried wholeheartedly, talking out loud, wanting answers - no - needing answers. She could not care less that the killer could get to her; hell, it might be better to just let him kill her, too. After all, the only person she had left was Emmie, and they were going to take her, too. Donna crawled into a ball on the bed and cried for hours.

Finally, her stomach started reminding her that she hadn't eaten anything since breakfast. Sitting up, she decided to see what there was to eat within walking distance. The small motel wouldn't have room service. Looking out the window, she could see a number of fast food places. Picking up her shoes and purse, she decided to walk the short distance to a small café. She had no thoughts of the killer watching her. She really didn't care.

Jade couldn't wait for the sun to go down. She would be going to her home, her man. What a thought...her man. She liked the idea very much. She'd had the typical high school boyfriends, the crushes every girl experiences, but never had she felt for anyone the feelings that were stirring over Ryan. Was this love? She was anxious to get home. What was Ryan doing right now? Was he comfortable in her home? Did he like her taste in furniture, colors, and style? Did men actually pay attention to those things? Her mind was a whirl of thoughts. She was getting antsy. Feeling her dad watching her wasn't helping.

Ryan sat in the living room playing cards. Losing again, he put the cards back in the box and got up to stretch his legs. Looking over at the big, comfortable sofa with all the cushions lining the back, he began to think about Jade and about them being alone tonight. His heart started hammering in his chest. Was he falling in love? He was feeling something he had never felt before. She was an extraordinary woman. One thing for sure, a future with Jade would be filled with uncertainties. Her visions and need to act on them would give him plenty to worry about. What if they had children? Would they have visions, too?

Whoa, where the hell was that coming from? "One step at a time, Ryan," he said to himself out loud. Going up the stairs, he found a linen closet and removed some sheets, a blanket, and a pillow. He might as well get a bed made while he could still see. He knew he could take care of that after Jade got home, but, feeling restless, he wanted to keep busy. This was all he could think to do in the darkening house.

Donna walked into the small cafe. Sitting down in a dingy corner booth, she looked around at the people that were eating. Not too many people; certainly none that looked like killers.

The waitress walked over and handed her a menu. "What can I get you to drink?" she asked with a half smile on her face.

"Just coffee, please." Donna took the menu and began looking at her choices for dinner. She didn't have much of an appetite, but her body was letting her know she needed something.

The waitress came back with a steaming hot cup of coffee. Setting the cup and a dish of creamers on the table, she asked,

~ 300 ~

"Are you ready, or do you need more time?"

Closing the menu, she said, "A garden salad with ranch will be fine." Then she handed the greasy menu back to the girl.

"That's all?" The waitress stood waiting for more. Surely this woman wasn't going to eat just salad and coffee.

"Yes, that's all." Donna sat there looking around again at the people in the small diner. The waitress went to get the salad, thinking that this would be a small tip. She could always tell the tippers from the cheap ones.

Donna thought again about Nora and Annie's blaming of James. That was crazy. Lost in thought, she began to tear up again. Reminding herself where she was, she vowed not to think about James right now.

The waitress brought the salad, set it down, and walked away. Donna looked at the small bowl without interest. Forcing herself, she poured the ranch dressing over the salad and began to eat.

~

George stood up and said, "Let's get this show on the road."

Jade jumped up, a bright smile lighting her face. She walked over and kissed her dad's cheek. "I'll be fine, Dad, I promise."

"You better be. I don't like this one bit." Walt hugged his daughter tightly. "George, is Ryan going to bring her back, or are you going to call? I mean, how do I know when this is over?" Walt struggled.

"We'll call you as soon as we have him," George promised.

"Let's go, guys. I'm ready," Jade said, showing them the car keys in her hand.

George, Danny, and Jade walked outside. Danny had his arm around Jade as they walked to the car. George stopped on the sidewalk and waited. Jade unlocked the driver side, and Danny opened the door. Leaning down, he kissed her cheek.

Jade blushed.Llooking at Danny, she said, "Tell George to keep my dad calm." Jade was making it look as though she were telling her lover something important.

"We'll take care of him, Jade. You just take care of yourself and Ryan." Danny smiled and patted the door. Walking back to where George stood, the two of them watched Jade drive off, both men looking around to see if any cars were pulling out to follow.

"Come on. Let's get inside, or he may not follow her," George said.

Jade was nervous, looking in her mirrors constantly. Would he see her and follow? She wasn't sure if she hoped he would or not. She knew she wanted this over and done with, but this was nerveracking. Could she remember what to do with the gun if she were face to face with the killer? Would Ryan be safe? What had she gotten them all into? She drove on, keeping watch and trying to keep herself under control.

Walt went to clear the dinner dishes. He had to do something. He couldn't just sit there. Nora got up and followed Walt into the dining room.

"I'm going to help you," she stated flatly.

"Nora, I appreciate that, but I need to be busy right now, and if you help it will go too quickly." Walt looked over at her with a grateful expression.

"I understand something is going on that you don't like, and I figure if I'm in here with you, then you can fill me in. Maybe I can help."

Walt smiled and took an armload of dishes to the kitchen. When he was coming back, Nora just smiled at him as she walked past to the kitchen. Walt shook his head and continued to clean up. The two finally had all the dishes on the counter, and Walt was filling the sink with soapy water.

"You're not going to use the dishwasher?" Nora asked.

"No, this will take longer."

"Okay, let's have it. What is going on?" she demanded.

Walt filled Nora in on the newest plan to catch the killer.

"I don't like it. Not one bit," Nora said, looking at Walt.

"Me either, but what choice do I have?"

"Well, you're her father. Why didn't you stop her?"

"She was going to do this with or without my blessing. What could I have done?"

Nora looked at Walt with such worry. What had her family gotten this sweet man and his daughter into?

"I'm truly sorry, Walt. I wish you and Jade had never been put in this ordeal to begin with."

"It's not your fault, Nora. Jade is always getting involved where her visions are concerned. It's just never been this dangerous for her before."

"I just don't know what to say."

"Do you want to wash or dry?"

"I guess I'll wash. I'm not sure where everything goes." Nora began dipping dishes in the water. Nothing more was said between the two for a short time, as each was saying silent prayers.

Nora dropped a glass, and it shattered in the sink. "I'm so sorry," she said as the tears began to fall.

Walt took the dishcloth away and set it in the water. Taking both of Nora's hands, he turned her to him. "Nora, this is going to be over soon. We'll all get through this. Please don't blame yourself." Gently pulling her into his arms, he held her while she wept. Wondering how to get through this, he just held her. It felt good to hold Nora. He liked the fit between them. He gently patted her back and told her to cry it out. He hated that all of them were suffering so bad. She had been so strong. He'd known it was just a matter of time before she cracked.

~

He saw the girlie leaving. Where did she live? They thought he was stupid. Well, he would follow and watch. He knew what he was doing. He had been in these situations plenty of times, and the cops were never smarter than he was. He opened the window and quickly but quietly made his way down the trellis.

He ran to his car. Catching up to her was easy. He slowly drove behind her, two cars in between them. He could safely watch everything she did.

Jade knew he was back there. She could feel him. Which car was he in? She would watch when she turned onto her street. The car that turned with her would be the killer, she was sure.

As she turned, she watched. Two of the three cars turned with her. Maybe he did have a partner. She began to panic again. Would he try to kill her dad since she wasn't going to Annie's? She pulled into her driveway and waited for the garage to open.

He went past, not even looking at her. She lived right across from the park where he had murdered that thieving fucker and his stupid wife. Interesting, he thought. So that was how she knew about it. Did she see him? No, he was too careful for that.

Jade pulled into the garage and waited for the door to close before she opened her car door. Making sure she locked the doors, she waited. No one slipped into the garage. She was safe. Getting out, she opened the door leading into her laundry room. Locking the deadbolt behind her, she ventured into the kitchen. Turning on the light, she looked around. Where was Ryan? Calling out to him, she stood there and waited.

"Hey, down here. I can't stand up with the light on." He was crouched down between the island and the double ovens. "Don't look down here; just turn off the light and go into the living room. The shades are down, and I'll crawl in there."

Jade turned the light off and walked past him. Feeling in her pocket for the gun, she felt reassured. She walked in and turned the lamp on. Ryan came around the corner on all fours and smiled up at her.

"Can you get up now?" she asked with a smile.

Ryan stood and walked over to her. Taking her in his arms, he held her, telling himself she was safe, she had made it. "Hey, are you okay?" he was holding her tightly and could feel the slight shaking.

"I don't know if he followed me. I had three cars behind me, and two of them turned when I turned."

"Oh, he followed you, you can be sure. Did you get a look at either one?"

"I tried, but when they both turned, I began to panic, thinking maybe he does have a partner."

"No, that was just good timing on his part."

"I would never get over anything happening to Dad because of me."

"Hey, don't you worry. You trust me, right?"

"Yeah, but..."

"No buts. George will take care of Walt, and I will take very good care of you," he said, still holding her tightly.

"Can I call my dad?"

"That's a good idea. Let him know you're here with me and safe."

Jade went to the phone and called her dad. Walt released Nora to get the phone.

"Dad, I just wanted to let you know I'm here with Ryan. I'm made it safely."

Walt felt his heart swell. "Jade, thank God! I have been worried about you getting from your car into the house."

"I drove into the garage. Everything is going according to plan. Is George still there?"

"Yeah, I think so."

"Ryan wants to talk to him."

"Hang on a minute." Walt stepped into the hallway and yelled for George.

"What is it?" George asked, coming to the kitchen.

"Ryan wants to speak to you." Walt handed the phone to George.

After a short conversation, George hung the phone up. He had a good feeling about this plan. He hoped this would be it. They would finally have that bastard. Dead or alive, he didn't care. George walked back into the living room and told Danny what Ryan had told him. They decided they would both stay with the family for a while longer.

George called Doris and told her he would be late again. Doris was pretty good about the hours he spent away from home when working on an important case. They had been married a long time, and he had been a cop when they married.

Walt and Nora finished the kitchen and came to the living room with everyone else.

"Annie, do you want me to bathe Emmie and get her ready for bed tonight?" Nora offered.

"Yeah, Aunt Annie, Yeah!" Emmie yelled, jumping up and down.

"Thanks, Mom, that would be wonderful. Are you sure you're up to it? We've had a long day," Annie said, looking at her mother and trying to see if she was tired or if she just needed busywork.

"I'm sure, honey. It will do me good to keep busy for a while."

With that settled and knowing that Jade was safe for now, Walt decided he needed to take a walk. Going to the door, he grabbed a light jacket and went out. George stood to see what Walt was doing. He realized Walt needed some time alone and let him go. This was going to be a long night for all of them.

27

THE killer went down the street, made a complete block, then drove by again. The light was on in the house. This is where she lives, he thought, licking his thin lips. He parked near her house and slid down in the seat, waiting.

He had time to wait as long as he needed to. The wicked thoughts of what he would do to her before he killed her were rampaging through his evil mind. He would love every single minute with that lovely little girl.

~

Jade was going to have to talk to Ryan about her thoughts, which were tying her stomach into knots.

"Are you worrying about your dad, Jade?" Ryan asked after watching her frown lines deepen around her brows.

"No. Yes. I'm worried about all of us."

"This will be over soon, honey, I promise." He pulled her tightly into his arms, not wanting to see the worry etched in her face.

Jade stood there holding him tight and wondering where to begin.

"Come on, babe. Let's sit down and relax," Ryan suggested. They both moved to the sofa, and as they sat, he pulled her close to him. Just sitting there together would be enough for him. He liked having her close; enjoying her unique scent was comforting to him.

"The quiet is killing me." She got up and paced the floor. "Where is he?" She walked over and, moving the blinds aside, looked out at the still night.

"Babe, he isn't going to come storming through the door," he said, knowing she was nervous and had never been through this before.

"Well, when?" She put the blinds back in place and stepped back.

"In the middle of the night, most likely." Patting the cushion on the sofa next to him, he tried to get her to relax.

"How do you do it? I mean, the sitting and waiting makes life feel like it's moving in slow motion. I don't know how you do it day after day." Picking up the TV remote, thinking a little noise would help, she clicked the power on. She knew nothing would really help but catching him. Giving up, she tossed the remote to Ryan and went up the stairs.

Flipping through the channels and giving Jade some space was all Ryan could do. He knew how hard this was on her but was unable to do a damn thing about it. Wishing the killer would strike and end the madness for her was heavy on his mind. He couldn't make anything happen; he could only be there to keep her safe if it did happen.

"I'm sorry," she said, coming back down the stairs. "I just feel so damn helpless."

"Give it some time, Jade. I know how hard this is, and I wish I could make him come through that door right now, but I can't. We just have to wait it out." He patted the cushion again, and this time she sat. Leaning over and brushing his lips across her mouth, he said, "I wish I could take this all away for you."

"It's just so unfair. Look at me. I'm sitting here having a pity party when I have no right to." Leaning her forehead against his, she asked, "So what do you wanna do to pass the time?"

"That's a loaded question." He took her face in his hands and smiled down at her. "I'll give you three guesses, and if it takes more than one, you're not the girl for me".

"Oh, it won't, but no, we're not doing that." She laughed.

"Okay, your loss," he said, rolling her away from him and picking the remote up again to flip through the channels. He had successfully lightened her mood.

~

Donna finished her measly meal and paid for it, then walked back to her motel room. Not giving any thought to a killer being around, she took her time and enjoyed the clear, crisp, evening air.

She was beginning to feel better now that she had her own space. She had no ill feelings toward Nora or Annie; she knew they were hurting just as much as she was. Everyone said things they didn't mean when they were hurting. She wasn't a vengeful woman. She would forgive Annie.

Maybe they were right, though, about Emmie. Maybe she was too old. Emmie would be a bundle of energy, and she really wasn't as young as she used to be. She would agree to let Annie raise Emmie; heck, she would even send her some money every month to help with the expenses. Maybe Annie would let Emmie come and stay with her during the summer. That would be fun. She would tell them tomorrow.

Donna went to her room and dressed for bed. Lying there silently and talking to James, she promised she would be a better person tomorrow.

~

Walt walked the neighborhood, enjoying the crisply cool evening and putting his thoughts in order. Ryan would take care of Jade, he knew. He just wasn't thrilled about them using her like this. After tomorrow, maybe everyone could get back to their normal lives. He wondered how long Nora would stay once the funeral was over. He would have liked to get to know her better, but California was too far. It just wasn't meant to be, he thought. Walking back home, he felt a little better. He knew he wouldn't get much sleep, if any, worrying about Jade. "Just let them both be safe, God," he prayed.

~

Nora got Emmie into bed and kissed her forehead. "Sleep tight, my little one."

"Goodnight, Nanny." Emmie snuggled down into the big bed.

Nora turned to leave. Looking back at her adorable granddaughter, she turned off the light and left the door open halfway. Walking into her own room, she decided to get some sleep herself. Tomorrow would be a hard day. She would try to talk some sense into Donna tomorrow, too.

After getting into her nightclothes, she walked to the bathroom. Taking her makeup off and brushing both her teeth and hair, she looked at her reflection in the mirror. She thought about how old she was getting, about how lonely she was, and how she hadn't fully realized it until she met Walt. She went back to the bedroom and crawled in bed, lying there but a minute before sleep took over.

Annie decided she'd better go check on her mom and Emmie. It sure was quiet upstairs. Telling George she would be right back, she walked to the stairway.

Walt opened the door as she stepped on the first step. Jumping and turnin,g she grabbed hold of the railing. Walt saw the look of surprise on Annie's face and laughed.

"Sorry, kiddo, it's just me."

"Thank God. You could have knocked me over with a feather. I think my heart stopped," she said, laughing, and continued up the stairs. Looking in the bathroom first and not finding anyone there, she went to her bedroom. Emmie lay on the bed fast asleep. So sweet, Annie thought, then went to check on her mom. Looking in her bedroom, she saw Nora sleeping and softly, deeply breathing. Annie closed the door and went back down the stairs.

"Everyone's asleep already. Guess I'll go to bed, too," she said. looking at Walt. "You gonna be alright?" she asked, knowing he was worrying about Jade.

"I'm fine, honey. Sweet dreams," Walt told her.

"Goodnight" was all Danny said.

"Night, Annie," George chimed in.

"Let me know if we hear anything tonight." She turned and walked away.

"Walt, do you want us to go so you can get some sleep?" George asked.

"I don't plan on going to bed anytime soon, George. I don't see sleep in my near future." Walt turned back to the TV.

George looked over at Danny, and he just shrugged his shoulders. They all sat there, quietly watching the late show. George didn't think the killer had followed Jade when she left. He and Danny had watched out the windows for any movement. The only thing they saw was the man nextdoor leave. Of course, the view from the window didn't show the entire street, and he could have been parked out of sight. George could only hope that their plan was going to work.

"I hate to call it a night, but I have to work in the morning," Danny said, standing.

"You all go ahead. I'm fine here. Just gonna kick back and watch some more TV before calling it a night myself," Walt said.

George stood, not wanting to leave until they knew if this was going to work. He had planned on camping out most of the night in Walt's living room. He understood Danny had to be in early. They should have brought separate cars. That was happening a lot lately. "I'm gonna check in with Ryan before we leave. Get an update," he said, going to the phone. "I need a number, Walt." He waited. Walt gave him the number, and after a brief conversation with Ryan, George told Walt all was quiet at Jade's. "Of course, we didn't expect anything this early. He probably won't make a move until sometime in the middle of the night." George wanted to make sure Walt understood.

"Thanks. I know what you're trying to do, and I appreciate it." They shook hands as Walt walked them to the door. Going back to the living room, Walt decided to laze on the sofa while he watched more mindnumbing TV. This was going to be a long night and, he hoped, a successful one.

~

Ryan reached over and kissed the top of Jade's head. "I'll bet he's sitting out there watching the house. Why don't you go on up and get ready for bed?" Ryan walked her over to the stairway and gave her a push. "You might want to stay in your jeans, honey. We don't know what's going to happen and when." Ryan smiled at her.

"You're probably right," she agreed. "Are you going to be okay on the couch?" "Yep, I'm a light sleeper, so don't worry about a thing." He doubted he would get any sleep at all, but he wanted to put her mind at ease.

"Well, okay then." She went up the stairs as Ryan turned the downstairs light off. She could hear him stumbling to the sofa. Turning the comforter and sheet down, she crawled onto the bed. Knowing he was out there watching her was a creepy feeling. Turning off the nightstand lamp, she let exhaustion take her away.

Ryan lay there wondering about the night and what it held. He kept thinking she was worried about what would happen tonight. He was worried, too. He knew he could keep her safe; he just wondered if the killer would make an appearance and if he would catch him this time.

~

The man sat there watching the light in the upstairs window. He was so smart, and they were so stupid. He liked the excitement of taunting women. He knew where his shit was and could get it so easily, but what fun was that? He could afford to play cat and mouse for a while. He so enjoyed it.

Cat and mouse. He laughed at the memory of the cat lying bleeding, unseeing, in that bathtub. It thrilled him to know he had the balls to do what he wanted. He was getting over his anger at Linderhoff. He had blamed him for putting him through all of this, but now he was thankful. It had been a while since he'd had the chance to have so much fun. He knew he could be cruel and brutal, even, if only she was alone.

He could wait for a while, anyway. His supplier hadn't started demanding money yet and still had no idea he'd been fucked over. Yeah, he could play for a while.

He watched the light go off and wondered if the cop was up there fucking her. That thought pissed him off. He wanted her. He would have her.

~

George and Danny headed for the station. The night air had taken on a cool breeze and it smelled like rain. Looking up, neither moon nor stars could be seen. That meant clouds.

They drove on in silence. George was thinking about Donna and wondering how she was faring on her own. Should he try to find out which motel she'd gone to? He decided he would. Picking up his telephone, he called the taxi service that had picked her up. "This is Detective Dunleavy with the St. Joseph Police Department." He waited till the dispatcher that answered recognized him.

"Yes, detective, how can we help you?"

"One of your cabs made a pickup early today..." George went through the incident. "I need to know where the fare was dropped off," he explained.

"Hold on for me, sir, and I'll see what I can find for you." The dispatcher placed George on hold.

"I was wondering if you were going to follow through on that," Danny said.

"Well, I wasn't going to, but then I thought better of it."

"Sir? That fare was dropped off at the Savory Palms Inn," the dispatcher said when she came back on the line.

"Great, thanks for your help." George hung up and turned the car in a U-turn. "The Savory Palms! What a hole in the wall. You sure can tell who knows the area by where they stay, you know?"

"The Savory Palms?" Danny asked with despair.

"Yeah, guess she didn't know any better. We're gonna run by there real quick and check on her."

"Sure thing. As a matter of fact, I would worry if you didn't, and I don't even know the lady."

The inn wasn't too far, and George knew he would feel better knowing she was tucked safely in her room. He also decided to leave word for her at the desk for tomorrow.

They pulled into the parking lot, and George looked around for any suspicious looking vehicles or people. Not seeing any, he told Danny he would be right back.

Walking in the front door to the small, grimy lobby, he observed a small man sitting on a stool, staring at the TV set

~ 313 ~

behind the counter. The lobby was dirty, and the walls were badly in need of paint. The paint that had been there was old and faded with years of dirty handprints and spilled food. The lone fake plant in the far corner had seen better days. The furniture boasted of an old brown leather couch with duct tape holding the leather together in more than a few areas. The two chairs were definite matches to the couch. The tables were scarred wood with water rings and hadn't been polished in this decade. The bell over the door rang, but the man didn't look over. "Excuse me," George said, standing at the counter.

"Yeah?" The man still hadn't looked at George.

"I need to leave a message for one of your guests."

The man got up slowly and looked at George. Realizing almost immediately that George was a cop, the guy forgot the TV and reached under the counter for a small tablet. "Do you want an envelope, too?"

"No, this will do," George said, taking the tablet. He quickly wrote a note telling Donna he would pick her up at the motel at promptly at one tomorrow. Then, handing the folded note back to the clerk, he said, "I don't know the room number, but this is for Mrs. Donna Linderhoff."

"Yes, sir, I'll see she gets it." The clerk turned and put the note in the small key box for room 114.

"Thanks," George said. Taking another look around, he turned and left the lobby.

Entering the parking lot, George looked around. What a dirty area filled with pimps and prostitutes, dirty bars and passed out bums. He was sure the area had surprised Donna. The occasional fast food place and one small café were the only reputable businesses in the area. The police were hard and heavy-handed in an area like this, and it didn't surprise him to see two units parked under an old closed bank drive-through, probably waiting for their next call.

Shaking his head, he walked back to his car. Danny watched him coming toward the car and knew Donna had not changed her mind when she got here.

"She's still here, isn't she?" he asked as George folded himself in the car.

"Yep, I don't get it, a classy woman like Donna pulling up to a shithole like this and staying."

"Upset as she was, she probably didn't even notice," Danny said.

"Maybe." George drove off.

~

Walt stood up. He was too old for this sofa. Stretching his back muscles, he decided to go up and get comfortable in his own bed. He knew sleep would not be possible right now, but he couldn't take the TV noise another minute. He could always read for a while if he could concentrate.

Securing everything for the night, he climbed the stairs, thinking how strange it was to have occupants in the other bedrooms. He wished one of them were Jade.

Falling in bed, he felt exhausted and frustrated. He picked his book up off the nightstand and opened to the page he had dog-eared. He relished a good mystery and congratulated himself when he figured them out before the author gave up the guilty party. He was more than halfway through this book and hoped it would last long enough to make him sleepy.

Settling in, he began reading.

~

Ryan lay there. Tossing and turning was out of the question. The sofa wasn't big enough to move. His feet hung over the end in an uncomfortable fashion. He thought of Jade in her big comfy bed, all alone.

There were two more bedrooms up there, but only one held furniture for an actual bedroom. The other Jade apparently used as an office. He didn't take the other bedroom because he wanted to be downstairs near the door. Now he was having second thoughts.

Looking at his watch, he pushed the light button. Two in the morning. He needed sleep. Getting up, he looked out of the window. Not seeing a thing suspicious, he decided to go upstairs to the spare bed and get some sleep.

Moving quietly up the stairs, he was careful not to wake Jade. Looking at her bedroom door, he couldn't resist a peek. Slowly, he pushed the door open and stuck his head in. She lay there asleep, breathing deeply. Standing there a moment longer, he resisted the urge to crawl into her bed. Finally, he closed the door and went to the spare room. Not bothering to turn the covers down, he was asleep before his head hit the pillow.

~

The night passed quickly and uneventfully. The killer watched the paperboy throw the paper on the doorstep. Once the boy was out of sight, he silently left the cover of his car and raced to put a surprise on the paper for her to find, then headed back to Walt's attic before everyone woke up.

Jade woke up when the sun began showing brightly through the three windows in her bedroom. She got up and went downstairs to brew a pot of coffee.

Going to the sofa to check on Ryan, she began to panic when she couldn't find him. "Ryan," she called softly, thinking he was already in the kitchen. When she got no answer, she tiptoed into the kitchen. Checking doors and windows and finding each locked, she stood in the living room, wondering where he had gone.

Back up the stairs she went, deciding to check the other bedroom. Sure enough, he lay there sleeping like a baby. She closed the door quietly and went back to the kitchen.

Filling her coffeepot with water and coffee, she wondered why the killer hadn't tried to get her last night. Did he know she came home? Maybe he wasn't watching like Ryan and George thought. Maybe he waited near Annie's for her. Another night wasted. She knew today would have enough sorrow and suffering without adding more if something had happened. She picked up the telephone and called her dad.

"Hey," she said when he answered on the first ring.

"Hi. Everything all right?"

"Yep. He was a no-show."

"Don't sound so disappointed." Walt was totally relieved. It was wonderful to hear her voice.

"I know. I just want this over, you know?"

"Yes, I do, Jade, but prepare. Today will be rough day, too."

"That's one of the reasons why I'm calling, Dad. Do you want me and Ryan to meet you guys at the funeral or come to the house first?"

"I'll get these ladies there; you can meet us."

"I love you, Dad."

"I love you too, baby." Walt hung the phone up and drank his coffee. Smiling, he gave thanks to God that all was well with Jade.

Ryan came down looking like he had very little sleep. Rubbing his jaw and yawning, he smiled at the picture Jade made in the kitchen. "Good morning. Is the coffee done?" he asked, settling himself in a chair.

"Yep. Do you want a cup and something to eat?"

"Sure, best offer I've had in a long time," he said, sitting back and watching her move through the kitchen.

"I called Dad already. He said he would just meet us at the funeral home today."

"Really? He didn't want us to come there so we could go together?" he asked, surprised as he sipped his coffee.

"Nope, said he could get them there and that we should just meet them."

"I'll call George in a bit and let him know our plans."

They went through the ritual of breakfast and then cleaned up together. Jade was thinking how nice it was not to be alone first thing in the morning. This was something she could get used to. She liked knowing he was here last night, and then getting up and making them breakfast felt right somehow.

Ryan decided to shake her out of serious thoughts when he looked over and snapped the dishtowel at her leg, missing her on purpose but laughing like he connected.

"What the...?" She turned to see his bright face. "Wanna play that way, huh?" she said, grabbing the frying pan she had just washed.

"Whoa, I wasn't going to knock you out," he said, stepping out of swing range.

"If you can't hang with the big dogs, you better stay out of the kitchen."

"Oh, I can hang alright," he said, reaching for her. He put her in a headlock and gave her a fake knuckle rub on top of her head. "See? I can do whatever I want," he told her, laughing and holding her there.

Jade reached up and pinched the inside of his thigh, laughing till she fell on the floor when he let go. He was vigorously rubbing his leg. She gasped for breath from laughing so hard and said "You can, can you?"

"Damn, girl! I fake my moves with you, but you pinch for real. I see how this is going to be." He stood there still rubbing his thigh.

"I'm sorry. Here, help me up." She swiped the tear from her cheek and reached her arm into the air.

Ryan snatched her up so fast she didn't know she was in his arms until his mouth crushed hers. He heard her soft moaning and pulled her tighter. She tasted of coffee and bacon. What a combination! Good thing he wasn't still hungry, he thought with a laugh.

"What?" She shifted to look at him. "Why are you laughing at me?"

"I'm not." He looked serious.

"Well, what are you laughing at, then?" She was feeling a little insecure now.

"What's wrong with you? I was just loving the fact that you are so sweet tasting," he tried to reassure her.

"Why would you laugh at that when we're kissing?"

"I was just thinking it was a good thing I wasn't still hungry because you taste like coffee and bacon." He stepped back from her. Why had she snapped so quickly?

"I'm sorry. I guess I'm still on edge some, and I'm just so happy. I can't believe this will last, you know?" She smiled at him.

"It's going to last, babe, I promise. Come on, let's finish this up." He pulled her back to him and pecked her nose with a slight kiss. Then, reaching, he picked up a clean cup. "Where does this go?" he asked.

"Here." She moved past him and opened a cupboard door. They finished the dishes, and she went to the front door. "I'm going to get the newspaper," she said, turning the alarm off.

Ryan stood to the side of the door so he couldn't be seen from the outside. Jade opened the door and stopped cold. There beside her newspaper was a small wild flower. She stooped to pick the two up. Looking around, she closed the door and held the flower up for Ryan to see.

"What do you make of this, detective?"

"Where was that?"

"On top of the newspaper."

"He knows you're here. Why the hell is he playing these games?" Ryan snatched the flower out of her hand. Crumbling the flower in his hand, he walked to the kitchen.

"Set the alarm again," he called to her, and then he threw the flower in the trash.

Jade walked up behind him and put her arms around him. She said, "It's okay, Ryan. He's just letting us know he knows."

"He couldn't have known I was here. Why didn't he make his move?"

"He's smart. You'll get him. I know you will."

"Damn it, Jade, don't you understand? Something's not right. He knows too much."

"What do you mean, Ryan? Do you think someone is giving him information?"

"I don't know. I need some time to think." He turned and walked away.

28

WALT'S house was a busy place, women coming and going from the bathroom, Emmie yelling for this or that. Walt was ready to have a quiet moment and decided to step outside. Opening the front door, he stepped onto the porch, always looking around. No peace, not even here at home. How long was this going to last? He knew everyone was getting sick and tired of the roller coaster ride, and he was ready for it to be over, too.

Maybe today after the funerals, they could begin some semblance of a normal life again. Maybe the cops just needed to somehow let the killer know they had the drugs, and then he would leave them alone. Walt made a mental note to talk with Ryan.

~

Donna stepped out of the shower and looked over at her dress. The tears began to fill her eyes yet again. How long could a person cry before they dehydrated, she thought. After all, she hadn't done much of anything else since hearing the news of James' and Amy's deaths.

She walked over to the telephone and called to reschedule her flight home for today. She had planned to talk to Nora and Annie as soon as the funeral was over, then take a taxi to the airport. The sooner she left, the sooner she could begin the healing process. After the flight change was done, she began getting ready to leave.

She decided she would walk to the diner for a simple lunch, then call a taxi from the pay phone there. The funerals were going to be pretty quick. No one would know about them but the family, so the service would not take long, and the plots were right next to the small chapel they chose for the service. It's just better this way, she thought. At least they weren't going to be cremated.

She finished with her hair and began to dress. Packing wouldn't take long. One suitcase didn't hold that much; besides she hadn't emptied the suitcase last night. She'd just hung her dress for today. She wondered what everyone else was doing. Would Emmie miss her already? Probably not; she didn't see her that much anyway. Donna picked up the suitcase and took a long last look to make sure she didn't leave anything behind. Walking down the hallway, she tried to remember the name of the chapel. She had to remember, or the taxi couldn't get her there. Why didn't she write it down? She decided she would concentrate while she ate, and it would come to her.

Entering the lobby, she walked over to the counter. No one in sight, she rang the small silver bell and waited. A pretty young woman stepped out and smiled.

"Can I help you, ma'am?" she asked in a sweet sounding voice.

"I would like to check out, please."

"Sure. What room number?"

Looking at the key card, she said "114."

"Oh, are you Mrs. Linderhoff?"

"Yes." Donna was surprised.

"I have a message for you, ma'am." The girl turned and took the note from the key box. Handing it to Donna, she said, "It was left for you last night."

"Thank you." Donna took the note but didn't read it. Handing the key card to the girl, she said, "I should be paid up. I didn't use the phone or anything."

"Yes ma'am." The young girl handed her a receipt. "Have a great day, ma'am, and thanks for choosing the Savory Palms Inn."

"Thank you." Donna picked up her suitcase and turned to walk out. She decided it was probably bad news, and she didn't want to bother with it right now. Putting the note in her purse, she walked to the small cafe.

~ 322 ~

Ryan sat down next to Jade on the sofa. He took a deep breath, enjoying her scent. She was so small and lovely that he felt he could sit and watch her for hours. Picking up one of her hands, he turned it palm up and kissed it, then tipped her chin for a taste of her lips. The kiss was a gradual one, soft and tempting to part her lips slowly. Nibbling on her bottom lip, he heard her moan; taking that as his cue, he deepened the kiss, feeling around inside her hot mouth with his tongue, licking and tasting with each stroke. He released her lips and moved down her neck, hitting points he knew would excite her. Jade reached up and ran her hands through his hair, tingling with excitement and wanting more. Ryan was moving the robe to the side to get his feverish mouth on one of her breasts, suckling slowly, waiting to see if she would stop him.

Jade pulled Ryan's head onto her breast and felt the tingling go all the way through her body. She had never felt this panic or this wonderful sensation before. All she knew was that she wanted more. When Ryan pulled back to look at her, she groaned as if in pain. "Why did you stop?" she asked breathlessly.

"I don't want to do anything you aren't ready for." He gave her a moment to reply. He prayed with everything he was that she would want to continue; he had never wanted anything so badly in his entire life.

Jade looked at him with passion burning in her eyes and just lifted her arms to him. That was sign enough. Ryan kissed her again, then, taking her hand, he slowly walked her up the stairs. Laying Jade gently down as he kissed her, digging and delving with his tongue, he untied her robe. Folding back the sides, he raised himself up to look at her. She began to shyly pull the robe back together, and he grabbed her hands.

"No way. I want to see you," he said in a deep, desire-filled tone.

Jade let go of the robe and lay there watching his eyes smolder. Ryan leaned down, taking a nipple in his mouth and feeling her whole body tense with the raw heat he had just begun to build.

Taking his time, he held back, knowing this had to be tender, not rushed. He held himself in check. He moved slowly. Moving his hand down her stomach and onto her inner thigh, he lightly rubbed his fingertips up and down her thigh, then trailing kisses where his hand had been moments earlier, he could feel her pulling and tugging at him and his clothes.

Writhing as if in pain, Jade wanted something so badly, but she was not exactly sure what that something was. Thrashing side to side on the bed as Ryan continued with his mouth and tongue, she screamed out. She blindly reached for him, not realizing she was on the verge of a climax so intense she couldn't get enough of his hot mouth.

Ryan continued lathing her with his mouth as he removed his pants. Once he was naked, he slithered up her body and rammed into her so hard she froze with the pain of her hymen breaking. Ryan stopped and stared at her in disbelief.

"Oh my God, you're a virgin?" he asked, shocked.

"Not anymore." She stared into his face, seeing the shock and disbelief in his eyes. "Ryan, it's okay." She reached out to touch his face.

"Jade, I'm so sorry, why didn't you say something before?'" He didn't have the words.

"The pain is gone, Ryan. I wanted you, and if I had told you, we wouldn't be here now." She tugged at him again. "Are we going to finish?" she asked, laughing shakily.

"You shouldn't experience any more pain, I promise. My God, Jade I would've been easier on you if I had known." He felt like a total ass. Moving slowly and watching her face for any sign of pain, he moved in her, wanting to see her pleasure.

"I promise I won't hurt you again," he said, and he began working his magic.

She tried to speak, but she couldn't even form a sentence. This was the best feeling she had ever had. Every part of her body tingled with excitement. Taking every pleasure as Ryan gave it, feeling with every fiber of her being, she still wanted more. She called out for more, not even realizing she had done so.

Ryan answered her call, and together they rode the waves of passion. Afterwards, Jade lay in his arms, her heart still beating wildly, her breathing fast and shallow. Ryan held her to him. They lay there satisfied, not wanting the outside world in any form or fashion to intrude.

This was a moment of wonder for Jade amidst all the bad that had lasted for days. Rolling over to look at Ryan, she smiled and kissed him quickly. Pulling her robe back on, she stood up "I have to shower, and then we need to get to your place so you can change. We're going to be late." She rushed out of the bedroom to the bathroom in a whirlwind.

Ryan heard the shower start, and he lay there feeling like a barbarian. He had just taken her virginity, and yet she was acting like nothing had happened. He wanted nothing more than to spend the day right here in Jade's bed with her, making love until nightfall. He supposed she was right; he did need to get moving. He got up and got dressed so that when she was ready, they could leave. He was going to go downstairs and wait for her, he but decided he wanted to know what it was like to watch her get ready, so he made the bed and then sat back against the pillows to watch. He could hear her in the bathroom singing while she showered and knew that he could do this for the rest of his life.

~

Donna pulled the note out of her purse after placing her lunch order. It was from George. She didn't need to call a taxi. Looking at her watch, she realized that she still had an hour or so. It was thoughtful of him, and she was grateful he would pick her up. She really didn't want to go in the chapel alone. It would be the hardest thing she'd ever had to do, and she was not going to have to do it alone. The people she had met since being here were the kindest people she had ever met, she thought. She would have to keep herself under control and try to make this as easy as possible for Emmie. She would mourn her son for some time to come, but she would do so with dignity. She folded the note back and put it in her purse when the waitress brought her food. Sitting there alone, she ate as she watched the people around her.

~

The killer sat ever so quietly in the sunlit attic room, listening to all the commotion going on. So the funeral would be today. Should he attempt to watch them all mourn the bastard and his stupid wife? No, he would wander around the house and try to find out as much as he could. Maybe he would even go to the girlie's house and show her he knew where she lived, too. This was fun. Maybe he was in the wrong business. He could get in and out of places so easy, scare people, make them know they weren't safe. The evil thoughts that would get in his head sometimes really excited him. Killing wasn't hard; maybe rape would be pleasurable, too. Laughing quietly, he decided to give it some thought. After all, he didn't do drugs, so he didn't need his suppliers. They needed him. He did need to return the unsold drugs, though, or they would be looking to kill him.

~

Jade finished getting ready. Watching Ryan watch her was exciting. This was the way it would be if she were married. Was she ready for a step like that? She knew she loved him, and she knew he accepted her visions without question, but did he love her? The thought made her stomach do a flip. The lovemaking had been exceptional to her, but she knew it wasn't new to him. Was she just another conquest? No, Ryan wouldn't treat her like that. She needed to stop this train of thought and pull herself together. This was the beginning of something really good, not just a fling without meaning.

"Ready?" she asked, looking at him.

"Yep." He leaped off the bed and kissed her briefly. "Let's go to my place," he said with a smile.

"Only if you behave yourself. You know we have to be on time." Loving the playful looks and ease with him were new, too.

"I will, but just for today." He took her hand and walked down the stairs with her beside him.

~

Walt was ready and sitting in the living room waiting patiently. Annie walked in with Emmie, who looked like a beautiful china doll, dressed in a dark chocolate brown dress with a matching ribbon holding her long locks back. She walked over to Walt and, without saying a word, crawled up on his lap. Leaning back, she laid her head on his shoulder. Walt wrapped his arms around the child and smiled at Annie. Annie knew this was going to be a difficult day for Emmie, but they would all get through it together. She just hoped that Donna would forgive her. She'd had no right to say the things she had said. They were true, but that hadn't been the way to handle the difficult situation. She would make a point to tell Donna how sorry she was and to beg for forgiveness if need be. Annie sat down and waited for her mom.

Nora was still looking around the room, trying to remember if everything had been taken care of. Did they do everything that needed to be done? Why was she feeling like she was forgetting something? She was nervous. Would she be able to help Annie and Emmie through this? Her baby Amy was dead. The thought hit her so hard she had to sit down. Crying was the last thing she needed right now. Pull yourself together, she ordered. But it didn't work. She hadn't allowed herself to fall apart at all yet. She had planned on doing that when she was home alone. Annie needed her now. She stood and walked to the mirror.

Wiping her eyes and all signs of the tears away, she grabbed more tissue, stuffing her purse with them. They would get through this; then, she could have her time to grieve.

As Nora came down the stairs, Walt set Emmie down and stood up. Annie stood and picked up her purse, then took Emmie's hand, and they all walked to the foyer. Walt opened the door. No one said a word. They walked to the car and settled in.

Walt turned to Nora, saying, "I just want you to know I'm here for you, for all of you." He looked in the rear view mirror at Annie. They both gave him a smile to show they knew he meant it, but they said nothing. Nora reached over and squeezed his hand. Then, folding her hands, she looked out of the passenger window and held her breath, trying to control the tears.

~

He looked out the attic window and watched them drive away. "Bye-bye," he said out loud, and then he laughed evilly. He thrilled himself with the promise that he would have the golden-haired beauty today to celebrate the day of the dead.

~

George arrived at the inn as promised. Donna was standing there waiting for him. He got out and took her suitcase from her. "I was hoping you got my message," he said.

"I was going to call a taxi. George, I can't thank you enough for this. I couldn't even remember the name of the chapel," Donna said, and she started crying.

"We're gonna get through this, Donna. I'm here for you to lean on," he said, taking her hand and helping her into the car. Women's tears always had an effect on him. He knew sometimes they were an act to get out of whatever trouble they might be in, but not this woman. Her tears were from the pain she was suffering, and he would not leave her to suffer alone.

He drove to the chapel, letting Donna silently cry her tears and knowing he would be there for her, for all of them. Today would be hard as hell, but it was the beginning of the healing process, too. With the burials done, they could start to put it all behind them. He tried to imagine, if he and Doris had been blessed with a child, what it would be like to lose that child. He could not fathom the depth of pain and despair a parent would feel at such a loss. He quit trying. He would just be there for them.

~

Jade and Ryan were the first to arrive. They sat in the car to wait for everyone else. After all, this wasn't their family, or even longtime friends, for that matter. It wouldn't seem right to go on in.

Walt drove into the parking lot and saw Ryan's car. He felt a moment of relief. That didn't last long. Getting out, he waved at them and opened the back door for Annie and Emmie. Ryan and Jade walked over. Jade leaned down and hugged Emmie. Ryan reached an arm around Annie's shoulder. Walt helped Nora out, and they all stood there for just a minute. George pulled into the parking lot and beeped to get their attention.

As George opened the door for Donna, he saw another sedan pull into the parking lot. Ryan looked up to see Danny Miller park his car.

"What's he doing here?" Ryan asked George.

"I don't know," George said.

Danny got out of the car and approached everyone. "I hope you don't mind my being here," he said. "It's just that after the short time I spent with you last night, I felt somehow it was right for me to come." He looked at Annie, who smiled at him.

"Thank you for coming," she said.

"Of course, thank you," Nora also put in.

Donna still didn't know who he was, but she did remember seeing him at Walt's last night before she left. She just timidly nodded to the young man. Then they all walked into the chapel together.

The service was sweet. The preacher didn't know James or Amy, but he delivered a very nice service. The caskets were closed, and Emmie asked several times to have someone open them. Both Nora and Donna were in agreement that it would not be wise. The time since the deaths had taken a toll on the bodies. Even though they had been prepared and were still preserved well enough, the mothers didn't want them shown.

Annie thought it might be easier if Emmie actually saw her parents and could say goodbye, but she didn't argue the point. The graveside service was serene, and everything went smoothly. Emmie was unusually quiet, and Jade wanted to help her but knew it wasn't her place. She stayed in the background with Ryan and desperately controlled the urge to comfort Emmie.

Danny sat with Jade and Ryan, wanting to be with Annie but knowing the time was not right. He would slowly push his way to her until they got to know each other. He would take his time and give her the space she needed, but he'd let her see he was there when she was ready.

Walt stayed by Nora's side, just as George stayed by Donna's. After the service, everyone went back to Walt's house.

Food and drinks were served, and conversation was smooth. Donna told Nora and Annie that she agreed with Emmie staying with Annie. She even told Annie that she would send money to help out. Annie wholeheartedly apologized for her hateful words the day before. Donna let her know it was something she had to hear because she'd had no idea that James had gotten that mixed up with drugs, much less that he was selling them. She didn't acknowledge the fact that he had put them in Emmie's baby doll.

Emmie was very quiet and spent her time on the floor with Harry. Harry lay there while Emmie petted and rubbed him, not making a sound himself.

Ryan and Jade sat on the sofa, watching the child and the rest of the people around them. Conversation was steady but not excited.

Annie turned to Danny to thank him for today and realized he was standing behind her chair. He had not been too far from her the entire day. Instead of saying anything to him, she began thinking about that. He was a nice man, not to mention very handsome. He had been so attentive to her throughout the funeral, and she had not even noticed until now.

Walt, of course, was still hosting everything, worrying about whether everyone had something to drink and if there was enough food out. Ryan reached over and took Jade's hand, pulling her up with him. She just looked at him and followed.

Taking her to the sunroom, he said, "When this is all over, I want you to go away with me for a while."

"I have to go to work, Ryan. I really should have already, but I just couldn't yet."

"No, I have a proposal on that, too, but I want to wait before I say anything. The timing has to be right," he said with a smile.

"What are you talking about, Ryan?"

"Just think about going with me. I really want you to meet my family, and we both could use some time for just us."

"Meet your family?"

"Yeah, I thought if you were ready and it was okay with you, then I want my mom to meet you. Are you up for that?"

"Sure, but I didn't know you weren't from here. Where does she live?"

"It's only about an hour or so south of here. I just don't get home much with my schedule."

"I would love to meet your mother."

"My brother and his wife, too. Oh hell, I forgot to tell you. I'm going to be an uncle. I just found out yesterday."

"That's wonderful, Ryan, a baby! I can't think of anything that brings a family closer together than a baby." She was flushed and happy. He wanted to take her home. This was going to be a step in the right direction. Her heart was soaring, and she couldn't wait to tell her dad.

Ryan hugged her to him and placed the sweetest kiss on her lips. Then he sat his head on top of hers with his eyes closed and knew in his heart this is where he wanted to be forever.

He felt her stiffen and stepped back to get a good look at her. She was a million miles away again. This happened more often than he'd thought. He stood there, holding her, waiting.

"I see you, girlie. You can't hide from me." The taunting *voice was coming closer. Jade was behind a box in the attic at her*

~ 330 ~

dad's house. The third floor was one big open area where long-forgotten items were stored.

It was getting dark. The light coming from the windows was fading, and she was there alone. How did he get in? Why was he there?

"Come out, come out, wherever you are!" He was laughing.

She could feel cold steel in her hands. She squeezed tighter, making sure her shaking hands wouldn't drop the gun. He wasn't far from her now.

"Where's my dope, girlie?" he asked.

"Jade, are you up there?" She heard Annie's voice calling to her. If she answered, he would know exactly where she was. She stayed down and quiet.

"Jade, I'm coming up," Annie yelled.

"Oh, goody, I get two for the price of one," he snickered. "I guess you better tell her to stay away, girlie, or I'll kill you both." He looked around while he roughened his voice to sound menacing.

"Jade, I was hoping to talk to you..." Annie stopped talking as she entered the attic and saw the hooded figure standing there. When she turned to run, he lunged for her, grabbing her and knocking her to the floor. He fell with her.

"Well, well, sister, it's nice of you to join us."

Jade stood up, the silver gun glinting in the dying sunlight. "Let her go." Her voice didn't sound like hers, not even to herself.

He rolled a little to see where Jade had been hiding. "Well, what do you plan to do with that? You gonna shoot me, girlie?" He sat up, pulling the hood down to keep his face covered.

Annie saw the gun and was crying hysterically.

"Let her go." Jade was calm. The shaking was gone.

"No," the evil voice said.

Jade felt her finger squeezing the trigger.

Shaking her head as if to clear the cobwebs, Jade stood frozen in Ryan's arms.

"Hey, welcome back, love." Ryan tried to sound like this shit didn't faze him. Truth be told, it freaked him the fuck out.

"Ryan, the visions are all different. I don't know which one, if any, will happen. This one was in Dad's attic. He had Annie and me in there, and I had my gun, and I ...." She was shaking and struggling with her tears.

"Shush, it's okay, honey, I'm here." He tried to sooth her. This was the third vision she'd had where the killer was close to her. "Do you want me to go check the attic out for you?" he asked.

"No, that won't do any good. My visions are in the moment. In other words, he could be there when this takes place, but not before. Does that make sense?"

"I think so. What you're saying is that in your vision, he's there because the time is right, but right now, the time may not be right." He held her to him. "Jade, this is the third vision you've had recently, so how do you know which one is right?" He was confused.

"I don't know. I don't usually have options like this. I'm not sure where or when he'll turn up, but I know it will be with me." She shuddered.

"Well, I just won't let you out of my sight, then. Until we figure out what's going on, you're sticking to me like glue, got it?" He looked down into her face.

29

HE snuck out of the attic and squatted at the top of the stairs to listen to the conversations and plan his next move. Funerals over, everyone should start going their own way, he thought. She would be easier to get to, and he would get everything he wanted, including his drugs. They would give them back to save her life, especially now that the cop was sweet on her. Yep, this would be over soon. He just had to get her alone, and then he would take her with him. He would figure a way to get to her. Maybe if luck held, it would be today.

"I suggest everyone move to the backyard and get some fresh air. The conversations are beginning to quiet down, and everyone is falling into a slump. I want Emmie on the swing and having some fun. This has been a hard day on her," Jade told Ryan.

He agreed as they went back to the living room. "Hey, everyone, why don't we move this to the backyard and enjoy the fresh air for a while?" Ryan asked.

"That's a great idea, partner." George stood up as everyone picked up their drinks and filed out the back door. Emmie didn't get up; she just continued to pet Harry. Harry barely lifted his head when everyone began to stir. When he realized his little mistress wasn't moving, he laid his head back down. He would not leave her. Jade came back inside and looked at Emmie.

"Emmie, come outside and I'll push you on the swing."

No, I like it right here." She didn't even look up.

Jade walked over and sat next to her on the floor. "Emmie, I know this has been hard on you today, honey, but the sooner you start playing and laughing, the better you're going to feel. I promise."

"Jade, I don't want to play. Harry's tired, too, so we don't wanna go out." "

Well, you know what? Harry probably needs to go to the bathroom, and he won't go unless you do. Don't you think you should at least take him out to do that?"

"He barks when he needs to go out."

"I know, but right now, he knows you need him, and he won't leave you even for that. So what do you say we go out for a few minutes anyway?"

"Okay." She stood up and grabbed Harry's collar. "Come on, Harry, let's go." She pulled until he stood up. Then they went out the door together. Harry ran to the back fence, and Emmie laughed. "You were right, Jade. Why didn't he bark?"

"Because he wanted to stay with you. That dog loves you, Emmie."

I love him too."

"Well, since we're out here, do you want to swing?"

"No."

"Come on! Let's go turn the tire in circles, then."

Emmie thought about it for a minute, then was off and running to the tire swing. "Come on, Jade!" she yelled.

Ryan stood on the porch with Walt and Nora, watching Jade and Emmie. "I'm glad she's good with kids," Ryan said, laughing and looking at Walt.

"Oh, she is, and she wants a houseful," Walt replied.

"Good, so do I," Ryan said, not missing a beat.

Walt and Nora just looked at Ryan and then at Jade.

"Young love. Nothing like it," Nora said, leaning over to whisper in Walt's ear.

He just responded by putting his arm around her shoulders, not even knowing he had done it. Standing there holding her next to his side just felt right. Nora didn't move. Her heart was fluttering like a schoolgirl's. Realizing how lonely she had been was hard for her. She would move here, she knew, but knowing the time wasn't right for such a conversation, she decided to keep the idea to herself a while longer.

Jade was spinning Emmie around and around, the rope getting tighter and tighter. Then she let go. Emmie whooped with laughter as her little body swung around on the swing. Closing her eyes tightly, she held on. Jade was laughing at Emmie's face, fear and excitement both apparent. She looked up to see Ryan watching her. He had that beautiful smile on his face. She smiled back at him and waved. He waved back.

Walt was watching the two and seeing the ease that had developed. He wondered when that had happened. Realizing he had his arm around Nora, he looked down at her. She was watching Annie and Danny sit quietly in the lawn chairs and talk. He wondered what she was thinking. Should he suggest she stay awhile and give them a chance to see what might happen? Was she feeling the same attraction he was? He would think about that for a while and decide.

~

He knew everyone was outside. He opened the attic door that led to the upstairs hallway. Slowly coming out, he listened. Not hearing anyone, he ventured all the way out. Going directly to Jade's room, he had a look around, opening drawers, picking up items from the shelves, taking his time and enjoying the feel of being in her private space. It was delicious to be standing in there when everyone was just a short distance away. He almost laughed out loud. He knew he would win; they all feared him. He couldn't wait to get his hands on her. In fact, he began to realize he wanted that more than the drugs. The drugs really didn't mean much to him, but he knew if he didn't sell them or return them, he was as good as dead.

~

Emmie and Jade were still at it. The tire swing had been such a wonderful idea. Her dad was right to put it up, giving Emmie some fun. It never failed to amaze Jade what a wonderful father she had been blessed with.

"Jade, I want my baby fixed," Emmie said as the swing stopped.

"We will get her fixed for you, honey, I promise." Jade looked at Emmie's sad little face.

"I want to hold her. I think she needs me."

Jade knew the child just wanted to hold onto something. She decided to see if her box with her own special baby doll was still here. "Wait right here. I think I have something to help you till we get Molly fixed." Jade walked over to her dad. "Dad, is that box with Weezie and my baby quilt still in the attic?"

"Yes it is. Why?"

"I'm going to get Weezie for Emmie."

"That's a great idea! You want me to help you find the box?"

"No, I can find it easily enough. Just keep an eye on Emmie. I'll be right back." Jade turned to go in and Ryan stopped her.

"I'll go with you," he said, opening the back door.

"No, I can get her. I'll be right back." Kissing him quickly, she went in.

Going up the back stairs, she wondered if Weezie would be a good replacement for Molly. Little girls were particular about their favorite babies. Smiling, she walked up the stairs.

He heard someone coming. He stopped going through things and stood very quietly, listening.

Jade made it to the top of the stairs and stopped. She got chill bumps all of a sudden. Waiting, she just stood there. She was in front of the attic door when he stepped out of her bedroom. She froze. He stared. It was just the two of them.

How sweet, he thought. "Well, well, girlie," he sneered.

Jade wasn't sure what to do. She knew she couldn't make it back down the stairs before he reached her. She stood there with wild thoughts running through her mind, not able to say a word.

"What a delight to finally see you close up. You are every bit as beautiful this close as you are from a slight distance." He was licking his thin lips. Should he take her now and make them deliver the drugs to him? He was thinking and planning.

Jade reached behind her and opened the attic door. Running up the stairs, she knew she could hide in here. She was running up before he realized she was going to run. He slowly went up the stairs, quietly stalking his prey. She couldn't get away from him now. He hadn't planned everything out in detail, but he was good at winging it.

Jade saw the boxes lining the wall and ran to hide behind them.

He came in and stopped. He listened, trying to hear her breathing. The pause gave his eyes time to adjust to the dim light.

The attic was a large room with three windows in the front letting sunlight stream through the bare windows. The room was filled with scattered boxes and trunks of different sizes. There was antique furniture no longer used scattered here and there, with boxes and trunks mixed in. This was a favorite place for Jade to play as a child. She would spend hours in here going through her mother's trunks and playing dressup.

A light layer of dust lay here and there on the wooden floor. The room smelled like an old bookstore, kind of musty but inviting. Some boxes were stacked six feet high. Not knowing what all her dad had kept up here, Jade was amazed by the number of boxes and trunks.

"Come out, come out, wherever you are, girlie!" He smiled as he said it. This was just too thrilling. He was getting very excited.

Jade held her breath. Reaching in her pocket, she felt the cold steel of the handgun. Holding the gun tightly in her shaking hands, she pulled it out. She remembered her vision and prayed silently that Annie wouldn't come in. Could she kill him? She was shaking and wondered how long before Ryan or her dad came to look for her.

He was moving ever so slowly, breathing hard, panting almost. He was getting excited in a fascinating way. This was a turn on for him. He could almost smell her fear. Stopping, he listened intently. He was sure if he waited, he would hear her gasping for air. He knew the air in her lungs was lacking the sufficient amount needed to survive.

"Where are you, girlie?" he whispered. "I want to play with you!" A light, menacing laugh escaped his thin wet lips.

Looking around behind the wall of boxes, Jade struggled to hear where he was. The room was so large it allowed sound to travel and bounce off the wall and floor. Learning his whereabouts was impossible, but that would be true for him, too. Pinpointing her would not be easy. If she was quiet and he had to search, that would buy her time for someone to miss her.   "Come on, girlie. I don't have much time. We need to go." He began moving boxes and trunks, beginning his search.

Go? Where was he taking her, Jade wondered. Why did he want her? She didn't have his drugs and had nothing to do with James. What was he thinking? Maybe he wanted Annie and had her mixed up with Annie. Maybe if she asked him who he thought she was, he would tell her it was Annie he wanted. Right, and just let her walk away. Shit. Shit. Shit. What was she going to do?

"I'm not leaving without you." More boxes scraping. "Hello, my pretty." He was pushing trunks and boxes that were too heavy for him and was grunting, breath labored. He could feel his blood pressure rising. "You're pissing me off, girlie. I will have you, and if you keep this up, I will hurt you more. I'm going to do things to you that you've never dreamed of. I can be quite inventive with my torture." He tossed a box, smashing the content.

Jade jumped. The box landed a few feet from her, and the taf torture had her keyed up. Come on, Ryan, Dad, George, someone, she pleaded to herself. Hell, at this point, she would take Annie. Anything to get his attention away from her. She had a gun; she knew how to shoot. The question was, would she?

Stopping dead not five feet from the wall of boxes Jade was behind, the killer listened for a sound to give her away. He knew he had heard something a second ago, and he thought it had come from here.

"I'm going to fuck you until you split in two. Then I'm going to peel your skin back and sprinkle you with salt. Do you know what that will feel like, girlie?" He thought that if he scared her enough, she would try to escape him. He needed to find her; time was running out. He was sure someone would come looking for her soon. He had to get her and get out. He would just have to move every fucking box and trunk in this room. He would find her.

"Tell you what I'm going to do. I am going to move each box until I find you, girlie. Then, because you made me work like this, I'm going to make you suffer like you've never suffered before."

"Emmie, sweetie, where did Jade go?" Annie asked. She was going to suggest that Emmie take a nap but hadn't realized that Jade had left.

"She went to get something for me."

"What, sweetie?"

"I dunno. She just said to wait right here."

Annie looked around the yard. She saw everyone but Jade. "Walt, do you know where Jade went?" Annie asked, walking up on the porch.

"I believe she's looking for one of her dolls to give to Emmie. She's in the attic."

"Oh." Annie said going inside. At the bottom of the stairway, Annie yelled, "Jade are you up there?" Not getting an answer, she said, "I'm coming up."

Jade panicked. This was going to happen. Could she shoot him?

"Oh, goody, I get two for the price of one," he snickered. "I guess you better tell her to stay away, girlie, or I will kill you both." He looked around while he lowered his voice to sound menacing.

"Jade, I was hoping to talk to you…" She stopped talking as she walked into the attic and saw the hooded figure standing there. When she turned to run, he lunged for her, grabbing her and knocking them both to the floor.

"Well, well, little sister, it's nice of you to join us."

Jade stood up, the silver gun glinting in the dying sunlight. "Let her go." Her voice didn't sound like hers, not even to herself.

He rolled a little to see where Jade had been hiding. "What do you plan to do with that? You gonna shoot me, girlie?" He sat up, pulling the hood down to keep his face covered.

Annie saw the gun and was crying hysterically.

"Let her go." Jade was calm. The shaking was gone.

"No."

"I said let her go. I will kill you." Jade stood there, knowing now that she could kill him. She couldn't shoot just yet, though; she was afraid she would hit Annie.

"I think the three of us should take a little ride. I want my dope, and I will get it. You are going to help me. I have plans for you, remember?" He snickered and sneered, those thin lips disappearing behind yellowed, rotten teeth. He struggled to stand up, pulling Annie with him.

"I doubt you're a good enough shot to miss sister here." He was sure she wouldn't try, but to keep her thinking, he put the crying Annie in front of his body.

Jade felt her finger squeezing the trigger, aiming at the center of the hood. Not thinking about missing, she pulled the trigger all the way. The shot rang out loudly. Annie fell to the floor.

Ryan, George, and Walt ran for the stairs.

He lay there in a puddle of blood, the face still covered by the hood. Annie was rolled into a ball, crying on the floor. Jade, standing very still, afraid her legs would give and she would drop to the floor, lowered the gun to her side.

The three men reached the second floor and saw the open door to the attic.

"What the fuck?" was all Ryan could say. Seeing Jade standing there white-faced with no color and Annie lying on the floor crying made his blood run cold.

George and Walt were on his heels.

"Jade, Jade!" Walt yelled as they ran up the attic stairs.

Ryan walked over to Jade and took the gun from her. Grabbing her tightly in his arms, he told her, "It's alright, honey. You did good." Remembering her vision, he felt his heart drop.

George bent down to Annie. "Annie, it's over. It's okay now." He gently rubbed her back.

Walt stood there, his heart beating so fast he couldn't think. His little girl had just killed someone.

Danny was there before anyone realized he had run right behind them. He walked over and stooped to remove the hood. The shot was a brilliant one, right between the eyes. The lifeless eyes looked up at Danny. He knew this guy. He had talked with him on several occasions about narcotics and the different drug busts that had been made. He couldn't believe this. Turning to Ryan, he said, "Is this the killer you two have been looking for?"

"It's gotta be. Check his right hand for a tattoo." Ryan still held Jade, hoping to stop the shaking that was wracking her body.

Walt walked over to Jade to take her from Ryan. "You better go call whoever you need to, and let's get this cleaned up. I got her. You go ahead."

Ryan was more than hesitant to let Jade go. He knew he had to put his cop mind to work and get this taken care of, but he wanted to be the one to comfort her. "George can take care of that." He refused to let her go. Walking her to the door, he decided to get her out of there.

George lifted Annie and handed her to Danny. Danny turned to carry her down the stairs.

"George, there's a tat in the wedge of the right thumb and forefinger. It's some type of Chinese symbol."

George and Walt stood there looking down at the man who had caused them all so much pain, fear, and frustration.

"Hard to believe it. He's not much to look at, is he?" George said.

"No, he's not." Walt was still trying to get his mind around the thought that his daughter had shot and killed this man.

"I wonder how he got in here," George said, looking around. There was a blanket and pillow in the corner near the window. He walked over and took a closer look at the area. There were fast food bags and wrappers laying there along with an empty drink cup, a cell phone, and a pack of cigarettes. "Good Lord, Walt, he's been staying in here."

Walt walked over to see what George was talking about.

"How the hell did he get up here?" George was thinking out loud. "The window's unlocked. I guess he used the rose trellis, the smart son of a bitch. He has been listening to us. That's how he stayed a step ahead."

Walt was pissed. He couldn't believe the killer had been in his house all this time and no one knew.

George dialed his cell phone and told dispatch to send a crime scene unit to Walt's address. "Come on, we'll go down and check on everyone while we wait. I don't want anything moved or interrupted until the scene is processed." They left everything just as it was and went downstairs.

Nora was fussing over Annie. Danny was standing next to the sofa where Nora was talking quietly to Annie, trying to calm her down. Donna was sitting in a chair, holding Emmie. Ryan was forcing Jade to drink. She looked as though all the blood had drained from her body.

"What the hell happened up there?" Ryan asked as George entered the living room.

"We didn't dig through anything yet. I called for a crime scene unit. We'll just have to wait until Jade is able to fill in the blanks."

Jade sat there, just staring into space. Had she really killed someone? Her mind was screaming at her, but she didn't want confirmation so she didn't ask out loud.

Walt walked over to Jade. Putting his hand in her hair, he asked, "Honey, are you alright?"

She looked up into her dad's face. Seeing the concern in his eyes, she numbly shook her head. Not sure her voice would be steady, she wasn't ready to talk. Taking slow sips of the strong drink Ryan had brought her, she felt her limbs growing weak. The shaking was subsiding, but she was still weak. Her mind was going over everything over and over. She couldn't stop the movie playing and replaying in her head. Annie was still crying softly, and Jade's heart went out to her, but she couldn't go to comfort her. She was not steady enough to talk, let alone try to stand.

Ryan sat back down next to Jade. Taking the drink from her, he pulled her into him and held her tight, realizing how easily he could have lost her today.

Thank God she had the gun with her. He didn't even know she had it on her. She was a smart woman. He had emotions running rampant through his mind and body. He just wanted to keep her close.

Nora got up to refill the glass for Annie, and Danny immediately took her spot next to Annie. He put his arm around her and held her to him. Talking softly to her, he was reassuring himself as much as her.

George stood back to watch everyone. Nora had Walt, Jade had Ryan, and now he could see that Annie had Danny. He went to the front door and took his cell phone out again, this time calling for the coroner. After the scene was processed, they would get the body out of here.

He wanted to ask Danny about the guy, since he seemed to know him. He just didn't want to ask in front of everyone and get them going again. Walking back into the living room, he saw Nora giving the glass to Danny for Annie.

The sun was going down, and the day was wrapping up. The crime scene techs were working furiously to get everything done so the body could be removed. George and Ryan were upstairs with the crime scene team.

"No identification on his person, George," Randy Martin said. "Do you know who he is?"

"No, not yet," George replied. "Tell the coroner he's John Doe for now."

"That bullet couldn't have hit better if someone had walked up and stuck it in his face," Randy said. "Who shot this guy?"

"My girlfriend," Ryan said with pride. He had not noticed how good a shot it had been until he went back up there with the team.

"Hell of a shot, Ryan," Randy said.

Ryan didn't say it was probably just lucky. Ryan also didn't know that the killer had been holding Annie in front of him.

"Well, I think we're pretty much done here, fellas," Sofie Ramirez said. "Anything else you want before we wrap it up?"

"No, I think that should do it. Thanks. If you don't mind, go ahead and send the coroner and the funeral home guys up so we can get him outta here," George said. "Ryan, you okay?" George looked at Ryan just standing there looking down at the stiff.

"Yeah, I just can't believe it's over."

"It's not over yet. We have to identify him."

"I know. We don't have to worry anymore about when or where he'll strike, though; that's what I meant."

"You think Jade will be ready to talk soon?"

"Yeah, she just needed to calm down and get herself under control. She's a tough lady, George."

"Yes, she is. You're a lucky man."

Ryan looked at George and saw the smile on his partner's face. "That I am," he said, smiling back.

After the coroner did his thing and the funeral home guys did theirs, Ryan and George cleaned up the mess. This was one mess they wouldn't leave. The family has been through enough, they both thought, and weren't bothered by the clean up. They had been in this job a long time, and neither had ever had to clean up the brain and blood splatter before. It really wasn't that tough since didn't know or care about the dead person.

They both looked around to make sure they hadn't missed anything. Ryan saw a box marked "Jade's toys." He walked over and pulled the tape loose.

Opening the box, he saw an Atari game, three or four dolls, two boxes of puzzles, and dressup clothes, complete with high heels. Laughing, he reached in pulling one of the dolls out. "Do you think this would be Weezie?" he asked.

"I don't know," George said, laughing. "What's a Weezie?"

"Jade's best doll." Ryan took the doll, and he and George went down the stairs.

Walking into the living room and taking a good look at Jade, noticing her color was better and she looked better, he asked, "Jade, is this Weezie?"

"Yeah, bring her here." Jade took the doll from Ryan. This had been her favorite baby. It was still dressed in a pajama jumper, and a hair net still held her hair in place. Jade held her out to Emmie.

"I love her, Jade! Thank you!" Emmie said, taking the baby and holding her close. "You will still fix Molly though, right?" she asked, holding the doll to her chest.

"Yes, honey, we'll get her fixed. In the meantime, I want you to take care of Weezie for me, okay?"

"Okay, I will." Emmie took the doll and sat down next to Harry. "Harry, you can't hurt this baby, okay?" she said, holding the doll out for Harry to sniff.

Annie turned and looked at Jade. Her color was back, and she was no longer crying. The look in her eyes was sorrow. She wanted to thank Jade for so many things; most of all, for saving her life. Jade was so strong, and Annie envied that. She got up without saying a word and walked over to Jade. Leaning down, she hugged her tightly. "Thank you for everything," she said as meaningfully as she could. "You saved my life."

Refusing to let the tears start again, she backed up and looked at Jade, smiling a bright smile. "I'll never forget what you did up there."

"You gave me the strength to do it, Annie. I don't know that I could have shot him if he hadn't grabbed you."

"He grabbed you, Annie?" Danny shot up out of his seat.

"Yeah, he was holding me in front of him when Jade killed him."

All eyes turned to Jade. Walt's had pure fear in them. Nora felt disbelief, Ryan felt pride, and George was questioning.

"He held Annie in front of him, and you pulled the trigger?" George had to ask.

"Yeah" was all Jade said.

"You didn't worry about missing him and shooting Annie?" George asked, still needing answers.

"No, I didn't even think about it. I just aimed and pulled the trigger."

Donna, who had been sitting quiet as usual, stood up and walked over to Jade. "You are a very brave girl," she said, taking Jade's hand in her own. "We all owe you so much."

"Jade, we need to get you and Annie separated and get some statements taken. Do you feel ready for that?" George asked.

"Yes, I can give you a statement whenever you want." Jade was feeling herself again. She really had been in control when she fired that shot. Realizing that, she knew she could finish this.

"Annie, are you ready?" George turned to Annie.

"I guess so." Annie looked to Danny. "Will you come with me?"

"Of course, if you need me."

"Walt, we're going to use the sunroom and the kitchen, if that's alright," George said, getting everyone up and moving.

Ryan led Jade to the kitchen, and Danny took Annie to the sunroom.

"I think these should be verbal first, so I'll go get two tape recorders from the car," Ryan said.

"I think you'd better take Annie's, and I'll get Jade's," George suggested.

"Yeah, that way there's no conflict." Ryan went out the front door.

"George, I want to stay with Annie if you don't mind," Danny said.

"I don't see a problem with that, Danny, but I think you and I need to talk about the deceased pretty soon. I get the feeling you knew him."

"Yeah, I talked to him sometimes. I don't know his name or anything, but he worked at the car detail place, you know, the one where we take our patrol cars on Broadway."

"We'll talk."

Ryan came back and handed George a mini recorder and a tape. George went to the kitchen where Jade was waiting, and Ryan went to the sunroom where Annie was waiting.

Ryan explained the interview process and asked Annie if she had any questions.

Danny reached over and took Annie's hand in his and held it tightly. "I'll be right here with you, Annie," he told her.

"I really appreciate your being here, Danny." Annie smiled at him.

Ryan started the tape recorder and gave the needed information to begin the interview. George was doing the same thing.

Walt got up and walked to the hallway closet, taking out his light jacket. He turned to tell Nora and Donna he was going for a walk.

~ 345 ~

"Want some company?" Nora asked.

"Sure, that would be nice. I just can't sit here while they interrogate the girls."

"I'll keep Emmie in here with me. You two go ahead," Donna said.

"Thanks, Donna. We won't be long." Walt was glad Nora wanted to go with him. He enjoyed her company.

Nora picked up her sweater, and Walt held it while she put it on.

They walked along, not talking, just enjoying the quiet. Walt reached over and took Nora's hand. He waited for an objection, but when she didn't object, he settled into the comfort of having her close. They walked a few blocks to the corner park, where a fountain in a small pond was the focal point and there were benches set here and there for people to sit and watch the dance of water and feed the ducks.

"I hope they aren't being too hard on our girls," Walt said.

"I think the girls can handle it. They both seem to be tougher than we give them credit for." Nora thought after her statement that it sounded like they were talking about daughters they shared. It was a natural thing that parents discussed, but, after all, she and Walt were parents, just not of the same children.

She wasn't about to break the spell that seemed to have been created. Maybe he needed normalcy as much as she did right now. How nice it would be to have the chance to stay and get to know this man, she thought again. If he would only ask her to stay or consider moving here, she would jump at the chance. She supposed it would be too forward for her to suggest it, so she wouldn't. Even if he didn't ask, she was still considering the move just to be close to Annie and Emmie.

"What are you thinking about?" Walt was looking at her.

"Just how quiet and peaceful it is here," she lied.

"Quiet and peaceful, huh? Then why the frown lines between your eyebrows?"

She smiled and hoped the lines went away. "Okay, I was wondering how the girls are doing." Still a lie, she thought.

"They're fine. You said so yourself just a few minutes ago." He put his arm around her shoulders. "This is nice, isn't it?"

"It is. It's rather comforting sitting here with you like this." There! She put that out there. She couldn't believe she'd said that.

Walt looked at her again, this time with tenderness in his face. "You know, Nora, I'm glad the killer is gone, but at the same time, I kind of regret it, too."

"What?" She was incredulous.

"Well, now that everything is pretty much over, I figure you'll be going back to California, and I have gotten used to all of you being in my house."

"Oh, I see." So that's how it is. She felt her heart grow heavy. He was just lonely, not interested. How could she blame him for that?

"I don't think you do see. I've gotten used to having you around."

"Walt, what are you saying?" she began to hope again. Her heart started beating faster.

"Well, what I'm trying to say is that I'm going to miss you. I was hoping for more time to get to know you."

They both sat there, afraid to say any more, both knowing they wanted more time, at least. The ducks began walking and quacking to get attention. They were used to people sitting there feeding them. Nora began to feel uneasy. She wondered if the ducks would bite. She scooted closer to Walt. He laughed and shooed the ducks away.

"They're used to getting fed, so they're not afraid of people," he said casually.

"Do they get aggressive if you don't feed them?"

"No, they will just go away after a few minutes when they know you're not going to give them anything."

She began to relax again.

"Don't you have ducks in California?" he laughed.

"Of course we do. Are you making fun of me?" She smiled at him.

"No, I wouldn't do that." He liked having her snug against him. Maybe he should have left the ducks alone instead of shooing them away.

"I don't take the time to feed the animals, none of the animals," she said, laughing.

"I see. So, what do you take the time to do, then?"

"I stay pretty active helping at the local nursing home and delivering Meals On Wheels."

"Wow, you volunteer a lot then?"

"I like to help people. It makes me feel useful. What do you do with your time?"

"I golf and hang out with my pals."

"Walt?" she asked in a very quiet tone.

"Yeah?" He turned his head to look at her.

"This is nice, isn't it?"

"Yes, Nora, it is." He felt her lay her head on his shoulder, and, leaning just a bit, he could smell the lavender scent she washed her hair with. Should he ask her to stay a while longer? Maybe she needed to get back to her normal routine. "We've been gone a while. Maybe we should head back." Walt moved to stand up.

"Already?" Disappointment was evident in her voice.

"Aren't you ready to go?"

"I am if you are. I was just enjoying the sound of the water falling and the quiet. You know, relaxing for the first time in what seems forever."

"We can stay a little while longer if you want to." He sat back down.

"No, you're probably right. We should get back." They both stood and walked hand in hand back to the house.

30

GEORGE and Ryan finished about the same time.

"We'll get these typed up, and then you both need to sign them," George explained.

"I'm glad this is over with," Annie said, looking directly at Danny.

"So am I. You have had a rough day." He looked down at her. Wanting to reach over and kiss her was hard to resist. He knew things were moving quickly, and he told himself he needed to take it slow. She had been through hell lately, and he didn't want to cause her any undue stress. He took her hand again and walked her into the living room.

"Where's Mom?" she asked Donna.

"She and Walt went for a walk."

Annie and Jade looked at each other. Both had bright smiles on their faces.

"Too bad she lives in California," Ryan said.

"Why?" Annie asked.

"Beause I think she and Walt could have a love connection," he said, laughing.

"Maybe she'll move here," Annie thought out loud.

"Really? Do you think she would?" Jade asked.

"I don't know, maybe." Annie was thinking now. It would be nice to have her mother close. She could be a big help with Emmie. Maybe she would suggest it. The thing with Walt could only help in that direction. She knew her mom was sweet on him.

The front door opened, and they heard laughter. Jade walked to the foyer and saw the flushed faces of both her dad and Nora. "Where have you two been?" she asked.

"We had to get out of here for awhile," Walt answered.

"Uh-huh, and where did you go?" Jade continued the tirade.

"We went for a walk," Walt said.

"Just a walk?" Annie came around the corner and asked.

"Yes, just a walk," Nora said. All four stood there and began laughing.

"We are adults, you know, and we can go anywhere or do anything we want to," Nora advised them.

"That's right. You tell them like it is." Walt shoved Nora forward.

"Okay, okay, we give up. We were just poking fun at you guys. No need for arguing. We don't care where you were or what you were doing, do we, Annie?" Jade said.

"Nope, sure don't." Annie turned and went back to the living room.

Everyone sat around talking about earlier. Emmie was busy playing with Weezie and not paying attention to the adults.

Donna remembered she was supposed to catch her flight earlier and hurried to the telephone. After explaining the emergency she had dealt with, they agreed to change her flight to the next day. She wrote the information down, and when she turned around, Walt was standing there.

"I didn't mean to eavesdrop or anything, but since you're not leaving until tomorrow, would you like to stay here tonight?"

"Walt, that would be so nice, and I just want to apologize for my actions yesterday. I don't mean to make you think I'm ungrateful for all you and Jade have done for us."

"Don't give it a second thought. We're glad to have you back." Walking away, he smiled. At least for tonight, he would have a full house. He would worry about the loneliness tomorrow.

George knew this case was almost over. He was going to miss these people. Mostly, he was going to miss the cases. He had decided this would be his last case. He was waiting to tell Ryan. Doris was the only person that knew he was retiring after this one. They could wait to finish this up tomorrow; he was going home to his wife. This had been a tough, trying time, and he wanted to get home. "Well, I hate to say it, but I'm going home. Ryan, we'll get together in the morning and wrap this case up. Danny, we'll talk tomorrow. I'm tired." George stood up. Walking over to shake Walt's hand, he thanked him for all of his help and generosity.

"I'll walk you out." Ryan stood up, too. Once outside, Ryan asked how Jade's interview had gone. George assured him she wouldn't have to worry about a grand jury indictment.

"She did good, Ryan," he said.

"Hell of a shot, huh?" Ryan beamed.

"Yeah, hell of a shot." He slapped Ryan on the back and got into his car.

"See you in the AM, partner," he said.

"Okay, be safe." Ryan turned to go back in the house.

"Well, Dad, it's getting late, and I think I'm ready to go home, too," Jade said as Ryan walked in.

"Sure, baby. I know you've had a rough day."

"Ryan, will you take me back to my house?"

"Yeah, are you ready?"

"I just need to tell everyone goodbye, and then I'm ready." Jade walked over and hugged Walt, then leaned down and gave Emmie a kiss on the forehead. "I'll see you all tomorrow."

"Bye, guys, the boss says we gotta go." Ryan waved at everyone and laughed. He had hoped to get Jade alone. He was worried that she still had a long way to go before the shooting actually hit her. He knew these things sometimes took time, then, wham, the person would have a reality attack and realize they had taken a life. Jade was being too calm, and he knew it hadn't hit her yet. He couldn't believe it when Annie told him the killer was holding her in front of him when Jade shot him. Annie said that was why her legs buckled and she fell on the floor. She couldn't believe she hadn't been shot. She said her ears were still ringing, but she would forever be thankful to Jade for having the courage to take the shot.

Opening the door for Jade and then settling himself in the driver seat, he decided to talk to her about the shooting and see if he could help her get through the shock quickly. "Are you tired, honey?" he asked.

"Yeah, a little bit."

"Do you want me to drop you off and go?"

"No, I want you to stay with me. Will you?"

"Sure. If you need me, I'm there."

"I like having you there when I wake up. Kinda silly, huh?"

"No, it feels right."

They drove a while in silence, both in their own thoughts. Jade was wondering what Ryan thought about her killing that guy. Did he think she was coldhearted? Should she bring it up? She didn't like the idea that it wasn't bothering her. She was feeling no remorse and a lot of pride at the fact she'd shot him while he held Annie in front of him. She still couldn't believe she'd done that. Smiling to herself, she looked over at Ryan.

"What are you thinking about that put that pretty smile on your beautiful face?" he asked.

"Seriously?"

"Yeah, I wanna know."

"I was just thinking about the shooting, actually."

"You wanna talk about it?"

"I'm just amazed, that's all."

"Amazed?"

"Yeah, I can't believe it's over, you know?"

"I can't believe you shot him right between the eyes."

"I know. When you talked with Annie, was she alright with that?"

"She's thankful to you. She said he was going to take the two of you with him."

"Yes, he was. I really didn't think. I just reacted. Crazy, huh?"

"No, that's usually what happens. I didn't know you had the gun with you."

"I put it in my pocket earlier. I've kept it in my purse since you gave it to me. I don't know why I put it in my pocket."

"I'm glad you did."

"Ryan?"

"Yeah."

"Do you feel differently about me now?"

"What do you mean?"

"Well, you know, I took a life tonight, and it doesn't seem to bother me."

"It will. It just hasn't sunk in yet."

"No, I don't think it will. I mean, I'm not sad or upset at all."

"He caused you a lot of fear. You didn't know him, either; that helps. You did what you had to do, and you did a damn good job of it."

"Can you believe I shot him with Annie standing in front of him?"

"That was hard to swallow."

"If I had waited, he would have killed her."

"I know."

"What do you make of Annie and Danny?"

"They're cute together."

"Yeah, it happened fast, didn't it?"

"What?"

"The two of them."

"They're not a couple, Jade. He's interested in her, but I think she's just being nice."

"Really? Why?"

"Well, did you watch them? He was very attentive, and she was, I don't know, just kinda there."

"Hmm. I'll have to watch more closely next time because, to me, it seemed like they were getting awfully cozy."

Ryan wasn't sure why the change in subject. He decided to let the shooting go for now. Maybe she just had to get the ball rolling and just feel him out a little. He would take his time with her where all that was concerned. He wanted her to deal with it in her own way.

The conversation was over, and both were in their own thoughts again. She knew he was okay with the shooting, and that was all that mattered right then. She didn't want to think about it anymore and certainly didn't want to talk about it.

She wondered if he would still want to take her to meet his family. The case would be over with by tomorrow, and then she would find out. He'd also said he had a proposition for her but wanted to wait till this was over. She wondered about that too.

~

Danny was sitting next to Annie on the sofa. He wanted to get her alone but knew the time wasn't right. She'd had a tough day, and he was going to take his time. He didn't want to scare her off. He decided to call it a day, too. Standing up, he stretched like he was tired.

"Well, I hate to go, but I think it's time," he said, looking at Annie.

"Danny, thanks for all your help today. We were glad you were here," Walt said.

Nora didn't say anything. She just watched the way Danny and Annie were looking at each other. If she didn't know her daughter better, she would think there was something brewing between the two.

"It was my pleasure, Walt. Well, not pleasure, but you know what I mean," he said, feeling ignorant.

"Annie, would you mind walking Danny out? I think that little walk did me in," Walt said, winking at Nora.

"Sure." Annie got up.

"Bye, Emmie," Danny said with a smile.

"Goodbye, Danny." Emmie barely turned her head away from Weezie.

As they walked to the door, Danny remembered that Donna was leaving, and he might not get a chance to say goodbye. He stopped and turned. Stepping back into the doorway, he said, "Mrs. Linderhoff, in case I don't see you before your flight takes off, I just wanted to say it was nice meeting you, and have a safe flight."

"Why, thank you, Danny. I'm glad I got to meet you, too. You keep your eye on our Annie, won't you?" She smiled.

"I would be happy to." He walked out, smiling at Annie standing near the door.

"What are you, some kind of magician or something?" she asked.

"Why do you ask that?"

"Everyone just fell in love with you. You're so charming."

"Is that so wrong? Do I have to be magical for you to like me?"

"No, of course not. It's just that you show up at a really bad time in all of our lives, and yet you just fit right in, no qualms."

"Just because people are having a tough time doesn't mean they're going to be rude." "No, that's not what I meant, either. Never mind. I'm tired, and I guess I'm not making any sense. Thank you for being there for me today."

"Don't thank me, Annie. I wanted to do it."

"You're a really nice guy, Danny, and I'm glad I met you."

"Whoa. You sound like you're not going to see me again. Don't think you're getting rid of me that easy. I plan to get to know you very well if you don't mind spending some time with me."

"I would love to spend time with you, but right now, I have to focus on getting back to school, getting a job, and taking care of Emmie."

"You still have to have time for yourself, Annie."

"I don't see how. I have new responsibilities, and Emmie has to come first."

"Well, we can get to know each other with her around. I don't mind."

"I just don't know if this is good timing."

"Don't say it. I'm not going to go away that easily. We'll work something out." He leaned over and whispered in her ear, "Just don't shut me out." Lightly kissing her cheek, he stepped back.

"We'll see." She opened the door and gave him a smile that said goodbye.

He stood there for a few moments, looking her in the eye, then smiled to himself "You're damn right, we'll see." He walked out the door.

Annie closed the door and leaned against it. She wanted more than anything to have time to pursue Danny Miller, but she knew she wouldn't.

Ryan pulled into the driveway at Jade's. She had been so quiet the rest of the way home that he was worried about her. He hoped she wouldn't put up a front for him.

"Well, here we are," he said, getting out. He walked around and opened her door. Taking her hand, he helped her out of the car, then caught her up in a lip-tingling kiss.

She tightened the hold on him and kept the kiss going longer than he had intended. He looked in her eyes when the kiss was over, trying to read her feelings. She looked good. She looked normal. They walked to the front door hand in hand.

"Are you sure you want me to stay?" he asked.

"Yes, I'm sure. I'm going on up. You ready?"

"Right behind you."

They went in and straight to the stairs. No lights were needed; there was nothing to fear anymore. Going into her bedroom, she flicked the lightswitch and walked to her dresser.

"Is it okay if I wear a nightgown tonight?" She smiled slyly.

"You won't be wearing it long, but go ahead if you feel the need." He sat down on the bed and began taking off his shoes.

"What's that supposed to mean, Mister?"

"Well, you don't expect me to lay here next to you and not make love, do you?" He had on the most innocent face that he could muster.

"Why, Detective Douglas, are you telling me that you're going to take advantage of me after all I've been through?"

"Yep."

"Okay then, no nightgown again tonight."

"Sweet." He stood up and started taking his clothes off, watching her to see if she would undress or give him the chance to undress her. She didn't miss a beat. She turned off the light and undressed as she walked to the bed. They met in the middle, both ready and eager.

After a long, slow, well satisfying love session, they curled up, so comfortable with each other that no words were necessary. He waited a while, then asked, "Are you still going away with me?"

"When?"

"I figure we'll have the case wrapped up sometime tomorrow, so the next day."

"I'm supposed to go to work soon. I'll need to call them again."

"Yeah, about that... What do you think about working with me?" There, he'd said it.

"What? I'm not a cop!" she declared loudly.

"No, I know, and I don't want you to become one, either. Why don't we work together? You know, my expertise with your gift. We could rock."

"I'm not following, Ryan. We would be doing what?"

"Private security work, honey."

"Would that be lucrative?"

"It would be, what we made of it."

~ 355 ~

"You mean you would quit the force?"

"Yes, and spend all my time with you forever."

She sat up and looked down at him. "Ryan, are you asking me to marry you?" She hoped she wasn't making an ass out of herself.

"See, my love, you do catch on quickly. Will you?"

She couldn't catch her breath. She just stared at him. No words would come to her mind. She didn't open her mouth because she knew she would stutter. Turning slowly away and getting up, she walked to the bathroom.

Ryan sat up, worried he had blown it. "Jade?"

No answer. He got up and walked to the door. "Jade? Honey, are you alright?" Still nothing. He was scared now. He knocked, but no sound came from within. Pushing the door open, he saw Jade sitting on the floor with her back to the wall, crying like a baby.

"Jade, what is it, honey?" He rushed to her. He been foolish thinking she was over the killing already. He had known he should give her time, damn it. "Jade, baby, we will not even think about marriage until you're ready. No worries, my love. Please stop crying."

"What? No, Ryan, it's not that, it's just that I can't believe you want to marry me. I don't usually fall apart like this, but I can't help it." She cried harder.

"Jade, I love you, and I believe you love me. When two people feel the way we do, they usually get married. If it's too soon for you, I can wait. Just talk to me, honey."

"Oh, Ryan." She flung herself up to him and cried hysterically.

He didn't know what had brought this on, but he held her until she quieted. Then he slowly wiped her face with a washcloth. Looking her in the eyes, he said, "Jade, we'll take this as slow as you need to. Just don't say no."

Finally, with the tears gone and her face composed, she looked at Ryan. "I don't plan to.

Taking his hand, she walked him back to the bed. Without a word, they made love slowly, sweetly, and completely. Then she rolled over to look at him. "Ryan, I love you with all my heart, and I would marry you tomorrow."

A rush of relief flooded his heart. Kissing the top of her head, he held her until they fell sound asleep.

Donna had gone to bed and put Emmie in with her. She wanted to be with her for her last night there. Emmie didn't mind; she loved sleeping with her grammy.

Annie had the big bed all to herself. She went over the day's events and lay there crying. She was so glad this was over. The killer was dead. Now she could take Emmie and go home, get their lives on track. What was Danny thinking? If it had been any other time, maybe it could've worked, but not now. Now she had to concentrate on Emmie. She wasn't even sure she could continue her schooling; she needed a job and money. Well, she'd had enough thinking for today; she needed rest. It would work itself out. Rolling onto her side, she quickly fell asleep.

Nora and Walt were still sitting in the living room. Nora was ready for bed, but she didn't want to leave Walt just yet. She sat there next to him, watching TV.

He would have to bring up the subject of her staying. She wouldn't do it. She sat there waiting, not really watching whatever was on the tube, just waiting and hoping. Finally, Walt stood up.

"Well, I guess I'll call it a night. Do you want anything before I go up?"

"No, I think you're right. We've all had a long day, and I'm getting tired, too. See you in the morning, Walt." She went up the stairs first. Okay, she thought, so maybe it wasn't meant to be, but it was nice while it lasted. She at least knew now that she wouldn't spend the rest of her life alone. No, she wanted companionship, and she wouldn't settle for less.

Walt went to his room. Laying there in the dark, he thought about Nora. She was someone he could spend the rest of his life with. He hadn't remarried after his wife died; he'd had Jade, and that was the most important thing at the time, but now that Jade was starting her own life, he didn't want to finish his by himself. He would talk to Nora tomorrow. Maybe he could persuade her to stay for a while. He went to sleep with a smile on his face.

The day began with birds singing and the sun shining through the windows. At first, Ryan thought he was dreaming. He rolled over and got up, pulling on his pants as he went. Jade was still sleeping, and he wanted to surprise her with breakfast in bed. Hurrying down the stairs and being as quiet as possible, he made his way to the kitchen. He began brewing coffee and then decided on pancakes and bacon. Frying them up, he put together a beautiful tray with fresh flowers he had picked from her garden. He hoped she wouldn't mind because they did add a nice touch. He went back up the stairs quietly, hoping to catch a glimpse of her sleeping. Her beautiful face was peaceful and radiant. He moved the tray under her nose to tease her awake. She lay there sniffing and smiling. Slowly opening her eyes, she said, "You made me breakfast?"

"Yes, for you in bed. Sit up and I'll let you eat." He set the tray down and began fluffing pillows behind her.

"You are the sweetest man, Ryan Douglas."

"Yes, I am, and you're the luckiest woman, Jade

Hamilton." Laughing, he set the tray in her lap and went around to get in beside her. This was the way he wanted to spend the rest of his life, and he hoped she would be ready soon.

After they had eaten, he gathered the dishes and tray and went down to clean up the mess that he had made. Jade was behind him, and when she saw the destruction, she started to laugh. "So this is what a good cook does to a kitchen," she said.

"Yep, you gotta give to get." Laughing, he pulled her to him for a kiss.

"Okay, for that, I'll help you clean this mess up," she said, smiling up at him.

"Good. This would take the better part of my day, and I still have to go to work." They finished the kitchen in no time.

"What are you going to do today, love?" he asked as he walked to the door.

"Well, I'm not sure yet. I think I want to sit in the quiet for a while and try to figure out what my next move is." She was beside him at the door.

"Why don't you pack for our trip tomorrow?"

"How long will we be gone?"

"Oh, I figure two days. I don't want to share you longer than that."

"Okay, I'll be ready in no time. Are you coming back here tonight?"

"Do you want me to, or do you need some alone time?" He was afraid of the answer but had to allow at least that.

"I want you here with me."

"I'll be back as soon as I can, then." He kissed her lightly and opened the door.

"I'll be waiting." She stood there while he went to the car. Watching him drive off, she had a feeling of satisfaction.

Walt and Nora had finished breakfast before anyone else came down. When Donna walked in the kitchen, they were sitting companionably at the table, drinking coffee.

"Good morning, Donna," Nora said.

"Good morning, all. Is there still coffee?" she asked.

"Of course. Let me get you a cup." Walt stood up.

"No, I can get it. You sit." She walked over and, getting a cup down, filled it with coffee. Looking at the clock, she realized she still had two hours until she needed to be at the airport. "Nora, do you think Annie would mind taking me to the airport? I'd like to keep Emmie with me as long as possible," she said.

"I wouldn't mind at all, Donna," Annie said, coming into the kitchen.

"Oh, I didn't see you there, honey." She blushed.

"I know. Did Emmie sleep alright last night?" Annie asked.

"I guess so. She's still out."

"Good, she needed a good night's sleep. I appreciate you taking her with you last night. She loves you very much, Donna, and with everyone leaving, I think it's going to be hard on her."

"I love her, too. I hope you will let her come to New York to visit me, and I'll come see her here sometimes."

"Of course she can; you're her grandmother, and I would never keep the two of you apart. She's going to need all of us." Annie sat down and patted Donna's hand.

"Well, I better go get my suitcase packed. I'll be ready in an hour if that's okay with you." Donna stood to leave.

"That's fine. I'm sure Emmie will be up and moving soon." Annie got up to get a cup of coffee.

Walt and Nora just sat there.

"So, how are you two this morning?" Annie asked, coming back to the table.

"Fit as a fiddle," Walt replied.

"Good as gold," Nora said.

Annie just looked at the two of them; then all three started laughing "My, aren't we in good moods this morning?" Annie said, sitting down with her coffee.

"Yes, I am, at least." Walt was feeling pretty good. He had decided to ask Nora to stay longer and was just waiting for the right time.

"I better get some breakfast for Emmie. I expect she'll be down any minute, since Donna went to finish packing." Annie rose and went to the stove; seeing the French toast batter and the bread, she decided to make some for herself, too.

After breakfast, Annie got Emmie ready to go to the airport. Nora offered to go as well, but Annie told her no. She thought it would be better if she handled it on her own.

~

Ryan arrived at work and was surprised to see George drinking coffee. He'd figured they'd go to Denny's again. Of course, he had already eaten, but he wasn't about to tell George that. George knew he never cooked for himself, and he wanted to keep Jade's reputation unquestioned. Instead of suggesting Denny's, he went to get a cup of coffee, then sat down at his desk and rifled through some papers.

"By the way, Ryan, we have his name now. He was Duran Carruthers. Have you ever heard of him?"

"Duran Carruthers... No, I don't think so. Is he in our system?"

"No, apparently this piece of shit is clean as the driven snow."

"No way, he has to have something in his background."

"Nope, I guess flunkies like James have always taken the rap for him."

"Did you get the statements typed up this morning?"

"Yeah, they're both ready."

After some thought, Ryan suggested, "Why don't we let Danny take Annie's to her for her signature?" He smiled at the idea.

"You bet. That saves me a trip. I assume you'll get Jade's signed?"

"Sure. Okay then, what's left?"

"Nothing. Now we wait to see what the Grand Jury will do."

"Yeah, I'm not too concerned with what the Grand Jury will do. It was a righteous shoot. Did you find any family for Carruthers?"

"No, I guess he was on his own. He worked for Shipshape Car Detailing. Danny said he talked to him a few times while he had his unit in for maintenance."

"Have you talked to anyone there yet?"

"Yeah, just got off the phone with them just before you walked in. They don't know of anyone to contact either. They all seemed shocked that he was dead, but they weren't upset."

"Surprising. He was such a nice man," Ryan snickered.

"Yeah, it must be a bitch to live your whole life, then not even be missed or grieved over when you die."

"I believe you get what you give, and he was slime."

"I agree." Sitting quiet for just a moment, George then continued, "Hey, while you drink your coffee, I have something I wanna say."

"Alright, go ahead."

"Ryan you know I've enjoyed working with you, and we make a great team."

"Yeah." Ryan looked up to see the intense look on his partner's face.

"I think it's time you get a new partner."

"What? Where the hell did that come from? I won't work with any of these idiots. No. George, don't go there! Are you upset with the way I handled this or something? I mean, I know you're not supposed to get involved personally, and I fucked up there, but ..." Ryan was watching George's face. There wasn't anything wrong. He could tell it was more than that. He shut up before he said something he would regret. Waiting for George to finish, Ryan said nothing more.

Reflecting on his bright young partner and knowing Ryan had come a long way in the short time he had been in investigations, George said, "No, Ryan, I don't think you did anything wrong." George looked Ryan in the eye "I'm just ready to retire, and Doris and I agree the time is right."

"Retire?"

"Yeah, you know, sit on my old ass and do nothing."

"I'd hate to see it, but I know you've earned it." Shaking his head, he continued, "Damn, I'm going to miss you."

"This is the last case I'm working. You're on your own now, kiddo."

"I won't partner up with anyone here. I guess I'll go private and take a partner of my own choosing."

George sat back and looked at Ryan. "You already have a plan, don't you?"

"Oh, how well we know each other. Yep, I figured it was about time for you to spring this on me, so yeah, I've planned ahead." Ryan explained his idea to George. George thought it would work well, and he encouraged Ryan to get Jade on board, assuring him he would be there for bouncing ideas and helping out.

"You know the best thing about this case, kiddo?" George loved calling him kiddo because it riled the shit out of Ryan.

"What's that, old man?"

"That fucker died knowing we had his drugs." Laughing, George got up and put his jacket on. "I'm done. I'm going home."

"Me too," Ryan said, and he walked out the door with George.

"Nora, since it's just you and me for a while, I was hoping to have a talk," Walt said, bringing drinks to the porch where they had been sitting.

"Oh? What about, Walt?" She held her breath, not sure what to expect.

"I've thought about this long and hard, and I know I don't have the right to ask."

"Ask what?" Her heartbeat quickened. Dare she hope?

"I want you to stay longer, Nora. I want some time for you and me to get better acquainted."

Nora stood up and walked to the edge of the porch. Taking a deep breath, she said, "I thought you'd never ask, and just in case you didn't, I'd already planned on taking time to help Annie and Emmie adjust to each other." She turned to see his face.

Walt stood up and took her in his arms, kissing her for the first time. It was every bit as sweet as he'd anticipated. "This is exactly where I want you to stay," he said to her, pulling her tighter in his arms.

"I'm not going anywhere."

They sat down on the settee instead of the chairs they had been sitting in separately. Cuddling, they both enjoyed the closeness they shared.

"I know you want to be here to help ease Annie and Emmie's way, but promise me you'll make time for us," Walt said.

"I'm staying for us. I just said if you didn't ask, I was going to use Annie and Emmie as an excuse. I don't plan to leave you alone too long," she said, putting her hand on his chest and leaning over for another one of those delicious kisses.

Annie pulled into the airport parking lot. "Donna, are you ready?" she asked.

"As ready as I can be. Emmie, you know, just because Grammy is going back to New York doesn't mean we're not going to see each other. You are going to visit me, and I will visit you, okay?"

"I know, Grammy. Aunt Annie already told me. I can come see you maybe next summer, and you're gonna visit me here, too."

"Yes, baby, I am. Now you listen to your Aunt Annie. She's going to take good care of you. I love you, baby." Donna held Emmie close. She knew she needed to get out of the car before the tears started again. "Annie, if you will just help me get my luggage, I'll get moving."

"Sure, Donna." Annie got out of the car and pulled the luggage from the trunk. "You take care of yourself. I'll have Emmie call you every week, okay?"

"Thank you, Annie, for everything."

They hugged each other while the skycap took the luggage. Donna waved at Emmie and turned to go. Annie got back in the car and turned to Emmie. "Are you okay, honey?"

"Yeah, I'm okay." She picked up Weezie and hugged her tightly. "Aunt Annie? Is Grammy going to be okay?"

"Yes, sweetie, she will be just fine, and you can call her whenever you want to." They drove off. Annie was feeling a little better now. Donna was on her way home, and Emmie was still here. Now she just needed to figure out what she was going to do about Danny.

~

Ryan was on his way back to Jade's when he thought he should call and make sure she was still there.

"Hello?" Jade picked up the phone on the second ring.

"Hey, babe, what are you doing?"

"I was just going out to pull weeds in my backyard flowerbeds."

"Do you want some company? I'm done with work for the day."

"You know it, sexy. Just come on in. I'll be out back."

"I'm on my way, but I have a stop to make first. See you soon."

Walking to the drawer where she kept her garden gloves, Jade decided work was exactly what she needed. She grabbed her green kneepad on her way out.

Ryan found her on her knees pulling weeds, so deep in thought that she didn't even realize he was standing there. Afraid he would scare her, he let the door close loudly.

Turning, she saw him standing there. "I'll be finished in a few. These weeds have gotten a little out of control."

"Do you want some help?"

"No, I'll just be another minute or two. Get a drink and sit. I'll be there in a minute."

He went inside and poured two glasses of lemonade. Bringing them both out to the patio, he sat down and waited for Jade to finish.

She pulled the last of the weeds and went to say a proper hello. "I'm glad you're here," she said, kissing his pale pink lips. "You have the sexiest lips I've ever seen." She bit at them, then grabbed her glass of lemonade. "For me?" she asked sweetly. Taking a long drink, she set the glass down and pulled her garden gloves off.

"For you," he said, standing. Without another word, he picked her up, taking her off her feet and swinging her around. He laid a kiss on her that had her toes curling. "Now I have something else for you. Have you been good while I was away?" he asked, setting her down.

"Of course. What else could I do?"

He reached in his pocket. Taking out a small velvet box, he took her left hand. Kneeling down on one knee and looking up at her, he said, "Jade, I know we haven't known each other for very long, but I feel like I've known you my whole life. I've just been waiting for you. Now that I have you, I don't ever want to let you go. I love you. Jade, will you marry me?"

She stood there looking down into his gorgeous face, and a tear slipped silently down her cheek. Smiling, she said, "Yes, Ryan, I will, and I love you, too."

He placed a circle of diamonds on her finger and kissed it. "This ring is a neverending circle, just as our love is." Standing up, he kissed her long and hard. "I really have waited my whole life for you, Jade Hamilton."

"Ryan, I'm so happy. You have no idea how much I love you." She was beaming with happiness. Caught up in his embrace, she looked at the beautiful ring over his shoulder. The neverending circle of love: what a beautiful thought.

Annie and Emmie went to Walt's house to get their belongings and Nora. Annie thought it was time to get settled into their new life. "Come on, Emmie. Let's go thank Walt and get our things. It's time to go home."

"Are we going to my home, Aunt Annie?" A look of fear crossed her little face.

"Your home is with me now, sweetie, and that will be in my apartment for now."

"Your apartment?"

"Yes, is that alright?"

"Uh-huh." Emmie hoped she could take Weezie with her.

Everything would be fine, Annie told herself. She was going to ask her mom to stay a while longer. Walking to the door, Annie rang the doorbell for the first time.

When Walt opened the door and saw Annie and Emmie, he stepped back. "Annie, why did you ring the bell?"

"This is your home, not ours; it's time we start treating it that way. We're going back to my apartment today. Is Mom around?"

"She's out back. Honey, you don't have to move back yet. Don't you want some time to adjust?"

"That's what I want to do, adjust, but in my own place. I want you to know how much it means to me, Walt, everything you've done for us. I don't think we would have gotten through all of this if you hadn't been there. Thank you." She grabbed him in a hug and kissed his cheek.

"Come on, your mom's out back." He stepped aside and let both Annie and Emmie walk in front of him.

~

Jade and Ryan were sitting snuggled up on the sofa. They were going to Walt's to let everyone know they were engaged. She was absolutely giddy. What a word, she thought. Giddy. Huh. She was going to ask Annie to help her with the wedding plans. She couldn't believe she was going to spend the rest of her life with this beautiful man. She was excited and so ready to share their news. They would be going soon; she just needed to be patient.

Watching her emotions run across her face as she thought, Ryan decided it was time to bring her back to Earth. "Are you ready to go to your dad's?" She had been daydreaming for awhile now.

"Yes, I can't wait to show my ring off." Holding her hand out in front of her, she stared at the beautiful circle of stones.

"Should we call first?"

"No, he'll be there." Jumping up, she pulled him to his feet. Smiling, she tossed him his keys. "Let's go."

They drove, making plans for the future. Ryan told Jade about George's upcoming retirement, the new business he planned to open for them, and the visit to his mother's. Everything was finally falling into place. Arriving at Walt's, they saw Annie's car.

"Good, everyone is here," Jade said. "Let's go tell them." She was so excited she couldn't wait. Ryan had to hold her hand to keep her from running.

"Honey, they'll still be there when we get in. Slow down, you're going to hurt yourself." He was laughing.

The two rushed inside and spilled the news. Walt and Nora were excited for Jade and Ryan. Annie was hysterical. She could not believe that this horrible situation had brought two such nice people together.

Emmie was in awe over the shining stones. She kept turning the ring around and around on Jade's finger. "They're so shiny," she said.

Nora explained she was staying for a while longer and tried to use the excuse that it was to make sure Annie and Emmie were fine, but everyone knew the truth, and it made them all happy.

Walt looked around at all the smiling faces. He finally had a house full of family.

CPSIA information can be obtained at www.ICGtesting.com
Printed in the USA
LVOW050300260911

247833LV00001B/7/P